THE WICKED SOULS DUOLOGY

CANDACE ROBINSON

BOOK ONE

VAULT
OF
GLASS

For Nate and Arwen,

We make up the ultimate Three Musketeers

PROLOGUE

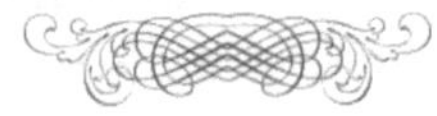

Overwhelmed with boredom, Vale stared down at his fingernails. He could only spend so much time tormenting those he encountered in the afterlife. When his work was complete in making them as miserable as possible, he found himself needing to search for new prey.

The fire beside him flickered and gave off a comforting heat. To Vale, it felt like a warm blanket against his cool skin. He hummed a melody to himself as the fire crackled, accompanied by a chorus of screams that continued to grow more intensely.

Vale should have felt something, yet he was incapable of compassion. It made his torture of others necessary, and with no complete spectrum of true emotion, their agony provided him with a sick sort of pleasure. It was the only real feeling he had ever truly known.

He picked at his nails a little longer with a sharp instrument until they were back to their pristine condition. The one thing he couldn't tolerate was the filth and grime that built up under his nails. One might consider this an oddity. After all, his experiments usually ended up being the cause of his distress.

Studying his nails one more time, Vale set the tool down

next to a row full of other torturous devices—giving him another thrill. When so many of his experiments resulted in such beautiful messes, he could forgive himself the lapse in hygiene.

Rows of cages filled with useless souls lined the walls of his domain. They would help him to crush the mortal lives he needed to flood the earth. After the time he had spent in his dark place, he grew tired of tormenting the ones who "deserved" it—he wanted them all.

The time had finally come to bring down humanity—he wished it could be as simple as a snap of his fingers. Vale didn't like to do things the easy way, though. No, he liked to do things the way that brought him the most pleasure. This time he was going to be known as Quinsey Wolfe. This time he would make sure the world ended in flames while orchestrating its demise and rebirth. There must be a space between his underworld and the human world, where the new souls could become immortal with real power. It would take time, but he would build this place. Then, he could discover the ones he truly wanted. Hearts would surrender, souls would suffer, and at the end of it all—he would watch it burn. From the ashes of its undoing, Vale would recreate it all in his image.

ONE

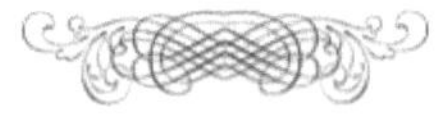

The mirror was a foggy mess as Perrie stepped out of her, literally, five-minute shower. She'd let her damn alarm continue to go off when she should've woken up right away, so that meant less shower time. With hurried motions, she drew a flower—a weepy-looking daisy, to be exact—on the glass.

Perrie's mom used to do this together with her when she was younger. It was before her mom ran off several years ago with another man, to another state, and never spoke to Perrie's dad or her again. For some strange reason Perrie upheld this so-called mirror-drawing tradition of theirs—possibly to remember something that used to be different.

The one thing her mom left her was her maiden name as Perrie's first name, yet it defeated the whole purpose since she spelled Perrie with an "ie" instead of a "y." Perrie preferred the spelling how it was, that way she was connected to her mom as little as possible.

"Dad!" Perrie yelled.

After throwing on a pair of jeans and an old Queen band tee, Perrie rushed down the hallway. Sometimes she could catch him before he left for work, but he was already gone.

In the center of the table rested a red velvet cupcake and a note beside it. *Have a good day at school! Happy Eighteenth Birthday!* A grin spread across her face.

Since Perrie's mom left, she'd told herself over and over not to care, but she knew her dad still did. There was a picture of them together on his bedside table from when they were maybe sixteen and high school sweethearts. Her mom was looking off to the side laughing, genuinely amused, while her dad was staring at her with such an expression of love and admiration. It used to make Perrie's heart skip, but not anymore.

Perrie knew what that kind of love felt like, and she'd missed it for the past six months. She tossed those feelings of that particular guy into her personal, little trashcan inside her head—almost completely hidden away.

Grabbing a small bowl for her breakfast from the cabinet, she padded over to the pantry where there were at least ten varieties of cereal to choose from. Her dad couldn't get over her cereal-stocking obsession. But she couldn't control how the different sugary shapes on the covers called to her. *What else can I say?*

Biting her lip, she decided to go for the bag containing only colorful marshmallows—no healthiness included.

As she reached for the cereal, feeling like Willy Wonka, a sudden poke came at her shoulder. Releasing a squeak, she flailed in her panic, effectively sweeping her bowl off the countertop. Then she thanked all the fish in the sea that it was plastic as it hit the floor with a *thump-thump*.

Perrie's back smacked hard against the granite countertop when she flipped around to face the intruder. Maisie, her best friend and cousin, stood a few feet away, smirking. Perrie rolled her eyes. Maisie just loved to scare the living daylights out of her when Perrie least anticipated these situations. It wasn't like this hadn't happened before. Odds were, she should've expected this. Maisie lived next door and they'd been playing at carpool for as long as Perrie could remember.

Maisie grinned from ear to ear while Perrie rubbed her stinging arm. Her cousin's one, bright-blue eye twinkled with mischievous intent. The other eye, which Perrie was sure contained a twin expression, was safely hidden behind an eye patch. Maisie usually pulled her long black hair away from her face to highlight that one accessory, but her locks relaxed around her warm brown skin today.

When Perrie's mom left, Aunt Krista offered up the house she owned next door. The tenants had recently moved out, so she'd asked her brother—Perrie's dad—if he wanted to rent the place. Ever since then, Aunt Krista had been more of a mom to Perrie than her birth mother ever was.

"One day, you'll have it coming, Maisie Jaser." Perrie cocked her head and fought a smile. Despite being an adult now, she was still determined to best her cousin at least once in her life. "I do have a key to your house, you know."

"You've been saying this pretty much forever, and I'm still waiting," Maisie said while laughing. She brushed a hand against her latest hot pink eye patch, where yellow stars and a moon were sewn onto its diamond shape.

Perrie motioned at the newest addition to Maisie's two-year-long parade of endless eye patches. "What's going on with this one?"

Maisie scrunched up her nose as if she was thinking incredibly hard about this. "So, I was in the mood for a night sky, but I wanted the sky to be pink because black is, well, you know?"

Perrie arched a brow. "Well, no, I don't know."

"Oh, you know." Maisie shrugged. "It's just such a dark color sometimes."

"You also realize you're still not blind, right?"

Her smile grew even wider. "I know, but I have to show support to those who only have the one eye." She pointed her index finger at the patch like she was actually missing the damn eye.

Ever since she started reading books about characters who wear eye patches, Maisie had been on this kick. She even started an online store where she'd sold quite a few. Perrie wasn't sure if these people legitimately needed an eye patch, or if they were using them for costumes, but either way, the accessories could make any outfit stand out.

If Perrie needed a patch, she would wear the shit out of the ones Maisie created. She still didn't get why Maisie wore an eye patch *all* the time, but whatever—it was her quirk.

"You keep showing that support." Picking up the bowl from the floor, Perrie tossed it in the sink. There wasn't time left to eat cereal, so she grabbed two granola bars out of the pantry and threw one baseball style to Maisie, who easily caught it. Perrie had to admit, her cousin still had remarkable reflexes with only one eye.

At the table, a small green box sitting beside the salt and pepper shakers drew Perrie's attention. Maisie must've set it there before sneaking up on her.

"What's in the box?" As Perrie started toward the table, Maisie flung past her to the gift and lifted it.

"Happy Birthday!" she yelled, thrusting the gift at her.

Perrie plucked it up just before Maisie whipped out a tiny yellow noisemaker from her pocket and blew loudly. The screeching sound caused Perrie to grit her teeth, while Maisie was panting as if she'd run a marathon. Perrie didn't receive a lot of gifts for her birthday, so she always anticipated Maisie's, even if they could be on the strange side.

"Is it another wood chip creation like the lion you made me that one year?" Perrie asked. Several years back, Maisie's parents were going to clear out their flower beds and replace the old with rubber mulch. Maisie objected and found a way to repurpose the mulch for her crafts. The one she'd made for Perrie looked just like a lion and still sat on her bookshelf.

"No, my parents are still all about the rubber mulch."

"Too bad," Perrie said as she inspected the dark green box, wrapped in a delicate, yet vivid green bow of a different hue. She peeled it open slowly, first removing the ribbon then the lid.

Tucked inside was a banana-yellow eye patch. Upon closer examination, there was an image of a roaring lion on the front. She could tell Maisie had stitched it herself using fur-like pieces surrounding the outer edges to create its mane. It was beautiful, and Maisie knew how Perrie had a slight decorating obsession with the fierce beasts.

Gently, she set the patch aside and pulled another gift from the box. It was another lion, though this one smaller. This lion was crafted with twigs, then hand-painted with a miraculous amount of detail, and washed in bright greens, hot pinks, and brilliant blues. Perrie didn't know how Maisie had managed to blend the colors together so artfully.

She envied those skills.

Tears gathered on her lashes, knowing how much time and effort Maisie had put into these gifts for her. Perrie tugged her into an awkward but perfect hug. "Thanks so much. These gifts are everything."

Maisie leaned back and locked her gaze with Perrie, her expression serious. "Are you going to wear the patch now?"

Snorting, Perrie shook her head. "No, but you know what? I'll wear it tonight, just for you."

Suddenly remembering the time, Perrie booked it for her room and shoved a pair of black boots on. She took one last look at herself in the mirror hanging on the back of her door, before pulling her brown hair into a low ponytail. She didn't have time to do anything exciting with it, and it wasn't like she would anyway—that would take effort. Besides appearing a little tired, her chestnut-colored eyes were a little lighter this morning. *It's a step up from a zombie, so it works.*

"Perrie! Hurry the heck up!" Maisie shouted.

Blowing out a breath, she grabbed her backpack and

coveted cello from the floor beside her desk chair. With the combination of a heavy backpack and even heavier cello case, she was guaranteed to have a bad back by the time she reached twenty. A practical person would have dropped the cello, but not her. She'd been obsessively playing the instrument since sixth grade. After her mom left, playing music was her escape, her healing process.

"Come on, Perrie. We need to get going." Maisie was already standing on the porch, holding the door wide open when Perrie came bounding out down the hall.

They piled into Maisie's car, and Perrie relaxed in the seat, munching on the granola bar. Maisie finished chewing hers and ditched the granola wrapper, while Perrie had barely taken one full bite. With that kind of speed, she bet her cousin could win an eating contest … if she didn't choke first.

"So, did you hear there's another person missing?" Maisie asked as she turned down the next road.

Perrie's lips parted as she met her stare. "No. Is it someone we know?"

"No. I don't think so. His name's Ben Johnston. He's a twenty-three-year-old from the University," Maisie answered while chewing on her left thumbnail, flipping her gaze back to the odometer to check her speed.

There were two major things Perrie knew about Maisie, one being that she absolutely had to go the *exact* speed limit. It didn't matter where she was, she kept to one speed at a time. Second, she had the habit of chewing on her nail when there was a riddle she needed to figure out, or a puzzle she wanted to slide the last piece into.

Leaning her arm against the car door, Perrie rested her chin on her hand. She scanned through the people she knew from memory to see if she recognized the name from anywhere. It wasn't a long list of names either. "Yeah, I don't recognize the name, but I don't remember many people who graduated before us besides the ones I was in Orchestra with."

Lately, strange things had been happening in her neck of the woods. Not that Deer Park had many wooded areas... But a few months ago, there had been an increase in disappearances in the city, and even more so over the last few weeks. Ben Johnston was another name and face to add to that list. The local police department had been investigating, but they *claimed* there was no clear answer. No predictable method or motivation, and the victims' ages and genders all varied. Thankfully though, no one she knew personally had gone missing, so it just made it seem less real.

Despite her own calm, her dad, on the other hand, was a worried mess. Perrie's midnight curfew, as well as Maisie's, had been cut back. It wasn't like they had anything to do to stay out that late for anyway, but it was still a blow to their potential social lives. The last time she'd stayed out late was a month ago when her dad and Aunt Krista extended their curfew for prom.

Perrie hadn't been in the mood to go to the dance at first, but Maisie bugged her about it endlessly. Even with offers from a couple of guys and girls, Maisie politely shot them down and convinced Perrie to go with her instead.

Maisie rubbed at her chin, and Perrie could sense her detective skills itching to come out. *Hell, mine are, too.*

"Maybe we could question friends or family who know these missing people?" Maisie asked. "Nothing is getting done here."

"I'm not sure that would go over well, even if you did have a badge. One day you'll have plenty of time to solve any crime you want."

"Yeah, I guess you're right about that." Maisie pulled into the parking lot of the school, managing to find a good spot right away.

Maisie sighed, and Perrie could tell she was still thinking about the missing people. Her cousin had once told her she wanted to pursue a career in fashion design when college started, but these days she seemed to be leaning more toward lead detective.

Perrie was an official adult according to "society," but it didn't feel like much had changed. That was probably because high school still had a few weeks left and she didn't have a good job. Hell, she couldn't even find a part-time job. But she was also still figuring out what college classes to take in the fall, as well as what career she wanted. Apparently, the college she'd been looking at didn't offer miming as a major, which she would be all over. She'd even find it useful wearing one of Maisie's patches while working her hands across an imaginary wall. But seriously, the only thing she had at the moment was an orchestra scholarship.

I have the rest of my life to figure things out though, right?

TWO

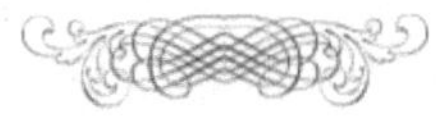

Opening the car door, Perrie threw her heavy backpack over her shoulder and grabbed her cello out of the trunk. A wave of mixed emotions flew through her, and she just knew it wasn't going to be a shit day.

As they headed toward the school, with her hands thrashing all over the place, Maisie asked, "Are we going to the horror film festival? It's next month!"

"Hell yeah, I'm all over it. I think the guy who plays Pinhead is supposed to be one of the guests there. If only some of the classic horror greats were still alive."

Maisie's hands continued to thrash ridiculously. "I know, right? Boris Karloff is practically my baby."

Vincent Price would be Perrie's.

When they finally breezed into the school, Perrie made the mistake of turning her head away from Maisie. Her smile and laughter vanished. The first bell hadn't even rang yet and she already spotted the jerk.

Neven Lee. Formerly known as "Nev." Once her Nev. Then he'd ripped her heart into a thousand tiny pieces, cutting those little morsels even smaller before lighting them all on fire—until they were nothing but ashes.

Neven stood off to the side with his black hair overgrown and shaggy, his warm brown eyes catching hers. He tried to give her a close-lipped smile and Perrie turned her head away, but not as quickly as she should've.

Maisie's eye followed the remnants of Perrie's gaze. "Just ignore him. We're almost done with school, and then you won't have to see him again."

Her cousin was being sympathetic, but Perrie knew she still missed him. She never actually told Maisie she couldn't talk to him. But Maisie felt just about as betrayed as Perrie did, and she wanted so badly to scrub that part of her brain clean to forget about him. It had been six months. Six whole months since her heart had been left for dead. She was being overly dramatic, but she didn't care.

"Easier said than done." Perrie turned her head one more time, noticing Neven walking toward them. *Damn.* Maisie scratched the side of her face. Then she looked at the ceiling and off to the side, seeming not to know exactly what to do.

Forget Maisie. Perrie needed to get out of there. Her surroundings offered no escape, and she was completely rooted in place. All her nerve endings lit up, and a slight panic formed in her chest as his large hand delicately enclosed her bicep.

"Happy birthday, Perrie," Neven said hesitantly.

She yanked her arm out of his grasp, as if his touch would melt her skin away. "Don't touch me." Her voice was just a whisper.

Hurt radiated across Neven's face, as it always did when she lashed out at him. For the first two months after she'd stopped speaking to him, he tried every single day to talk to her. Then it turned into every week, then every month, and then he didn't try anymore. *Until today.*

He never stopped looking at Perrie in school, though. It was almost as if he was waiting for her to approach him. That would never happen, and he could stay being an asshole for all she cared. *Yes, I believe asshole is still the correct word at this moment.*

Like always, she had to crane her neck to see his tall hovering form. "Don't give me that look, Nev. It isn't going to do you much good. And don't expect me to feel sorry for you."

He had the nerve to smile a wide grin, displaying each and every annoyingly perfect tooth. "You called me Nev. Not 'Neven' like you have been."

Flexing her fingers at her sides, she brought them to her palms and dug them finger by finger into a fist. She wanted to punch him—*hard*. But she didn't. She couldn't because she still saw a friend in his face, and she shut that thought down fast.

"Neven," she said through gritted teeth. "Leave me alone. I'll never forgive you."

He scowled, frustration written in his expression. He ran his hands through his hair and grabbed it like he wanted to rip it out—most likely to throw the strands at her face. They glared at each other until he calmly lowered his hands to his sides.

"Damn it, Perrie. How many times do I have to tell you that I have no clue what the hell you've been talking about for the past six months? Anyone else would've given up already, but you and me"—he pointed back and forth between them—"we're the real deal. If I have to wait an eternity for you, I will." He tipped his chin at her and walked off.

"Well," Maisie said in awe.

Whirling around to face her, she hissed, "*Well?*"

Maisie shook her head like she had sand or something in her hair and was trying to get it out. "Oh, yeah. Screw that loser!"

Sighing, Perrie nodded. Summer couldn't come soon enough. No more Neven, no more school.

The bell rang then and they headed to their first-period

English class together.

Their teacher, Mr. Carter, was possibly the only instructor who she found to be awesome. Perrie's writing skills were average at best, but he could turn anyone's work into a masterpiece.

After Perrie finished writing a short story on why classic horror movies were an art form, she watched from her desk as Mr. Carter drew a picture resembling the Mona Lisa in Paint. He did this every day after he taught the lessons, and she was always flabbergasted that he could use a computer mouse to do it. She tried once and gave up after attempting the letter P, which was when she realized her handwriting had been much better as a three-year-old.

The rest of her classes before lunch passed way too slowly. During Math, she finished her homework, so she didn't have anything to do besides stare at Mrs. Briggs's seventies-styled hair. It wasn't seventies cool either, it was rough—try Farrah Fawcett with a curling iron and electricity. Perrie wasn't quite sure if her teacher was stuck in an older era or invented one herself. Either way, she had no intention of ever visiting it. Her stomach let out a monstrous rumble. It had been repeating the broken-record process since she walked into class.

Inwardly groaning, she watched as the second hand on the clock slowly forced itself to the number she needed before the bell rang. *Thank fuck!* She practically wanted to do three fist pumps instead of one. That was how much she loved feeding the monster in her belly.

Having already packed up her binder and other belongings, Perrie collected her backpack and started to stand up. Out of habit, she reached for her cello, then she remembered she'd dropped it off after first period in the music room.

As she headed out the doorway, she spotted a familiar face. August.

Green eyes locked on hers, and in an instant, they both smiled at each other. August was about as relaxed as she'd ever seen him in black Chucks, jeans, and a baseball tee. The sight of him made her heart kick up a notch.

She practically ran into his arms and backed him up against the lockers. Chuckling deeply against her ear, he hugged her back with just as much force.

With her friend August, she didn't have to look up as far as she'd had to with Neven to see his face. She was about to say something when her eyes drifted to the Devil passing them in the hallway. If looks could kill. Neven didn't so much as glance at her—his dagger-throwing gaze was for August alone. They used to talk a little, but not anymore.

"So, I got you something for your birthday," August said against the side of her face. His breath brushed her ear, and her skin absorbed the warmth.

Perrie pulled back, lifting her brows. "You didn't have to get me anything."

He released her to unzip his backpack and fished out a tiny box. "Don't worry. It isn't an engagement ring."

Laughing, she took the box from him and opened it. She gaped, her heart swelling at the sight. Tucked inside was a silver necklace with a cello-bow pendant, encrusted with small, sparkling sapphires.

"You can also read the back." He grinned.

Perrie flipped it over and read the engraved two words: *I'm here*.

Taking a deep swallow, her heart pounding even more, she pulled him to her and kissed his soft cheek. "Thank you!"

She didn't know what it was, but lately she'd been *feeling* something more for August. Unfortunately, she didn't want to have feelings for anyone. After breaking up with Neven, Perrie's goal was to get through high school, do the college thing, and see what happened after that.

August had been making it harder. They may have started out as friends, but something was changing. In the past, Perrie had chosen to ignore it for as long as humanly possible by reminding herself she'd hated him before all of this.

When August moved here and started his senior year at her school, Perrie had never thought she could hate someone so much, so fast. There was no real reason—he hadn't attacked her per se. He just waltzed into Orchestra class and took over first chair, *her* first chair, like his name was written on it. She'd been undeniably *pissed*. That first day of senior year, she was happily sitting in her seat from the prior year. And as class began, their teacher introduced the new student, August, and stated that he had a late audition. It was a surprise to everyone when he took over first chair right then and there, like he was a king or some shit.

Cello was the one thing she excelled at, and she knew it was her one ticket to a scholarship for college. She still got one, but back then she'd thought everything would be wrecked.

Perrie had wanted to rip him apart. She couldn't believe that this guy, with his perfect face and perfect curly blond hair, had taken her spot right out from under her nose. He sat down next to her without so much as a glance, even though she'd been staring multiple daggers at him.

When the bell rang, and the class had emptied except for them, Perrie had waited as far away from the offender as possible.

Neven had been running late after basketball and her teacher had already left for the day. It was just the two of them and that alone made her even more furious.

Finally, he glanced Perrie's way, and the look he gave her held zero emotion. Then the fucker had turned around. It was almost like he couldn't have cared less.

Her brows lowered, her temper rising.

Picking up her expensive bow, that her dad had saved for her last Christmas present, Perrie took it and slowly approached him. As she came upon him, he was completely oblivious, polishing or maybe tuning his instrument—which made her anger pulse harder. When he finally glanced up from his cello, confused by her aggression, she looked him straight in the eye and tapped her bow to his chest.

"So, you think you can just magically come in here like some kind of magician and poof your way into first chair?" She stood so close she could smell his soapy scent. It was an addicting smell, sort of like how gasoline could be, even though it shouldn't.

At that very moment she could tell he didn't think of her as *nothing* anymore.

His lips puckered and his head tilted to the side. "First off, you haven't even heard me play. Not that I'm Mozart or anything, but I earned first chair."

He was fighting a smile at that point, but his words took shape in her head. That was true. She hadn't heard him play a single note of music. Everything inside her was driven by an idiotic amount of jealousy. Tantrum be gone.

"Well then, play for me."

He just stood there, so she said it again as a question, "Will you play for me?"

"Sure. But I can't play if you have that bow jammed into my chest the whole time." His head cocked to the other side, playfully studying her "weapon."

He was right though, so Perrie dropped her hand back to her side, removing her bow. Heat rushed to her cheeks in embarrassment—truth be told, she had been more anxious to hear him play. She shifted from foot to foot, waiting to hear the notes.

As August played, her opinion changed. He was better than her by a landslide. He played with fluidity—everything about the way he moved, from his fingers, to the way the bow went across the strings, was close to Houdini-level magic. Perrie could try and try, and she would never be able to play like he did that day.

When he finished, she knew he had rightly earned his

place.

"Congratulations on first chair," Perrie had said while turning to pack up her things and leave.

"And you are?" he asked.

She slid her bow into its case before responding. "Perrie Madeline."

"Perrie." He tried the sound of it like he was testing a brand-new instrument. "I'm August Hartley."

She couldn't contain her high-pitched laughter as she'd spoken, "Oh, I know. The second Mr. Hamm said we had a new first chair, I made sure I got the name."

August smiled. It was everything a smile should be—real, warm, and welcoming. Perrie knew she was going to like him. When she'd looked back at him from the classroom door, she'd given August one last quick wave.

Who would've thought that glaring daggers at someone for a full class period would gain a new best friend?

Perrie shrugged off the memory, its purpose no longer helping, and accepted August's gift before they met Maisie for lunch.

"Help me put it on?" she asked.

As soon as the cool silver of the necklace rested around her neck, latched at the nape, another crack against what she'd come to think of as her stone heart struck.

THREE

The lunch line in the cafeteria wrapped around the wall but it moved fast. Perrie grabbed a basket of hot fries, and August got his usual variety of pretty much everything.

Perrie spotted Maisie by the flash of her eye patch, consisting of reds, whites, and blacks. She'd already changed into a different one, as she was known to do throughout the day. It resembled a deck of playing cards with hearts, spades, clubs, and diamonds.

"Hey, guys!" Maisie practically yelled.

August and Perrie sat down next to each other, directly across from Maisie.

"Nice patch," he said, pointing his fork at her right eye.

She brushed her hand across it as if in thought, which Perrie guessed she was. "Thanks. This one was getting rather lonely in my backpack, and the other one was tired of working its shift."

"That totally makes sense." Perrie nodded with a smile. *Of course it makes sense, minus the fact that a patch* doesn't *have feelings.*

"So, have you guys heard about the other missing person?" August asked right before he shoved a piece of pizza into his mouth.

Perrie's stomach sank at the question. "Yeah, Maisie and I were just talking about that this morning. We don't know him, but this is getting pretty sketchy with all these disappearances."

August set down what was left of his pizza. "I thought he looked familiar, but I don't think I've seen him around or anything."

Maisie couldn't contain herself and dove into a list of her theories about the disappearances. "If the missing people were kidnapped, it could be someone like Jeffrey Dahmer, although it isn't only men who have vanished. Or possibly Ed Gein! Maybe the suspect is also digging up bodies from graves. Although, no bodies have been found yet is the problem."

August remained focused on Maisie, clearly intent on hearing every single one of her theories.

"Unless the kidnapper is like Charles Manson and sending people to do his or her dirty work," Perrie piped in, making the mistake of glancing over at Neven's table. At a nearly full table, he sat with some of the other guys from basketball. As if he felt her looking, his gaze met hers, locking.

Perrie glanced down and forced herself to not peer back up in that direction. It wasn't that she missed "them" because she was over that aspect with him. But she missed his friendship.

On the first day of ninth grade, students from the other junior highs in the area came together for high school. Neven, being one of those students, was the first person she'd met that day.

Perrie had no idea where she was going. Feeling completely lost, she'd bumped into Neven who offered to help her find her class. He'd said she looked like a confused tourist in a new country and pulled the schedule from her hand. Neven noticed they had first period together and proceeded to drag her along with him. Even though he'd already known some students in the class, he'd chosen to sit next to Perrie. After that, they'd become friends and he'd gotten along perfectly with Maisie's quirkiness.

The summer before eleventh grade, things began to change between Perrie and Neven. Their friendship grew into something new and different. His dad had passed away from a freak accident at work, and she was there every day with Neven to help him get through it. She'd known from experience how to grieve over a lost parent.

It was July, and Perrie had been leaving his house. When he'd come in to give her a hug, he instead pecked her lips, then instantly pulled away, as if he hadn't meant to do it at all. They'd stared at each other for several long moments before he leaned in to kiss her again. And she'd let him.

Neven Lee was her first kiss and her first everything else to follow. She'd loved him with all of her heart, until he split it in half. Perrie's heart wasn't as broken anymore, and after the bruises and cracks that were left behind, she'd wanted it to remain like stone.

"I think the Manson-esque theory could be possible." August's words knocked Perrie out of her reverie.

It was possible. She met Maisie's gaze and they both nodded in agreement.

"I think it has to be a guy, though," Perrie said.

"That's sexist." Maisie shook her finger at her. "Equality when it comes to kidnapping."

"I'm sorry, but most females can't lift some of these muscular human specimens." Perrie tapped her chin. "Unless there could be more than one."

"Like in the movie *Scream*?" Maisie's eye shone with excitement over the mention of one of her favorite nineties slasher films.

"Precisely." Perrie grinned.

"You two are virtually insane. That movie sucks." August grabbed Perrie's trash and tossed it away. With a horrific remark like that, he may have just destroyed any remaining possibility of them becoming more than friends. But she couldn't help but stare at his backside, the way his muscles flexed, the easy way he carried himself.

"You're ridiculous!" Maisie yelled to his back.

August shrugged without turning around. After he walked back to them, they left the cafeteria and headed to class, discussion about missing people forgotten.

"See you in last period," Perrie called to August as he stopped outside his next class.

"Battle of the cellos, doll face. Me and you!" he shouted back, her heart fluttering in her chest. It always did when he called her that.

Almost every day during their free time in Orchestra, August and Perrie battled it out. Sometimes she won, but only because he secretly let her.

The next period crept by at a sloth's pace. Perrie mainly watched Maisie doodle in her notebook to take up time. The little skeletal drawing looked like a masterpiece, while Perrie's doodles were just a bunch of repetitive circles drawn together that she continuously retraced. Shit-art, Perrie preferred to call it.

Last period finally arrived, and when Perrie walked into class, an unfamiliar face slid into view. A substitute teacher, which meant she would practice whatever the hell she was in the mood for.

August hadn't made it to class yet, so she strolled to the instrument closet, grabbed her cello case, and settled into her chair. As she struggled to pull out the instrument, a blond head passed through the door right as the bell rang. Perrie's chest tightened and she attempted to push the feeling away, but it stood its ground.

She opted to distract herself and focus on messing with her cello, checking to make sure everything was in tune to ignore the butterflies fluttering about inside her stomach. August took his seat next to hers, raking a hand through his hair, and the nervousness subsided.

Perrie's emotions around him were unpredictable, especially when she was trying so hard to fight them. August drew his cello out of its case—the instrument was far more refined compared to hers, not a single scratch or scuff mark on its smooth body.

"What's up with that guy?" He nodded in the direction of the teacher.

Right off the bat, Perrie knew exactly what he was talking about as she focused on the substitute again. How had she not noticed before? The guy looked like he just strolled out of the 1920s, wearing a suit that had to be authentic from the era. His dark brown hair was slicked back, glistening under the light, and far too perfectly shaped around his head.

"I feel like he's going to whip out one of those old bowler hats." She laughed a bit too loud. The substitute examined them and she tried to cover her mouth to muffle her laughter. His eyes narrowed in her direction. Perrie played it off and went back to tuning her cello, still smiling.

Despite her efforts, she couldn't manage to tune it. Even though she could usually get it right away with a tuner.

"Here, let me see what's going on with it." August took the instrument from her, his fingers softly brushing hers. Perrie's cheeks warmed, and she felt like a pubescent teen.

Attempting to tune a cello without a tuner never worked for her. She couldn't ever get the sound right by ear like some people could.

August, however, was a master at this. He plucked at the strings carefully, and she watched how he closed his eyes, noting the focus on his face as he listened to each vibration. Her lips parted in awe as she studied his ease.

He twisted the peg and plucked the string again, releasing a perfectly tuned note that was pure bliss. The sound of it struck her soul in a way only music could. He held the cello out for Perrie to take, pulling her out of her trance.

"There," he said with a smirk.

Perrie took the instrument and cradled it like a newborn baby. "Thank you. You're a god!" she said dramatically, bowing her head in praise of his abilities. August rolled his eyes and chuckled it off.

After what had happened with Neven, Maisie and August had been everything. Perrie liked to think they'd become the Three Musketeers of Deer Park High School. Not the classical musketeers either, but the perfect blend of chocolate and fluffy nougat wrapped up in a flashy wrapper.

For the rest of class, they bickered about musical notes and best horror movies. As soon as the bell rang, Perrie packed everything up and Maisie sauntered into the classroom. The three of them made their way out to the large, empty parking lot, where August's car appeared to be missing.

She whirled to August and frowned. "Where's your car?"

"I woke up with a flat tire this morning." He rubbed his eyes and sighed loudly. "Didn't feel like working on it until after school today. My parents had already left for work, so I walked to school instead."

Maisie straightened, seeming prepared to save the day. "We can give you a ride home!"

"It's all right. It's not that far of a walk." He shrugged nonchalantly.

"Anyway, August—you're coming with us." Perrie rolled her eyes, grabbed his arm, and pulled him with her. He put up absolutely no resistance as they piled into Maisie's car and took off. August only lived a couple of minutes out of the way from their destination.

Maisie took a turn down Oak Street, which Perrie had always found ironic. The street was lined on both sides with tall trees, each one reaching their crooked branches toward the other as if longing for their touch. For a town called Deer Park, Perrie had seen more trees on a street corner than actual deer. *Not* one *single deer, to be exact.*

Out of nowhere, Maisie slammed on the brakes and Perrie's chest struck hard against the seat belt. Then she smashed back into the seat just as hard. *Are my organs still intact?* It was the only thing she could think about in that moment. Seriously, they felt like they were bleeding profusely.

"What the hell?" August and Perrie said at the same time. Maisie didn't reply—she was staring across the street to the left.

"Look!" she exclaimed.

Perrie followed Maisie's pointed finger and stilled. Across from them stood an enormous gray stone building, unbelievably tall, and its walls lined with huge rocks along the base. Among the rocks, it appeared there were absolutely no windows of any kind. A curving archway framed an entrance with one of the tallest wooden doors she'd ever seen. *Creepily unusual.*

"Impossible," Perrie breathed.

"This has never been here before." August's jaw hung open.

He was right. He was beyond right. There was no way in hell this place was magically built overnight. Even if it were possible, the building was obviously old, at least over a hundred years old.

"Maybe we never really noticed it before." Maisie unbuckled herself and opened the car door, completely taken by the sight of the building.

Perrie's eyes widened, and she threw her hands up, waving them like a lunatic. "*Never* noticed it before? This *giant* stone mansion?"

"Perrie has a point, Maisie." August continued to examine the building with his brows up his forehead.

With hesitation, Perrie stepped out of the car, August following behind her. They walked around to stand near Maisie, completely speechless as they prolonged their staring marathon at the place. It really was an unusual structure to be sitting in the middle of her town. How had it not drawn major attention from the locals?

"We should investigate!" Maisie moved before either of them could protest.

"Just a quick look," Perrie said, her interest piqued. She fell into step beside Maisie, and her fingers itched with curiosity.

Perrie walked to the door at a leisurely pace, as if she had all night to see what was going on. They inched closer to the arched doorway, where overgrown grass met a block of cement, and two things popped into her line of sight. First, a golden plaque on the door with words on it written in an elegant, yet outdated black script.

Quinsey Wolfe's Glass Vault

Maisie tilted her head to the side, seeming skeptical of the plaque. "Not sure what a glass vault is."

Perrie motioned at a sign to the right of the door, then shifted closer to see what was written on it.

The illustrious Quinsey Wolfe presents a wonder of the world, a true sight to behold in his infamous glass museum. A forewarning to onlookers and wanderers—beware of your imagination and curiosity. This is not for the faint of heart.

"Not for the faint of heart?" August repeated the line. "Pretty cliché for my taste, but okay."

"I'd have to agree," Perrie said with a quirked eyebrow.

Maisie pushed Perrie to the side so she could get a better look. She lifted her eye patch to rest on her forehead and examined it more thoroughly. "I like the sound of that."

She would.

August reached for the doorknob and jiggled it. "It's locked."

"Oh, look." Maisie tapped a paper sign just below the description. "It also says opening soon and that they're hiring. I can message this Quinsey Wolfe guy at this email address."

Maisie unzipped her purse and pulled out a small notepad and pencil. *Of course* she carried around a pencil and small notepad. How could she not? She always had an idea or something brewing that she needed to write down, so she or *Perrie* didn't forget.

"What's with the notebook?" August asked.

Maisie studied the sign while writing. "Because you never know when you're going to need one."

"You aren't really going to apply, are you?" August pressed his shoulder against the door, his arms crossed over his chest.

Maisie brought her eye patch back over her eye. "Heck yes, I am! I've been looking for a job I would like, but nothing holds my interest. This place sounds awesome."

"Right," Perrie drawled. "So, this place just grows out of the ground overnight? I like strange, but I don't know about this. I say we get the hell out of here."

"Although," August started, "now that I'm looking around, there are a lot of trees that have been cut down. Maybe it's just been hidden all this time?" He stepped in front of them and inspected the ground further.

It was true, obviously there were trees here before and had since been cleared out. Perrie still found it odd that they wouldn't have noticed some old, historical-looking mansion when they'd gone down this street before.

"So, it's settled. I'm going to email this Quinsey Wolfe as soon as I get home!" Maisie bounced in place.

"You do that." Perrie rolled her eyes. She was going to search for a job soon, but this place didn't look like her cup of tea. It did seem to be Maisie's though.

Unease lingered in her chest as they headed back to the car. Perrie glanced back one more time at the aged mansion. The hairs of her arm stood on end as the building seemed to be watching them in return.

Only silence filled the car for the rest of the ride to August's place. When Maisie pulled up in front of his house, he reached around the passenger seat and gave Perrie a hug.

She held onto him longer than necessary as he said, "I hope the rest of your birthday is spectacular, doll face."

After he released her and stepped out of the car, Perrie grasped the necklace at the base of her throat and thoughts of the odd museum vanished from her mind.

FOUR

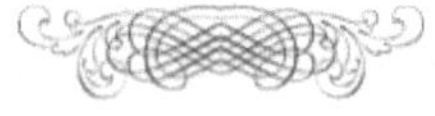

"Are you ready for your birthday dinner?" Maisie asked, turning onto their street.

"My monster is," Perrie said as she patted her stomach.

Every year Perrie's aunt made her a birthday dinner, and it was no small feast. Leftovers would last for almost an entire week—it was more than a two-person household could handle.

"You better get to the red velvet cake before I scarf that entire thing down." Maisie chuckled. She would do it too.

Once Maisie parked in the driveway, Perrie dropped her school things off at her house, then headed back to Maisie's through the freshly cut grass.

Maisie was already somewhere inside her house—most likely eyeballing the cake.

Practically leaping over the steps, Perrie burst inside. Her dad, still wearing his chemical plant uniform, stood by the table with a soda in his hand, obviously surprised by her dramatic entrance. He always took off a little early from work on her birthday so he could make it for this occasion. It almost brought a tear to her eye that he, along with her aunt and uncle, put in so much effort for her. But Perrie's main concern at the moment was the food.

"Hey, sweetie." Her dad walked over to her and gave her shoulders a squeeze, then kissed the top of her head as if she was still his little girl. "Happy birthday. How does it feel to officially be an adult?"

Pulling back from the hug, she laughed. "I feel the same as yesterday."

"Don't worry, you have the rest of your life to feel like an adult and trust me, you younger people have it made."

"Okay, Dad, you're talking like you're seventy. Adulting is fine."

"*Fine*?" Aunt Krista shook her head and waved her hand dismissively. "Not once you get the bills every month."

Since her mom had left, Perrie had wished so hard to have a mom like Krista. She treated her like another daughter, and even though she was great, it wasn't the same.

"You guys ready to cut the cake?" Her dad must've sensed Maisie pining for it.

"Finally!" Maisie sighed dramatically.

"Maisie, please." Aunt Krista glared.

"Yes, Mom?" she asked sweetly.

"Manners?"

"Oh, just give the girl some cake already," Uncle Jaron interrupted, his dark eyes settling on the dessert. "Actually, give me some cake."

Aunt Krista swept her long hair over her shoulder and lit the candles on the cake. Everyone then joined in to sing *Happy Birthday*. Awkwardness washed over Perrie, but it always did when the focus was on her. As soon as the song ended, the feeling left and she grabbed a plate.

Her aunt really outdid herself with the birthday party this year. Any kind of dip Perrie could imagine rested on the table. Aunt Krista knew her so well. Perrie could literally drink the cheese dip and eat the guacamole alone. Every counter and table showcased sandwiches, cupcakes, cookies, cake, and chips. Anyone who saw it would think the food was for a party of fifty instead of the five of them.

As Perrie bit into a cupcake, Uncle Jaron mentioned their summer plans. They would be going to visit Maisie's grandparents in Turkey for their annual trip. She almost wished she could go, but Maisie said it really wasn't that exciting. Perrie's dad agreed to watch the house while they were away, which really meant she'd be the one checking in and doing the chores.

"Hopefully the police will get a solid lead while you're gone," her dad said. All talk of summer vacation was out the window as the conversation took a darker turn. Perrie guessed they were on to disappearing people now. "It just has me worried that no one has turned up." He sighed. She knew what he was more worried about, what he didn't know how to say out loud. *Me.* He was worried about her. He wouldn't know what to do if she disappeared too.

Aunt Krista placed a hand on his shoulder. "Don't worry, James. They'll find the person responsible."

I hope they do, too.

Uncle Jaron nodded in agreement. Aunt Krista was the practical thinker in the family, and Uncle Jaron usually followed her lead. She knew just what to say at the right moment to comfort anyone, but her dad's shoulders remained stiff, his smile gone.

Her dad peered down at his watch. "I think it's time for us to head home."

Perrie helped Aunt Krista pack up the leftovers and gave everyone a hug before leaving. She and her dad moseyed on back to their house to hang out in front of the TV for a little while. He flipped on the news first thing and watched the screen flicker absently with stories about animals dressed like chickens and a woman arrested in a shopping center for "public indecency."

Biting her lip, Perrie could tell he wasn't all there.

"You all right, Dad?" she asked, dragging the blanket

closer to her chest.

"Yeah." His gaze was vacant, still worrying about the missing cases.

Perrie decided not to tell him about her run-in with Neven, August's gift, or the strange mansion on the way home. When he was in this mood, everything stayed a one-word answer. So after about an hour, Perrie kissed him on the cheek and headed down the hall to start on her homework.

Luckily, she didn't have much to do since she finished her math homework in class. All she had left was a paper for English, which she finished in less than an hour. While she waited on her slow ass printer, she checked her email.

Nothing too special ever popped up in her inbox, mostly junk mail. She had a wretched habit of subscribing to pointless websites when they offered discounts on free shipping. Eventually she would unsubscribe from some of them, but for now she started deleting the emails. Except for the one that was a few dollars off admission to the horror film festival next month.

As she scanned the rest, her stomach sank as her gaze settled on a familiar name. Neven. She debated whether or not she should read or delete it, but curiosity always won with her.

Hey Perrie,

I just wanted to tell you that today made me realize just how much I miss you. We've been together on your birthday for the last three years. Could we at least start talking again?
Love Always,
Nev

"What a douche," she muttered, reading it again. *Okay, maybe he isn't being a douche at the moment, but he still is one.* She held the cursor over the delete button, but then an impulse made her change her mind and decide to give him a quick reply.

Neven,
I'll think about it.
Perrie

Short and simple. Perrie hit send and signed out of her email. Shuffling to her dresser, she reached for the clasp of her necklace from August. She took it off and left it to sit neatly on top of her dresser.

Her thoughts rotated back and forth from Neven's email to August's gift, and how she'd lost one friend but gained another.

Perrie had been about two months into her senior year. She didn't want to go to school the next day, but she forced herself to anyway. Her goal that day was to continue to avoid Neven like the Black Plague. Fear and anxiety had taken over her limbs, though, and it felt like they were going to fall off at any point.

Once her first class was over, she'd been fine the rest of the day … for the most part. Well, not *fine*, she just told herself she was going to get through her classes. She was like a stone statue, cold and unfeeling, and that was all she'd wanted to be.

That same day she decided to stay late after Orchestra to practice and to escape, while being alone with music. Perrie remembered walking to the instrument closet to grab a music stand, then becoming frustrated. She couldn't find the stand she'd wanted, the one she *always* used, and suddenly it all felt like too much. It seemed stupid now, but her mind was a jumbled mess back then and her heart ached.

Perrie's legs collapsed and she'd curled into herself. That was when the tears came. It was the first time she'd cried about Neven. She cried like never before. When her mom left, back when she loved her, she didn't cry as hard then as she did that day in the music room. Everything about that day, that time, that place, overwhelmed Perrie from the second she stepped into her first class that morning.

August had barely made a noise when he found her sobbing and huddled up against a wall.

With him standing there so close and her heartbroken, it had made her tears flow even more. Perrie shifted away from him, but he didn't leave. Instead, he sank down beside her on the carpeted floor and pulled her onto his lap. His warmth, his comfort, made her tears slow.

Perrie and August hadn't spoken to each other outside of casual conversation about school or music. He would sometimes talk to Neven after class when he would meet her there. They'd been sort of friends, but more like acquaintances. He was the first person that she'd told everything—before she'd told Maisie.

When her crying ceased, she was holding onto him like she'd known him her entire life. There were questions written all over his face, but he never asked them.

After that day, she and August grew closer and closer. She'd been so sure they could just be friends.

Now, Perrie didn't know. It was so strange how a friendship could begin so fast in a single instant, but it could, and it did. August's thoughtful gift was a reminder of that change.

She shook her head and snapped her fingers. *No more Neven or August tonight.* This wasn't a love triangle or any other weird love-shaped fictional bullshit. It was her moving on from one guy, where the feelings were already dead, to fighting her emotions for someone else.

Tearing off the day's clothes, she threw on her old tattered T-shirt and baggy polka-dot pants before wandering back into the living room. Her dad was already getting up from the couch and heading to bed.

"Good night, sweetheart. I hope you had a great day. Happy birthday one last time." It was the longest sentence he'd said to her that night.

"I did. I love you, Dad." She waved him good night, then flipped on the TV.

"I love you, too." He yawned and disappeared into his bedroom.

Snatching the flowered quilt from the edge of the couch, Perrie pulled it to her chin and turned on *Dracula*. It was the black and white version, and those ones were always the best.

About five minutes after the first woman on screen screamed, a gentle tap sounded at the door. It could only be one person at this late hour. Tossing off the blanket, Perrie padded to the door and looked through the peephole. *Yep, I was right*. Maisie stood there in her pajamas, her fingers tapping her thighs. Perrie whistled a birdy signal like they'd started when they were younger. Maisie released a high-pitched one in return and Perrie threw the door open, tugging her inside.

"What are you doing coming over so late? Is everything all right?"

"I have the most exciting news." Maisie was practically beaming in her bright yellow pajama pants and her long-sleeve banana-print shirt. An eye patch shaped like a banana covered her eye, matching her clothing.

"I have three questions. First, do you sleep in eye patches? Second, couldn't you have just sent me a text or called? And third, can we sit down?"

"My answers are… No, they would get in the way while I sleep. I could have, but for absolute expression, I can't do that over text—emojis aren't a replacement. Last, yes, let's sit down because I see you're watching one of my favorite movies ever."

Maisie plopped down on the couch, snatched the blanket, and covered her legs. Perrie shut the front door, then sat beside her and grabbed the edge of the blanket to cover herself. "Okay, what's this big news?"

She frowned as her gaze settled on Perrie's face. "Hey, where's your new eye patch? Remember, you promised to wear it."

With a huff, Perrie left her comfortable spot and located the patch on the table. She then slid it over her eye, the fabric soft like silk. "There. Happy?"

"Yes! Now, remember the Glass Vault?"

"Of course I remember the old, creepy mansion that appeared out of nowhere! How could I forget?" Perrie rubbed the side of her head and pretended to look lost. Maisie ignored her sarcasm.

"Anyway, as soon as we finished up dinner, I emailed my resume to Quinsey Wolfe. He emailed me back in record time and said I have the job." She paused for effect. "I start this Thursday, nine o'clock sharp!"

Squinting, Perrie nodded in confusion. "Wait a second, so you're starting work at nine in the morning? We have school."

Maisie shook her hand wildly in front of her face. "No! No. He wanted me to start at nine at night."

Her jaw dropped. That seemed like odd hours for a museum to keep on a regular day-to-day. They also hadn't officially opened yet. Maybe they were getting everything in order for whenever they planned to open, though?

"I don't know. That seems pretty late for a school night— or any night—to go into work at a museum. It's not a bar or strip club here, or is it?" Perrie paused. "Did he say what time you would be getting off?"

She shrugged emphatically. "I told him I could work till midnight for now until summer starts, which is almost here anyway."

"What did your parents say? I'm willing to bet they aren't overly thrilled about the late exotic dancer-like hours."

Maisie stayed silent and looked off to the side to try and hide her guilt.

"You didn't tell them, did you?" Perrie wasn't surprised.

Maisie had been looking for a job that met her impossibly high standards for a while now. Besides selling her eye patches, she didn't have any real work experience, and she refused to do anything that involved food. Hell, Perrie refused to do anything that involved food. She supposed working at the possible freak show of a mansion must've meant a great deal to her cousin if she hadn't said anything to her parents yet.

"You can't either. This is like my dream job!" Maisie brought her thumbnail to her teeth and chewed nervously.

"Dream job?" She laughed a little too loudly and she hadn't meant it to sound so harsh. "The whole thing seems sketchy. We don't even know what a glass vault is! A museum grows out of the ground, a guy you haven't even met, no interview, hires you, and he wants you to start right away? It doesn't make sense."

Unfazed by her questioning, Maisie said, "But, Perrie, he sounded so desperate in the email! It's so new to the area, barely anyone has applied. He wants to open soon and needs the help. It's perfect timing!"

Of course no one else had applied. She'd had no idea the Glass Vault even existed until this afternoon.

"Fine." Perrie relented. "I won't say anything, but you have to get August and me in for free once it opens. I want to see what this place looks like."

"Deal." She grinned widely and drew an exaggerated cross over her heart with her finger.

They stayed up a little longer and finished watching the rest of the bloodsucking goodness. When it was over, Perrie walked Maisie to the door and waited until she made it home safely. After her cousin had crawled through her bedroom window, Perrie waved good night and shut the door.

Once she locked the door behind her, she yawned and removed the lion eye patch from her face. She turned it over and over in her hand, thinking about the Glass Vault and what kind of things waited inside.

FIVE

School that day was as mundane as it could get. Maisie had a group project she needed to work on with a few people in her class, so Perrie caught a ride home with August since he'd fixed his tire.

"Do you want to come inside and hang out for a bit?" Perrie turned to August as he pulled into her driveway.

He was rocking the wind-blown look, his blond hair a curly mess and sticking up all over the place. A smile spread across his face and her cheeks warmed *again*.

Enough of that shit already.

"Yeah, sure, I don't have to be at work until later." August was a janitor at his dad's law firm and cleaned the building a few times during the week.

The house would be empty since her dad was working overtime, so he wouldn't be home until later this evening. Not that she planned on doing anything besides them hanging out. *Or do I?*

She couldn't help the image coming to her of her straddling August in the driver seat, her hips rocking against his as he gripped her waist. Their mouths coasting over one another, his tongue dancing with hers.

Perrie didn't look at him as she stepped out of the car, a heat spreading through her, lower and lower. She cleared her throat and told herself to calm the hell down.

"Do you want something to drink?" Perrie asked as she opened the door and entered the foyer.

He shrugged out of his jacket. "I'll take some water."

Perrie grabbed them each a room-temperature bottled water from the pantry. She then chugged hers almost all the way down as she went back into the living room to where August was waiting.

"Thanks," he said when she handed a bottle over to him.

"Sorry if it's too warm. Cold water just rubs me the wrong way."

"Yeah? We're in sync then." He nervously fiddled with the cap. "So, Perrie, I've wanted to ask you something."

"Oh, yeah? What's up?" His rambling had gotten her full attention. He was totally focused on her face and she could practically feel the intensity of his stare. Did he *know* what she'd been thinking earlier?

"I was wondering if you wanted to hang out sometime?"

She frowned, a little unsure of what he was trying to get at. "Sure, but we hang out all the time. We're hanging out now."

He raked a hand through his hair and took a deep breath. "I mean like go *out* out."

"Do you mean like an actual date?" She bit the inside of her cheek, feeling like a deer caught in headlights.

He inspected the floor as though he was searching for something. She hoped she didn't just embarrass herself by asking if it wasn't what he'd even meant.

"Yes, doll face, like you and me. An actual date." Her heart slammed against her rib cage as he continued, "I like you. I have for a while now, but I wasn't sure when would be a good time. If you don't want to, if this is too soon, I understand. I don't want anything to get weird, but I had to try."

Perrie's heart pounded harder as her gaze locked onto his green irises. The stone in her chest cracked even more. Perspiration pressed against her shirt as she swallowed her remaining sip of water. She'd told herself she wouldn't get in this position again for a long time, but the truth was she liked him. This was her chance to tell him she'd give it a shot. Perrie had been hiding under the surface of her feelings for too long. She needed air, and August was oxygen.

But then the fucking doorbell rang.

"Hold that thought, okay?" Ragged breaths escaped her as she rushed to answer the door. She was prepared to tell whomever it was to get lost when she pulled the door open to Neven. The words were knocked right out of her, and her stomach plummeted to the earth. She should've checked the damn peephole first.

Anger coursed through her veins, and her words were trapped in her throat for a moment. "What the hell are you doing here?"

"We need to talk."

"Sorry, pass." Perrie motioned to the living room where August stood. "I have company. This will have to wait." She began to shut the door, but Neven stuck his foot in to stop it from closing.

Perrie clenched her jaw and was about two seconds from pulling the door back open to slam it on his foot, when he reached out to touch her. "It's important. Please?"

The worried look on his face made her halt, think. "Fifteen minutes." Maybe the sight of him wasn't bothering her as much anymore, so she decided to let him in.

Neven stopped dead in his tracks when he spotted August. "Alone?"

"Anything you have to say you can say in front of him," Perrie said and crossed her arms. August rocked back and forth on his heels, clearly uncomfortable.

"It's fine, Perrie. You can call me later." August started to collect his things.

Perrie rushed over and tried to stop him, not wanting him to leave. "August, you don't have to go."

"Don't worry about it. Just call me later, all right?" He threw his jacket over his shoulder and she walked with him to the door. Neven remained in the background watching them quietly.

"Okay. Talk to you later." She smiled, trying to ignore the awkward situation.

Closing the door behind her, Perrie pressed her back to it and took a deep breath.

"This better be good." When she looked at Neven, she couldn't control the past from coming to her in a rush.

The day everything went downhill with Neven was six months ago. Everything in Perrie's life had felt perfect. She wasn't as worried about the future and college because life at that moment was great.

It only took one mistake to ruin everything. Neven had called her one morning to say he wasn't feeling well and wouldn't be at school. She'd told him she would check on him after.

Perrie remembered every minute detail about that day. She could recall the crisp smell of the fall air, the caress of the light breeze, the sound of the leaves and branches brushing together, and even the crackle of Nev's neighbor grilling meat outside.

Maisie had dropped Perrie off at his house on the way home, and she should've told her cousin to wait, but she'd never needed to before.

Nev's car had been the only one in the driveway, and the door to his house unlocked. He'd always left it unlocked for her when he knew she was coming over, so she didn't think anything of it at the time.

After grabbing a bottled water from the cabinet in his kitchen, she'd headed upstairs. Loud music echoed from his room, the way it always had when he was home alone. As she inched closer, *noises* came from inside the open door. Perrie had known what the sounds were from the second they struck her ears, but still she persisted. She needed to confirm her worst nightmares and torture herself further.

When she reached the doorway, her gaze first landed on male and *female* clothes scattered about the room. Perrie swallowed her anxiety. Nev was right there in his bed with a redheaded woman who she'd never seen before. Then again, she couldn't see her face, but she would've recognized that hair anywhere—it was the color of fire. She was on top of him rolling her hips against Neven's naked body, his fingers digging into her waist, his eyes closed, his lips parted. Neven's hands drifted up to cradle her breasts as he groaned, the redhead arching in pleasure.

It hit Perrie all at once and she couldn't take it anymore. She hightailed it out of there. Thinking back now, she should've done or said something. She should've pulled the redhead off him and slapped Neven hard across the face. There was always the should've, would've, could've, but instead, she'd chosen to leave.

Perrie had walked all the way home, dazed and disoriented, the tears never coming.

Neven called several times that evening, but she refused to answer the phone. The whole night and the following day numbness consumed her. She robotically went through the motions of brushing her teeth, showering, dressing, and so on. It wasn't until later in the orchestra room she'd let go and allowed herself to feel everything—the hurt, the betrayal, and the brokenness.

When Neven had called that evening, she told him it was over, to leave her the fuck alone, and never speak to her again.

The sound of Neven rambling on about something interrupted her thoughts, but she couldn't focus on what he'd said.

"Well?" Neven blurted, instead of explaining himself, shifting from one foot to the other.

"Well, what?" she snapped, even though it was her fault for not listening.

He slid his hands into his pockets, seeming hesitant to say anything else. "Have you been down Oak Street lately?"

Perrie's heart lodged in her throat, her voice coming out in a rasp. "You saw the Glass Vault?"

His eyes widened at the mention of it. "Yes! I went down the street this morning on the way to school and noticed it. When I asked the guys at basketball, they had no idea what I was talking about."

"Why didn't you just send me another email? Or a text? I do have a phone. You didn't have to show up here."

"Would you have responded?" He shrugged and pursed his lips.

"I did email you back the last time, didn't I?" she bit back.

He waved it off, as if that detail wasn't important. "So you saw the Glass Vault?"

Perrie rubbed her chin with her thumb and forefinger. "I was with Maisie and August yesterday when we stumbled on it. Maisie already has a job there."

"She's gone inside the place? When I stopped there this morning it was locked up tight." He sighed.

"No, she emailed the owner, Quinsey Wolfe. He hired her right on the *internet* spot. It's incredibly odd."

His eyebrows shot up. "This creepy building appears out of nowhere, and Maisie gets a job there, even though she has no idea what's inside or what she'll be doing?" Neven shook his head. "It sounds just like her."

"It so does." Perrie snickered.

Their conversation was at least about the Glass Vault, but then the silence became tangible.

Neven let out a long breath. "Is there something going on between you and August?"

Fucking great. She crossed her arms. "No. Not at the moment. There could be, but I don't think that's any of your business."

Neven laced his fingers at the back of his neck and released a frustrated groan before throwing his hands into the air.

"Come on, Perrie! I still don't understand what I did wrong. You said I cheated on you, but I don't know when or how I could have if I was throwing up all day."

"But you went for a run? Who the hell goes running after vomiting?"

"Apparently, I do."

"I saw you, Neven. You were fucking some redhead." Perrie tried to keep her voice as even as possible. If she worked herself up, she would explode and break everything in the house.

"What girl?" he shouted.

"I don't know! She was naked, you were naked"—Perrie pointed at her brown hair—"and there was red hair with both your clothes on the floor!" she screamed. How could he keep lying about this?

He gritted his teeth, and she didn't think she'd ever seen him so mad. "Either you've been making this shit up for the past six months to mess with my head, or there's something seriously wrong with you if you think I would've ever cheated on you. I don't even like red hair!"

"Well, apparently, you did that day!" She was anxious to meet his fury with her own.

"I told you I was sick that morning and then about an hour later I felt fine. It was already too late, so I stayed home. You know how antsy I get, so I decided to go for a run before you came over. When I got home, you never showed up, so I called you several times. I didn't come to school the next morning because I was sick again." Leaning against the wall, he appeared to try and cool himself down by once again explaining what had happened. She had heard this story too many times already.

Her head pounded from having the same conversation again.

Neven went on, "It doesn't make sense, but what if that wasn't me? What if that was someone who *looked* like me?"

Perrie couldn't keep from rolling her eyes.

"That's the dumbest thing I've ever heard! So, you mean to tell me that two people broke into your house to have sex on your bed? Not to mention one of them happened to have your face?" She waved her hand in front of her own face for emphasis. "Come on, Nev."

"I get it. There's something strange going on here and I'm going to figure this shit out. Please trust me this one time, Perrie. I'll prove it to you. I just want my best friend back."

"Damn it. Fine." It might've been foolish, but anyone could hear the sincerity and frustration in his plea. She wasn't foolish enough to doubt what she'd seen though, but she would let him do his thing and see what he came up with.

His head drooped, seeming heavy with the weight of this mystery. "You know you're not the only one who's pissed. I wish you could have trusted me. I loved you then, and I still do, Perrie."

She was confident she could burn a hole straight through his heart if she stared hard enough. *Why can't he move on already?*

As he turned to leave, Neven glanced over his shoulder one final time. "See you tomorrow, Perrie."

He was wrong, though. A strange feeling poured over her, making her think that she wouldn't see him the following day.

SIX

The phone rang and Perrie struggled to open her eyes. With a tired yawn, she reached to answer it.

"Hello?" she said groggily as she glanced at the time. It was only 6 a.m.

"Perrie?" a voice rushed out.

She blinked, trying to adjust her eyes to the darkness. "Yes?"

"Hello, dear. It's Julia, Neven's mom." Her words were blended together and Perrie could barely hear her name.

Neven's mom never called her, and Perrie had no earthly idea why she would be. But she was wide awake now. With the phone already pressed hard to her ear, Perrie sat up and leaned back against the headboard.

"Hello, Mrs. Lee."

"I'm sorry to disturb you, but it's important. I know you and Neven haven't been around each other for some time, but have you talked to him recently? I tried calling his friend David, but he didn't answer."

It was as if she'd dumped a full bucket of cold water over Perrie. She was asking her about Neven?

"As a matter of fact, Neven stopped by for a little bit after school yesterday."

"What time was that?" Mrs. Lee asked anxiously.

"I don't remember the time exactly, but it was sometime in the afternoon. Why? What's going on?"

She waited a few seconds before answering. "He never came home yesterday."

Perrie's heart practically froze in place. That didn't sound like him at all. He wouldn't just disappear. Neven and his mom always had a great relationship, more so after his dad died. He would've called her and let her know if he was going to be late.

"Are you sure he didn't stay the night somewhere and forget to call?" she asked, keeping her voice calm, but her stomach churned with apprehension.

"I don't know. If that's what happened, then he's in a lot of trouble for making me worry like this. Can you call me if you see him at school, or better yet, tell him to call me?"

Her hands shook. "Of course I will. I promise."

"Thank you, Perrie. I hope to see you soon too. The house just isn't the same without you."

Perrie missed Mrs. Lee, but she couldn't face being in that house after everything. So she lied and told her she would come over soon before hanging up.

Hands still shaking, Perrie shot Neven a text.

Perrie: Call your mom.

Perrie: And text me back to let me know you did!

Her thoughts flew in every direction. The worst-case scenario being that he was part of the growing list of missing victims, but that was the last thing she wanted to consider. She hadn't prayed in a long time, but she was praying now that she would see him at school. Perrie would take anger over this nervousness and worry any day of the week if it meant Neven was safe.

Sleep wasn't a possibility any longer, so she flicked on the lights and tossed on the first clothes she found in her closet.

Maisie needed to know, so she reached for her phone and called her.

"Hello!" Maisie sang, already wide awake and in a good mood.

"Maisie!" Perrie practically screamed into the phone.

"Perrie? What's going on?" The bounciness left her voice.

She rushed to tell her the story of what had happened on the phone call between Neven's mom and her, and how he'd stopped by yesterday.

"Hold on. Neven stopped by yesterday and you didn't *tell* me?" Maisie said with exasperation before switching to detective mode. "He probably stayed at one of the guys' houses from basketball. Didn't you say Mrs. Lee couldn't get a hold of David?"

He would stay at David's sometimes during the school week, but something about how he'd forgotten to call his mom rubbed her the wrong way.

"All right, Perrie. Let me finish getting dressed and we can leave for school now and see if he's there."

"Yeah, okay. See you in a few," she said and ended the call.

Neven still hadn't texted her back, so she messaged him again.

Perrie: Neven, quit being a jerk and text me back already!

She ran a brush through her hair, threw on a pair of shoes, and hit the steps as fast as she could. Maisie was already waiting for her in the driveway when Perrie hurried to meet her. Throwing open the door, she flung her stuff in, sat down, and buckled up as quickly as she could.

"Let's go!" Perrie said, chest heaving.

Maisie hit the gas, all safety protocol tossed to the wind. Normally her cousin would've finished buckling before the car moved, as she always drove the *exact* speed limit. However, she avoided the snail-pace routine and booked it. Perrie would give her a proper thank you later for her massive sacrifice. Squinting her right eye, Maisie stayed focused on the road. Her left eye was comfortably hidden beneath a doughnut-shaped patch, with little sprinkle jewels glued on it. A nude piece of colored cloth rested where the doughnut hole should've been. *Yes, the patch did distract me for about ten seconds from our current dilemma.*

Perrie noticed then that they were some of the first students pulling into the parking lot. As soon as Maisie threw the car in park, Perrie leapt out of the passenger side with her cousin hot on her heels.

"Gym first!" Maisie called out.

Twin minds. Sometimes Neven practiced basketball before school started.

Inside the gym, several guys were bouncing basketballs around, but not one of them was Neven.

"Look, it's David." Maisie tapped Perrie's shoulder and pointed toward a guy wearing a blue jersey.

"Hey, David! Can you come here for a second?" Perrie called.

David halted his dribbling and glanced up at the pair of them like they were lost. He then jogged over and stopped just short of bumping Maisie. "What's going on?"

Maisie was already prepared. Somehow, in their mad dash to get to the gym, she'd managed to fish out her small notebook and pen.

"Have you seen Neven?" She scribbled down the question and peered back up, awaiting his answer.

David exchanged a confused look with Perrie, skeptical now of the notebook and their business with him.

"Well," he started, "I saw him at school yesterday."

"And what about after school?" Perrie asked before Maisie could write his first answer down.

Worry lines appeared on David's forehead. "Is there something wrong, Perrie? You've been ignoring Nev. Why are you asking me where he is?"

"That doesn't matter right now!" Perrie shouted.

His eyes grew wider as he seemed to come to his own conclusion. "Wait. Don't tell me he's missing?"

"No!" Perrie's hands flew up to her face. "I mean, I don't know. His mom called me and said he never came home from school yesterday. You know Nev—he always checks in with his mom if he's going to be late."

He nodded in agreement, then shifted his focus to Maisie. So far, she'd been writing everything down.

"What's the deal with the notebook?" he asked her.

She just smiled and winked. "Wouldn't you like to know?"

A crooked, flirtatious smile spread across his face. He seemed to be mistaking Maisie for another girl. Knowing her, she winked at him because she thought he wanted to see her written notes. Perrie had been around her long enough to know when to pull out.

"Okay! So, let us know if you see Neven." She grabbed Maisie's arm and tugged her to leave.

"See you in class, Maisie," David called.

Before parting separate ways, Perrie returned with Maisie to her car for their things. Perrie spent the first half of the day searching for Neven between classes and asking some other students if they'd seen him. She even went to the bathroom during her first-period class to purposely pass by his classroom to see if he was there. No such luck.

When the bell rang for lunch, Perrie found August waiting for her.

"August, you really need a cell phone. Have you heard the news about Neven?" She then spilled everything to him. From the conversation with Neven, to the crazy shenanigans this morning—she didn't leave out a single detail. "I'm really worried."

"Don't worry, we'll find him." He pulled her into his arms and rested his head on top of hers.

She inhaled his comforting soapy scent. "We don't know that. What about all those other missing people?"

He drew back and cupped her chin with a warm hand. "Perrie, relax. We have to try to be positive here."

Positivity, smositivity! she wanted to shout.

"Do you want me to come over after school?" he asked.

Perrie wanted him to, but she really should go and see Neven's mom. "How about I call you at home later?"

August gave her one last squeeze and they walked to lunch, but her appetite was nonexistent. The day remained a perpetual blur, and Perrie found herself repeating a cycle of self-pity. At first, she was mad at herself for yelling at Neven the previous day. Then, she was angry with Neven for making her mad at herself. Then, she was back to being mad at him for making her angry in the first place. It was a vicious cycle.

After school, Maisie drove them to Neven's in record time, but Perrie was surprised to see they weren't the only ones visiting. Parked right at the edge of the driveway was a police cruiser.

Maisie slowed to a stop in the street, and they were both a little unsure of what to do.

"Should we turn around and go home?" Maisie asked.

Perrie mulled it over yet decided against it. They were already here anyway.

"Let me go alone." Maisie opened her mouth to protest, but Perrie shook her head. "I don't want it to look like an ambush."

"Wave at me if you need me. I'll be right here waiting for you." She ducked down low in her seat, trying to become invisible.

Climbing out of the car, Perrie slowly made her way up the long drive. Her heart was pounding and she could hear the rush of blood in her ears. She didn't think she could take any more heartache if anything truly awful had happened to Neven. Regret poked at her, for her earlier words and calling him a jerk all the time.

Perrie flexed and unflexed her fingers before ringing the doorbell and patiently waiting. Mrs. Lee answered within seconds and Perrie wasn't sure what to expect. She'd never seen her so disheveled. Her blonde hair was an untamed mess, and her brown eyes—which were the exact shade of Neven's—were bloodshot.

Neven was a perfect mix of both his parents. He had the balanced combination between his mom and the Chinese on his dad's side.

"Hi, Perrie. Have you heard from Neven?" she asked anxiously, still wearing her pajamas. Even in her sadness and exhaustion, Mrs. Lee was incredibly beautiful. The small amount of hope glimmering in her eyes was killing Perrie.

"No, Mrs. Lee. I was hoping you had better news for me." She wished she could tell her he was all right, but she wasn't so certain. He still hadn't answered any of her texts.

Mrs. Lee's shoulders slumped and the hope she'd held was gone. "No. I was just answering Officer Rodriguez's questions."

Peeking around Mrs. Lee and the door, Perrie tried to get a better look at her guest. A petite female officer stood in the living room, her black hair pulled up in a high ponytail. She looked as if she would be able to hold her own, despite her small stature. The officer whipped her head around and caught Perrie staring.

"Are you Perrie Madeline? I heard Mrs. Lee call you Perrie." *Damn. So much for going alone.*

Perrie's muscles went taut, and the hairs on her neck stood on end. "Yes, ma'am. I am."

"Can you answer a few questions for me?" Officer Rodriguez stalked toward them with her notepad and pen at the ready. The whole thing reminded her of Maisie this afternoon—only this was an actual officer in a real investigation.

"Yes," Perrie squeaked, then cleared her throat. "Yes," she said again.

"Julia here tells me you saw Neven Lee after school yesterday. It appears you're the last person to have seen him."

Oh, God. Panic rushed through her veins. *Does she think I did something to him?*

Beads of sweat formed on her back, and her shirt was starting to cling to her skin.

"Yes, I did," she sputtered. "But I have no idea what happened to him after he left."

"Relax. I'm only trying to figure out where he might have gone so we can try and locate him. Can you tell me about yesterday?" Officer Rodriguez's tone was gentler this time, less intimidating.

Perrie took a deep breath and told her how he'd stopped by for a few minutes, then how a conversation about a new museum turned into them fighting about their past relationship. She didn't seem surprised by any of it. People argued all the time and didn't murder them. Although, some did…

Officer Rodriguez finished up her notes and handed them both her card before she left. Heavy tension remained between Perrie and Mrs. Lee, palpable and stifling.

"Would you like to come in? I was just about to put on some tea," Mrs. Lee asked, unable to muster a smile.

Perrie probably could, but she just couldn't.

"Actually, Maisie is in the car waiting for me. I just wanted to stop by and see how you were doing." She pointed toward Maisie's parked car across the street.

"If you hear anything, please let me know," Mrs. Lee begged.

Perrie nodded. "I promise. If I hear anything at all, I'll call you right away."

The walk back to Maisie's car felt longer, heavier, because there were zero answers.

"Finally!" Maisie said after Perrie opened the car door. "I was going out of my mind with worry. When I saw that officer walk out, I ducked down again as fast as I could. I wasn't sure what the heck to do."

Perrie smiled at Maisie's craziness, even though her eyes were filling up with tears. She tried to push them away as she attempted to forget the rest of this damn day.

"You always know just what to say, Maisie."

SEVEN

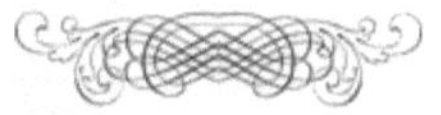

After going over the talk with the officer and Mrs. Lee on the way home with Maisie, Perrie had called August on his landline for him to come over.

"Ladies, I'm at your service," August greeted her and Maisie with a sack full of chips and candy bars.

Perrie sifted through the plastic bag. "Sorry, Maisie. No cheese Doritos, but there are these." She whipped out the ranch style and Maisie wrinkled her nose.

"All mine then." Perrie's sudden enthusiasm deflated as she took a seat beside Maisie on the couch.

August lowered himself on the floor in front of her and leaned against the table, his curls falling across an eyebrow. "So, no news about Neven?" he asked, stealing a handful of chips from Perrie's bag.

"No," she started. "The cop doesn't know much yet, either." If Neven didn't show up that day, who knew how long it would take the police department to find real answers.

"Any theories?" Maisie sipped on a can of soda.

"I'm leaning more toward the *Scream* factor now," August said. "Neven's pretty big and I don't think one person could take him down."

"Unless they knocked him out with chloroform," Perrie pointed out.

"I can actually see that."

"I don't want to see that." Neven was no André the Giant, but she wouldn't deny he could hold his own. If it really was more than one person, though, then it was possible he'd been overpowered. Perrie didn't want to dwell on that aspect too much.

"Do you think it might be someone we know?" Maisie asked with the question already written on her notepad.

Perrie shook her head. "If he's part of the group who has gone missing, I'm going to say no. Especially since we don't even know any of the previous people. There's just no connection."

The conversation veered off into stupid territory when they started relating circumstances to Jigsaw, and so she was done. Maisie turned on the first *Saw* movie just in case they could get some ideas from it. But Perrie couldn't focus on the film.

Halfway through the movie her dad walked through the door. Maisie and August then picked up their things and left.

"Are you hungry?" Perrie started for the kitchen. "I can make us something to eat. Spaghetti?" It wouldn't take long to cook, but her mind would stay occupied. She didn't wait for him to respond, so she gathered everything she would need.

Her dad set his lunchbox on the counter. "That sounds good."

"So, Mrs. Lee called this morning." Perrie wanted to lay this on him gently.

"Neven's mom? I didn't know you two were talking again." He unpacked his lunchbox, quirking a brow.

"We're not, technically." She blew out a breath. "Neven's gone missing."

Her dad's hands stopped their methodical chore and dropped to the counter. He squeezed his eyes shut and frowned. Perrie needed her dad to say something, to make her feel better—the same as he had when she'd gotten a scrape in her younger years, when he would say it was all okay. But things weren't really okay.

"Neven? Missing? Are you sure?" He pursed his lips and removed his work badge, resting it beside the lunchbox. Another hard thing about her breakup with Neven was that her dad really liked him.

"Yeah, I went over to see his mom and we talked for a bit. I spoke with a police officer investigating the case, too." She turned back to her task and filled one of the cooking pots with water. The sound of running water was strangely soothing.

"Is he part of the other missing people?" His question was the same as her own.

"I—I don't know." Tears stung the corners of her eyes. She hated doing this in front of her dad.

"Oh, Perrie." He sighed and wrapped his arms around her. "It'll be okay."

She peered up at his face, seeing his apprehension. He knew the same as she did—that it wasn't okay and most likely the same as the other cases. But he squeezed her one more time before releasing her.

"Let's get dinner going. I'm starving!" He clapped his hands together and the edges of her lips tugged up a fraction.

After dinner, stuffed from two servings of spaghetti, Perrie headed to bed early. Once in bed, she cried to herself, trying to muffle the sounds out with her pillow and blankets pulled up, covering her whole face. She didn't want her dad to hear her, to worry more.

She barely slept a wink, tossing and turning all night, reliving those last moments with Neven. What more could she have done? Should she have invited him to stay longer? Asked where he was going? With a groan, she threw one arm over her face in frustration.

Perrie rolled over and stretched for her phone. She attempted to text Neven a few more times but to no avail. All she wanted was to stay in bed, so she shot Maisie a text too.

Perrie: No school for me today.

Maisie: Try to hold your head up, jellybean. I'll talk to you later.

The last thing she wanted to do was go back to school. Around the time her dad woke up, she told him she wasn't feeling well and she would probably stay home. He didn't question, only wanted her to get some rest.

But she didn't. She stared at her ceiling for hours until her phone ringing drew her out of her nightmare of a reverie.

Maisie.

"Hey," Perrie answered.

"It's August. Maisie let me use her phone. I just wanted to check in on you. The school works in mysterious ways when your face isn't here."

"I know, I know, my face deserves the attention. But I'm fine, I'll see you tomorrow." She just needed one full day to be alone, even though it wouldn't have been the worst thing to have him in bed beside her with his arms folded around her.

"If you need anything, I'm here. Maybe I'll eventually become part of the social circle and get a cell phone." He paused. "Nah, I like the freedom. But for you, anything."

"I agree. It's too overrated." All she had was a basic phone from her dad without a camera, and honestly, she didn't even care.

"See you tomorrow, doll face." He understood. He always did.

A knock sounded at the door around four in the afternoon. Perrie forced herself out of bed to see who it was. She spied Maisie through the peephole and swung open the door.

Crimson stained Maisie's cheeks, and her hair was all over the place. Her cousin must've gotten home and rushed over—not that the run over here took more than a few seconds.

"How are you doing?" she blurted.

"Oh, you know. A day full of nothing is like a day at the circus."

Maisie grunted, slid in past her, and booked it for the fridge. Before Perrie knew it, Maisie pulled out several slices of cheese and a juice box. "Compared to my day, it very well could've been."

Perrie's brows shot all the way up. "Is that negativity I hear? Coming from the queen of all things positive?"

"Yeah, whatever. You weren't there to deal with David all day. He's worried, I'm worried, we're all worried, but I had to comfort *him* throughout third period. Then August left early during lunch, so David came and sat with me. That human specimen has drained all things positive from my very soul."

"Wow. So, I take it you aren't into David then?"

Maisie offered her a slice of cheese, but Perrie dismissed it with a flick of her hand. She shrugged and plopped onto one of the barstools at the breakfast bar.

Her cousin seemed to contemplate Perrie's question further, sipping quietly from her juice box. "Um, no thanks. Anyway, David talked to Neven's mom and she's even more panicked. There's still no sign of him and everyone's on edge."

Perrie took a seat next to Maisie on the other wooden barstool, where she was unfolding another piece of plastic from a cheese slice. She removed the slices and folded them both into smaller squares before sticking the entire thing into her mouth.

"I get it. I've been replaying the whole day over in my head and I still don't understand what could've happened."

Maisie patted Perrie's shoulder. "We have to breathe and take a step back. We can't overthink how we're feeling until we know something solid."

That was exactly what she was going to do.

"Speaking of circuses, you don't think it's possible Neven could've joined one, do you?" Perrie asked, her shoulders slumping forward.

"If only we could all join the circus, Perrie. If only." Maisie shook her head, chewing on her thumbnail. She stayed a little while longer to chat and finished her snack, which included two more slices of cheese. Then she stood from the stool and stretched before leaving.

Perrie attempted to keep herself occupied after Maisie had gone, opting to snack on something while watching TV. She could barely focus on the screen, which was sad considering the movie was *Dr. Jekyll and Mr. Hyde.*

A couple hours later, another knock sounded at the door. Perrie peeked into the kitchen and looked at the clock as the pendulum swayed. It was just a few minutes before eight and her dad was working until nine tonight.

"It's just me!" Maisie shouted through the door, then birdy whistled.

Perrie's shoulders relaxed. She birdy whistled back as she unlocked and opened the door for her. "Back already?"

"Yes!" She squeezed past her again.

Perrie got a good look at her, noticing she was wearing black from head to toe. Black leggings tucked into boots and a lacy baby-doll dress. Dark, little felt buttons were dotted down the center of the dress for decoration. It was a *very* Wednesday Addams look.

She'd completed her ensemble with a matching black eye patch lined in lace and silk trimming. The patch was calm in comparison to her other eye, which had been made up with black eyeshadow, bringing out the blue in her iris. Perrie supposed black wasn't a dark color for Maisie this time.

"Are we going to rob a bank tonight?"

Maisie snorted. "No, silly. I start my job at the Glass Vault, remember?"

Perrie totally let that slip her mind and had forgotten all about the new job. Worry stirred within her.

"Are you sure you don't want to skip it tonight?"

She scrunched up her nose. "If you don't want me to go, Perrie, I won't go."

There was a distinct sadness in her cousin's offer and she could tell Maisie wanted this job. Maybe it would be a good distraction for her. Personally, Perrie wished she'd applied with her and had the diversion right now.

"No, it's okay. I know you want to go." Perrie sighed. "But you have to promise me you'll be *extra* careful. Seriously, don't stop for anyone. Drive straight there and straight home."

"Deal. Now, I'll need your help getting the car backed out of the driveway," she said. "I'll put the car in neutral and then we can roll it onto the street. We'll have to take it a few houses down before I can start the engine again."

"Wait, what?" Perrie jumped upright. "You still haven't told your parents?"

Resting her hands together, she batted her eye innocently. "No, but I promise I'll tell them tomorrow. I just want to get a feel for the place first. I don't want to get my hopes up if it's not going to work out. It's not like I'm going out partying—I just want a job."

"Damn it, fine," Perrie grumbled. "Just a heads up, if they come over here asking me where you are, I'm going to tell them. Aunt Krista can see through my lies, no matter how hard I try to tell them. She's like a human lie detector."

"I know! I don't know how she does it." Maisie giggled.

"All right. Let's get that car ready. The sooner you go, the earlier you can get back and let me know what really isn't for the "faint of heart" in there."

They snuck as quietly as they could next door and managed to get the car on the street. There were a few times they almost gave themselves away with laughter. But success came as they rolled it down the drive without a problem. Perrie helped Maisie walk the car a few houses down before her cousin got in and started it up.

"Good luck." Perrie reached through the window and high-fived Maisie. She watched the car roll away, her stomach in tight knots. A gut feeling told her this was a bad idea.

A light pulsing throbbed at Perrie's head, waking her up. The beeping of the alarm buzzed a few seconds later, and it wasn't making her head feel any better. She took some Excedrin, washed it down with water, and got dressed.

Grabbing her things for school and a quick bite to eat, she made her way over to Maisie's. She couldn't wait to ask her all about her first night on the job and find out exactly what was inside the Glass Vault. Knowing Maisie, she would have plenty to spill, not one detail spared.

Perrie stopped short of the front door and noticed Maisie's car wasn't in the driveway. She looked toward the street to see if maybe she parked against the curb. Maisie hadn't.

Did she leave for school without me? Impossible.

Uncle Jaron's truck was still parked in the driveway, and she knew her aunt's car was in the garage. As she raced to the door, Perrie tried not to overthink. She rang the bell several times and banged on the hard wood in between, her nerves bouncing like crazy.

Aunt Krista answered the door in her pajamas with a scowl crinkling her forehead. It was obvious she'd woken her aunt up. "Perrie? What's going on? Is your dad okay?"

"Where's Maisie?" Her heart was pounding ferociously, seconds from jumping out of her chest.

"She probably just overslept. Let me check on her," Uncle

Jaron said, appearing behind Aunt Krista, looking crisp in a pressed suit with his dark hair slicked back. As he walked away, her aunt peered out toward the driveway and scrunched her nose when she noticed the missing car.

"Did she already leave for school?"

Perrie cupped her mouth and shook her head frantically. "No, I don't think she came home last night."

Uncle Jaron returned frowning. "She isn't in her room."

"What do you mean she didn't come home last night? She came home, did her homework, and went to bed early," Aunt Krista noted aloud.

No. No. No. Fear and worry consumed Perrie in that moment. She ran her hands through her hair, gripping hard as she tried to make sense of this. Uncle Jaron and Aunt Krista were talking, but she couldn't hear what they were saying. It was all noise. She needed to tell them.

"Maisie started a new job last night at this place called Quinsey Wolfe's Glass Vault over on Oak Street." Perrie laid her confession before them like a neck exposed to the guillotine, waiting for the blade to come down.

"What are you talking about?" Aunt Krista barked.

Perrie hadn't seen Aunt Krista this mad in a long time. The last time she'd been this angry was when she and Maisie accidentally broke her aunt's three-piece set of unicorn figurines. They'd been playing with a ball in the house and had gotten a little too reckless, then blamed it on the dog, of course. But she'd known in a split second they were lying. Now Perrie just wanted to crawl into a dark hole and find a way to reverse time.

"Perrie, tell us exactly what happened." Uncle Jaron's tone came out calm.

Perrie started with telling them about Monday, the day they'd found the new glass museum and how they were hiring. She then confessed to them how Maisie emailed the owner, Quinsey Wolfe, and how he'd hired her right away.

Taking a breath, she also spilled the beans about last night being Maisie's first day. She purposely left out the fact she'd helped her move the car for her cousin's grand escape plan.

"Thank you," Jaron said for her honesty, as if she'd just performed a miraculous deed. She turned to Aunt Krista, who studied Perrie with narrowed eyes. *No pat on the back from her.*

"Let me try to call her, okay? Just relax." Uncle Jaron produced his cell and raised it to his ear. Perrie took hers out and shot Maisie a text.

Perrie: Maisie, call me now!

When no answer came, Uncle Jaron left a short message and hung up.

"This is what we're going to do first"—he placed a comforting hand on Aunt Krista's shoulder—"we're going to go to the school to see if Maisie's car is there. Maybe she went to school early and forgot to tell Perrie. If she isn't at the school, then we'll stop by this Glass Vault and look for her there. Okay?"

Perrie and Aunt Krista nodded in unison. Uncle Jaron grabbed his keys and Aunt Krista slipped on a pair of sandals. They all hurried out the door to his truck and climbed in.

Before Perrie could buckle, Aunt Krista rattled off a hundred questions. "Why didn't you tell us Maisie started a new job? Who is Quinsey Wolfe? When was she supposed to be back? Why didn't she tell us about this?"

"I don't know the first two. I think she should've been back around midnight. She knew you guys would say no."

Aunt Krista gave her "the look" and Perrie wished she would just stop for a minute. "That's right—we would have said no," she shouted. "There are people missing, your friend is missing, and not to mention it was a school night. There's no way we would let her work a job that late at night with everything going on. I don't care how close she is to turning eighteen."

Silence filled the truck for the rest of the ride to school. Perrie slumped in her seat, unable to stop the miserable emotion consuming her. Her phone hadn't buzzed once from Neven and now Maisie wouldn't answer. Uncle Jaron kept his cool, but she knew he was as disappointed as Aunt Krista. No telling when they would get her dad involved, but she was sure it wouldn't end well.

Uncle Jaron pulled into the school parking lot a few minutes later. He circled it twice, and Maisie's car was nowhere in sight.

"Where is this place? You said on Oak Street?" Aunt Krista peered around the front seat.

Perrie could barely find air to breathe as she said, "Yes. It's right off Oak Street."

Her uncle was already leaving the school parking lot when Aunt Krista asked, "Are you sure? That doesn't seem like a place for a museum."

"That's what we said, but it's there."

With Uncle Jaron speeding down the road, it didn't take long to arrive at Oak Street.

"Slow down so we don't pass it up." Perrie leaned forward in her seat to focus. "Stop! This is it." She pointed.

Uncle Jaron slammed on the brakes and they all lurched forward.

"Where?" Uncle Jaron asked while Perrie jabbed her finger at the air.

When her eyes finally refocused, her hand faltered. Quinsey Wolfe's Glass Vault was nowhere to be seen. There wasn't a trace of a building—it was as if nothing had ever been there at all.

EIGHT

How could the Glass Vault be gone? There was no way. Perrie knew she hadn't imagined it being here. Swinging open the car door, she ran to the edge of the curb and stared at the cut-down trees. Aunt Krista jogged up beside her and placed both hands on Perrie's shoulders. Those two hands did nothing except weigh her down.

"Are you sure this is the right place?"

Wriggling out of her grasp, Perrie spun to face Aunt Krista and her uncle—who now stood directly beside her.

"Yes, I'm sure! We were here Monday after school and there was an old stone building right there." Perrie pointed at the empty space. "Neven saw it too. There was a big wooden door with a plaque that said Quinsey Wolfe's Glass Vault." She trudged through the grass. "See, there are trees that have even been cut down."

"Who knows when those trees were cut down. And if it was here, it's gone now," Uncle Jaron said skeptically.

"It wasn't a traveling carnival on wheels!" Perrie yelled, her breathing ragged.

Aunt Krista tried to rest her hand on her arm again, but Perrie pulled away before she could.

"Well, maybe it was"—she shrugged—"or maybe you're just confused. Either way, we need to go to the police. We have to find out where Maisie is."

Perrie didn't respond. There was nothing she could say that would make them believe her, not when her proof had vanished into thin air. She knew the Glass Vault had been there and she knew what she'd damn well seen. A mixture of anger and confusion stormed through her veins, and in that moment, she couldn't even begin to imagine how Maisie must be feeling.

"Come on, let's go to the police station." Uncle Jaron sighed. He ran a hand across his forehead, his expression grim, as if someone just died. Maisie wasn't dead. Neven wasn't dead. Even with all these people gone missing, there hadn't been any bodies found.

With a heavy heart, Perrie followed them back to the truck. Her panic had subsided for the time being, but she'd been left with an incredible feeling of doubt.

First Neven, and now Maisie. Who's next? What's next? Nothing was adding up.

Aunt Krista couldn't keep it together and cried all the way to the police station. Perrie wanted to comfort her, but she couldn't even keep herself from rocking anxiously in her seat. Uncle Jaron looked as confused as he was hopeful, which was an odd expression. At least he was holding it together better than Aunt Krista and her.

Again, Monday played over and over in Perrie's head until she'd exhausted her brain. She couldn't let her imagination play tricks on her. *Maybe I'm crazy.*

When they finally pulled up to the station, the three of them hurried inside and approached the lady at the front desk. She wasn't the type of person Perrie would expect to be manning the front end of the station. Hot-pink lipstick stained her lips, and she loudly smacked her gum. Uncle Jaron explained the situation and she lazily handed him a missing person's report to fill out. After the report was completed, they were pulled back to speak to Officer Rodriguez in her office. She seemed to recognize Perrie immediately.

"Hello, Perrie. I would ask how you're doing, but I know these circumstances have a way of turning that question into a disaster," she said as she ushered them inside her office.

Perrie couldn't argue with her.

Officer Rodriguez's brows lowered as she read over the missing person's report. She took a quick sip from a navy-blue coffee mug with little white birds on it before making eye contact with any of them.

"Have you heard anything about Neven?" Perrie was too antsy to hold back her impatience.

"No, not yet," she answered. "We may have some promising leads, though."

Shifting her gaze toward Aunt Krista and Uncle Jaron, she asked, "What exactly is going on?"

They explained to her everything they knew, which wasn't much. Aunt Krista told her about this morning. She started with Perrie's frantic visit, Maisie's new job, and ended with their realization that Maisie wasn't in her room when Uncle Jaron went to check on her.

"It appears you're the last person to have seen Maisie. Can you tell me exactly what occurred last night?" Officer Rodriguez fixed her dark eyes to Perrie, searching her face for a hint of understanding. She tried incredibly hard to maintain eye contact, even though it was a struggle.

Something in her brain clicked and she wanted to curse herself for not thinking about it sooner. In both cases, Perrie was the last person who had seen Maisie and Neven before their disappearances. Nausea bubbled up her throat with the notion of being a suspect in her own cousin's missing person's case.

Sweat formed on Perrie's palms, and she rubbed them against her jeans nervously, but they started to perspire again.

So, that was pointless. "Yes, let me start from the beginning."

Before speaking, Perrie inhaled deeply, then began with the trip down Oak Street on Monday, how she'd seen this building that seemed to have come out of nowhere. She told her about Quinsey Wolfe's Glass Vault, the strange description, and job listing. Then, how Maisie emailed the owner about the position on the same night, and a man named Quinsey replied back, letting her know she could start working that Thursday night. After that, she mentioned how the Glass Vault was the same new museum that Perrie had talked about with Neven. She ended it with the last time she'd seen Maisie, which had been at her house the night she'd disappeared.

The tale was becoming a shitty walk down memory lane because everyone in the room was staring at her. Perrie's hands shook and she didn't know what to do with them. So she tightly folded her arms across her chest, wishing she were back at home in bed and this was all a damn nightmare.

Aunt Krista voiced her disappointment in Maisie for not telling them about the job, but Uncle Jaron calmed her before that anger could take root again.

"You said you saw this building going down Oak Street?" Officer Rodriguez asked, seeming to be her best attempt to ease the growing tension.

"Yes, ma'am."

She leaned back in her chair. "I just went down Oak Street this morning and I didn't see a building. In fact, I go down Oak Street every day and I've never once seen anything except for trees. Maybe you're mistaken about the street?"

"What about the freshly cut-down trees?" Perrie tapped her fingers against her knee in anticipation.

"Yes, I did see those, but there isn't a building there."

This shit storm was going nowhere. "I know. We just drove down Oak Street before coming here. There was no building, but I swear to you I saw it."

Officer Rodriguez tilted her head to the side. She rubbed

her index finger against her temple as her thumb rested on her chin. "Are you sure it wasn't some type of trailer?"

"That's what I was thinking!" Aunt Krista blurted. "It would make sense! Maybe it was a lure and when Maisie went in, someone took her."

Perrie knew what she'd seen and it was an actual building. A building with a stone structure like that would've been impossible to move, even if it was on wheels. Unfortunately, she had no proof and nothing to say. She'd told them her story and that was all she could do. No one was going to believe her unless this place reappeared from whatever hell it had come from. She should've thought to take a picture of it Monday with Maisie's phone.

"I'm going to look into this. I'll search around Oak Street this morning, but for now, keep your eyes and ears open. There's always a chance she ran away. I've seen so many cases where the family thinks their child has gone missing, but it turns out they've made the choice to leave."

"Perrie, do you know if Maisie was talking to anyone?" Uncle Jaron turned to her suddenly.

"You would know better than anyone," Aunt Krista piped in.

The gears in her brain started to turn, first clockwise, then counterclockwise. She tried to think about this objectively. Maisie didn't date. She'd never shown interest in anyone, at least no one Perrie knew about.

"No, not that I know of."

Officer Rodriguez studied her with curiosity. "I know we've had a lot of missing persons lately, but I was thinking about how close Neven and Maisie's disappearances are. Is it possible that they were romantically involved? Could they have run away together?"

Her jaw dropped. She hadn't even thought about that. *Why would she even think about that? There was no way. I would have known, right?*

"No." Perrie shook her head. "I mean, they used to be friends, and I dated Neven for a long time, but they aren't like that."

"She's right," Aunt Krista snapped. "Besides, Maisie would have never run away." She also knew Maisie would never have done that to Perrie, even if she wasn't with Neven anymore.

"We have to look at all the possibilities." Officer Rodriguez reached for her business cards and handed one to each of them. Perrie pocketed the card again, even though the officer had already given her one at Neven's. "Like I said, keep your eyes and ears open. I'll check things out on Oak Street this morning. I'll even track down the company that cut down the trees. We're going to do our best to find out exactly what's going on."

On the way home, Aunt Krista sobbed uncontrollably. Uncle Jaron was a worried mess and Perrie was freaking out. It didn't help that she was already worried over Neven's disappearance, but now she was a key player in her own cousin's missing case. Her aunt and uncle would never say it aloud, but she was sure they blamed her for not telling them sooner. She was the last line of defense and she could've stopped Maisie from leaving.

Once outside her aunt and uncle's home, Perrie's shoulders hunched forward as she walked inside and plopped down in the living room. For the first time in a long time, it was awkward to be around each other. She assumed they were all wondering on some personal level about what could have been done differently. The silence was overwhelming, so Perrie escaped by giving her dad a quick call.

He rushed home from work and came right over, then they revealed everything to him.

"You should've told us Maisie was going out last night," Perrie's dad pointed out.

Groaning, she slid her hands down her face. "I know. I

even told her if Aunt Krista or Uncle Jaron found out she had left that I was going to tell them. I didn't think she was truly in any danger. It wasn't like she was going off to a club or a party. She was going to work, so I wasn't worried."

That was only partially true. She'd had that gut feeling about something bad happening, but she didn't think it truly would. Especially nothing like this. She never dreamed Maisie would go missing, not once.

The rest of the afternoon and evening was spent with Aunt Krista and Uncle Jaron. Dad tackled dinner and sent Perrie to the house to get ingredients. She believed he did it to give her a breather and a moment to herself, which she was silently thankful for.

They tried to sit down for a meal, but no one could eat. Perrie picked at her food until Dad said, "I think we'll go home for the night."

With very few words, Perrie left with her dad and headed up to her room. She flopped onto her bed and stared up at the ceiling once again.

All day Perrie had been thinking about Neven and Maisie, about what more she could do, and then it finally came to her. She had a plan. With a grin, and a stirring of fresh determination, she jerked forward. She grasped her phone and called August's home number, praying he was there.

"August!" she shouted as soon as he answered.

"Perrie, are you all right?"

She scooted to the edge of her bed and rested one arm on her leg. "No, I'm a fucking mess."

"I knew you probably weren't up to coming to school again today, but where was Maisie?" Worry flooded his voice.

And then, she finally broke down. A helplessness enveloping her—she couldn't manage to get one single word out. August patiently waited until she'd relaxed a little.

"Do you need me to come over?" he asked once she was finished sobbing.

Wiping her eyes, Perrie shook her head and realized how fucking stupid that was because she was on the phone. "I do, but I need you to wait until my dad falls asleep."

"Oh? So, it's going to be *that* kind of hanging out," he teased, lightening the mood.

A hint of a smile played across her lips, the first one she'd had all day. It quickly faded as she told him everything. For the fourth time that day, she relayed her story about Maisie and the disappearance of the Glass Vault. She could hear the shock in his breathing, same as hers had been, then he launched into a series of questions for which she had no damn answer.

"Maisie's gone? What do you mean the Glass Vault disappeared? And what the hell is this about the building being on wheels? Didn't you tell them it was huge and had *stone* surrounding it? I'm not sure any wheels could carry that entire building off in less than twelve hours! Are you sure you told them *everything*?" he exclaimed.

"Of course I did! No one believes me, August. They heard me out, but everyone thinks it's a trailer or something that can be moved." Perrie fell back onto the bed, her body lightly bouncing. "It doesn't really matter what they believe. We need to find Maisie and Neven ourselves."

He paused for a few seconds. "Then that's what we'll do."

Curling herself around a pillow, she squeezed it tightly. "Maisie means everything to me. She's practically my sister. Neven used to mean so much to me, too." She supposed her feelings of friendship with him never truly disappeared. "We can't sit here and do nothing."

"It won't hurt to take a look around where the Glass Vault was. I'll pick you up around eleven."

"That works for me. My dad is a sound sleeper, but I'll still meet you outside."

Living with her dad didn't give her too many options. Perrie couldn't just go out, so that really only left her with the sneaking out option. She understood the situation from his point of view, but going after Maisie was the right thing to do—she knew it.

The rest of the night, she kept to herself, basically twiddling her thumbs while watching the pendulum on the clock swing. Right at nine, her dad's door closed, and she counted the minutes until it was five to eleven. She was suddenly grateful to all that was holy that her dad's bedroom was at the opposite end of the house, because sneaking from her room to the front door was easy.

Wind ruffled the end of Perrie's ponytail as she stepped out into the night. She peered up at the dark sky while crossing the damp grass into the street. The few stars she could see shone brightly, seeming to watch her every step.

As she crept closer to the end of the street, Perrie spotted a flash of silver. August was already there waiting for her, so she picked up the pace until she reached his car. He'd left it unlocked and she slid easily into the front seat. August looked like he was on edge, as if his day had been just as stressful as hers. His blond curls were everywhere, and his eyes were dull with heavy bags beneath them. He might not be as close to Maisie as she was, but he cared about her, too.

"Are you all right?" she asked.

"Yeah, it's a lot to take in, you know?" he replied.

Perrie knew exactly how he felt. She leaned her head against the back of the seat and buckled up. "Let's just go and hope Quinsey Wolfe's Glass Vault isn't really gone."

NINE

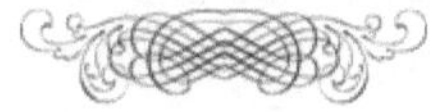

Perrie and August sat in silence the whole drive over to Oak Street. The silence helped her to refocus her thoughts and concentrate on Maisie. She didn't realize it before, but she was beyond exhausted. If she could look into a mirror right then, she was certain she wouldn't recognize the zombie-looking person staring back at her. If Maisie were there, she would know just what to say to lighten the mood.

When Oak Street came into sight, Perrie shoved aside her fears and worries. It was so frustratingly dark and not a single street lamp lit either side of the road. Farther up ahead, though, a flicker of bobbing light caught her attention.

"Wait! Look down there. What is that?" Perrie squinted her eyes to try and see better.

August leaned closer to the wheel to get a better look. "I have no idea. Let me get near it." As he inched forward, her eyes grew into saucers.

"Holy Mother." *Yes*, there was a light, but not only that—the looming silhouette of the Glass Vault. It appeared the same as she remembered. Large stone siding, big door, and windowless walls—it was all there.

August parked near the curb. "Okay? It's still here."

"Apparently, it is," she said sarcastically.

He barely acknowledged her. His eyes were trained on the stone building and the single light radiating from the porch. On the other side of that door, there was no telling what was inside.

August drummed on the steering wheel. "What do we do now?"

"I don't know. I didn't think that far," she whispered.

"Why are you whispering?" August whispered back.

Clearing her voice, Perrie spoke in her semi-normal voice. "I don't have an answer to that either."

He relaxed his head against the seat for a minute, then straightened. "Do you want to go home or take a look at the door *again*?"

"Is that sarcasm?" She smiled. "This is the one time I wish my phone had a camera. Honestly, I hate photographs." Her dad had gotten her a basic phone a few years back because of all the "nudes" teens sent of themselves. She could've had an upgrade this year, but hadn't cared enough to get one.

"You're in luck, doll face. Look what I picked up this afternoon." August produced a sleek smartphone from his jeans pocket.

"So you gave in to society's demands?"

"Sometimes you have to." He held the new white phone up and snapped a picture.

Perrie leaned across her seat, pressing her chin against August's shoulder. His clean soapy scent struck her nose and she wanted to shift even closer.

The photo of the building on his phone darkened. "Why's it black?" she asked.

He squinted at the screen, as if it would make the picture turn out this time. When it didn't, he snapped another photo. And another. And another. Black. Black. *Black*. The images were there for a nanosecond and then *gone*. Even if she'd taken a picture on Monday with Maisie's phone, it would've been pointless.

With a frustrated sound, August placed the phone back into his pocket. "Are we even sure this place was gone this morning?"

"Yes, I'm sure of it."

His lips twitched, like he was trying to hide a smile.

"Spit it out, August."

He pressed his head against the window. "This isn't the time or place, but I was just thinking that there's no way this building could have wheels hidden underneath."

She snorted loudly. "Seriously, and obviously, there's no way this is a trailer."

Silence surrounded them for a few seconds longer, but Perrie was itching to let the damn cat out of the bag. "I have a plan."

"Oh? Let's hear it, then."

"For the record," she said, clasping her hands together, "this may be the stupidest thing I've ever done. It's like we're in a horror movie and the audience knows we're about to rush right into danger. But we have to go inside regardless, right? Most people would just leave and go home, back to where it's safe. I would be that person calling out how stupid they were, too.

"Maybe the Glass Vault has nothing to do with Maisie and Neven's disappearances, but I have to know for sure. I want to go inside and investigate. If we don't find them, if there aren't any clues, then we leave it up to the police. I'll understand if you want to wait in the car or go home. I won't be mad, August."

August reached over and gently pried her hands apart. He moved his other hand up to tenderly stroke the right side of her cheek. Her body heated, and her heart accelerated. Even though she couldn't make out all the details of his face, she could see the sincerity in his smile plain as day.

"Perrie, you're an idiot." Her shoulders slumped at his

words, and she started to move back from his touch, but he pulled her closer, refusing to let her look away. "But, I'm an idiot, too. I'm with you every step of the way. So, if you want to get out of the car, I'll follow you. However, I must warn you that I'm no knight in shining armor. I don't have any of those skills."

She let out a loud laugh and dragged August to her, folding her arms around him. "Neither do I, August. Neither do I."

Before releasing him, she stared at his face a moment longer than she should've, his lips mere inches from hers. Then she drew back because they needed to get inside the museum.

As quietly as she could, she stepped out of the car, except when they shut the doors. Even though they tried to close them as softly as possible, it sounded like a gunshot echoing down the entire street.

"Shit," August said at the same time Perrie ducked to the ground. "Did you just crash to the cement and leave me in the open?"

With nonchalance, she popped back up from the hard ground, as if it had never happened. "I have no idea what you're talking about." She smiled, meeting him on the other side. "Let's do this."

Clenching the back of August's shirt, Perrie followed him to the door while damp grass brushed against her ankles. Besides the sounds of their footsteps, they were surrounded by the uncanny melody of chirping crickets and croaking frogs.

Except for the small ball of light illuminating the porch, she couldn't see anything. The tall wooden door came into view, daunting as ever. The same words were scrawled across the front:

Quinsey Wolfe's Glass Vault

The job posting was no longer listed. In its place, it now

read one word: *Open*. Yet, there were no hours of operation written anywhere.

She and August exchanged glances, giving each other a similar look of surprise. "So, I guess they're open?" Perrie asked.

"Only one way to find out." He shrugged.

The golden knob flashed under the light and Perrie reached to turn it. She gasped. *Unlocked*.

As she pushed the door open, no squeaky hinges greeted them, which wasn't what she'd expected. She thought there would be darkness, but they were instead met with a row of lit lanterns hanging on the wall in a long and narrow hallway.

Perrie stilled, swallowing hard. "Should we keep going?"

"Yeah, or we can stand here all night and admire the hallway."

"Good point," she replied, rolling her eyes. "Guess I'll go first."

Quietly, she stepped inside. August followed suit and softly closed the door behind them. There was nowhere to go but forward. A musty smell filled her nostrils as she took stock of their surroundings. The walls on either side of them were decorated with red-and-gold leafy-patterned wallpaper, highlighted even more by the lanterns attached. The lanterns guiding their way seemed to float and move with the eerie shadows they cast around them.

Perrie listened for the echo of footsteps or distant voices, anything that would point them in Maisie's direction. Nothing … only the soft padding of their own footsteps against the flat blue carpet.

She and August walked side by side, like equal partners. At the end of the hallway, there was only one way to turn, a sharp left. August went first, gripping her hand and bringing them down the next hall covered in solid-gold tile.

This place was beginning to feel like a miniature maze because of the narrow halls leading them in a certain direction.

She suppressed the urge to turn around and run away—back to August's car.

I am not a coward. Maisie needs me. Ignore the voices in your head telling you otherwise.

Refocusing her thoughts, Perrie noticed the hallway had changed. These walls were blue with a gold trim dividing them. Instead of lanterns casting light, expensive-looking crystal chandeliers hung above them. The smell was beginning to remind her of an old library, except no books lingered.

"I'm starting to feel like this place is all hallways and no rooms," August mumbled as he looked ahead. There was obviously going to be only one way to turn again.

"I just hope we run into someone soon," she said.

Maybe, if they could find the owner, he would tell them how his building could vanish into thin air, or why their photos wouldn't appear. Then again, she wasn't entirely sure she wanted to know any of those details.

"If we ever get out of these hallways." August ran the tip of his fingers along the wall, barely touching the surface. Bits of dust floated off into the air.

They reached the end and their only option was to turn right. The flooring transitioned from tile to another flat carpet, but with a strangely unique Victorian pattern, containing threads of browns, golds, and oranges. Again, she noticed the walls had changed their pattern. The blue-and-gold wallpaper had become green, the deepest, most luscious shade of it she'd ever seen. It almost reminded her of the wrapping paper Maisie had used on her birthday present.

"Look!" she whisper-shouted. Up ahead, at the end of the hall, was an opening.

Perrie latched onto August's arm and gripped it so hard she feared she might break it in half. He picked up the pace and she stayed attached like a baby sloth. As they got closer, she took a long, deep breath. The hallway spilled into a large room, and the first thing her gaze landed on was the shimmer of a thousand colorful glass statues. They were *everywhere*.

The room itself formed a complete circle and different displays were placed next to each other, one after another in the same fashion.

Perrie didn't know what August was thinking, but she was both disturbed and enchanted. Everything in the room was made of glass or made to appear like it. She wanted to get a closer look, but she was planted in place by the warning signals going off in her mind. *Ignore them.* There was no one here, and unless they were hiding in the displays, then they were completely alone. Perrie's hands shook when she noticed there was no other door, window, or way out besides the way they'd come in.

"August." She hesitated.

"Yeah?" He attempted to move forward, but she grabbed his arm and yanked him back.

"Did you not notice the, um, lack of exits?" Her gaze continued to search for another way out, maybe even a trapdoor on the marble floor. There wasn't one. Tilting his head, he scrunched his eyes, seeming to try to recall each one of their steps from the moment they'd come through the door.

"Well, now I do," he said finally.

"This is too strange."

He gripped his curls and scratched his head. "I couldn't agree more. There also appears to be no one here."

"Let's take a look around then." She took a cautious step to her left and August followed.

Maybe they were missing something—a secret door or clue that would tell them where to go next. Perrie was ready to believe anything, even the possibility there might be an invisible door. Maybe they would find someone. Maybe they could find this Quinsey person, if he even existed, so they could ask him about Maisie. Unfortunately, that was one too many maybes for her.

This museum was unlike anything she'd ever seen. The

displays each contained frighteningly life-size glass statues with realistic, human-like characteristics. Perrie would never have known that glass could be molded to reflect life, both physically and in color. They were all made that much more unique by the precise coloration of the scene they were playing out. It was like they'd been caught in the moment, as if a photographer had captured them as the action occurred.

They were undoubtedly beautiful, but spine-chilling in the stories they were trying to tell. The displays were from some of the best horror films to date, historical events, and gruesome fairy tales.

Perrie came upon the display of a creature with long, distorted nails standing over the bed of his dreaming victim. The victim's eyes were pressed tightly together and her mouth was crafted into a frown. She must've been having a nightmare and didn't even realize the worst of it was about to come true.

Moving onto the next one, she studied a display with a wolf that was equal parts man, in shredded clothing, howling at the moon. Beneath him, Little Red Riding Hood was sprawled out on the ground with her red cape twisted and mangled like her body. Her eyes were left wide open. Unpleasant chills tingled down her spine and the hairs on the back of her neck rose.

What is this place? She shuddered.

Perrie and August walked in continued silence, his hand clasping hers. Neither of them could bring themselves to speak to each other, so she kept her eyes busy.

There were many, *many* more. They passed a display of kids with white hair and glowing eyes, a cemetery surrounded by ghostly figures, the witches of Salem ready for revenge, and then she halted. Frankenstein's Monster was hard to miss in the menagerie. He faced the wall, back to her, so she was unable to see his expression. She maneuvered around for a better look at his kneeling figure. Stitches covered his glass body, mended wounds that would surely leave behind scars if he were a real person. The way he held himself told her he'd lost everything.

Perrie didn't know why, but she felt sorry for him.

August led her away and onto the next display. These particular scenes she was familiar with, as they were all fairy tales, twisted to be obscure and obscene. Mother Goose ripping the feathers from her beloved goose, Alice setting fire to Wonderland, Hansel and Gretel eating the witch they'd cooked, Ariel halfway finished cutting off her own fin to become human, Pinocchio had sewn a suit of what appeared to be skin to wear over his wooden body, and plenty others that she couldn't find the right words for.

A large sign in her peripheral vision caught her immediate attention.

Welcome to Sleepy Hollow

A glass girl knelt beside it with her hands over her face, as though she was crying. Behind the girl was the Headless Horseman mounted atop his horse, a long blade in his hand. Perrie looked to the right of her, finding the next display to be Jack the Ripper.

Perrie was about to walk toward it to get a better look at what was inside, when something tugged on the front of her shirt. She inhaled sharply and peered down. Nothing was there.

"August, I felt—" She tried to catch his attention, but he was focused on the Sleepy Hollow sign.

A strong force pulled her right leg and Perrie crashed to the floor, landing hard on her side. She quickly rolled to her stomach to get back up, but she couldn't.

"Perrie!" August stooped down and grabbed her hands, but before she knew it, they were being dragged forward. He tried to yank her back, but the force tugging at them was too strong. It was almost as though an invisible wind was drawing them toward the Sleepy Hollow display.

"Please don't let me go!" Perrie screamed at August. She didn't know what was happening, but she did know she didn't want him to leave her there.

His face was flushed red from attempting to haul them in the opposite direction. "I'm not letting you go! Just keep holding on to me."

Perrie squeezed as hard as she could, but then another powerful rush of wind sent them crashing into the Sleepy Hollow exhibit. She was sure they would have to pay for whatever they broke inside this vanishing death trap. Closing her eyes, she prepared for the impact of body against glass. She'd been expecting to hit it hard, so when the wind ceased and she collided with soft grass, a gasp escaped her mouth. August fell on top of her, knocking her sideways.

"What the hell was that?" Perrie shouted and scrambled to her feet.

"No idea." August shook his head and pushed himself up.

"We have to leave. *Now!*" Panic seeped its way through her, down to her bones.

"I'm with you"—he grasped her hand—"but how do we leave?"

His words caught her off guard. *The exit of course!* Except … there was no exit. When she looked around them, they were no longer in the exhibit. In fact, they weren't in the museum at all, and she had no idea where they were.

TEN

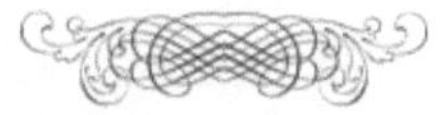

Perrie and August now stood in a forest, surrounded by a fog so heavy she couldn't see anything past the trees directly in front of them.

How are we not in the museum?

"You okay?" August poked her hand with his pinky, waking her out of her staring spell.

"Yeah, I'm fine." Chest heaving, heart pounding, she walked back in the direction they'd come from. Something thrust her backward before she could go any further. She shot August a confused look.

"What the hell?" August tightened his fists and took a few steps back, then jolted forward, hitting the wall of invisibility. As he bounced back, he caught himself before falling to the ground. It was as though there was a wall made of rubber in place of their exit.

Feeling dazed, Perrie shook her head to clear it before her gaze settled on August. "Hold on. What are you wearing?"

Forget the wall, what is with his ridiculous getup? He wasn't dressed in the same clothing as before. August wore black trousers with a button-up black vest and a white collared shirt underneath. A long black coat swept around him, ending where a pair of tall black boots began. Besides the eye-catching quality of his ensemble, she had no clue what era it was even from. But it was old.

August eyeballed her and pointed at himself. "What do you mean *me*? What are *you* wearing?" Shuffling forward, he lifted a lock of her hair. "And when did you get curls?"

Inhaling sharply, Perrie snatched the strands from him and examined it. One long, curly hair twisted in her fingers. Dropping it, she quickly ran her hands over the top of her head and felt the newness of it.

What is going on? Seriously, she was in full-on panic mode as her hands trembled. She took a look at her clothing next, shocked to see August was right.

Perrie wore a long black dress with a big skirt and sleeves that came to her elbow. A layer of lace flared out at the ends and brushed the skin above her elbows. The bodice was cinched tight with decorative buttons trailing down her middle. She skimmed her hands up from her stomach to her neck where she could feel the collar squeezing her throat.

Never in her life had she been claustrophobic, *but she was now* with all these buttons. The dress almost dragged on the ground and she lifted it away to see her shoes. *These shoes*! They were charcoal gray, with pointed toes and skinny heels. Perrie had never worn real heels in her life! Actually, the last time was her princess dress-up shoes back in preschool—they didn't count.

Even when Perrie had gone to the prom with August, she'd chosen flats over heels. Using caution, she took a couple steps and, thankfully, they weren't as uncomfortable as they appeared. Shaking her head, she dropped the skirt to cover her feet. They needed to find Maisie and the last thing she needed to worry about were shoes.

"I don't know why I'm wearing this, honestly. I sure didn't have time to change or magically find these clothes in the one-second transition from where we were—to wherever we are now," she snapped more to herself than August.

"I need a picture of this." August reached for his pants pocket but realized he didn't have any. He patted his hips and backside down. Nothing.

Their cell phones were *gone*. Her dad wanted her to have a phone for emergencies. Well, where was the damn thing when she needed it? Even the necklace August had given her had vanished. She was at a loss for words and it seemed August was, too. Perrie's legs slowly carried her back to the barrier, while she held her arm out with her palm up and fingers spread apart, until her hand contacted the invisible wall. It was like rubber mixed with gel. There was no breaking through it. She pushed, clawed, and scratched as hard as she could.

Using her miming skills around the barrier, she first went to the left, then again to the right. August copied her movements until they realized they were practically surrounded. Their only option was to go in the other direction, toward the forest in front of them. She hesitated.

"I really don't want to just sit here." August sighed.

Perrie had no intention of sitting there and waiting for who knew what. This whole week had been a fucking mess, and this place was about to put her over the edge. She didn't know where she was or what the hell was going on.

Is this a nightmare? Perrie pinched herself on the arm like they did in the movies to wake up. *What a waste of time.* All that did was make her arm hurt.

"We're not going to sit here," she said. "Let's try going forward, since that appears to be the only direction to go." There was little to see except bushes and trees, so she let nature lead the way.

August motioned her forward. "Ladies first."

"Why thank you, August. Aren't you just a gentleman? I'll let you know if I see a werewolf in the forest so you can, you know, run first." She smiled, lifting her skirt and trudging ahead.

Surprise washed over Perrie by the level of comfort in her pointy *hiking* shoes. Still, she wished she had on something more practical. Climbing over tree limbs wasn't exactly a tea party.

"Let me go ahead of you then. Wouldn't want anyone to mess up that pretty face of yours," August said, reaching to move a tree limb so she could pass through. The long limbs were covered in green leaves, dotted in between with shriveled red berries that she was sure were poisonous.

August's jacket snagged on a branch, but he didn't seem too worried. He was looking ahead, far too focused on that than disentangling himself.

"No way," she breathed.

Before her, on the other side of this forest, stood another large wooden sign. This one was different—it curved and was secured on either side by tall, round wooden posts. The sign was so old, rotted and worn from harsh weather. She was impressed that it had any life left in it at all.

Even though she could see the large letters, Perrie squinted hard to read what was written across it to make sure she wasn't dreaming.

Welcome to Sleepy Hollow

"That's the same sign we saw in the exhibit on display." She cupped her mouth and clenched August's shoulder.

"I realized that when I saw the sign," he said sarcastically with a grin.

She slapped his arm. "Stop trying to be funny."

Swallowing, she stepped closer to get a better view when, rising out of the fog, two rows of houses appeared beyond the sign. Straight ahead, past an ordinary field, the houses continued to stretch to the left with its twin set on the right, becoming a village.

They looked like old cottages, practically falling apart with crooked roofs and leaning structures. She had no clue how they were still even standing.

Perrie threw her hands in the air. "Where are we? I mean, *seriously*, what's going on?"

August glanced up at the sign again. "I feel like we already have our answer."

He was right. This was the exact sign from the display. It didn't seem possible, but somehow, they'd been transported to Sleepy Hollow. And nothing here was made of glass.

Just to be sure, Perrie brushed her hand across the grass and picked one small, single blade, then rolled it between her forefinger and thumb. Its smooth texture grazing against her skin was as real as it got. Satisfied enough, she threw the blade of grass on the ground.

"Maybe we'll find someone here who can help?" Perrie suggested.

"As you wish, milady." August bowed.

She rolled her eyes and smiled. "I'm pretty sure that's a different era."

"Are you sure?" He chuckled, flicking his gaze back to the houses.

"No, not exactly."

August walked ahead and Perrie followed, taking one last glance at the sign above their heads. The world was as silent and intimidating as the thick fog encasing them. Finding it hard to see very far in front of her feet, she kept her eyes trained on the back of August's head.

As they approached the first set of houses, they decided to go left and knock on the doors. Maybe *someone* would be inside.

They walked up the couple of wooden steps of the first house and managed not to fall through the stairs in their dilapidated state. No one answered when she knocked, so August tried turning the knob, only to find it locked.

After about ten houses, Perrie was starting to believe no one was home. They trekked to the next house, her fist in midair and ready to knock when a male voice shouted from inside, "Leave now!"

Startled, Perrie jumped back. Thankfully, August caught her before she fell down the stairs.

"Please, can you open up? We're lost," she said.

A man's voice shouted again, even louder than the last time. "I said, leave!"

"Look, we need help, and we're lost. My friend here is injured and needs somewhere to rest," August lied.

Perrie shook her head. "Injured? What am I going to say I have, a fucking stomach ache?"

"Just go with it."

After a pause, the man responded. "No. Go find someone else. If you don't get off my property, I'm going to have to shoot you and your friend. Do you hear me?"

That did it. Perrie scrambled down the stairs with August—imaginary injury be damned. She wasn't ready to take a bullet for something like that.

"What now?" she asked as she leapt down the last step.

August cocked his head. "I guess we can try a few more houses? Investigate more. I mean, there has to be a way out of here."

The word 'investigate' reminded her of Maisie and her notepad. Had she gotten magically sucked into this hellhole too? If she had, then there was a chance she was hiding somewhere in one of these houses. Maybe she was too afraid to come out, but no, that wouldn't be Maisie. Perrie could feel the hope in her heart building to a catastrophic letdown.

She placed her arm in front of August. "Do you think Maisie might be here? She did go to the museum that night."

"Honestly, I hope not, Perrie. But it's a possibility." August's gaze shifted up ahead past the field. "Do you hear that?"

"Hear what?" Perrie tilted her head, trying to listen.

"Exactly, I'm not hearing *anything*. No birds, insects, nothing."

"I haven't been paying attention to sounds since we've been, you know, a little busy trying to find people." She thought about it a little harder. "But the wind doesn't seem to be blowing anymore."

August tensed, his eyes scanning the landscape. "Something's off, even more than it already is."

They moved on to the next house and like the others, no one answered. There had to be someone inside one of these homes. Especially since they'd encountered some crazy down the cottage strip who'd threatened them already. She wondered if locals weren't answering the door because they were frightened of them.

It dawned on her then when she remembered what she'd seen in the display. Gasping, she whirled to the side and grabbed onto August's coat and stopped him.

"What do you know about Sleepy Hollow?" she rushed out.

"Ichabod Crane"—his eyes widened—"The Headless Horseman."

"I think we're inside the story. I've never actually read it, only seen the movie, but I know the basics." Perrie's thoughts ran wild and suddenly the locals' behavior made sense, or … the one local they'd encountered.

The Headless Horseman wasn't real—she didn't think—but who was she to say what was real and what wasn't anymore.

A strong sense of urgency flowed through her veins as they walked up to the last house. August rapped gently against the door, while she wanted to pound it like a madman. Same as with the others, nothing happened. Perrie was almost tempted to run back up the field to the first cottage and take her chances with the other guy. If he hadn't threatened to shoot them, that was, she would've kept bugging the piss out of him until he'd let them the hell in.

"You have to hide now," whispered a meek female voice.

Perrie's head jerked up. Did she imagine it? There wasn't anyone here. "Is someone there?" she asked. When no one answered, she turned around.

The door creaked, and Perrie whipped her head around so fast that lightning wouldn't have been quick enough to strike. A small hole opened up in the middle of the door. The lone eye of a local peeked out at August and her, unblinking.

"What do you mean hide?" Perrie said. "Can you let us in? We're sort of lost." They were more than lost, but she didn't doubt this stranger would believe them if they told her the truth.

"It is only I here," the woman said. "If I let you in, you must promise to do as I say."

August shared Perrie's skepticism, like he didn't know what kind of creature this woman was, yet they both agreed to her terms.

The tiny opening closed and at least a dozen bolts ground together on the other side as the stranger unlocked the door.

"Uh, maybe we should go back to that guy with the gun," August muttered.

Perrie glared daggers at him, and he just smiled wide at her dirty look with that maddening grin she loved so much.

The door slid open and they were greeted by a young woman in a gown that was once fashionable, but now moth-eaten. Perrie peered down at the stranger's bare feet. She was not what she'd expected—not at all. Beautiful, golden hair fell in waves around her cherubic face. If it weren't for the fact she shared Perrie's height, she would have mistaken her for a child.

The young woman waved them inside, and they hurried into a small living room. With a practiced hand, the stranger locked each one of the bolts, then turned around to face them.

"Thank God!" Perrie exclaimed, relieved by the fact they were no longer alone. "I'm Perrie"—she motioned from herself to beside her—"and this is August."

"Pleased to make your acquaintance." The young woman slowly nodded. "My name is Katrina Van Tassel."

ELEVEN

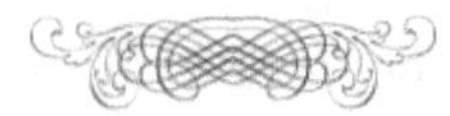

Katrina Van Tassel.

Perrie might not have read the Sleepy Hollow story, but she recognized that name from the movie. Even her face looked familiar, like she'd seen her before, but maybe Katrina just had one of those faces. Either Katrina was mad, Perrie was mad, or they were all entirely crazy here. She wanted to hysterically laugh at this circumstance, but then she remembered Maisie and Neven were missing.

"Hi, Katrina, it's a pleasure to meet you, too." Perrie was unsure if she should bow or what, so she stood awkwardly beside August.

Strolling over to a circle of wooden chairs, Katrina sat and motioned for them to do the same. "I would offer you a refreshment, but we need to wait until it passes."

"Until what passes?" Perrie asked, just as confused as August looked.

Katrina's face paled. "The Headless Horseman."

She has to be joking.

"You've got to be shitting me." August clasped the back of his neck.

Swaying, Katrina gazed dreamily at the ceiling. "Yes. He

has taken everything from me—my father, mother, my love, and everyone else I have ever cared about. The taunts continue one by one, until he decides it is my time."

The hairs on Perrie's arms rose like needles. The way Katrina talked—it was dazed and absent-minded, as if she wasn't all there. She believed in something that wasn't even real. Perrie wanted to ask her if she knew about the Glass Vault, or if she'd seen Maisie, but this wasn't the right time or place.

August gradually leaned forward, as if he was approaching a frightened kitten. "What year is it?"

"Seventeen-ninety. Why?"

Perrie sucked in a sharp breath and her eyes widened. Seventeen-ninety? They couldn't have traveled through time. *The Legend of Sleepy Hollow* was just a story.

August shifted back, his expression blank. "Excuse us, we have been on the road a long time and have lost count of the days. We were unsure if the New Year had already passed."

A much better answer than she would've thought to give. She didn't have the mind for coming up with lies on the spot. It was why Aunt Krista could always call her out when she'd lied.

When Perrie scanned the inside of the cottage, there wasn't much to the living room—four chairs, a large rug, and a kitchenette, complete with a wood-burning stove and dated cookware. They really weren't in Deer Park anymore—that was for sure.

"Where do you hail from?" Katrina asked.

"Well, we uh, come from the East?" It came out more like a question than an actual answer. Katrina tensed and dropped to the wooden floor and flattened herself against the dust.

"Lie down on the floor. Don't make a sound until I tell you to," she said anxiously.

"Is there something wrong with the East?" Perrie furrowed her brow.

"Shh! Get down!" she whisper-shouted.

August laid down flat on his stomach, and Perrie followed right next to him, inching closer until their shoulders were pressed together. She didn't want to find out what would happen if they didn't follow her instructions. Straining her ears, she listened for anything out of the ordinary. It wasn't hard to pick out the strange noises when this whole world had been silent. Outside, the noises grew louder, and louder, until she could almost make out the source of it. The sound of a horse's hooves beat upon the ground in a steady cadence.

The ground quaked around them as the horse drew nearer. Perrie's heart was pounding so rapidly that she worried whatever was outside could hear it. August must've sensed her growing fear and looped an arm around her waist, tugging her even closer to his warm body. It calmed her enough.

Perrie glanced at Katrina, who watched the door like a bird of prey. A sheen layer of sweat dotted her forehead and rose-red lips. Katrina knew exactly what waited outside her home, as if it was her daily ritual.

Then the noise outside came to an abrupt stop. The horse and its rider had to be in front of Katrina's house. It whinnied loudly enough that it reverberated in Perrie's ears like a powerful musical note. The sound was so deafening that she cringed into August's side in an effort to shield herself, while he didn't so much as flinch.

Someone jumped to the ground from the horse with a heavy thud. Hefty footsteps followed.

Thump, thump, thump.

Perrie clenched her jaw so tightly she was afraid her teeth would break. She wasn't sure how much time went by, but it must've only been several seconds before the rider turned around. The boots hit the steps as they walked back to their horse.

The horse let out another loud whinny before galloping away. Perrie didn't even twitch. August lifted his arm from around her and started to move, but Katrina was faster and whipped out her hand to catch his wrist.

"Not yet!" she said in a desperate whisper.

August's lips parted like he was ready to argue, then seemed to see the seriousness on her face, and relented.

BOOM!

Perrie's fingers dug into the wood at the sound of the gunshot, and she snapped her eyes back to the door, hoping they were not under fire.

BOOM!

Another sounded, but it was different this time. The echo of the gunshot was nearly drowned out by a man's deep, aching scream. Perrie trembled, holding her breath until her chest burned and she thought she would pass out. She'd never in her life heard the strangled sounds of someone suffering.

She wanted to run to the door and help whoever was in need, but she had no weapon or combat training, and didn't even know what the hell was out there.

Only hushed silence filled the air, followed by the hard stomping of hooves as they drew nearer and nearer. They passed by their hideout, then drifted farther into the distance. The beat of the wind whispered once more as it blew against the house and the three of them were alone.

Katrina rested her head against the floor and breathed deeply. "We can move now."

"So what's going on? Who was that?" Standing took some time from how rigid she was, but Perrie lifted herself upward, albeit shakily. She was beginning to believe Katrina wasn't so crazy after all.

August pulled up beside Perrie and stretched his arms to the ceiling. "It can't be who we think it is, is it?"

Gnawing on her lip, Perrie turned to him. "It has to be the Headless Horseman, but how is that possible?"

"Think about it, Perrie. We're in a place that makes no sense—the impossible could be possible."

Katrina lifted herself up and quickly tidied the messy strands of her hair. "The tales of the Headless Horseman are most certainly true. There is no certain time he arrives, but when he does, he continues to take us one by one. Mr. Roberts, God rest his soul, and I were the last ones left. Now it is only the three of us."

"Mr. Roberts? I think he may've been the man who wouldn't open the door for us earlier," Perrie said.

Katrina sighed. "He has not opened his door in quite some time, not since his wife and two children were taken."

"I'm confused." August stumbled back to the chairs and sat. "Why don't you just pack up your things and leave?"

Perrie wondered that too as she plopped down on a chair. If a headless psychopath was going around taking people, she sure wouldn't have stuck around.

"I can't leave. I have tried" —Katrina took the seat across from August—"but the both of you can."

"We didn't—" Katrina interrupted her before she could explain.

"I know the two of you are not from here, or the East as you say. There have been others like you who have come and gone. When I have tried to follow them, something always keeps me here."

Perrie rested her hands on the arms of the chair and gripped the edges. "What do you mean?"

The young woman before her withered, as though she'd resigned herself to remain in Sleepy Hollow for eternity. "If you continue following the field and pass through the graveyard, I believe you can cross somewhere else. When I have tried to do the same, a force pushes against me, and I am unable to pass."

August hunched forward, hands on his knees, seeming to anticipate her next words. "What about the Headless Horseman? Have you seen him?"

"I have. It is true he is without a head, but I have never

seen him take anyone's," Katrina said, not meeting their eyes as she busied herself with the lace cuffs of her sleeves. "My true love, Ichabod, was the first to be captured. I was with him that night and taken by surprise. The Headless Horseman emerged from nowhere. Ichabod told me to run, and so I did, deserting him. That was the last I ever saw of him. After that night, the Headless Horseman has come when it pleases him, picking us off one by one."

Her eyes grew distant, and Perrie shuddered at the idea of being taken by this *thing*. Maybe there was a way to save Katrina and themselves.

"Could you show us the way to the crossing?"

"Perhaps in the morning. It is too late and he will have returned to the graveyard by now. It will be safest to go at dawn."

Perrie's eyes fluttered wildly. "We have to pass where he lives?"

Katrina pursed her lips and nodded. "I am afraid so, but that is your best chance. When he returns for me, I pray the two of you will be far from the danger."

"Will you come with us?" August asked.

"I will try."

The whole point of them going into the Glass Vault was to find Maisie and possibly Neven. She was still unsure if Neven even came to the Glass Vault. "You said others have passed through. Was there a girl named Maisie or a guy named Neven? The girl possibly wearing an eye patch?"

"No." Katrina touched her cheek. "No, I cannot recall those names. I am certain."

The little bit of hope Perrie had evaporated from her chest. But she couldn't give up. She wouldn't.

Katrina sagged her shoulders tiredly. "In the meantime, I will feed you and grant you the spare bedroom tonight for some rest."

Exhaustion hit Perrie at that moment, and she had no idea

when they would eat next, so she agreed. Katrina heated up some food that she already had prepared in a large pot. While the meal was cooking, Perrie decided to confess the truth to her.

She and August alternated explaining to Katrina where they were from, the date, and the glass museum. Katrina took it all in stride and didn't seem that surprised. In a place where a man with no head kidnapped people, it didn't appear that far-fetched to be able to believe something seeming out of the ordinary.

Katrina handed them steaming bowls filled with a warm meat and vegetable stew. Perrie took a small bite and was surprised by how delicious the flavor was.

After dinner, Katrina led them to the spare room. Based on the time frame, Perrie wondered what Katrina thought about them staying together, but the young woman obviously didn't seem to care.

"Rest easy," Katrina said softly.

"Thank you." Perrie smiled.

She felt like they'd hit a dead end. If Maisie wasn't here, then where was she?

TWELVE

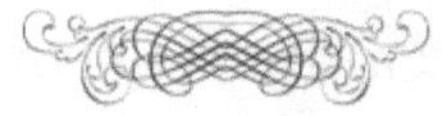

The spare bedroom that Katrina gave to Perrie and August was cramped and only held a few things in it. On one side of the room, a chair and small writing desk, with several blank sheets of paper sprawled across its surface, took up a corner. Then on the other side of the area stood a dresser and a decently sized bed, complete with a handmade quilt to keep warm.

August lowered himself to the floor.

"What are you doing?" Perrie asked.

His lips pulled up to one side. "I was going to let you have the bed."

Perrie drew the covers back. "August, just because we're in a different century doesn't mean you have to act like the perfect gentleman and sleep on the floor. Just get in the bed and be quiet."

He didn't think twice about it and removed his jacket and boots before sliding right into bed. She repeated his motions with her shoes and settled beside August. Surprisingly, her dress wasn't as uncomfortable as she'd first thought. Maybe she would be able to sleep.

August laid on his back, staring at the ceiling with his

hands tucked behind his head.

"What are you thinking about?"

He rolled over to face her. "I'm thinking about tomorrow and hoping I can get us out of here and back home."

"Where do you think Maisie and Neven are? Katrina hasn't seen them."

"I honestly don't know," he said. "I don't think they're here. Katrina has been here longer, so I'm sure she would have noticed someone like Maisie passing through."

"Maybe Maisie didn't stop here?"

"If that's the case then she could've found her way back home already."

"What about Neven? People go missing every single day, so what if something terrible happened to him? What if he isn't here?"

August reached over and pulled her to him and she rested her head against his chest. "One day at a time, okay? Let's stay positive and start fresh tomorrow. Once we get the hell out of here, that's when we can worry about everyone else."

He was right. She would do it for Maisie and Neven. If she could stay positive about this then she could remain focused. Although, she wondered if her dad, Aunt Krista, and Uncle Jaron had discovered she'd gone missing too.

Perrie placed her hand on August's cheek, turning his face to meet hers. "Thanks for coming with me tonight, August. I'm glad you're here. This would be a messed-up place to be alone."

"I wouldn't want you to be alone here, either. Hell, I wouldn't even want to be alone here." His lips brushed her forehead, and Perrie nuzzled into the crook of his neck, drawing in his soapy scent. For the time being, she felt safe.

"Good," Perrie said, breaking into a wide smile. She looked up one more time to find him grinning, too. As she lay back onto his firm chest, she was unable to stop smiling.

"Good night, Perrie."

"Good night, August."

As she shut her eyes, she waited for exhaustion to creep in and slip her into a deep sleep.

Someone was chasing her. Perrie was back at her house running from someone, something, and there were no lights to guide her. She hurried to her room and attempted to turn on the light there. But as she flicked it up and down, no light came, so she ran into her closet to hide.

The door banged open and the shape of a person now stood in the doorway. Nothing was visible, not even when she squinted her eyes to try and see. This darkness was different— it had a life of its own that swirled and twirled around her, enveloping her until she was a part of it.

He found her. The person in the doorway grabbed Perrie and she still couldn't see him. Pulling her from behind, he dragged her while she bucked and kicked at the floor to lessen his hold. Even her scream was weak, barely any sound escaping, the volume so minimal that no one would be able to hear it except for him.

By the touch of his strong hands and the feel of his large body, Perrie knew it was a man. His hands smelled of something putrid and decomposing. She gagged, but nothing came up.

Screaming was getting her nowhere. When they reached her front door, outside stood a horse on a road lit up from the beams of street lamps.

He hauled her onto the horse with him while Perrie continued to scratch and claw. Then she finally got a look at her captor. Swathed all in black and cocooned in a cloak of obscurity, but where his head should've been, there was nothing—only a void.

Her body froze, locked in place, but then a cold brush of metal rubbed against her neck. She was on her side, and he raised his arm to pull back what looked like a long sword. Closing her eyes tightly, she hoped and prayed she wouldn't be able to feel this. The wind roared against the blade as it fell.

Something brushed across Perrie's face, and she was barely coherent, bringing her hand up to swat it away. A few seconds later, the same something tickled her cheek, and her eyes flew open when she remembered the nightmare.

A soft sigh escaped her when she found August holding one of her long, brown curls caught between his fingers. He went to brush her face with it again, but she knocked his hand away before he could.

His laughter rumbled deeply, and she shoved his shoulder, which only made him laugh even more.

"I heard Katrina moving around, so I thought I should wake you up to get ready." He yawned. "Although, I wouldn't mind watching you sleep some more."

"You were just sitting here watching me sleep?"

"Well, no, I was actually sleeping until your snoring woke me up."

Perrie kicked his leg softly, her cheeks heating. "I do not snore!"

He leaned his head into her shoulder and chuckled. "Sure you don't, Snoring Beauty."

The fact that he'd called her beauty took away all the embarrassment.

"Whatever." She smiled.

They lay there for a little while longer as reality soaked in and then they forced themselves to get up. Perrie didn't know why but she'd thought she would wake up in her own room, as if this had all been a nightmare. August slipped on his boots while she laced up her pointed shoes. He waited for her at the door and opened it after she finished.

Katrina sat at the kitchen table, wearing the same tattered dress. They joined her for breakfast, which consisted of stale bread and half an apple each.

"It's all I have left," Katrina said.

"It's perfect," Perrie replied.

"I agree." August shoved a piece of bread into his mouth. The three of them ate their share in silence. Perrie tried to savor the taste of the apple, to make the stale bread last, but it was hard to do that when the monster in her belly demanded its fill.

"Are we ready to go?" Perrie was the first to stand, anxious to get moving before they were no longer alone. She hoped they would make it out and find Maisie.

Katrina folded her arms and nodded. "There is nothing left for me here. I only hope I can follow."

Perrie hoped so, too. The key word was *hope*.

As Katrina led them out the front door and onto the porch, the day appeared the same as it had yesterday. Trees rustled, and fog covered the ground, making it hard to see anything that wasn't immediately in front of her.

Perrie flinched as the stairs creaked and moaned with the weight of their footfalls. They stepped into the early morning dew blanketing the grass, and waited for Katrina to continue leading the way. They hadn't walked for long when a graveyard formed in the distance, the headstones seeming to go on for miles. The land appeared dead with only leafless trees and blackened dirt.

As they drew closer, the shapes of the headstones became clearer and a chill raced down her spine. She was beginning to get a shitty feeling about this.

Then the scent of decay struck her nose.

"Oh damn," August groaned, wrinkling his forehead.

Katrina came to a horrified stop and dropped to her knees. Large black beetles scattered across the dirt ground as she covered her mouth. Perrie could tell there was a scream anxiously trying to dig its way out from Katrina.

It wasn't only headstones covering the graveyard, but severed heads sprinkled everywhere, like seeds waiting to be planted. There were no bodies, just a never-ending graveyard of scattered bloody heads and grave markers.

Perrie closed her eyes and counted to five, foolishly hoping they would be gone when she opened her lids. *Nope*. They were all still there. Her gaze darted to Katrina who remained on her knees, rocking back and forth. August bent down beside her and said the words Perrie wished she could get out. "There's nothing we can do, Katrina. They're all gone. We have to be strong and get out of here."

Perrie crept closer, kneeling in front of her. "He's right. We're going to have to run through there. As hard as it is, avoid looking down and don't focus too much on anything except what's ahead."

"Okay," Katrina said breathlessly. "We are going to have to run."

That was a start. Now Perrie just needed to get her own nerves in check.

They sprinted through the graveyard and avoided the heads the best they could. She spied more of the color red, pooling where the severed heads lay. The headstones appeared mostly old, broken, and cracked, but she didn't have time to admire them—she brushed past everything.

The trees' rustling slowed to a stop—frozen in time. Perrie made the mistake of staring toward a spot where a tree had quit moving, causing Katrina to do the same.

Shifting her gaze to the ground, Katrina screamed in despair. "Ichabod!" She lunged to a fallen head, resting on its side under the tree. The dark-skinned head wore a hollowed-out expression, charcoal-colored hair, and eyes the color of ebony. Katrina reached out to grab it, but August dragged her back.

"We can't stay here," Perrie said. "Let's go. Now."

Tears rained down Katrina's cheeks, but her strength managed to take over.

From behind them, sounds came alive. The same hoofbeats from the day before approached. Perrie couldn't see through the fog, and she wasn't going to linger there either. They didn't look back. They ran.

The beats drew closer and closer, and there was no way in hell that all three of them were going to be able to outrun a horse.

August stayed ahead and Katrina was in the middle. Perrie glanced back, gasping. To her horror, a headless rider pushed out from the fog. It wasn't that she was shocked by the fact the Headless Horseman did exist, it was how he looked exactly as he had in her nightmare. A demon swathed in black.

She pumped her legs even faster, but she had never been a good runner. The horse's hooves pummeled the earth, taking its rider beside them, the headless creature holding the same shining blade from her dream. August looked back for the briefest second and saw how the Horseman was trying to cut them off. The blade was coming for her. She knew it.

Her legs were growing tired, heavy. The Headless Horseman wouldn't let up his speed when he neared, and he lowered his blade to her neck level as he pursued. Perrie should've dove to the ground, but she wouldn't be fast enough. Katrina gave her a hard shove to the side, just in time to keep Perrie's head on her shoulders.

Somehow, between Perrie hitting the ground and looking back, Katrina was in his grasp, her excruciating wails reverberating through the fog. Perrie grabbed for her, but missed.

"Run! Get out of here before it is too late," Katrina yelled.

Two arms snatched Perrie from behind, and she shrieked. All she could think about was her nightmare. She was next, this was it for her, and now she would never find Maisie or Neven. With a brutal twist of her shoulders, she tried to break free but couldn't.

"It's just me," August whispered, and she relaxed slightly.

The Headless Horseman held Katrina with one hand, and with the other, he raised his blade.

Perrie didn't see what happened next because August drew her forward, urging her to run even faster than before. The path where they were headed was unclear, but then she didn't have to wonder too hard. Just like before, back in the museum, a strong force pulled her toward it. The wind yanked at her entire body, then August shoved her from behind.

Their fingers brushed as she reached for him, but it was too late.

There was no going back.

THIRTEEN

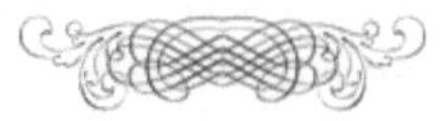

$\boldsymbol{\mathcal{A}}$s Perrie pried open her eyes, the whole world spun.

She lay on the floor of an unfamiliar room. A bed rested beside her, covered in silky sheets, and a small dresser stood across from it.

The graveyard was gone. Katrina was gone.

"August?" She forced herself to stand, but she didn't see him anywhere. Lifting the bed skirt, she looked under it, but found nothing.

Groaning miserably, Perrie fell to the bed. Her dress made a loud crunching noise as she sat and peered down at her lap. She inhaled sharply. It wasn't the same dress as before, but an entirely new one. The black material had become a vibrant green, like the color of the purest emerald.

As Dorothy would've said, *There's no place like home.* And she still wasn't there. *Where are those damn red ruby slippers when you need them?*

Perrie kicked the skirt of her dress out in front of her and the gown seemed to weigh her down. Layers upon layers of shiny green fabric made up the skirt. Even the bodice was finely crafted with little buttons and ruffles.

What the fuck is happening here?

On the wall, a single oval mirror hung, and she hurried over to it to take a better look at herself. A ton of skin and cleavage were on display, more than she'd ever shown in her life—aside from a bathing suit, which the last time she even wore one of those was in junior high before she developed.

She pulled the skirts aside and a heeled shoe protruded. *Heels again?* This time ankle length and laced up at the front. Her hair was still curled, but instead of hanging at her waist, it was now just below her shoulders.

Her hands flexed—she thought she would've been back at home, and now she was somewhere else. She needed to get the fuck out of this room and find August and hopefully Maisie if she was here.

Perrie's gaze fell to a door by the dresser, and she opened it wide enough to peek out. No one was there.

Breathing a sigh of relief, she opened the door wider.

"Not so fast, Mary," said a gruff male voice.

She whipped her head to the left and took a deep swallow. A tall man, dressed in a black suit and gloves, with a wooden cane in one hand, loomed above her like a gothic tower. He was an older man—maybe in his late fifties—with peppered gray hair and an impressive mustache. The man was physically fit, yet she wasn't going to be intimidated.

"Sorry, you have the wrong person. I'm not Mary. Maybe you could try another room down the hall?" Taking a measured step back, Perrie looked into his dark-brown eyes. She didn't like the way he was looking at her, as if she was his next meal and he was starving.

When she spoke, she realized her voice wasn't her own. Apparently, she'd adopted an English accent in favor of hers. It wasn't any stranger than anything she'd experienced so far, but it was still startling.

He studied her as if *she* was the crazy one. Mary might rhyme with Perrie, but there was no way the two could be confused. She'd never seen this man before in her life. He stepped forward, and she took another step back. He waggled his gloved index finger in front of her face, scolding her like he would a naughty little child.

"Oh, Mary, Mary, Mary. I didn't know tonight is to be our role-playing night. I believe we only do that on Fridays."

What is this asshole talking about?

"I told you my name isn't Mary, so I think you need to leave, or better yet, *I* need to leave." Perrie attempted to take a step around him, but he grabbed her by the arm, pushing her back toward the bed, and she stumbled.

His expression turned predatory. She was about to vomit on this bastard's face if he put his hand on her one more time.

"What should I call you then? How about *Helen*?" His head fell to the right. "Or *Margaret*?" He rubbed his right hand over his left that was squeezing the top of his cane. "Or maybe *Rose*?"

Anger blossomed inside her and she was sick of this fucker already. He needed to back off.

"Look, man, I don't know who you are or what's going on, but I'm not going to sit here and play this sick game of yours. I'm out of here, so find someone who actually wants to play and get you off," Perrie snapped.

There wasn't time to think, so she attempted one more time to dart around him. He jabbed his cane forward and hit the middle of her chest, stopping her in place.

Who does this guy think he is? Perrie threw her hand up to shove the cane away, but he was too fast. He bumped it harder against her chest and she fell back onto the bed. A deep throbbing came against her sternum, making her want to cry. She held her chest and a ragged breath escaped her.

"Tonight, Mary, I am going to call you *Victoria*." He smiled, showcasing a crooked incisor that was single-handedly laughing at her.

Screw this guy. Perrie pretended like she was still grabbing at her chest in pain, then rolled to the side, but the stupid big dress slowed her down. He shot his cane to the side to block her path.

Perrie's instincts kicked in and told her to try again, so she attempted to maneuver around his cane, but he was there, his arms slamming around her shoulders. He was even stronger than he looked.

"Naughty, naughty, Victoria. The fun hasn't even begun yet. Remove your dress, then I'll fuck you slowly before getting rougher. Maybe."

Perrie couldn't breathe as he tossed her back on the bed, waggling that damn finger at her again.

"No way in hell. For the last time, I'm not the person you're looking for!" she shouted.

"I *said* remove your dress"—his voice became harder—"or I will do it myself."

Perrie needed to come up with a plan to get away from this beast. So, she one more time went to dive around him, when he grabbed her by the throat, thrusting her backward once more onto the bed.

"You smell like honeysuckle on a sweet spring day." He caged her in with his arms on both sides, so she couldn't stop him from leaning forward to sniff her neck.

His body smelled strongly of odor and alcohol. "You reek of piss," she spat.

"Sweet, Victoria"—he laughed as if she'd told him the most hilarious quip in the world—"I wonder if you taste as good as you smell."

He leaned forward and skimmed his lips along her neckline. His tongue slid over her flesh, licking from the base of her throat to her left ear in a long, slow stroke. And then she felt his hardened length pressing into her. Perrie kicked, thrust, and screamed, but he was too heavy for her to knock away.

The edge of Perrie's skirt inched up her thigh as his hand traveled against her leg. Her stomach twisted into never-ending knots. A true feeling of terror washed over her at what he was going to try to do next, when the door burst open.

"This room is already taken."

"August!" she cried.

August stepped in, wearing gray slacks, a black jacket with only a few buttons at the front fastened. The jacket was longer in the back and concealed a high-collared white dress shirt with a gray tie. A black top hat covered his blond hair. "Sir, I am sorry I didn't catch your name? I believe this is the room I am supposed to be in."

"This room is mine for the evening." The man pushed himself off Perrie and her body relaxed immediately. I really don't think my name is any of your business."

August stroked his chin, as if what the crazy said was worth thinking about. "You seem to be mistaken, sir. I have already paid for her services for the entire week. Therefore, I believe it is time you take your leave. There are many other ladies here to fulfill your needs."

What is August talking about? Where are we? She could take a couple guesses herself, but she was sure that none of them would be what she wanted to hear.

"Mary?" The man whipped his head back to her so fast he might have pulled something in his neck—his eyes were bulging. "Is this true? This can't be true, can it? We always have Mondays and Fridays together."

Swallowing, Perrie mustered the most apologetic smile she could and casually shrugged. "It is true. I'm so sorry, but he offered to pay a better price and I accepted it for the entire week."

"Mary, you are nothing but a filthy, lying whore—like the rest of them." His eyes narrowed and he clenched his fists tightly to his sides.

"Hey, let's not call the lady names." Slowly, August walked forward with his hands spread before him, as if trying to calm a wild beast.

The frown left the crazy fucker's face the instant he turned to August. The way he behaved, spoke to him, it was like they were old friends out strolling in the park.

"No hard feelings, just watch your back with this one. That whore"—he pointed at her—"will feed you lies, and then throw you away like trash for the next person who will offer her something better."

The man sneered at her with disgust in his voice. "Mary, don't expect me to come back, even when you are begging on the ground for me to help you again. I am going to Irene. That is a woman who can help me feel like a real man."

While nodding, she attempted a solemn expression. "Good evening, then." *You crazy asshole.* "Truly, I am sorry."

He went without saying another word but still reached out to shake August's hand, as if they'd made a business deal together. *I guess they kind of did.*

Once he was out in the hallway, August shut the door after him and closed the distance between them in three long strides. He gently took her face in his hands and scanned her up and down.

"Are you all right? He didn't hurt you, did he?" Worry lines etched his forehead.

"I'm fine, but I'm most likely going to bruise here where he thrust his cane." Perrie's hand drifted to her chest and rubbed the spot where she was hit. Despite that, she already felt so much safer with that lunatic out of the room.

"He *what*?" August shouted.

She covered his mouth with her hand. "Shh! I don't want anyone to hear us."

August sat beside her and placed her hand into his lap, holding it there. "If I see that guy again, I'm going to beat the shit out of him, just so you know."

"That makes two of us." She really wished it would've been three. "I wish Katrina could've escaped with us." Perrie knew the Headless Horseman had Katrina in his grasp, but she didn't know what happened next. She could only assume the woman suffered the same fate as the others.

August straightened. "Katrina saved your life, Perrie. She wanted us safe. *You* safe. So what she did for us back there, for you, don't beat yourself up about it."

"Okay," she murmured, wishing there was something more they could've done.

"That's better." August squeezed her hand with an encouraging smile.

"On another note, where are we this time? How did we get separated?" Perrie asked as she reached to remove his top hat. Like her dress, it was finely made.

August took it back and ran his finger across the edge before setting it down beside him, deep in thought. "I think it may have been because we weren't touching," he said finally. "I mean we were, but then I lost hold of your hand and ended up in another room. Oh, and by the way, I like you with or without an accent."

She bumped his shoulder with hers. "The unexpected is to be expected, I guess. But this place isn't what I think it is, is it?"

"Oh, it is. It's a brothel." He waggled his eyebrows, followed by a semi-expression of apology.

Her body tightened at his words. "*What?*"

FOURTEEN

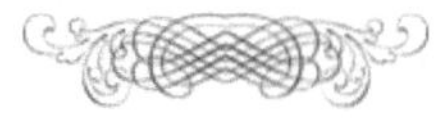

"What are you talking about, August?" Did he say *brothel*?

"I landed in a room further down the hall in a lady's bedroom." He arched a brow. "I had a front-row view. Kind of hard to misinterpret that."

Perrie's pulse quickened. "And?"

"And, she had on a lot less clothing than you're wearing. She kept asking me for her money up front. I told her I had no idea what she was talking about, and then she told me I only had an hour to 'get on with it.' I told her I was sorry, that I had the wrong room, and I left."

Jealousy pricked at her, but she pushed it aside. "How were you able to find me?"

His lips twitched with the slightest hint of amusement. "I didn't know if you were in here or outside somewhere. I started checking all the rooms, which was a big mistake. People do some acts in those rooms that can't be unseen.

"Then I heard a scream, and I recognized the sound of your voice, following it until I was led to this room. Made it just in time, right?"

"That you did." Leaning in, she wrapped her arms around his waist and held him tight. "And I guess you didn't see

Maisie?"

"No." He shook his head sadly. "I wouldn't—" A blood-curdling scream coming from outside their door interrupted August. They both jumped to their feet, startled.

"What do we do?" she asked.

"Check it out?" His answer came out more like a question.

Perrie led him out the door and into the empty hallway, where he followed her down it to a flight of stairs that took them to a large area.

The front room of the brothel served as a pub, and several glasses filled with alcohol were spread across the counter. The thick stench of cigar smoke and alcohol burned her nose. A group of people stood scattered in a circle around a hysterical middle-aged woman.

Perrie cautiously approached the group, careful to keep her distance.

"He got her! He got her!" cried the woman. "I saw a figure hovering over her and then she dropped dead."

August broke through the crowd. "Did you see who it was?"

Everyone in the circle turned around and stared at them. Perrie wanted to pull him back and smack his arm for putting all this attention on them.

"It's Jack, of course." A young woman, maybe in her early twenties, pushed her way through. Her red hair was pulled up in a once fashionable bun where it poofed in the front. "He isn't stopping, and he won't stop unless we get him before he gets us. He is bringing us down one by one."

The realization hit Perrie like a speeding train. "You're not talking about Jack the Ripper, are you?"

A tall, broad-shouldered man stepped beside the young woman. "Who else do you know of going around murdering whores?"

August stiffened beside her and ground out, "There's no need to call them that. For most of these women this is their only option to make a living."

"Call them what you want, but a whore is a whore, and you are no better than me, *sir*," answered the broad man. He glared at the both of them and then stepped around the group, leaving.

The red-haired woman rubbed Perrie's shoulder in sympathy. "Watch your back. I know out there they say not to trust anyone, but it's hard for our type to do that when what we do is part of our survival. This is the only way to get food in our mouth."

All right… Perrie needed a minute of silence so her brain could catch up. She'd left Sleepy Hollow and wound up with Jack the Ripper. Thinking back to the museum, she remembered seeing the Jack the Ripper display set up beside Sleepy Hollow. When she crossed out of Sleepy Hollow, instead of jumping back into the museum, she jumped to the next display. They had to be traveling between them then, so the next question was, how do they instead jump back into the museum? Still, as much as she wanted to go home, she wanted to find her cousin more.

As the woman started to turn away, Perrie asked, "Have you seen a girl named Maisie? Dark hair, brown skin, blue eyes with an eye patch covering one?"

"Does she work here?"

"No, I'm not sure if maybe she passed through here, though." Perrie scanned the room and no one here looked anything close to Maisie.

"No, I haven't heard that name. A lot of these girls are faces without names."

"Thanks," Perrie said as the woman moved to sit at a nearby table.

She should feel relieved that Maisie most likely wasn't in the Jack the Ripper display, but she still wasn't close to finding her.

At least she knew quite a few facts about Jack the Ripper. Maybe not the minor details, but she and Maisie had once done a research paper on him for English class. His true identity was never discovered. And for the most part, Perrie remembered the names of the women he'd murdered. Doing her best Detective Maisie impression, she approached the woman once again.

"So, who was it that Jack got this time? What was her name?" Perrie grabbed the stranger's sleeve, hoping to get some answers.

The other lady, the witness to the murder, had stopped crying long enough to be led toward the stairs. She looked like she could use an escape. The redhead waited until the woman was removed from the room to speak.

"Elizabeth. Elizabeth Stride. He managed to hold her still long enough to slit her throat, and the bleedin' was enough to do her in." Her voice was low, solemn.

Perrie wasn't sure what to do, but unlike Sleepy Hollow, this wasn't a work of fiction. *True crime section at the bookstore all the way*. Ripper was a real dark creature of the night. She knew the history, and it was her own personal key she could use to at least warn the next victim and avoid another murder.

"I'm so sorry." Perrie frowned.

The young woman held her hands gently. "Just be careful, Mary, it's all I ask. I don't want anything to happen to you."

Mary again?

"So you know who I am?" she asked, a little more delighted than she should be.

"Are you well?" Her brows drew together, and she brought a hand to her forehead. "Of course I know who you are. You're Mary Kelly, and my name is Fannie Caldwell."

Mary Kelly. It almost felt as though the pressure building in her head could push her eyeballs right out of their sockets.

"Yes, I'm sorry, Fannie. This whole situation is playing with my head." Perrie scrambled for the words she needed to pull herself together.

"Just go on back to your room and get whatever rest you can." Fannie nodded in understanding and shooed her off.

"Thank you and be careful yourself. Good night." Perrie gripped August's hand and gave him a hard tug. He'd been watching them the entire time, probably unsure of what was going on.

"What was that about? What's with that look on your face?" he asked in a hushed tone.

"I'll tell you as soon as we get back to the room."

Once they were back where they'd started, Perrie ushered him into the room and locked it up tight behind them. She collapsed onto the satin-covered bed, joined seconds later by an anxious August.

"Spit it out," he said as he searched her face for a clue.

"You know who Jack the Ripper is, right?" Perrie folded her hands in her lap and squeezed them together until her knuckles turned white. She then gazed into his green eyes.

"Of course I know who Jack the Ripper is. Who doesn't? His case is one of the most famous in history."

"What do you know about his victims?" She questioned, ready to burst with her answer.

"Not much. I know they were all ladies of the night, though."

She shook her head, almost smiling. *Almost.* "Nice way of putting it, August."

"Well, they were."

Sighing, Perrie brought her hands to her forehead. "Anyway, the point is Mary Kelly was one of his victims, and I *am* Mary Kelly. I'm one of Jack's victims—he's going to fillet me like a fucking fish!"

August's eyebrows shot up. "First off, that's not going to happen, and second, you're not food—no slicing and dicing for you."

She puckered her lips. "August, I'm serious."

"So am I, doll face."

Perrie fell backward onto the bed with a great sigh. August did the same, his top hat falling off his head and bumping hers. She rolled over and propped her head up on one arm, tossing his hat to the floor.

"Elizabeth Stride was murdered tonight."

"Right?"

She ticked off the murders in her head. Martha Tabram, who might or might not have been a Ripper victim, Mary Nichols, Annie Chapman, Elizabeth Stride, Catherine Eddowes, and Mary Kelly. That meant there was one left before her. In the real world, Elizabeth and Catherine were murdered the same night.

She went over the list of victims with August, then said, "We have no clue if the time frame is going to work the same here. There was no mention of Catherine Eddowes, only Elizabeth Stride."

"I don't know, Perrie. Maybe the people down there just haven't heard about Catherine yet, and how do you know this, anyway?" August rubbed his temples, whether from a developing headache, thinking, or both.

"I had to do a research paper on it with Maisie." Her heart stuttered at the sound of her cousin's name, and she hoped Maisie was somewhere safe, being her usual quirky self. "When Maisie does a research paper, she has to know every single detail, right down to the nitty-gritty. Therefore, *I* have to know every single detail."

August was about to open his mouth when she stopped him. "Wait!" Perrie told him her theory about how she'd seen the Jack the Ripper display next to the Sleepy Hollow one, and how they must be jumping from one display to the next.

"I don't know if we're going back in time, or if we're somehow stuck in a world inside of the displays. Whatever it is, is fucked up," August said as he raked a hand through his hair.

"I don't know, but the events in Sleepy Hollow weren't

accurate from what I know. Well, from the movie, anyway. And you know just how well Hollywood matches film to book. *Poorly*. However, I know the entire town wasn't missing in it, so I don't think we're going back to a true time."

August sat up. "Agreed. So, you said you fell in this room, right? Did you search around for a portal?"

"No, I didn't. I just looked for you, and then that asshole came in." Perrie leaned forward and pushed up from the bed.

August patted around the walls. "Let's look in here. I already searched in the room where I fell in with that woman and didn't find anything there."

Perrie moved to the opposite side of the room and knocked on the walls. Finding no exit, she headed toward the bed and tapped the floor underneath, slapping it several times with her hand just to be sure, but she felt nothing.

This wasn't like last time. When they'd appeared in Sleepy Hollow, the barrier was right where they'd been standing. This time it was like they were spat out and then it completely vanished. *Is our escape somewhere outside of the brothel?*

August halted his search and brushed his partially gelled hair back from his eyebrow. "I say for now we just get some rest since it's still dark. In the morning, we can go search around the city and try to find a way out of here."

"Then what? Are we going to go home, or are we just going to end up in the next display from the museum exhibit?"

Perrie wanted to get out of this one. When she thought of what had happened to Mary Kelly, her entire body shuddered. What happened to her was only something that the sickest of individuals could've done. Mary was pretty much skinned and dismembered.

Even if they ended up in another place that wasn't home, she would prefer it to having a meet and greet with Jack the Ripper. Especially since she *became* Mary this time—*however the hell that happened*. And if Maisie was in a different display, then how would they find her? There was no way they could go home without her.

August placed his hands behind his head and looked up at the ceiling. "Perrie, I know as much as you do, but we're going to find a way out of this. If I have to tear this city apart bit by bit to find that damn portal, I'm going to get you out of here."

She let herself smile. Even during the hardest times, he knew just what to do or say. August was . . . she couldn't even put into words what she felt for him anymore. "No, we're going to find a way *together*, and we're going to get out of here *together*."

FIFTEEN

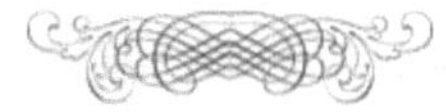

Exhaustion consumed Perrie from head to toe. A crazy asshole and an unsolved murder were enough excitement for one day. She didn't fight the need for sleep, so she lay down next to August and closed her eyes. They forfeited warmth and chose to sleep on top of the blankets. Who knew where these sheets had been and what horrors they'd seen anyway.

August pulled her close and wrapped his arm around her stomach. Taking hold of his arm, Perrie tugged it up to her chest and shut her eyes. It felt nice to be held again. It felt even better knowing that August was the one keeping her close. Her body heated at the thought.

Perrie didn't want to think about murder or Jack the Ripper right now. She wanted to think about a time when everything, mostly everything, was fine, and possibilities were endless. Yet something terrifyingly good could happen. So she chose to think about that night at the prom when her feelings had started to change for August.

After everything that had happened with Neven, she hadn't wanted to go to the prom. She was never big into dances or anything like that, yet Maisie was, and her cousin hadn't wanted to miss the prom. Perrie insisted she take someone, but

Maisie told her she wanted to go and hang out with her. Perrie had been extremely reluctant to cave to her begging. Then, when Perrie wouldn't budge, Maisie made a desperate play at lunch one day.

"August, will you go to prom with us?" Maisie asked.

Perrie had been sitting beside him at the time and was totally caught off guard. He was in the middle of swallowing a french fry and choked from surprise. She started patting his back and he grabbed his water bottle and started chugging. "You guys are going to prom?"

Maisie leaned forward with her strawberry eye patch and said, "Yes, if you'll take us?" She hadn't even given Perrie a chance to answer.

Perrie looked at both of them. "There's no way I'm going. If you two want to go, then more power to you. I'll be at home in my pajamas, most likely having a personal movie marathon."

"If Perrie doesn't go, then my duty will be joining her at this movie marathon." Grabbing Perrie, August hauled her to him in a side hug. He stroked her hair with his other hand while shrugging at Maisie.

Maisie threw up her hands, squeezing her fists in front of her, and begged, "Please!"

"Fine." Perrie sighed in defeat, wiggling out of August's arms. "I refuse to wear heels, though."

"Yes!" Maisie pulled her arm in a downward fist pump.

Perrie rolled her eyes and laughed.

August had picked them up for the prom that weekend. Perrie hadn't gone too fancy with her attire, opting for a relaxed curl in favor of an expensive updo. Her dress was red and strapless, tight on top with a wicked flared skirt right above her knees. Like she'd told Maisie, Perrie would not be wearing heels and had chosen a pair of black flats instead.

Maisie, on the other hand, stole the show. She wore a similar style dress of sapphire blue with one shoulder strap.

Peacock feathers lined the strap, and across the bottom of the dress, were more feathers woven in, hanging from the front, all the way to the back.

Her hair was curled and tied in the back into a loose bun. Maisie's eye patch was the same blue shade as the dress, except around the edges of the patch were miniature peacock feathers. She'd looked beautiful.

Once they'd arrived at the dance, they took prom pictures together. It was the first and only time she'd ever felt a twinge of jealousy toward Maisie. While Perrie watched August, she knew if he wasn't already hot for Maisie, he would be now.

He never looked at Maisie that way, though. Even that night, it was only like a friend, and Perrie had felt relieved. Then she'd wanted to slap herself for that moment of jealousy, not knowing why she should care if August liked Maisie.

August wore a black suit with a green tie, and it made his eyes stand out, drawing her into them more than ever that night.

When they'd sat down, August went to get them drinks and that was when she'd spotted Neven. He'd come in with some of the guys from the basketball team. Most of them with dates, but Neven and David didn't have one.

As soon as Perrie saw them, she examined her fingernails to pretend she was doing something.

David approached her table, and Perrie glanced up when she heard him talking to her cousin. "Maisie, you look interesting tonight. Do you want to dance?"

Perrie gave him the biggest what-the-hell look. That was the best he could come up with? *Interesting*? He'd been trying to get with Maisie forever, and his lines hadn't gotten any better.

Maisie told him okay, but she'd said yes to anyone who asked her to dance that night. She even asked the guys who were alone to dance since they'd been standing by themselves. That was what Perrie loved best about her cousin—the fact she didn't care what anyone thought, and just wanted to see everyone happy.

After Maisie left with David to dance, Perrie was done playing the examining nails game, so she glanced up and just happened to lock eyes with Neven. He looked so pitiful, and at that moment, she felt bad for him, then got mad at herself for feeling bad.

Neven got up and started to walk to her table. Thinking back, she didn't know if she would've talked to him if he'd tried. She probably wouldn't have and would've gotten mad like she always did for what he'd done.

He never made it to her table, though. August had come back with the drinks just in time.

"Do you want to dance?" He looked shy for the first time when he'd asked her, which made her say yes. She would've said yes anyway, though. Perrie had never seen August like this before, and she'd found it adorable.

As they got to the dance floor, Perrie looked back for Neven but he was already gone. The crisis had been averted.

The song playing was slow, which was awkward for her at first since she hadn't danced before. Then August helped her get into it—he knew what he was doing. Perrie laid her head against his shoulder and wrapped her arms around his warm neck.

His hands at her waist had drifted down toward her lower back. A fluttery sensation bloomed inside of her stomach, like more than butterflies. It was a mixture of things: dragonflies, ladybugs, moths, and maybe even hummingbirds.

The whole dance Perrie had kept thinking to herself, *What if I just leaned up and brushed my mouth against his?* Something about the way his hand rubbed against her back told her that she didn't think he would have minded at all, but she wasn't that brave. Not that night.

After the dance, August walked both of them to Maisie's door before taking Perrie to hers. She'd been such a fool—it was another perfect moment. Instead, she rushed in for a hug and squeezed him goodnight, avoiding looking at his face. Before she closed the door, he was smirking at her—a daring one that let her know he'd wanted to kiss her. Leaning her back against the door after shutting it, she'd sighed but smiled so big that her face had to have been outlined in cracks.

Half asleep, half dazed, Perrie rolled over to August. He was lying on his back, and she lifted herself, then pressed her lips to his, a spark igniting in her—his mouth was soft and perfect. She wasn't sure if he was asleep, but his arm wrapped around her, and she leaned over to his ear and whispered, "Good night, August."

"Good night, Perrie," he whispered back. So, he *was* awake.

Perrie left his ear and placed a gentle kiss against the side of his warm neck. He inhaled shakily, and her body wanted to do more—*she* wanted to do more.

As if hearing her thoughts, August pulled her on top of him, his hands drifting down to her waist. She lifted her dress and her breathing hitched at the feel of his strong body beneath hers. And then his hands began to move with her while she slowly rolled her hips forward, feeling every single inch of him. Her lips found his once more, and this time their mouths parted, their tongues danced as she licked and nipped. His hands drifted under her dress to her backside, gripping her soft flesh. She ground her hips into him, harder, faster, eager for the blissful feeling to wash over her.

It would be so easy for her hands to lift his shirt, then drift down to the button of his pants, and have him inside her. But she didn't. Instead, this was what she wanted for now.

A rush of warmth spread through her until it exploded into a thousand shattered pieces. She moaned in pleasure against his beautiful mouth.

As her blissful moment came to a spectacular end, Perrie continued her pace so August could hit that same crescendo. But then his hands halted her movement.

She frowned, confused. "Don't you want—"

"Another time, doll face. I just wanted you to feel good tonight," he murmured, bringing his mouth to hers again. Although it was the lightest of kisses, one like no other, it seared her straight to her marrow.

With a smile, her legs like jelly, she peeled herself from him and rested her head on his chest. She inhaled his comforting scent as he pulled her body closer to him, and in this moment, the escape had been perfect.

In the morning, Perrie still lay comfortably in August's arms. She risked glancing up and he was already awake, staring down at her. The night before she may have been bold, but right then, her cheeks heated at the wonderful memory.

"Finally awake, sleepy head?" He smiled.

"Why didn't you wake me?" As she sat up, a cold brush of air hit her after leaving August's warm arms.

"Why? So I can bring you out of your lovely dream back to this hellhole?" He maneuvered himself to an upward position next to her, then twisted his body so he was sitting on the bed with his feet flat on the floor. August already had his shoes on and placed the top hat on his head.

"Thanks, I appreciate that." She leaned over and slipped hers on, guessing that neither of them was going to discuss the night before. But she still felt the ghost of his hands on her, the way he'd made her feel.

Downstairs, everyone was eating breakfast and socializing with each other. Perrie spotted Fannie, and they shuffled over and sat in front of her at a table. The young woman poured a little whiskey into her tea from a tiny, silver flask.

"I need something a little stronger than sugar in my tea this morning." Fannie answered Perrie's unspoken question.

"I completely understand," Perrie said. She wouldn't be surprised if these women drank all the time.

Fannie leaned back in her chair and shifted her attention to August. "So, I see you are still here?"

"I have her for the entire week and not only at night either." August stared at her, pointedly.

"A knight in shining armor, I see." Her eyes widened as she sipped some of her *special* tea. "As long as you don't have someone waiting for you at home like most of these men do."

"What? It isn't like that," he rushed on.

"We will have to see about that, now won't we?" Fannie clucked her tongue, her sarcasm thick as honey.

Laughing, Fannie offered them something to eat. Perrie thanked her and accepted the small portion of food and the *un-special* tea since she needed to keep a clear head. Fannie seemed sweet and incredibly smart. It wasn't her business, but Perrie wanted to ask her why she worked at a brothel.

"How did you end up here, Fannie? I don't think I've ever asked you that." Perrie hoped from whatever false memories she had of her that she hadn't.

Relaxing back in her seat, Fannie appeared to consider the question with a great deal of thought. Perrie wondered how many other people had asked her the same question, or rather, cared to ask.

"I lost my parents when I was fourteen, and I had no other family to take me in and nowhere else to go. My parents didn't have a lot of money. When they passed, I had nothing and had to live on the streets for a long time. I was just a street rat, taking food from what I could scavenge out of the trash. Eventually, I ran into two women who told me about this place. They took me in, and now here I am." She waved one hand in the air.

Perrie's face must've looked stricken because she rushed on, "Don't worry about me. This may not be the Queen's palace, but it has treated me better than I was ever treated on the streets. The ones who work the streets have it the hardest." She peered down at her tea, staring at it for a moment before lifting it up and drinking it again.

"Mary!" A loud shout interrupted Perrie's thoughts.

She only turned around because the voice had been so loud. Then she remembered *she* was Mary, and that crazy bastard from the day before was sauntering to their table.

"What do you need, sir?" August pushed out of his seat and stood in front of Perrie. She rose out of her chair and stepped next to August. Two were always better than one.

"I came to apologize for last night." He gazed dreamily up at the ceiling then back toward Perrie. "Thank you so much for everything. I know you did that so I would go and see Irene, and she fulfilled every single fantasy I have ever dreamed about."

Did I just vomit a little bit in my mouth? I believe I did.

"Irene can certainly work her magic," Perrie replied.

"I will be spending my time with her from now on. Please know our time together is something I will always cherish." If the earth opened up at that particular moment, she would kick him into the gaping hole.

"Mm-hmm." Her lips were sealed tight.

Smiling, he left with a final, "Good day."

"Wow," Perrie drawled to August.

"Well, he shouldn't be bothering you anymore," August said.

"I'm glad to say I have never had Thomas in my bed," Fannie piped in.

Ah, so the fucker has a name.

They spent the rest of their time finishing up breakfast. Everyone discussed Elizabeth Stride's death, but no one mentioned a second murder. Two well-dressed men threw out their thoughts on the situation, that it was the woman's fault. Perrie wasn't certain if the time-frame of the murders was the same here.

Brushing the crumbs off her dress, she prepared herself to explore the city, and hoped to find a damn portal leading to Maisie.

SIXTEEN

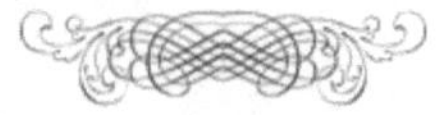

The door squeaked open as Perrie and August took their first steps out of the brothel. She was desperate to find the portal out of here that would lead them to her cousin—whether home or the next display.

But what if we don't find one? The little demon of misery knocked at her brain, and she flicked it away.

Tall stone buildings, with numerous windows, lined the street. The old street had only two directions, left or right.

"Where should we start?" Perrie asked.

August arched a brow. "Let's try left."

Left it was. The sun shone in the sky and the weather didn't have a single chill in the air. No people bustled about in the city, only them. Even the buildings appeared to be closed with no life within. And she wondered why.

Perrie walked to the closest building, green vines running up its length, and peered inside. Nothing except for a few dining tables and two settees.

"Where is everyone?" She glanced at August, then back toward the window.

August shrugged. "I don't even know. That seems to be the go-to answer these days."

"That it does." She sighed.

They set out down the graveled street again, reaching the end of the row of buildings where an intersecting street appeared. Before she reached it, the barrier knocked her back. August caught Perrie and helped right her on her feet again. It was the same as before—she could push against it, but she couldn't penetrate it.

"You take the right, I'll take the left," he said.

Perrie headed for the left row of buildings, with triangular roofs and tall chimneys, while he went right to the other set. She patted the barrier down like she'd done in Sleepy Hollow. They both did this until they were forced to turn where the barrier wasn't letting up. The route to the backside of the buildings remained inaccessible, even though she could see stone streets and other structures past them.

Chest heaving, Perrie met August back in the middle of the street. "Okay, so this seems to be like last time. I bet if we go to the opposite end, the remainder of the barrier will be there, forming a perfect rectangle."

"Agreed. That means the barrier should open up the same as in Sleepy Hollow since this side won't. Let's go." August didn't seem surprised by her logic. An idiot could've guessed the same thing.

Adrenaline took over while running to the other side with August. Everything remained a blur as she passed. She ignored the buildings and stayed focused on her goal, her heart thundering in her chest.

As they inched closer, a small village of houses slid into view up ahead. Thick smoke poured out of the chimneys of several.

Perrie smacked into something and realized they'd reached the end of the barrier. It launched her backward and she fell straight to the ground on her ass, scathing her right arm in the process of catching herself. August wasn't able to stop himself either and landed right beside her.

"Well, fuck." He shook his head, and his top hat slid off. Clenching his jaw, he stood up and kicked it. "That feels good."

In that moment, Perrie was just amazed that he'd been able to keep his hat atop his head while running.

Annoyance and confusion stirred within her—she didn't understand why the portal was still closed.

August clasped her hand to help pull her off the ground. She then brought her arm up and cradled it. His mood changed to one of concern, and he tenderly held her arm, inspecting it. "Are you all right?"

"Yeah, it's just a scrape. It'll heal."

Perrie's gaze flicked to the barrier. Scuffing her feet toward it, she pressed her palm against the rubber-like texture, thinking it might pull them through this time. But it didn't.

One name screamed inside her head. *Maisie.* What if Perrie didn't see her again because they were trapped here?

As she rubbed her palm against her face, a thought formed. "Maybe it only opens up at a certain time of the day or something."

"In Sleepy Hollow it was morning," August pointed out.

She cocked her head and angled her eyes toward the blue sky. "It's early now."

"Then how about we try nightfall?"

"What do we have to lose, right?" *Only Jack the Ripper may come out to play.*

On the way back to the brothel, they passed one of the tall gray buildings, a long crack running up the side. Vines and flowers with brilliant blues, yellows, and pinks covered a balcony on another. Underneath was a shoe-shining station sitting outside of a cobbler's shop. Not a single soul was around to have their shoes shined—its purpose defeated. Everything continued to stay quiet in this hellish town.

Once inside the brothel, Perrie's hope slipped, but she would maintain her grasp and hold onto it until nightfall. She hadn't had time to think about how her dad must be feeling with her gone. She didn't want him to feel abandoned like when her mom had left. But he was safe, so she pushed her thoughts of him away.

August took a seat at the small table they sat at this morning.

Resting her elbows on the scratched wood, Perrie placed her chin on her palms. "Now what do we do?"

August studied the bar. "Hungry?"

"Really? You can still think about eating?" She let out a small laugh.

"All the time." He stood and walked over to the counter, finding two bowls of stew, then headed back to grab them some tea. Apparently, money wasn't an issue downstairs at the pub portion. *Strange*. Perrie continued to stare at the swirling liquid.

"You're going to have to force yourself to eat whenever you can. Who knows when or if we'll be able to eat or drink anything again."

She ate a few bites from the bowl. "There, happy?"

"Thrilled." He smiled and waggled his eyebrows.

Unintentionally, her gaze traveled down each of his features to his mouth, the mouth she'd kissed the night before. He still hadn't said a word. There was nothing she could say, yet so much she wanted to. Her eyes drifted up to his cute and messy hair, wondering what it would feel like to have her fingers tangled in it. She should've done that last night when he'd sent her over the edge in pleasure.

Blowing out a breath, she ignored that matter for now and managed to finish half the bowl of stew. At least the monster in her belly was satisfied at the moment.

Perrie broke the silence and pointed at his head with her spoon. "I see you forgot your hat back there."

Pressing his hair down, he groaned, "Fuck that hat."

Before she could say anything else, the door flew open.

Fannie barreled in and screamed, "She's dead. The Ripper has done it again. Catherine Eddowes has been murdered."

Jolting up, Perrie rushed over to her. "Where is she?"

"She's down the street." Perrie tried to run past her, and Fannie took hold of her arm. "You aren't going to want to see this one. How could he do this to my friend?"

In an instant, August was beside her, heading straight for the door.

"I'll be right back," Perrie told her.

She stepped outside into the darkness and halted at the sudden change of lighting.

"How is it dark this early?" August asked. "We were just out here."

They hadn't slept late, and they weren't gone that long when looking for the barrier. It should've been nowhere near nightfall.

"Things aren't making sense any more than they have been," Perrie mumbled.

To her left, not far from where they stood, was a body with no one around it. No lookers, no help, no police officers.

"Are you sure you want to see? It isn't going to help anything." August pulled her back. She clenched the skirt of her dress, fingernails biting in deeply. No one, including her, wanted to see a dead body, but this was too important. Her theory needed to be confirmed—she had to know if she was next.

"I know, but I need to see for myself." She wouldn't back down from this. "Are you sure *you* want to look?"

"I'm going to be real honest here. Not really, but there's no way I'm going to let you walk over there by yourself," he said quietly.

With quick strides, they headed toward the limp body on the ground. August reached the victim right before Perrie did. A woman wearing a canary-yellow dress lay in a pool of blood. Perrie's vision blurred and the stew in her belly wanted to resurface. Red by her legs, red by her head, and red by her arms. Red, red, red. It was *everywhere*.

Perrie covered her mouth with both hands as August leaned down to check the woman's pulse, but there wasn't a point. The part of her face that Perrie could see was a mutilated mess. No one would be able to survive that brutal savagery. She couldn't look at the rest of her, but something in the woman's expression drew Perrie in for a closer inspection. The left side of the woman's face was undamaged for the most part. Long, silky black hair sprawled about her oval-shaped face.

Impossible... She recognized the victim. She'd spoken with her twice now.

"August, I know her," Perrie whispered.

He whirled to face her. "What are you talking about?"

"This woman, I *know* her." Hands shaking, she stared into his eyes.

"I've never seen her before in my life." He chewed on his bottom lip and shook his head.

"You haven't, but I have." She backed away a few steps from the body. "This is Officer Rodriguez."

August's left eyebrow slid up as far as it would go, like a flag being pulled to the top of a pole. "Well, how did she get here?"

"I don't know, genius. I suppose the same way we got here."

Lifting his finger, he pointed it up at the night sky and waved it like a sword. "Touché. Now keep going."

Gripping her hair, Perrie stumbled backward into a wall. "She was investigating both Neven and Maisie's disappearances. I told her about the Glass Vault and she said she would check it out later. My assumption is that she got sucked into this demonic prison like we did."

"But I thought you said the Glass Vault vanished?"

"I did!" she whisper-shouted. "But maybe it chooses when to disappear and reappear."

August rubbed his chin and asked, "So, Officer Rodriguez went out to inspect it, assuming she was alone, and the Glass Vault just . . . reappeared?"

"Maybe. You saw how even the photos on your phone didn't stay. Plus it reappeared for us." It was a little hard to believe, but it was what it was.

Perrie took another look at the unmarred side of Officer Rodriguez's strong, pretty face. If a well-trained officer couldn't escape Jack the Ripper, then how are they supposed to?

"We have to go back, it's not safe for us to stay out here any longer than we need to. Especially you." Because in this place *she* was Mary Kelly.

Latching onto his hand, she hurried with him back to the brothel. Her mind buzzed with a thousand different questions. How did Officer Rodriguez get here? Did the Glass Vault really just reappear when it wanted? If that was the case, then maybe Maisie was here after all. It had to be more than assuming. Unfortunately, she couldn't ask about Maisie now with Officer Rodriguez lying in her own blood.

Inside the pub, Fannie sat alone at a table with her head in her hands.

"Are you going to be all right?" Of course she wasn't, but Perrie tried to be sympathetic anyway. She couldn't tell her Catherine was really Officer Rodriguez. She couldn't even tell her that her friend, the real Catherine Eddowes, wasn't here. Fannie would look at her like she was crazy.

"No, Mary, I'm not. He's going to pick us all off until we are nothing. I don't want to be left worse off than being a street rat."

"You're not a street rat," August said robotically. Perrie almost rolled her eyes at how awkward he'd sounded.

"Not at all," Perrie chimed in.

"I know I'm not. But all men want to do is *use* us. Jack wants to use our bodies for his own sick purposes." Fannie tucked a red curl that had fallen loose from her bun behind her ear. "He's out there. He looks like a regular gentleman, too, with a top hat and cloak to match his suit and boots—all black. Be careful is all I ask."

"You too, Fannie." If Fannie had made herself known, then she would've most likely been killed and lying in her own puddle of blood in that old alleyway, too. Perrie knew how she felt. She didn't want to be like the other women, either.

August nudged her with his elbow and whispered into her ear, "Do you want to go to the room?"

"Yes." She glanced once more at Fannie, her expression distant, then they ascended the stairs back to the room. She had so damn much to think about. No matter what they did, it was all trial and error—no definite explanation. It was as if this place was a riddle without an answer, an experiment without a solution, or a lock without a key.

After entering the bedroom, Perrie collapsed against the foot of the bed, defeated. August slid down beside her and pressed his strong body next to hers, before leaning his cheek against the top of her head.

"Don't even think about it, Perrie."

She played with the hem of her skirt. "How can I not think about it, August? I'm going to be next."

SEVENTEEN

Perrie couldn't help knowing she would be next. Mary Kelly's death had followed Catherine's murder. She didn't like the idea of a torturous death, especially not her own.

August frowned so deeply it might actually stay that way. "I'm not going to let that happen to you."

"That's easy for you to say. You aren't Mary Kelly. You're not going to be hunted down and murdered by some sick fuck," Perrie said between clenched teeth.

"Well, you aren't Mary Kelly. You're Perrie Madeline, and *we* are leaving here just like we left Sleepy Hollow. Yes, we may enter a new hell, but then we'll get out of there together because that's what we do. We have been a team—we will always be a team. Hell, we were a team even when you hated me."

Rolling her eyes, she palmed her forehead. "Even then I don't think I actually disliked you—I was just mad."

"Oh no, you definitely hated me, doll face. That was loathing at its finest." He knocked his shoulder with hers. She leaned her head against him and tightened her arms around his waist to soak in his warmth.

"Okay, maybe just a little bit." She laughed. "I'm truly

sorry about judging you before I got to know such fine character in another human being."

"I'll take that answer." He snorted.

Perrie loosened her arms from around his waist. "So what if we can't get the barrier open?"

"Maybe it has something to do with not having seen Jack the Ripper yet."

"What do you mean?"

"When we went through the barrier last time, 'the Headless Horseman'"—he used air quotes to emphasize—"was chasing after us, so maybe Jack has to make some kind of entrance before we can make our exit."

It was hard not to laugh, but she kept her cool. She wouldn't want to interrupt his terribly important thought process.

"That has to be the least appealing thing you could've come up with. I, for one, do not have any intentions of coming face-to-face with one of the most notorious serial killers in our history."

August pursed his lips and blinked. Was he really considering this? Accurate or not, she didn't like the idea of facing off against Jack the Ripper before she could make an escape.

"So, you're fine and dandy with hunting up and down the street, calling out Jack's name to lure him from the shadows?" Perrie stared at him hard.

"Better than Jeffrey Dahmer, Ed Gein, and Charles Manson." He shrugged.

"One, those were nowhere near close to Jack, and two, Charles Manson didn't physically commit the crime. Also, who's to say Jack won't come barging into the room either?" She immediately wanted to take that back.

Perrie honestly didn't even consider that as a possibility until the words had flown out of her mouth. She just assumed people would have to be out walking the streets for Jack to hunt them down. It wasn't like anyone knew who he was. He could be a number of people. In fact, he could walk right into the pub and ask to have *her* for the night. No one would know his real purpose.

August toyed with his lower lip. "What if he was already here? What if Jack is Thomas?"

It made complete sense that Thomas was Jack—the sick bastard.

"You know what?" she started. "I think you might be right. It's already nightfall, earlier than expected, but I say we go ahead and try for the barrier. Maybe find a few weapons before we go."

"I'm all for weapons but be prepared to run like hell."

A gun would've been the ideal weapon, if they could find one.

They searched the room to see if they could find anything worth using. She located nothing that was suitable as a weapon, besides a stash of beads. Throwing beads at a full-grown man like it was Mardi Gras was a horrible idea.

"Maybe I should hunt down Thomas and steal his wooden cane from him while he's here undercover," August mumbled while searching under the mattress and coming away with nothing except air.

"Yeah, I don't know about that. He was a master with that cane. Who knows what other sick shit he does with it." If she saw him again, she would shove his cane so far up his ass that he wouldn't know what was happening. "But for all we know, Thomas could be anywhere."

"Good point. By the way, thanks for putting those cane images in my head." He knelt and searched below the bed, coming away with nothing yet again. "I admit defeat. This search is pointless. Let's grab something to use from downstairs."

First, there were heads sprinkled like dessert in the graveyard, then the lunatic in the bedroom who was most likely Jack, followed by graphic murders. It was pure insanity—horror movie style.

Perrie was the one who'd told the officer about Quinsey Wolfe's Glass Vault, and now felt partially responsible. She wasn't the one who'd murdered her, but there were so many "what ifs." What if she had never seen the Glass Vault that day? What if Maisie had never stopped, and they'd never gotten out of the car? What if she'd been honest and told Maisie she didn't want her to go to the museum?

If Perrie had been honest from the beginning, then none of this would be happening. Maisie wouldn't be missing, Officer Rodriguez wouldn't be dead, and she wouldn't be worried about saving her own neck.

She needed a knife. *Now.*

Giving up on the room, they moved on to their next best option, the kitchen. Downstairs, a few people sat around tables, but most of them must've been in rooms having sex or doing other business. Perrie and August easily snuck past them all. Unfortunately, the only weapons around were some semi-sharp knives and forks as backup. A knife was a knife, and she would take what she could get.

Exiting the pub, they walked outside into the night. The darkness curtained itself around the city, and a touch of wind folded and bended its way around her. Lanterns along the road lit up the street, guiding her in whichever direction she chose to follow.

Perrie clenched the utensils in her grip. "Okay, we're outside, and no one's here. So, do we just stand around out here and wait for Jack, or should we head right for the barrier?"

"I think we should try for the barrier—maybe we don't really need him there to pass through. It's only a theory," he said, and she hoped it was only a theory.

Not bothering to take their time, they hung a right and ran for what would hopefully lead them out of the Jack the Ripper display. As they crept up close to the barrier, Perrie slowed.

She took a couple of steps and hit the rubber-like surface—not passing through.

"Fuck. Fuck. Fuck." August gritted his teeth as he pressed his hand against it and nothing happened.

"Are we stuck here?" Perrie asked the invisible wall. Of course it didn't answer back. "As much as I hate to say it, we're going to have to try our next theory."

"Jackie boy, here we come." August held up his fork and knife, appearing more like a guy ready to eat than a guy ready to fight for his life.

She still smiled, but her stomach was sinking into a never-ending black hole. Maisie, Neven, and home. Those were the three things she needed right now. Perrie repeated them over in her head like a mantra as they turned back.

Once they reached the pub, August grabbed her elbow and his eyebrows flew up.

Her gaze followed his, and her mouth fell open. "August, where's the body?"

Was it gone when we left?

"Maybe someone moved her? Or maybe Jack came back to collect his trophy."

"Not the best time for jokes."

"I'm actually pretty serious on this one."

"You're right," she decided. "I'm sure some weird shit went down."

In the spot where Officer Rodriguez's mutilated body once was, now lay nothing but a stone walkway. No body, no blood, no nothing. It was as clear as day.

"I don't think someone cleaned up the blood that fast," August said, clenching his jaw.

"I agree." She doubted someone would be able to scrub all that blood away anyway. Besides, they hadn't even seen one person out on the street to hint at a cleanup crew.

A ticking sound stirred, and Perrie's spine tensed. "August, press your back to mine. Weapons ready."

"The poorly-made utensils are prepared," he said, his back firmly against hers.

"Did you hear that ticking sound?" Perrie cocked her head to the right and listened. Not a single peep that time. She scanned the front area while August did the opposite.

"What ticking sound?"

"Like a clock." She took a deep breath. "And it smells really bad over here." Not like a dead body but something else foul.

August inhaled and gagged a little. "I shouldn't have taken that deep of a breath. It smells like rotten piss."

"Can piss smell rotten?"

"This piss can. It's probably years built up of people coming out here and going on the side of the building."

"That's gross." Her shoulders relaxed. It must've been her imagination. "I'm feeling antsy."

August scratched his bicep with his fork. "Is your ADHD kicking in now?"

"August, you know I don't have ADHD," she huffed.

"Really? You could have fooled me."

A scratching noise filled the air. Their connected bodies stiffened at the same time as if they were conjoined.

"I know you heard it this time," Perrie whispered with knives ready in both hands.

"I wish I hadn't."

A ticking came from her right, but she couldn't see anything. Then another scratching noise erupted from her left. A long screech, a hundred times worse than nails against a chalkboard. She gripped her knives harder, and a couple of forks were ready in the sides of her shoes. Neither she or August uttered a single word.

Low, then higher and higher, a loud, slow creak, like that of a rusty door hinge, sounded. Perrie still couldn't see through the darkness resting in every corner. She wasn't dumb enough to actively seek out the source of disturbance, especially given her special circumstance.

"August," Perrie whispered.

"Yes?"

"Please tell me you've taken karate or something like that."

"No, but I can punch someone in the face." His head whipped as far around as it could go. "Well, we'll see if I can anyway. Have you?"

"No! All I took was ballet when I was like four," she groaned.

"Good, then you should be extra light on your feet."

Another creaking noise, followed by a sharp cracking, echoed. Then a *clack, clack, clack*, like running feet against the ground. Perrie didn't see anyone in the direction she thought it was coming from. Then it all occurred at once. A black shadow popped into her peripheral vision, and she pushed back against August. She shoved him out of the way, but she was too slow.

The shadow was really a person dressed all in black and wearing a dark cloak. The person—Jack—lunged forward and swung at them. Jack spun around and around, flashes of silver darting out like shooting stars in the sky. For a split second, Perrie thought of a magician at a magic show, then a stinging sensation throbbed against her arm. The knife in that hand clanked to the ground. Her hand clasped her forearm and the dark figure retreated in the other direction.

Warm blood coated her palm as it came away from her stinging arm. August refocused his attention on her and her damn arm instead of the murderer.

"We've seen Jack," she grunted. "Let's try for the barrier."

The adrenaline pumped through her veins, giving her momentum. August led the way as they headed back toward the barrier.

When they approached the brothel, which took only a minute, a woman stood outside. Not just any woman either, but Officer Rodriguez—intact. She was wearing the exact same yellow dress Perrie had just seen her lying in. Only, it was clean, not a speck of blood on it. Not a single mark marred her flawless face, both sides matching equally.

"Hey, Mary," she called, "How about you lend your gentlemen over to me for the night."

"Officer Rodriguez?" Perrie's jaw dropped, her brow furrowing.

"I'll even lower the price for the night, love." Her gaze settled on August, ignoring Perrie completely.

"Officer Rodriguez! It's me, Perrie Madeline." She jumped in front of August, both hysterical and relieved. "Don't you recognize me?"

She didn't.

"Mary, you know bloody well my name is Catherine. Don't act dense because you don't want to share."

What the fuck? "I don't have time for this. Come on, let's go." Perrie tugged Officer Rodriguez's arm, but she yanked it out of her grasp.

"We've got to go," August said quickly.

I tried, right? Perrie couldn't let herself feel guilty at the moment, not while they were under attack. She took off on a hard sprint with August again. They were only a few buildings away from the barrier when they were stopped in their tracks.

Jack the Ripper rose from the darkness to block their way. The collar of his cloak was propped high, and a black scarf was wrapped around his face, shadowing his features. He was smaller than she'd imagined he would be. Not that she'd put too much thought into his height.

Jack jolted at Perrie first, and she whirled out of the way at the last second. Her wounded arm throbbed to its own tune, and she tried to ignore the pain.

August lunged at him with one of his knives, and Jack somehow managed to knock them out of both of his hands. Jack dove to the ground and pulled August's legs out from underneath him. It happened so fast that she didn't have time to warn August until she saw him lying on the gravel.

Rushing forward, Perrie pulled on Jack's cloak with all her strength. She leveraged her weight against Jack, yanking harder, and he let out a small choking sound. August hurried to get up.

The Ripper's knife crashed to the ground as Perrie gave his cape one more good pull. August took advantage of the Ripper's momentary disadvantage, knocking the top hat from Jack's head to the ground. He grabbed the scarf and quickly unwound it, leaving her speechless. Wild red curls unraveled from the fabric, curtaining a familiar yet unfriendly face. Perrie's eyes widened to the size of full moons, but she didn't dare release her hold.

August stepped back, his head cocked, his voice low. "Definitely not Thomas."

Not Jack the Ripper, but Jackie *the Ripper.*

For a moment, Perrie was both shocked and stunned—she should've put it together. Fannie was the only person they'd ever seen who went outside, besides the dead body of Officer Rodriguez, and then her reanimated living body. Fannie hadn't seemed unhappy. In fact, her story was almost admirable. Why would she kill her friends?

Her head filled with so many questions that would never be answered—there wasn't time.

Grabbing hold of Fannie, August twisted her arms behind her back. She thrashed like wildfire.

"I am going to destroy you, Mary, from the inside out," Fannie spat.

Ignoring her, Perrie asked August, "What do we do now? Just throw her down and run?"

"Grab the knife first," he agreed.

Perrie picked up the long blade from the ground while August threw Fannie to the side like a sack of potatoes. They then hauled ass to the barrier.

A loud screeching erupted from all around them, but she couldn't let herself look back. She focused on leaving, finding Maisie, and getting the hell out of the Glass Vault. The darkness swallowed her view up ahead, but she knew she was close.

Then Fannie somehow appeared, blocking their way, twirling what looked to be a scalpel in her right hand.

They stopped dead in their tracks.

"Perrie, I'm going to distract her," August whispered. "You head to where you think the barrier might start and see if you can get through. I'll be right behind you."

"Don't be ridiculous!"

"Don't be stubborn!" August barked.

"Fine!" she yelled.

"Good!" August yelled back. He had his mind set on doing what he wanted, and she wasn't going to argue.

"Run left," he said softly.

Perrie took off as if she was heading straight for Fannie, but at the last minute, she moved to the left. Fannie was ready for it, and she turned to run toward Perrie. August yanked Fannie from behind by the cloak, but it snapped off.

With not enough air in her lungs, Perrie arrived at the barrier, and for a split second nothing happened. Then a suction tugged at her, pulling her forward again. The strong wind from the barrier blew her hair every which way. August made a desperate dive toward her and managed to wrap his arms around her waist.

The last thing Perrie saw before being uprooted was Fannie hitting the barrier and bouncing back.

EIGHTEEN

The ride through the barrier was all a big blur. It tossed Perrie out, throwing her in a field of grass with August's arms still wrapped around her. They hit the ground hard, knocking the wind right out of her, and broke apart.

"It looks like we moved on to a new display." She stood and dusted herself off, taking in their new surroundings.

August blinked and peered around. "Yep, circular vacation of death. This one may not be as bad as the last, but with the track record we've had so far . . ."

Relief crashed over her in waves. They were out of that hellish place—no Ripper. She should've paid more attention, shouldn't have trusted so easily. Perrie was so set on Jack the Ripper being a man that she hadn't even thought it was possible. She wanted to believe there was some good in this place, that Fannie was like Katrina, but she'd been wrong. If only she could've done more to save Officer Rodriguez.

"Hey, check out your arm," August said in awe.

She examined the wound on her flesh, but there wasn't one. "It's gone!" With wide eyes, she shoved it in his face.

"Thank fuck for that." He laughed.

"And I'm finally out of that dress." Once again, they were

wearing different clothing—there seemed to be a pattern here. Perrie was trying to be optimistic, given that her arm was newly healed and they were safely out of the Ripper's way.

"Technically, you're still in a dress." He motioned a finger up and down at the length of her body.

Yes, I'm still in a dress… But this one was much easier to manipulate and move in. The olive green blended in with her surroundings, and the material was cotton, possibly combined with another material, hitting right at her ankles. Her sleeves flowed slightly, until the ends cuffed at her wrists—a brown belt with a peculiar tribal design wrapped around her waist. The flat slip-on brown shoes she wore matched the same pattern of the belt at the front where her toes were. Perrie's braid lay right above her waist, and she grabbed it.

"This isn't exactly jeans and a shirt, but it works better than thirty layers of material for a suit." August studied himself and pulled at the end of his tunic.

The length of his hair came to about his chin, and she reached up, running her fingers through it before tugging at a lock.

"You rock the long hair." She let her hand drift away from his curls when he caught it, drawing her closer. Her chest tightened, remembering their moment in bed, him bringing her to bliss, even while still wearing her clothing.

"Do I?" August brushed a calloused thumb against her skin, her fingers, shifting even closer. With a smile, he reached around her waist and tugged the end of her braid. "I like yours too." He brought his hand to cup her cheek, his lips millimeters from touching hers. "Don't think I've forgotten about what happened between us. We need to go, but I just had to do this first." Then his lips were on hers in a searing kiss, the movements of his mouth fueling her to match his pace, demanding more. August's tongue flicked Perrie's and he nipped at her bottom lip, his fingertips trailing down her spine until they were at her backside, pulling her closer. All of his hardness was against her softness, teasing them both.

Too soon, he left her. But they didn't have time for anything else right then, even though she wanted more. His phantom touches still lingered, though.

Grinning, Perrie checked out the rest of him—tight brown pants, dark-brown boots and a green tunic covered his lean muscles. They almost matched, except for when she noticed a sword belted at his side.

"Hey, why do you get a weapon and I don't?"

August unsheathed the long sword and rotated it around and around as if he'd just won the lottery. The light caught and flashed across the silver surface, nearly blinding her.

While still holding the sword, he walked over and pulled out something tucked into the belt at her back.

"You do." He handed her a small dagger encrusted with red rubies.

"This isn't even close to being as good of a weapon as yours." She frowned. "I would have to be fairly close to what I'm attacking. It isn't like I can throw it since, you know, I haven't been trained in throwing daggers."

"Better than nothing." He smirked.

"True. Why do you think we didn't have weapons before?" She studied the dagger, turning it over. Better than being equipped with forks and dinner knives this time. Although a fork could do some damage, she much preferred this tiny dagger. She tucked it back into her belt and patted it several times.

"Again, I'm going to be real honest here, Perrie, and I'm willing to bet this world is worse than the last, based on our track record. So, you'll have to excuse me if I seem a little too excited about this sword." August carefully sheathed his blade.

This place seemed similar to Sleepy Hollow with its lush forest, minus the dense fog. They did the usual routine and checked the barrier. It wouldn't open or give way, so their only option was forward.

"It's déjà vu all over again." August shook his head with an annoyed sigh.

"Maybe we'll find Maisie in this one." *I hope.* "But now I don't know how many displays there are. She could be in any one."

"We'll see. I'm not sure how many of these we're going to have to get through to find her."

"Hopefully not as many as there were in the Glass Vault." But doubt after doubt washed over her.

Taking quiet steps, they trekked their way through the forest's rich land filled with skyscraping trees and bright green shrubbery. It was eerily silent, though. In the trees, a few scattered small birds nestled there, but not a single chirp or caw escaped their beaks. As if they were too scared...

They wandered a little farther until sunlight broke through the tall and narrow trees, guiding their way to a large opening leading out of the forest.

Once they stepped away from the last tree, a row of large gray boulders twice her height came into view. They stopped in front of the first one, and Perrie studied their odd lined arrangement. It almost looked as though they'd purposely been placed there like this. But, who could've moved boulders this big without some sort of machine?

The ground quaked beneath her feet, as if to answer her question. The intensity of the shaking rattled her bones and muscles, seeming to clack them against one another.

Perrie searched for cover, but there wasn't any. The trees weren't wide enough to hide behind, and with how fragile they appeared, she wasn't sure if the trunks would be standing after this. Perrie and August were exposed, and it was basically an open invitation to be attacked.

"Go to those boulders!" August pointed up ahead.

They tried to run, but the debilitating shaking made them stumble too many times before they caught themselves against a boulder.

Perrie dove down first behind a large boulder covered in green moss and dirt, cradling her knees to her chest. She had no fucking idea what was causing this, but then it stopped as fast as it had started. Above the ringing in her ears, booming voices echoed. Someone was speaking … or more like rumbling in another language.

For the moment, they were hidden enough behind the line of ten or so boulders. That was, until lurking danger decided to come searching for them… A large gap rested between each boulder, big enough for her to crawl past. August shimmied up to the open space and peeked through.

"What do you see? Maisie?" she whispered. He didn't seem to hear her, so she tugged on his shirt to get his attention. "August?"

He shook his head, placed one finger to his lips and slid over to the next boulder, motioning for her to follow. She lowered herself to where he once was, then pressed her hands to the boulder and peered out.

Perrie sucked in a sharp breath as she stared out at a huge bridge, built with white rocks and a wide stone pathway, sitting in the middle of a meadow, dividing the luscious green landscape. All in all, the structure was beautiful. The one thing missing was water beneath the bridge—only a sparse patch of dirt rested underneath.

Her heart pounded furiously in her chest as she took notice of what was there. It wasn't Maisie.

Three tall trolls stalked beneath the bridge, their skin sallow and dark brown in certain places along their bodies. It almost appeared like rotten flesh draped their skeletal bodies. These trolls—boney with sharp-looking features—were nothing like what she would've imagined one to look like— not that children's toys were good examples.

Stringy, dark hair caked in dry mud and dirt covered the heads of two of them. Perrie guessed those were the females, judging by their well-endowed breasts and the curls between their thighs. The other turned around, clearly male, his hanging length one of the largest she'd ever seen. Dirt and grime concealed most of their flesh, and from the looks of it, these creatures had never bathed a day in their entire lives. With lazy movements, they lumbered about until something caught their attention, the male pointing upward.

A *clack-clack-clackity-clack-clack* echoed.

Perrie's gaze traveled to the top of the bridge to where a little white goat walked. As it seemed to have a bounce in its step, the goat was one of the happiest things she'd seen since they'd fallen through. A sense of dread filled her as she now watched the goat, her eyes darting back and forth between its snowflake-colored fur and the trolls.

One of the females rumbled something to the others before slapping at her chest. The male nodded, and the other female retreated to the shadows, visibly enraged when she sank down to the ground, no doubt to pout about her loss.

The first female troll licked her thin lips with a long green tongue the color of the vomit that the little girl in *The Exorcist* spewed from her mouth. Perrie couldn't imagine the stench of what the troll's breath must smell like. The female crept to the edge of the bridge and pressed her palms against the stone, waiting now for the moment when the goat was close enough to snatch.

By now, the goat had reached the middle of the bridge. Its leisurely pace and beautiful surroundings appeared to distract the goat from the real sense of the lurking danger below the bridge.

Please run. Please run. Please run! Perrie chanted over and over in her head. But her attempt at mind control failed.

The female troll moved as quickly as a spider, skittering up the bridge, and snatched the goat in her hand with one swipe. An ugly cry tore from the goat's throat seconds before she snapped its neck.

The troll jumped down from the bridge and back to the pit.

From the ease of her movements, Perrie bet the troll had done it a million times before. With a loud thump, the female hit the earth hard and the ground rumbled. The quakes from earlier were the trolls—another mystery solved.

A ruckus stirred beneath the bridge as the female with the goat raised her prize and dangled its body proudly. The other sulking female troll hobbled over to her companion and spoke, loud enough for Perrie to hear clearly, but it didn't matter since she couldn't understand a fucking word.

Then the sulky female attempted to grab the dead animal from the Goat Killer. The male stood and shoved the female down, while the one holding the goat cackled so loudly Perrie's ears ached.

The sulky troll hit the ground with her fists—one struck right after the other, making the ground shake again. She stopped after the others ignored her tantrum and moved back to sit, her lips pulled back into a sneer. Perrie *almost* felt bad for her.

The Goat Killer took her dead prey in her hand and pounded it against the ground, blood spraying. Perrie gasped, so jarred by the action of it that she scooted back and covered her mouth. She watched in horror as the female ripped off one of the goat's legs with a loud splitting snap. At least she'd killed it first before doing that… The troll brought the tiny bloody leg to her mouth, biting and chewing like she was testing it out.

A true smile of satisfaction spread across her crimson-stained lips. The rest of the goat was gone in three bites, not even taking time to chew before swallowing the pieces whole.

Blood mixed with thick drool dribbled down her chin, and Perrie couldn't watch anymore. She whirled toward August, who was still watching the trolls, his disgust mirroring her own.

"Well, Perrie"—he sucked in a breath—"this just went from bad to worse."

NINETEEN

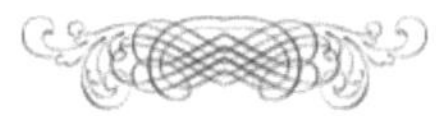

Perrie rested against a boulder, done with troll watching. "Is this what we're in for, August? Are these displays going to get worse the farther we go? This is more than *Three Billy Goats Gruff*. It's Bloody Fucking Troll's Gruff."

"What now?" August asked. He slid beside her and propped himself against another boulder, pulling his legs up and resting his forearms on top of his knees.

As if in response, her stomach growled.

"Really, Perrie?" August shot her "the look" and pointed his thumb back at the troll area. "After seeing that sick shit?"

It was poor timing, she knew. But like called to like, and perhaps monsters did the same since the one in her stomach was ravenous. A few feet from them sat a berry bush, and she nodded at them. "What about those? Do you think they're poisonous?"

He crawled forward to the bush. "They look okay to me."

"How positive are you about that *exactly*?" Perrie joined him and he plucked one blue berry. He inspected the berry, rotating it in between his thumb and index finger. Her fingers fidgeted with a blade of grass as he cut the berry in half with his fingernail and examined the juice dripping out.

"I'm going to say fifty percent sure." August grinned and popped the berry into his mouth before she could snatch it back. He chewed away at it as if he hadn't just risked his life.

"You idiot!" she hissed. It was her turn to give him the "what the fuck" look. "I could have given you that same percentage myself. Fifty percent chance leads to death, or fifty percent chance leads to staying alive."

"What can I say? I'm a daredevil."

"Yeah, well you're no Matt Murdock," Perrie teased. *But, what the hell*? She grabbed a berry and tossed it into her mouth.

About two minutes passed and they'd both eaten a few more berries. She didn't feel sick, but who knew how long poison took to kill someone. She was too hungry to care, so she gathered as many berries as she could in the folds of her dress, then crawled back to the boulders to eat.

They finished up the berries and oddly enough, they were still alive—for the time being. August and Perrie peeped through the hole to find the trolls sitting around. One of them threw a tantrum for no reason and pounded the ground, making it vibrate *again*.

She and August tried going back to the barrier where they'd come through, just to double check if maybe they could make an exit that way. The villains of this exhibit had been seen, more than she would've liked, so she thought that maybe the barrier would open. It didn't. Perrie punched the invisible wall over and over again with her frustration. They then came back through the woods and settled behind the boulders, and she knew their only option was to get across the bridge.

While waiting, two more goats attempted to pass over the bridge, and more blood was spilled. The two remaining trolls had taken their turns, the sulky female being the most vicious of them all, ripping the goat apart piece by bloody piece.

"I think the way out will be through the opening under the bridge. It's just a guess, but since the shape of the barrier is a rectangle again, and we fell through back there—" She pointed behind them.

"Then that means the way out could be straight ahead, right past troll territory, like in Sleepy Hollow," August finished.

"Precisely. Now the question is, how long will it take for them to fall asleep?"

The option she preferred was to attempt to go over the bridge and just hop off the side, but that wouldn't work because the bridge was too high. An issue that dampened another plan was the starting point seemed to curve right by the sidewall of the barrier, preventing them from being able to walk around to the other side of it. Somehow goats kept on appearing, though, the same size and shape. *But a goat's a goat, right*?

August busied himself with his nails, picking at them with a stick he'd found on the ground while they waited for the trolls—hopefully all of them—to fall asleep at once. Perrie remained vigilant, despite her exhaustion, and kept a trained eye on the bridge. She could feel her eyes fighting against the need for sleep as her lids grew heavy. Every few seconds she nodded off, when suddenly, her body straightened, her eyes fully open. A young guy appeared, walking across the bridge, no goats in sight.

"Where did he come from?" The guy was tall with the lightest white hair she'd ever seen, and his complexion was just as pale. He looked like a normal person from a regular village, dressed in a similar fashion to August.

"Who?" August dropped the stick on the ground and turned back to the hole. "Oh wait, I see."

As the trolls came to attention, perking up and listening intently to his footsteps above them, Perrie's heart raced. She fought the urge to run to him, to shout and warn the guy about the trolls. But, she was too afraid to tempt fate, and she wouldn't risk the possibility of saving her cousin.

"Doesn't he know about the trolls?" she whispered.

"Don't think so," August breathed.

They watched the trolls as they determined whose turn it was now. It appeared to be the first Goat Killer's turn again as she geared up to do her spider crawl.

Perrie glanced back at the guy crossing the bridge, recognition hitting her this time. It was clear to her now what was so familiar about him. His hair, that unique shade of white—she would've taken him for any random person if it were a different color. *He* was one of the missing people—she'd seen several pictures of him right after it was announced, after Maisie had told her about him a couple days ago.

"That's Ben Johnston."

August's brows lowered in confusion. "Who?"

"Ben Johnston. You know, that college guy who went missing? It was right before Neven."

He squinted his eyes at Ben a little harder, then he blinked several times in recognition. "I wouldn't have guessed, except for that hair."

"That's exactly what I thought!"

"His chances of making it back home now are slim," August said, his lips forming a thin line.

Perrie waited, hoping this troll was going to do something different this time, but the female slunk low like a spider and crawled. Ben inched closer, then she hopped over the side of the bridge, landing directly in front of him.

Not a single scream tore from his throat, nor did he fight back or run. *Why doesn't he do something*? Instead, he just stayed there, lingering like a fucking moron while staring at the troll.

The troll stood idle, studying her prey with hungry eyes, a smile spreading across her horrid face. Something wasn't right. She held out her gigantic hand to Ben, and he took it in his own. It was as if he was mesmerized by her and under her spell.

"August, what's he doing? No one in his or her right mind would willingly go to a creature that looked like that."

August wrinkled his nose. "Is he even in his right mind? How long has he been missing?"

"A week or maybe less."

The troll yanked Ben to her harshly, pulled him to her chest, then leapt off the bridge, landing roughly on the ground—causing it to ripple. He still didn't scream, only smiled while in her arms. It made zero sense.

The moment was short-lived as the troll tossed Ben to the ground like a toy.

"You're so beautiful!" he cried, his words echoing out from under the bridge.

"There's something wrong here. He has to be under some type of influence," August muttered.

"I agree. Maybe she's somehow enchanting Ben by locking eyes with him," she guessed.

The male troll stumbled toward Ben and picked him up off the ground with little effort. Then, like a whip, he slapped Ben against the side of the bridge, cracking his head wide open. Blood oozed out from the wound as the male beat him against the dirt.

Not once did Ben scream as his body was tossed ragged at the ground. There would never be any un-seeing this. The sounds of his body ripping, cracking, and tearing, reverberated throughout the forest. They wouldn't stop until he'd been taken apart, piece by piece, just like the goats. Blood covered Ben's broken body from head to toe, leaving no life in him.

August pulled Perrie to him, and she shakily pressed her head into his shoulder, holding him tightly. No one deserved this. She hadn't known Ben, but seeing him become their plaything would haunt her for the rest of her life.

"I really wish I knew what time it was," she mumbled. Wearing a watch didn't seem all that awful of an idea, considering how long they'd been here. *Although, who's to say it wouldn't have vanished with our phones?* Her necklace had.

After the incident with Ben, not even a single of his bones lingering, one of the females lay down to rest. Three more goats had followed after Ben's death, and the trolls continued taking their turns.

"Do you think we should try running for it? Maybe sneak up to the edge and run through?" Perrie monitored the situation, her gaze following the length of the bridge and halting. "Wait. *What the hell?"*

Grasping August's arm, she tugged him to the hole. He arched a brow, appearing skeptical at first, but once his gaze landed on what she'd found, he didn't look away. "No way. A reanimated corpse made from thin air."

As sure as her name was Perrie Madeline, she watched Ben Johnston cross the bridge again. Same as before—white hair, pale complexion, and clothing. Everything was in one piece. No broken bones, no missing limbs.

"Can't be a zombie if he was in the trolls' bellies," she said. "This whole place is making less sense than ever."

They chose not to watch any of what happened, not after the last time.

"Let me put my thinking cap on." August placed his hands against his head. After several moments, he looked up.

"What do you have?" She anxiously leaned forward.

He studied the trees for a brief period of silence and then, finally, opened his mouth to speak. "I've got nothing."

With a grunt, her body dropped back to the boulder. What made this world the same as the last? What were they missing?

She thought back to the other two displays they'd experienced. Like lightning, it all struck her at once.

"In the display with Jack the Ripper, AKA Jackie, we found Officer Rodriguez dead at first, right?"

"Right, and then we saw her magically appear alive. What's that got to do with anything?" August asked.

"So, she was dead and then she wasn't. We saw her after that, alive!"

His eyes widened, seeming to catch on.

"It's the same thing here," she continued, "except we didn't see Officer Rodriguez die again, but maybe if we'd stayed longer, it would've happened. The only two people we've seen die have come back to life."

"Okay, sounds fair"—he rubbed his chin—"but what about Sleepy Hollow? We didn't see any dead bodies come back to life."

"What if Katrina already died once before and we just missed it? Maybe we got there right as she came back to life." Perrie knew she was onto something big, something that could help them piece this place together.

August quit rubbing at his chin and rested his hand on his knee. "It's possible."

"Let's assume for the moment then. Now, what do they all have in common?"

"Ben and Officer Rodriguez went missing," he said absently. "Did Katrina look familiar to you?"

Perrie nodded. "A little. I thought I had seen her before."

August's eyes shifted from one side to the other, like a ticking clock. "I think I saw her on one of the flyers, but she may have had really short blonde hair, like a pixie cut."

"Oh. Oh!" Perrie snapped her fingers. "Josselyn Shaw. I remember seeing that flyer, but the picture was grainy. Those flyers were everywhere. She didn't really look like her photo at first, but I can see it now."

"That means each display we've been to contains a

missing person within it. The question left is, why?"

TWENTY

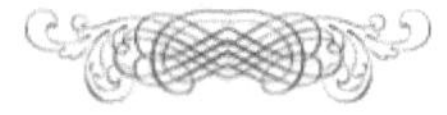

Somehow, there were missing people inside the Glass Vault. *Why? How did they get here?* If it was true, then Neven and Maisie must for sure be in here somewhere. Perrie still wanted to get out of this nightmare, but they were going to have to find Maisie and Neven first.

"I think we'd have to find Quinsey Wolfe to answer all of our questions, but I'm sure he's nowhere inside his own scenes of horror," Perrie whispered. But she didn't know if Quinsey Wolfe even existed. "More importantly, we now know Maisie and Neven both are in a display somewhere."

August was peering through the hole when he said, "The trolls might be going to sleep now. Let's get past them and see if we can find Maisie or Neven in the next display."

One of the female trolls was already lying down, making grunting and choking noises like she had something stuck in her throat. It was probably *only* a human or goat bone.

With light movements, the sulky troll patted the hard dirt, as if softening up a feathered-down mattress. *Ridiculous.* Even if she sat there and patted and smacked at the ground for an hour, it wasn't going to get much softer. Finally, she lay down on her side in her freshly patted dirt bed, dragging her legs up to her chest like a small baby. Her matted hair fell over her face, and Perrie couldn't really tell, but she thought the troll closed her eyes.

"Okay, we need a plan now," she said to August. He sat back and tapped the tips of his fingers together like a villain in an old cartoon.

"Ah yes, the plan." He paused for effect. "We'll go as far as we can to the left side of the bridge, get to the edge of the hole underneath, and dash through it like madmen."

"Great minds think alike. That was my plan, too. Now, what do we do if the trolls wake up?" She sighed.

"This would be a whole lot easier if there was only one troll," he groaned, crossing his arms.

"I know, right? Isn't it supposed to be one troll to each bridge? I've never seen multiple trolls sharing bridges. Not that I've seen a troll until now, besides in the actual nursery rhyme. And in that story, all the goats got across. That didn't happen here," Perrie huffed.

"The trolls are spaced pretty well apart. We walk as quietly as we can, and if one moves, we start running."

"Are you ready to do this?" Her hand shook unsteadily as she freed the small dagger at her waist. Perrie had zero experience using one, but she would swing it like fucking crazy if she had to find a way to her cousin.

"Better than dying behind a boulder." He unsheathed his sword.

They avoided any twigs that might snap or any leaves that could crunch. The sun's light was lessening as it started its descent, and Perrie hoped it stayed lit long enough to see as they passed through. August took his first step into a lush field with tiny pink flowers blooming everywhere. The place was beautiful, but the hidden ugliness gave nothing a real chance to live here. She wondered if the displays in the museum were real. And if they were, how were they transporting them to places like this? She couldn't focus on that now.

Perrie and August made their way to the bridge with no way of seeing the trolls ahead of them. Her hands had stopped shaking, but her heart pounded fast—so fast she couldn't believe she wasn't having a heart attack. She squeezed her dagger harder.

As August reached the rustic stone bridge, he stopped and listened. Only snoring sounded, so she advanced and joined him. While stopped, she took a few deep breaths.

August whistled quietly, signaling for her to move ahead of him before they continued. As they approached the opening under the bridge, the grass started to thin out. No more small flowers existed in this part of the grass. Then, there was no grass at all, only soft dirt that became hard earth.

Slowing down, she tiptoed quietly to the hole, and plastered her body so close to the wall that she imagined she was one with it.

Carefully, Perrie peered around the edge of the opening. *So far, so good.* The trolls still snored and gurgled in their slumber. Body odor and rot invaded her nostrils as she stretched a little farther around the corner. She gagged on the thick stench of it, grateful for their snoring to mask her disgust.

Beneath the bridge the lighting was dim, but enough rays seeped inside so she could see everything clearly. Long fissures marred the high ceiling, and she assumed it was from each time the trolls' heavy bodies scaled up it, causing its damage.

The sulky troll lingered in her fetal position, a huge puddle of drool running from her mouth to the ground, her matted hair soaking in it.

The second female rested on her back with her mouth wide open, and every single one of her sharp teeth on display. Black, green, brown, and yellow teeth all crooked and decayed. The urge to brush her own teeth had never been stronger.

The male twitched and his stomach gurgled. He shifted around on the floor until he appeared comfortable again. Perrie didn't dare move. *Yet.*

Aside from the overwhelming smell of the trolls' domain, they were clear to keep moving. Perrie signaled to August with a wave of her hand. As she started walking, August pulled her back and shook his head, pointing to himself, then at the troll nest. He wanted to go first, and she didn't waste time arguing. He grasped her hand and rubbed it softly with his thumb, as if to silently reassure her that everything would be fine.

Their steps were so quiet, calculated, that even a mouse wouldn't hear them coming.

Clack-clack-clackity-clack-clack.

They froze. Something was on top of the bridge, and from the sound of its steps, it was one of those *fucking* goats.

August's gaze widened at Perrie, telling her to run. Just as they moved, one of the trolls opened its eyes. Red. There were no dark pupils or whites outside the irises—it was as if blood had swallowed those colors.

The troll settled those orbs of blood on Perrie and August and barreled for them. They'd made it halfway to the end when August was thrown back. Whirling around, Perrie found a female troll's hands tightened around him.

She didn't have time to think—she ran with her dagger and stabbed the bitch's hand repeatedly. Red liquid spewed from the wounds. The troll released him and cried a monstrous noise, causing the bridge above to rumble.

August rebounded quickly, just in time, and darted forward with sword in hand. Another troll jolted for them. August maneuvered to the side and sliced the tendon right above one of the troll's rotten feet.

"Go," he yelled.

Perrie sprinted to the other side of the bridge, legs and arms pumping as hard as she could. August reached the barrier right before she did—the force of it pulling at him the second he came close. She didn't make it. A large, dirt-covered hand wrapped around her waist and yanked her back.

"August!" she screamed.

"Perrie!" He looked back in horror, pushing against the draw of the barrier. It was too late, though—and he vanished into thin air. Nothing was left except a field on the other side.

Perrie screamed again, unable to stop, gripping the dagger with such force for fear she might drop it. She wiggled and writhed to free her arm with the dagger, but it was trapped.

The troll tightened her fist. Lucky for Perrie though, the female switched her hold and freed Perrie's arm with the dagger. Then the troll lifted Perrie to her face, each getting a proper look at one another. *Fuck.* Perrie was in the hands of the one troll who seemed the most vicious of all. And the troll was *pissed*.

No time to waste. Perrie used what was left of her adrenaline and thrust the dagger right in the center of the troll's left eye. The female roared, the sound piercing Perrie's ears as the bitch stumbled back and dropped her. Perrie didn't hesitate when her body hit the hard dirt. She ran.

The ground vibrated, making her tilt sideways. Her body ached, but she had to keep going. The barrier was right ahead.

Please take me, she silently repeated inside her head. As soon as she reached the barrier and struck it, the wind swept her up and dragged her forward. The last sounds she heard were the wild screechings of the ravenous trolls.

Perrie's feet landed on solid ground. Falling forward, she caught herself with her forearms and hands, right before her face collided with the grass below.

She rolled over to glance behind her, making sure none of the trolls had made it through the barrier. Relieved to find not a single monstrous beast, she lay there and let herself breathe, hard and rapid, until she could think clearly. The pain from her fall to the ground in the troll display was gone, just like the cut to her arm from Fannie had simply disappeared. It seemed if someone was hurt in a single display, then moved to the next, the individual would be magically healed.

That answer she could deal with.

Laughter bubbled up her throat and she slapped the ground. Maybe she was losing her mind being in here too long, but she almost felt invincible in that moment. This world was completely fucked.

Finally, she sat up and looked around. More trees, this time pine and oak, enveloped her, and August was nowhere in sight. He'd gone in before her, so he had to have landed somewhere else, just like in the Jack the Ripper display. Even though she knew he had to be here somewhere, worry filled her.

Pulling herself up to stand, Perrie brushed the dirt from her dress. This time the bodice was dark red while the skirt was a darker brown, like the color of tree bark. Matching brown flats covered her feet and no weapons in sight. *Whatever, I'll use a tree branch for a weapon if I need to.*

Perrie turned around and touched along the barrier to see how wide it went. She yanked her hand away, afraid it would suck her back through. She had no intention of being chased by trolls again.

Taking a deep swallow, she took the path laid out before her and ditched the trolls. She hadn't walked very far from where she'd landed when she spied a cottage in the distance. *There's a cottage in the middle of a heavily wooded area? Why does that sound familiar?*

Gray smoke curled upward into the bright blue sky from the chimney on the roof. She wasn't even sure if she *wanted* to know who or what was in that damn cottage, but someone was home.

The trees in the surrounding area seemed tall and wide enough to climb. She glanced at the cottage and back up at the trees, then one more time toward the cottage. Shaking her head, she postponed the cottage and would attempt to climb a tree to see how far the forest reached. Perrie padded over to the nearest one where clusters of large beetles trailed its trunk. She'd seen much, *much* worse in the last couple of displays.

A branch dangled right above her head, and Perrie grabbed hold of it. She started to climb up the tree, but her feet caught on her dress and she slipped. *This is why I hate dresses.* Hiking up the skirt to the middle of her thighs, she knotted the excess fabric between her legs.

Perfect.

Again, she reached for the branch and managed to lodge her foot into the bark and swing herself up. Perrie climbed a few more branches, her new curls brushing her shoulders as they fought with the breeze. When she stretched for the next branch, she couldn't grasp it, and her hand connected with the barrier. She guessed that proved the barrier was more like a rectangular box. There were limitations, even when her feet weren't touching the ground in this prison.

Stepping down a branch, she surveyed the area and found no sign of human life coming from anywhere—except the cottage.

Could August be in there? What about Maisie or Neven? The cottage was the only other option she had.

A soft scratching sounded from below her, and she stilled. Before she could do anything else, a small furry thing scurried past her, and she almost lost her balance. Perrie risked glancing up and found the furry thing was only a squirrel. She breathed a deep sigh of relief.

As she carefully climbed back down, leaves crunched somewhere nearby. She gripped the branch tighter, when a small deer zoomed by beneath her—this place seemed to have more animal life than the other displays.

Perrie lowered herself to the ground and was proud of herself for not breaking her neck in the process. She untied the fabric of the dress, freeing it back to her ankles, and looked ahead. Something about the cottage had changed—a light illuminated from inside the glass windows. Someone was definitely home. She wondered if maybe it *was* August who could've been using the smoke to signal her. It was worth a look inside. Then again, what if he wasn't even in this display… What if he'd landed somewhere else?

Perrie thanked every tree around here that the cottage wasn't covered in sugary treats and frosting. She really didn't want to have to deal with a damn witch at the moment. Although, it was possible that a smart witch would leave her house unfrosted to better lure in her victims who didn't know about *Hansel and Gretel*.

"One thing at a time, Perrie," she told herself.

When she and Maisie were younger, *Hansel and Gretel* was their favorite fairy tale. Perrie was never afraid of it back then, even though the story itself could be disturbing for children. When she looked back, she was always so intrigued about a cottage made of desserts and sweets, regardless that the witch would eat the children's cooked flesh for meals.

They'd always played in Maisie's backyard. Maisie would grab a loaf of bread and tear up slices for crumbs, pretending their fake stepmother had abandoned them in the woods. Back then, Perrie didn't think it would be her real mom who would eventually abandon her.

Birds were never around to peck at the bread for them to pretend to lose their way, so they had to use Maisie's dog, Roosevelt. He wasn't alive now, but he'd gobbled the pieces of bread up just as well as any bird.

Maisie and Perrie would argue over who would be Gretel and who would be Hansel. Perrie would usually give in and be Hansel most of the time. Her cousin was persistent, always had been.

In Maisie's backyard under the trees, Uncle Jaron had built a small cottage for them to play in. It had been so much better than those cheap plastic ones.

One day, while they'd been pretending to be Hansel and Gretel, they decided to *decorate* the small "cottage". They'd snuck inside Maisie's house and grabbed anything they could find to make it look like a cottage of candy. They'd used just about everything, from condiments to potato chips. To draw the designs, they'd used ketchup and mustard, which were the brightest colors they could find.

They'd wanted to make it vibrant.

She and Maisie didn't go unpunished. Her aunt had made them clean the house up as best they could and help Uncle Jaron repaint it. Perrie wouldn't really have called it a punishment because it had been fun getting to redecorate it again. That time, they'd chosen the colors, and they made sure the house was brighter than before.

The little hammer inside Perrie's head knocked the memory away. *God, I miss Maisie.*

Using caution, she walked toward the cottage. The roof wasn't covered in candy. A normal roof sat on top of a normal green cottage. *Thank the display for this one common courtesy.* The house was a regular storybook home, complete with pretty flowers and lush green shrubbery.

Perrie attempted to peer inside the windows, but too much grime covered the glass to see anything. Swallowing her fear, she found her inner courage, which was buried very, *very* deeply at that moment. She marched to the front door and lifted a shaky hand to knock, rapping against the door three times, and each time it reverberated around the cottage. In case someone, or something, monstrous answered the door, she took a few steps back. The distance gave her a chance to take off running if need be.

No one answered, so she tried again and did the same thing, except this time she gave the door an extra knock before stepping back. She realized then that no one was going to answer.

"Guess I'll just let myself in then," Perrie mumbled. Grabbing the unlocked doorknob, she shakily opened it and stepped inside.

TWENTY-ONE

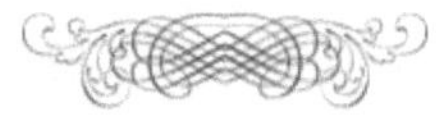

Once inside the cottage, the smell of death permeated the air.

The odor was so pungent and heavy that Perrie's stomach churned with nausea. She covered both her nose and mouth, hesitant to keep going. But she did, and turned the corner of the small foyer. A comfortable warmth enveloped her body inside the cottage, and she stepped into a large living area. Perrie stopped dead in her tracks.

A rocking chair sat in front of a fireplace, and a girl occupied it. Perrie couldn't see what the girl was doing with her hands exactly, but it looked like she was sewing or knitting something.

"Excuse me." Perrie balled her hands into fists, prepared to use them, or run if this went awry.

The girl didn't turn around. Instead, she continued to rock herself back and forth. Each slow creak of the chair echoed in Perrie's bones.

"Hello," she said even louder.

Nothing. The girl didn't even flinch. Heart pounding, Perrie inched closer to the girl and reached one hand out toward her shoulder.

Her eyes widened in recognition. "Maisie!" she gasped,

inhaling the thick scent of smoke and decay. The rocking stilled for a moment, but her cousin didn't look up.

Perrie bit her nails into her palms to calm her initial shock. Kneeling beside Maisie, she scanned her soft features. Her cousin appeared fine, changed even. Maisie's normally straight, black hair rested just below her chin in loose ringlets, making her look a lot younger than her almost eighteen years. She wore a remarkably similar dress to Perrie's, and her feet were bare.

"Maisie? What are you doing?" Perrie asked, her attention drawn to Maisie's hand where she continued her methodical stitching. It wasn't cloth she was holding, but looked to be some sort of animal skin, possibly deer.

Maisie stopped then, slowly lifting her head and focusing on Perrie with the strangest look on her face. "Who is Maisie?"

A solid blue patch that matched her dress covered one of her eyes. Although, there was nothing vibrant about it like her usual patches.

"You're Maisie." Perrie grabbed her hands, desperate for her cousin to recognize her. Maisie gently removed Perrie's hands from hers.

"Aren't you just the silliest? My name is Snow." Maisie giggled.

Perrie's eyebrows shot straight up, and she nearly toppled over. "Uh, as in Snow White?"

"Yes," she said sweetly, giggling an octave higher than before. "How did you know that?"

"Lucky guess." Perrie cringed.

Something was fucking wrong with her cousin. Her smile was too wide, her voice too sweet, and there was an overly dreamy expression on her face that made Perrie shiver. She took a careful look around the room, tuning herself into her surroundings now. All over the floor, piled up in one of the corners were dead animal carcasses, blood pooled beneath them.

Next to the animals, pushed into the shadows, rested seven little beds in a row. Seven beds meant seven damn dwarves. Perrie stood shakily and walked closer for a better look. Seven little men lay in their beds with the sheets pulled clear up to their chins. At first glance, one might think them asleep, but the blood on their slashed faces proved otherwise. The light red sheets on their beds were drenched in blood. She'd been too focused on Maisie to notice any of this sick shit.

She whirled back to Maisie, horrified. *"What is that?"*

"Those little men weren't very kind to me." Maisie shook her finger in the air. "Now they won't be mean to me anymore."

Tossing her head back, Maisie laughed hysterically. Perrie's chest tightened as she became more and more disturbed by her cousin's behavior. Maisie lifted the animal fur to flip it over and Perrie squeaked. Ruby blood, from where the underside of the fur had been laying, caked her cousin's dress.

"Um, Maisie?" Perrie rasped.

"You mean Snow." Maisie tilted her head to the side, grinning wide.

"Right, I mean Snow." She pressed her lips together and nodded. "You do realize you're getting your dress a little messy. Maybe you should put that down and find something else to wear. Do you have another dress?"

Perrie wanted to take the animal fur and toss it into the lit fireplace, but the burning smell would make the odor of the room even worse than it already was. So instead, she reached for the fur to set it on the floor, but Maisie moved it away from her hands. Maisie's brows drew together in a hard line, then she hopped up from her seat.

"Yes. I believe I do!" Maisie softly set the fur on the floor, as if it was fragile enough to break. She then skipped over to a wardrobe.

Hesitantly, Perrie followed Maisie, moving her hand

gently to her cousin's arm. "Snow," she started, "do you recognize me?"

At first, Maisie didn't look at her, she was too busy tossing out dwarf-sized clothing from the wardrobe.

"Snow!" Maisie looked at Perrie then, staring hard, as if this was the first time she was *seeing* her. "Do you remember the name Perrie? That's me. What about August or Neven? Does that ring a bell?"

"Perrie." Maisie sounded out her name like it was a new word she was learning for the first time. Perrie thought there might be recognition starting to form, but then her eyes lost focus.

"Let's clean," Maisie said with a wild grin, forgetting all about the dress.

"Let's not."

Her cousin seemed to not like that particular answer as her face contorted into a childlike pout.

"You know"—Maisie gazed over toward the beds—"they did an awful thing to me, and I taught them."

Perrie avoided staring at the massacred men. *Do I even want to know*? But yes, she had to know, even if she didn't like what Maisie was insinuating.

"What did they do to you?"

"When I first arrived, I didn't know there were people who lived here. I fell asleep in one of the beds and when I woke up to whispering, my wrists were tied together."

"Then what did they do?" Perrie's fear shifted to fire as anger coursed through her. She was certain she wasn't going to like the direction this story was taking.

Maisie reached for her eye patch and lifted it back. Perrie's hands flew to her mouth as a loud gasp escaped her lips, her knees weak. There'd been no time for her to prepare herself for the ghastly sight. She'd been beyond wrong and now she thought she was going to be sick.

"They took out a knife and removed my eye."

Her eye was gone. Maisie's beautiful whole fucking eye was missing, and in its place was a gaping hole. They'd mutilated her face. A mixture of emotions stirred within Perrie—rage, despair, fear. If those little men weren't lying there already dead, she would've slaughtered them herself.

"Don't worry"—Maisie giggled, pulling her eye patch back down—"after they fell asleep, I was able to free myself and get them all back. You see that bucket over there?" She pointed at the corner with a bloody bucket beside the pile of animal carcasses.

"Yes, I see the bucket." But that didn't mean she wanted to know what was in it.

"Take a look inside," Maisie said anxiously.

"I think I'm going to pass on that."

Ignoring her response, Maisie lifted her hands to cover her one remaining eye and patch. "Now they see no evil." Then she moved her hands and covered her ears tightly. "They can hear no evil." Finally, she drifted her hands in front of her mouth, and her solo eye opened wide. "And now they will forever speak no evil."

"Uh-huh." Perrie's lips remained parted in shock. What the fuck was she supposed to even say to that?

Maisie pointed furiously at the men and giggled with pure excitement. "Here, I'll show you my collection."

Clapping frantically, Maisie dashed for the bucket, tugging Perrie along with her. Before she had time to protest, the bucket was in front of her. Her hand fisted her mouth as she dry heaved and stumbled backward. Bloody eyeballs, severed tongues, and ears filled the bucket. This was… This was… *Insanity.* Maisie had gone insane. And being here had made her this way.

"They wouldn't sit still, so I had to put them to bed first," Maisie said, pointing directly at her heart. "I used the same knife they used to cut out my eye."

After seeing her cousin's wound, Perrie knew she

would've had to defend herself. But the way she was acting, and the way she went about it, wasn't like her at all. Perrie needed to snap her out of this trance. There wasn't much time to think, so she came up with the first thing she could.

"Snow, look at me." She approached her cousin and gently placed her hands on the sides of her face. "Do you want me to tell you a story?"

Maisie clasped her hands together at her chest and made it seem like Perrie had just given her the best birthday present in the entire world.

"I love stories!" Maisie steadily shook her clasped hands.

"Then you'll love this one, I promise." Perrie walked her cousin back to the rocking chair and helped her sit, kicking the bloody fur out of the way before Maisie tried to drag it onto her lap again. Once her cousin was settled and content, Perrie took her place in front of the fire and began.

"Once upon a time, three good friends traveled far and wide to attend the great carnival. They were—"

"What were their names?" Maisie interrupted her. "These three good friends."

Shit. "They were called—uh—Mais, Nev, and Posie."

Maisie nodded her approval and Perrie continued, "So, like I was saying, these three good friends—Mais, Nev, and Posie—traveled far to attend the great carnival. All Mais wanted to do was eat a funnel cake before going on their favorite ride, the Zipper.

"The three good friends ate their tasty pastry and took turns riding their favorite ride. Nev and Posie, when riding together, would watch as Mais rode with the new friends she made. Mais was a silly girl, but silly in every good way."

This wasn't only a story—it was a memory. Maisie had dragged Neven and Perrie to the carnival one summer for a fun night. They'd taken turns riding the Zipper with each other, and Maisie would ask some random person to hop on with her so she could keep going.

"Eventually, Mais wasn't feeling up for another ride. Nev and Posie asked if she was all right, but Mais ran off and lost her pastry. Never one to quit, Mais went on and on again, until she felt sick. Nev and Posie suggested she take a break and play some carnival games!

"Posie was not very good at these games, but because she loved her cousin, Mais, she tried to win her something anyway. She picked a game, the hardest one in all the carnival, and tried her best to cheer up Mais. When the game was done, Posie won the smallest baby dragon and gave it to Mais, who suddenly felt much better that day."

The stuffed dragon Perrie had won for Maisie was still proudly displayed in her cousin's room.

"Every now and then, Maisie, you talk about how that was one of the greatest days of your life." Perrie waited patiently, congratulating herself for a job well done. Her English teacher would be proud that she'd managed to sneak in a couple of rhymes, too.

Maisie pressed her fingers to her cheeks as if she had dimples there and laughed. "That wasn't a story at all. There weren't any animals or castles or anything."

Perrie dropped her chin to her chest and mumbled sarcastically, "There was a stuffed dragon."

"Do you have any better stories?" Her cousin's eye widened with enthusiasm and a glazed shine.

"No." Clenching her jaw in frustration, she tried to come up with another. "Okay, I have one." Perrie then told her the story about Hansel and Gretel, about the ketchup on the house, and Aunt Krista's reaction. After that, she went on about high school, the Halloween party where they'd dressed up as Hansel and Gretel. It was the same year they'd tricked Neven into dressing as the witch.

"You have to remember that, Maisie," she urged her frantically. "That was our sophomore year—it was the best Halloween of all time. You even said so."

The fog in her eyes cleared for the slightest moment, and then it was gone. Maisie jumped out of her seat and clasped her hands together once again, and Perrie waited to hear what she'd been hoping for. But then she yelled maniacally, "I love dessert!"

That was it. That was the last straw. Perrie couldn't keep this charade up anymore. She dragged Maisie out of the chair by both arms and shook her hard.

"Damn it, Maisie. I don't know what the fuck is going on here, but we're done with this shit. I can't sit here anymore and play these games with you like we aren't in some demonic house. This house is filled with the dead bodies of people you say that you slaughtered. Then there are the skinned animals." She pointed at the bloody furs in the corner. "Not to mention, the stench in here reeks of a thousand deaths. If I have to slap you repeatedly to get you to remember, I will. Snap out of it, Maisie!"

Perrie released her cousin's arms and raised her hand, ready to smack the crazy out of her.

Then Maisie's one good eye widened. "Perrie?"

TWENTY-TWO

Perrie had done it. She didn't know how, but she'd done it. Her cousin was back.

"Maisie!" Perrie rushed forward, practically crying as she wrapped her arms around her, and squeezed her tighter than she had ever before.

"How did you get here?" Maisie blinked, appearing a little disoriented.

Perrie explained to her how she and August went to the Glass Vault to search for her, but instead got magically sucked into the hellish displays. Maisie stayed focused as Perrie told her about the previous places—Sleepy Hollow, Jack the Ripper, and Billy Goats Gruff—about what she and August had gone through—how they'd discovered the mystery of the missing people.

"Between Ben, Officer Rodriguez, and Josselyn, none of them recognized themselves either," Perrie said.

Maisie considered the information, furrowing her brow, as if trying to puzzle the pieces together. "Where's August, then?" she finally asked.

"I don't know." Perrie sighed, her chest heavy with regret. "What about you? What happened? Do you remember everything?”

Maisie pushed her hair behind her ears. “I remember most of it. I think? I left your house and arrived at the Glass Vault, but when I came inside there was no one there.”

“Did you meet Quinsey?”

She shook her head. “No. I didn’t see anyone in the museum. It was like what you saw. I wandered down a bunch of halls and wound up in the exhibit. I waited for a little bit, figuring that he was either late or somewhere on the premises.”

Leaning her back against the wall, Maisie slid to the floor. Perrie sat on the wood floor with her legs crossed, facing Maisie.

“While I was waiting, I walked around and looked at the displays. I remember stopping in front of Snow White.” She closed her eye. “The seven dwarves were lying asleep in their beds and someone was peering in through their window. Then it felt like something was sucking me in, and suddenly I was in a forest, a little further away from this cottage.” She pointed in the direction Perrie had come from, which was interesting since Maisie hadn’t encountered the trolls.

“Is that all you remember?”

“I remember more, but a lot of it is a blur.” She toyed with the skirt of her dress, observing the red still covering it. Perrie had never seen Maisie so not herself. She almost didn’t want to ask her about her eye, but she had to.

“What about your eye? Do you remember that at all?”

“I do, but I don’t. It was like I was possessed by something. It’s as if the person who was speaking to you wasn’t me, yet was me at the same time.” She paused. “I know how it sounds, but you have to believe me.”

“I do believe you, I promise. Trust me when I say that August and I have seen some seriously fucked up things.”

“Okay, so the odd thing is, I was already missing my eye when I got here. I lowered the patch to get a clearer view of my surroundings. That’s when I discovered my eye was gone.”

She traced her fingertips over the blue patch, staying silent for a few moments.

"Maisie, it's part of the display. As soon as we get out of this scene, you'll have your eye back."

She shrugged and smiled. "I'm used to seeing with one eye anyway."

Perrie was sure Maisie was the only person on the entire planet who wouldn't be freaking out just a little bit over a missing eyeball. If it were Perrie, she would have lost her shit.

"What about the dwarves? They didn't attack you?"

"No. I came to the cottage as soon as I saw it. The men were already dead—their ears, eyes, and tongues were already missing, and in that bucket over there." She tilted her head in the direction of the bloody pieces.

"I didn't see the Snow-White display," Perrie said. "However, this earlier version of you that was here before the real you came back said she'd murdered the dwarves after they ripped her eye out. This could be the story of the Snow-White display that had already happened, and by you coming here, it's the continuation of the story."

"That does sound plausible. By the way, I like how you said *she* instead of you." She smiled a genuine Maisie smile.

"You may remember all the crazy stuff this person said, but that wasn't you talking. Quirky and crazy isn't the same thing."

"Why thank you, Perrie, I'm glad to know you enjoy my presence."

"You're one of a kind." She laughed. "What else happened after you came into the cottage, or have you just been here the entire time?"

Maisie bit her thumbnail and chewed on it. "There's something else, and it's too much of a blur. I remember having a semi-meltdown after finding the dead bodies and the animal carcasses in the corner with the pail of body memorabilia. It had me panicked, and I ran out of the house. Outside, I screamed and kicked a couple of trees to cool myself down."

Perrie's stomach dropped, and anger boiled within her for what Maisie had to face. When Perrie had come through the first display, she was with August. She didn't know what she would've done if she'd been alone. Even when she'd been alone with that Thomas asshole, she already had experience with this place because of Sleepy Hollow. Maisie had gone to the Glass Vault by herself, got sucked in by herself, found all these dead bodies by herself, and she was missing an entire fucking eyeball.

"After moaning and groaning for a bit, I gathered my wits and set sail through the woods, away from the cottage in my pretend escape ship. Then I remember seeing a man."

"What man?" Perrie asked, wrinkling her nose.

"I have no idea. He had dark, brown hair that fell to his shoulders. That's all I can remember. Then somehow I ended up back at the cottage."

"He wasn't a giant or a troll, right? Someone who can lift you up with one hand?" Perrie tapped the middle of her palm several times for emphasis.

Maisie squinted her one eye. "I'm going to go with smaller than a giant, but I mostly remember a well-structured face and hair blowing around."

"From your detailed account, there's a model running around somewhere in the woods."

"That would be a strong possibility," she said, pointing a finger in the air.

"And you haven't seen anyone else pass through here?"
She shook her head.

It made sense. Perrie had only seen one missing person in each of the displays. This wasn't including August or her, though. Finding Maisie was checked off her list. Now August was gone, and they still had to find Neven.

"We got separated once before, but we both wound up in the same display. I'm sure he's here somewhere. Nev will probably be in another scene, so we can work on him next." A new rush of confidence flowed through her. "Let's turn this plan into pure action and find the guys."

Inside the lone bedroom, Maisie discovered a dresser filled with rows of the same shoes, eye patches, undergarments, and dresses. Not much variety there.

Maisie tore off the bloody dress, then threw on a clean one and a pair of shoes in record time. "There, I feel a little cleaner."

On the way out, Maisie picked up a bloodied knife and wiped it semi-clean using the sheets on one of the dwarf's beds. Then Perrie grabbed them each a pickaxe propped against the wall near the dwarves. *This is definitely better than forks or knives.*

Once outside, they trudged through the trees beneath the overcast gray sky. Animals darted in and out of the woods, seeming to dance happily around them. With Maisie being Snow White and all, she must be attracting these creatures. *Weird.*

"It's like we're at a zoo with all the different animals we're seeing, minus the whole locked-up-in-cages thing," Maisie said in astonishment.

"A zoo without cages," Perrie agreed.

Maisie had been against zoos since she was small. She would never go near the cages, preferring to sit around and watch the nature wildlife shows, where those animals had some freedom.

When they were nine, Aunt Krista had taken them to the zoo, but Maisie wasn't having it. When they approached the bald eagle, it was in a smaller area than an armadillo had—her little nine-year-old self almost blew a fuse. After that particular visit, she started a petition and went around the neighborhood asking people to sign it. Perrie went along with her to show her support.

Maisie was quite proud of herself after getting fifty

signatures.

Aunt Krista had then taken them to turn the list in at the zoo. Needless to say, the bald eagle still remained inside of the same small cage, and all they'd received from the zoo was a sucker and a sticker.

Maisie hadn't been back since. She must've had an impact on Perrie, though, because she couldn't look at the zoo the same way anymore.

A rustling stirred from up ahead, interrupting Perrie's thoughts … and animal gazing.

"What is that?" Maisie turned in the direction of the noise. Perrie strained to listen and another sound, like someone struggling, making desperate grunts, came.

"Whatever it is, it doesn't sound good."

Maisie and Perrie exchanged a glance, pulling their pickaxes up over their shoulders and hurried in the direction of the sound. The grunting continued, growing louder as they ventured nearer.

A large pink flowering bush blocked whatever was behind it, so Perrie used her weapon to maneuver the branches back.

The source of the grunting was a face Perrie was *very* familiar with. "August!"

His eyes flickered with relief, despite the gag in his mouth. She raced to him and removed the black cloth, pulling it down to rest around his neck.

August breathed in the fresh air, his chest heaving as leaned back against the tree where his hands were bound. "Hurry and untie me. We have to get out of here before the guy comes back."

"A guy with long hair blowing around?" Maisie asked.

"Maisie?" August blinked repeatedly, finally acknowledging that she was standing next to Perrie.

"I know you're always too busy ogling Perrie, but come on, August, you had to have noticed the eye patch." She laughed and pointed at her eye.

"Good to see a friendly face," he said, biting his lip while looking about. "Now untie me before he comes back, please. And to answer your previous question, yes, he has long hair."

Perrie took Maisie's knife from its hiding place and cut the rope binding August's hands. He winced when he was freed and rubbed at his wrists.

"What happened to you?" Perrie tucked the knife into the sash of her dress.

"Not much. I landed somewhere over there." He pointed to the left of where they'd come from. "Next thing I know, I'm hit with something hard from behind and tied to a tree."

"Did you get a good look at the guy?" Maisie asked.

"Sort of? Big guy, too. Arms the size of bowling balls." He flexed his arms, which weren't near the size she was imagining of his attacker. Although, his arms were quite nice to look at, and strong when they'd held her. "He kept asking me about Snow. At first, I thought he was curious about, you know, the white stuff that falls from the sky. But then he kept asking me where the girl is."

Maisie's eye widened. The guy must've been the one Maisie had mentioned earlier. Only two men come to mind who would be searching for Snow White—either the Huntsman or the Prince. She was about ninety-nine percent sure there wasn't any fucking Prince Charming out here.

"Don't worry, guys, I'm totally prepared." Maisie lifted her pickaxe in the air.

Perrie helped August stand, his forehead slicked with sweat. He arched his back and shook his legs and arms out, seeming to try to rid himself of any stiffness. She would be too after sitting in that position for so long. Another person off her checklist—leaving only Neven.

"August, in case you didn't already know, meet Snow White." She waved her hand toward Maisie. Her cousin stepped forward and bowed slightly.

"I'm not surprised," August stated flatly then grinned at

Perrie. "I'd say it's a step up from working at a brothel, though."

Maisie's eye crinkled as she gave her a mischievous look.

Perrie sighed. "Seriously, don't even ask."

Twigs and branches snapped, one after another, interrupting what Maisie was going to say. The sound continued, as if an animal was running through the woods. It wasn't an animal, though. The pounding of feet against the earth matched the beating of her heart.

Maisie grabbed the pickaxe Perrie had left on the ground and handed it over to August. He shifted his weight and prepared his weapon for the strike. Perrie didn't want to stay here one second longer. They could look for the barrier later.

"Let's go," Perrie said sharply.

August and Maisie didn't argue. They made it a few feet, when something powerful yanked Perrie to the side, and she screamed as she dropped her blade, her only weapon for defense. She didn't understand. The noise she'd heard—she thought it was far enough away, coming from the other direction.

"Where is she?" A booming voice with hot breath pressed against her ear.

"Fuck," August ground out, turning around with Maisie right behind him. Perrie mouthed for them to run—neither one of them listened.

A strong hand pulled her face to meet his, and she couldn't see August or Maisie anymore.

His eyes were liquid gold, molten and rich in color, and his face square but strong. Most people would find him ruggedly handsome. Apparently, she was right when she'd guessed a male model from Maisie's earlier description.

"Do I have to ask again? Where. Is. The. Girl?"

"I'm a girl," Perrie answered stupidly, but it was a way to distract him from Maisie. She wouldn't let him have her.

"Don't play games with me. I saw you with Snow just

moments ago," he rasped.

"Let her go!" August shouted.

The man tore his eyes away from her and spotted August. "Either you're a wizard and freed yourself, you little rat, or perhaps this little tart here helped you escape." He squeezed her tighter.

"Sorry, not a fan of bondage," August said as he raised his pickaxe. "At least not with you. Now, let her go."

Her jaw ached with the pressure of the man's hand on her face. She scratched at his arms and kicked her feet, but it didn't affect him. He just gave her a shake hard enough to jar her neck. She looked around and realized that August was alone. *Where is Maisie?*

"When I have Snow White's heart in my hand, then you can have the little mousey," he growled. *Okay, definitely the Huntsman.* "Now, where is she?"

"August, go!" Perrie would rather die right here and now than let him lay one single finger on Maisie or her loving heart.

The Huntsman clamped down on her jaw, holding it in place. "Snow, come out now—I know you're here. I might have to make it so the little mousey will not be able to make a single squeak ever again."

His voice was soft, but dangerous. The threat beneath was subversive, but effective. As he spoke, his fingers slowly stroked her cheek. She wanted to bite them off.

"Here I am." Maisie appeared, leaving the safety of her hiding spot, and struck a warrior pose, complete with the pickaxe. She should've taken the damn opportunity to run away.

"Maisie! Run," Perrie tried to yell, but the Huntsman's hand tightened on her face, so much so that she feared her skull might burst into a bloody pulp.

"Ah. There you are, my little doe. I have been searching everywhere for you. You have made things quite difficult for me, and I don't like things to be troublesome," he drawled.

"I'm here now, so let her go," Maisie insisted. "Once she's safe, I'll come with you."

Oh, hell no, she won't. If he released Perrie, she could grab the knife she'd dropped on the ground and bring it up to stab him.

"How sweet. My little doe thinks she has a choice," he purred in Perrie's ear.

Maisie hadn't lowered her pickaxe. She looked prepared for anything, anything except his lightning quick reflexes. In less than a few seconds, he tossed Perrie to the ground and slid an axe from behind his back faster than she'd landed. He thrust it with one muscular arm and it swung round and round toward its target. The sharp end sliced clean through Maisie's neck perfectly, before slamming into the trunk of a tree at the same time her head tumbled from her shoulders.

Time stopped.

"No!" Perrie howled, her heart disintegrating. Her scream was louder than a thousand screams put together and longer than a thousand echoes. She crawled to Maisie's crumpled body, her hands shaking as she touched her cousin's pale face. There was blood *everywhere*.

While the crimson liquid poured out of her cousin, all Perrie could think was, *Let me put her back together. She'll be fine.* As Perrie lurched forward to try and reattach Maisie's head, two strong hands pulled her from her delusional thoughts. She flailed frantically in his arms, violently tossing herself around to break free. Her fists pounded against muscle that wouldn't give way. She was going to murder the fucker.

"Perrie, it's only me," August said gently, and she halted. "We have to go."

The ringing stopped and the world swung back into full motion.

"But, Maisie . . ." she croaked miserably.

The Huntsman, decked out in the furs of his prey, retrieved the embedded axe from the tree. His back remained turned to them and her knife in the grass gleamed. She could grab it and attack him from behind.

Perrie tried to loosen herself from August's grip, but his hold was like iron. Despite that, she broke away, reached for the blade shining in the grass, and snatched it.

"We have to get out of here now," August said hurriedly.

The Huntsman watched Perrie, smirking as if he was the devil himself. He already knew what she wanted to do to him, how badly she wanted to drive the knife into his heart. His eyes dared her to do it.

"Go on then, little mousey," he shouted, motioning to the cottage. "Before I change my mind and kill you both."

Neither one of them had the skills to throw a pickaxe the way he did, so, for now, they ran.

"I will see you again," the Huntsman called.

She didn't look back.

The run was a blur, the world spinning. Perrie kept seeing Maisie, whole one minute, then head severed the next. As if her brain wouldn't let her forget, she couldn't stop the replay constantly rolling in her mind. She'd always thought the mind would block out traumatic events like that, but she guessed not.

August stopped once to ask her for directions to the cottage, but she couldn't hear her voice as she answered him. She didn't want to go back there, but it was the only place that had water, shelter, and better weapons.

"I need a break." Perrie turned to lean against a tree, even though they weren't far from the cottage.

August slowed and walked back over to her, his face solemn. He pulled her away from the tree and tugged her to him, wrapping his arms around her. She was like a rag doll slumped in his embrace, unable to bring herself to hug him back.

"I'm not going to sit here and tell you everything is going to be okay, but we have to keep going." He stroked her hair.

"Even if we have to go back and stop others from coming into this place, we have to try."

Her heart ached. Maisie was more than her cousin—she was like her sister.

"She's gone." Perrie's voice was barely above a whisper.

Hot tears slid down her cheeks and the loss consumed every fiber of her being. Maisie was a major chess piece in helping Perrie become who she was. She was there for her through everything. The day they moved into the house beside her cousin, Maisie was there with a tray of rainbow cookies and a smile brighter than sunshine. She shared her mom with Perrie when she needed one—she was her best friend.

How could she be gone?

"Look at me, Perrie." August cradled her face, and she lifted her head, their eyes locking. "I cared a great deal about Maisie, too. I know for a fact she would want you to keep going, not just for her, but also for yourself and for your families. Do it for her, do it for me."

More tears poured down her face, and she found the strength to hold him. He rubbed slow circles against her lower back to try and soothe her. After a few silent moments, she was steadier on her feet. She wanted to leave this nightmare and be done with it for good.

"I'm ready." Perrie sniffled with a hollow spot in her chest that would always be there. But she had to push forward.

"I'm right here, doll face." He took her hand, interlacing their fingers and gently squeezed.

They spotted a well a few paces from the cottage, neatly tucked behind some flowers and bushes. August turned the crank—a loud, screeching sound poured out as the rope wound up.

A tiny bluebird darted right above her head—she ducked as it chirped and flew to sit on a windowsill a few feet away. The bucket finally reached the top and August handed it to her. They didn't have the luxury of cups around them, so she drank straight from the bucket. She hadn't realized how thirsty she was until half the water in it was gone.

Perrie passed it to August, and he finished the rest, wiping his mouth with the sleeve of his shirt. Three other bluebirds flew and chirped past them, joining the first one by the window. Their chirping struck her as oddly melodic, harmonious even. *Strange*.

A commotion came from inside the cottage.

It sounded like someone was singing.

TWENTY-THREE

A voice… A singing voice… How could there be a voice coming from inside the cottage?

"You heard that, too, I'm guessing?" August asked.

"Yeah, but I thought for a second I might be imagining it." Perrie focused on the window. The singing grew louder as someone belted out a long high note, lovely and sweet. A melody that could lure anyone in, just like a siren's deadly song.

"No. You definitely weren't hearing things."

Perrie didn't understand. Maisie was murdered right in front of them. There was no way she could just come back to life like the living dead.

No. Not like the living dead—something else. "We have to go in there and look."

"All right," August agreed, "let's go."

Perrie gripped the hilt of the knife to keep from shaking.

When they reached the front door, August didn't hesitate and went right in. Slowly, she followed behind him with her knife raised. The familiar stench of what she now knew to be bloodied animal carcasses and dead little men invaded her nostrils once more.

Perrie trailed August around the corner of the foyer and he paused. She peered over his shoulder, taking a sharp breath. In the wooden rocking chair, moving back and forth, sat Maisie. The same deer fur rested in her lap as she stitched it. It seemed impossible, but it wasn't.

"Maisie?" Perrie whispered, rushing to her. The rocking chair halted. "Maisie, what's going on? How did you get back here?"

She glanced up at Perrie with a big smile on her face. "Maisie? Who is Maisie? My name is Snow."

Perrie's heart withered. Maisie was herself only minutes ago.

"Oh, no. Not this shit again," Perrie hissed, bringing her hand to her forehead, both in relief and frustration.

August knelt beside her cousin, resting his hands on the chair. "Maisie, what's going on?"

"Why are you calling me Maisie? My name is Snow, silly." She giggled.

August stood and took a step back. "We just saw you, Maisie. You were *dead*," he said, brows lowered in confusion.

Maisie lifted her head, acknowledging the both of them with that same too-wide smile. Just when Perrie thought her cousin was going to speak, she instead burst into a spell of giggles. It went on for an uncomfortable amount of time. Then, as if the joke was no longer funny, she went quiet.

"You die here, you stay here," Maisie sang.

"What was that?" Perrie barely heard her.

"You die here, you stay here," she sang louder.

August turned back to Perrie and frowned. "This is the same as it was with Ben, isn't it?"

"I think so." Perrie nodded. "I was thinking earlier about why they can't remember who they are, but we can. It's because they died here, and we haven't. It's like they become a part of the story, doomed to repeat it so long as they're stuck here."

August rubbed at his chin. "So, if we die, then the same thing will happen to us."

"Mystery solved. Now what do we do?" Maisie still wasn't herself and the Huntsman was out there somewhere, waiting for them … or Maisie again.

"First things first," August started. "What's wrong with Maisie? How do we fix this?"

"It will take some *convincing*."

"What did you do last time?" He smirked.

"I yelled at her." She left out the part about nearly smacking her senseless, though. "But I don't know if it will work a second time."

"Won't know until we try, right?" August suggested.

Sighing, Perrie attempted to muster the same amount of frustration as last time and yanked her cousin out of her seat. Gripping her shoulders, she shook her as hard as she could. If they were lucky, maybe the jarring sensation would be enough to wake her up.

"Maisie, snap out of it!" Perrie yelled.

Maisie's lashes fluttered and her lips parted in surprise, but there was no trace of her cousin in her dreamy gaze.

Perrie whistled their birdy signal to no avail. "Help me," she pleaded to August.

He scratched the side of his head, seeming to not know what else to do either. There had to be a better way to get through to her.

"Look at me." Perrie locked her eyes with Maisie's. "I'm not going to waste my time here telling you stories about how we know each other. We tried that already and it didn't help."

Maisie excitedly clasped her hands together. "Oh, I love stories! Will you tell me one?"

"I just said I'm not going to tell you a story. Now listen, try to remember, we were in the forest and we were attacked by the Huntsman from the story of Snow White."

"What story? I am Snow White, you silly little thing." She

broke out of Perrie's grasp and took a seat back in her rocking chair. Perrie was about to unleash a loaded sentence of fury when August beat her to it.

"Maisie, knock this fucking shit off and come out of there already. Perrie had to listen to this bullshit once today. She doesn't need to deal with it anymore." His voice sounded deeper than ever from his anger. "I was tied to a tree for who knows how long, and I'm tired as hell of this place. If it isn't a prostitute killing other prostitutes, it's the Headless Horseman or a Huntsman chopping off heads! I don't want to hear the ramblings of a crazy person for another second. Wake the hell up!"

"Don't forget the trolls," Perrie added.

"That shit, too." He sighed heavily.

"Wow." Maisie gazed up at August in wonder, blinking several times and rubbing her temples. "Give me a second here. I've never seen you so angry before. I'm willing to bet Perrie enjoyed seeing this new side of you."

Perrie laughed, even though tears pricked her eyes again, but this time because of relief. It was true. That was one of the few times she'd ever seen August mad, not that she was complaining. Perrie never thought she would find anger so down right sexy.

"Maisie, you're the only person I know who could make this day interesting. Thank God you're back." Perrie launched her arms around her, not wanting to let her go, especially after watching her cousin die in front of her. "What do you remember?"

"Everything, mostly. I know the Huntsman was chasing us, and I think something bad happened." She stroked her neck with both hands. "He got me, didn't he?"

August and Perrie stayed silent. Maisie already knew the answer.

"Anyway, I remember everything with the exception of how I end up back here every time."

Every time? Does that mean this has happened more than once? At this point, she couldn't keep herself from grabbing her own throat. She couldn't begin to imagine how it would feel to lose one's own head like that more than once. *When the Queen of Hearts says off with your head, that's normally it—but that's a different story, I guess.*

"How many times?" August asked.

"I think this makes seven." She rubbed her eye. "Sometimes it takes me longer to pull myself together. I don't understand how Crazy Maisie takes over."

"Crazy Maisie won't take over again—we won't let it come to that." Perrie wanted to be as reassuring as she could, but based on what they knew, Maisie might be trapped here like the rest.

"Perrie, I'm not afraid. I've been putting the pieces together, even the missing ones." Maisie's conviction unsettled her. "This time it was an axe, before that it was a knife to my heart, then a knife at my throat, once it was my own pickaxe, and the list goes on. After I die, I come right back to this house and it starts all over again."

Maisie was too calm, too collected for someone who had died and come back to life multiple times. It didn't surprise Perrie, though. Her cousin adjusted her eye patch, and Perrie cringed a little inside about her missing eye.

August gripped the back of his neck. "Have you tried to leave?"

"A couple times, yeah. It was around my fourth 'death day' when I found the barrier. I had the pickaxe with me and managed to duck low and hit the Huntsman in the thigh. I didn't get much farther than that, though. I slammed right into the barrier and bounced back. Again, I tried, but it knocked me off my feet. Then the Huntsman was there with my pickaxe and the rest is pretty obvious." Maisie was not as phased by the repetition of death in this world as Perrie was. But not a hint of sadness lingered in her cousin's eye.

Maisie turned to August. "He didn't murder you, did he?"

"From what I remember . . . just the whole tied-up-to-the-tree situation. That about sums it up on my end."

She breathed a sigh of relief.

"That's good. Perrie told me earlier you guys have been able to pass through each barrier safely." Perrie already didn't like where she was going with this.

"Safely is an understatement." August's words made her think of her personal incident with Thomas.

"If I'm right, if I can't slip through, then all I can do is help you two get past the Huntsman. Hopefully, he doesn't take the only eye I have left this time," she said with finality.

"Are you insane?" August shouted.

"What are you thinking?" Perrie cried.

"I know I'm not going to get through. If you two can manage to get home, you might be able to figure out what's going on here. Not to be all gloom and doom, but if dying here is real, then I'm already gone." Maisie shrugged, as if it was really not that complicated or hard to understand.

Perrie's heart sank and sank. "What if you're wrong and you're not really dead?" She grabbed her cousin's forearm and squeezed it. "You don't *feel* like a ghost, and you're warm. You'll be here by yourself with that maniac on the loose. I can't watch you die again, Maisie."

Maisie seemed to fight to hide the grin on her face. "Have you ever even seen or felt a ghost, Perrie?"

"It's not the time, Maisie!" Perrie snapped.

"I'm willing to sacrifice myself to get you two out of here. Take it or take it. There's no leaving it."

"But—"

She shook her head. "But nothing. You're going to have to warn people, especially Mom, Dad, and Uncle James."

"That's going to go over really well. They'll probably lock me up in a mental institution." Perrie's shoulders slumped.

Maisie waved a dismissive hand at her and refocused her

efforts on August. "You know I'm right."

He didn't even *try* to argue.

"I need you to get yourself and Perrie out of here. Try and find Neven, maybe he's safe like you two. I'll go as far as I can to help you distract the Huntsman. When we get to the barrier, you'll both go through it without me. Once you make it out of here, and if I'm not really a ghost, then you can find out how to save me."

Perrie folded her arms. "I refuse to agree to this plan. I'll stay right here. I want to try and find Neven, but I won't leave you here."

August reached for her, his expression sympathetic, and she knew what he was going to say. She didn't want to hear it.

"I don't want to do this either, but Maisie is right. If we can get out of here, maybe we can find a way to release everyone from these prisons. We can't save anyone by staying inside the displays." He uncrossed her arms and took both of her hands. Tears stung the corners of her eyes.

"We're all they've got," he murmured. She didn't want to argue anymore—it would be pointless. Maisie would never give in.

Perrie was beginning to see the bigger picture, but she wasn't a superhero or anything otherworldly and neither was August. They were two regular people fighting for their survival against something supernatural. Yet, if there was a slight chance they could get out of here and find a way to rescue Maisie and everyone else, she was going to take that chance.

Perrie grabbed August's hand and Maisie's in the other.

"Okay then, let's do this."

TWENTY-FOUR

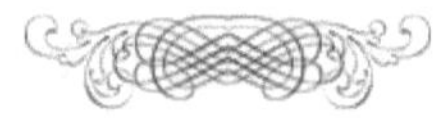

Perrie inhaled the outdoor air, the crispness and freshness slowly erasing the stench of decay.

Sliding out her knife, Perrie handed it to Maisie, who needed more protection since the Huntsman was after Snow White. Each of them had also collected a pickaxe before leaving the house of death.

To her credit, Maisie didn't look the least bit nervous. Her determination to get out of this place was aligned with Perrie's. But Perrie just hoped that when the time came Maisie would try to pass through the barrier, too.

Overhead, birds chirped loudly, flitting carelessly from one perch to another. Perrie and the others kept their steps quiet, careful as they trekked through the forest. The Huntsman could be lurking anywhere.

God, this fucking thing is heavy! Perrie switched the pickaxe to a different shoulder, taking turns to rub her sweaty palms against her dress.

August glanced back at her, giving her a steady, wide smile. Perrie wanted to bottle up that smile, tuck it into the deepest depths of her heart as she grinned in return.

Maisie didn't miss the exchange and leaned over to

whisper in her ear. "I know this isn't the time or the place, but he's a good guy, Perrie. He's good for you."

"I know," Perrie said. She'd known this for a while now. And she remembered his perfect mouth on hers, his strong hands on her body. Perrie wanted to tell her cousin more of what had happened between them, but there might never be a time to do so.

Maisie opened her mouth to say something when heavy footsteps snapping twigs interrupted. Her cousin quickened her pace ahead of them, readying her knife.

"He doesn't even try to conceal himself." Maisie chewed on her thumbnail and shrugged.

"Get ready to run," August said.

Perrie was getting tired of running—that was all they seemed to be doing these days. If they made it home, she would avoid it for probably ever.

A flash of movement came to their right, so they broke left and ran for it. Perrie had once heard somewhere to avoid being shot, that one should move in a zigzag pattern so the person couldn't get a proper aim on the target. But would that work when the attacker was using an axe? As something heavy struck her shoulder from behind, she wouldn't have time to find out. A sharp pain shot up her entire arm, feeling like she'd been hit with a baseball bat. Perrie stumbled, losing her balance and dropping the pickaxe. As she fell forward, she caught August, bringing him down with her and landing on the ground in a heap of tangled limbs.

Where the handle of the axe struck, her shoulder was on fire, pain radiating. Body trembling in panic, Perrie could barely hold back a scream as she pulled herself to her knees.

"Jesus." Perrie fumbled to August's side and helped him to stand. Blood oozed from his nose, but other than that, he was still intact, his pickaxe beside him and, at least, not *through* him.

"You are a lucky little mousey. The end of my axe only

grazed you," a loud voice boomed, closer than she wanted, like lightning crashing through the sky.

The Huntsman emerged in all his bravado from the thick brush. "I could have taken you down easily, making you bleed if you were who I was after. Now, *where is she?*"

Perrie searched around the forest and through the trees for Maisie. But she had no clue where she'd disappeared. Her cousin was apparently sneakier than the Huntsman.

"I have no idea." Perrie only had her fists and legs at the moment. Her weapon was on the ground, and he was already twirling another axe in his hand like a baton.

"Snow? Come out, little doe. I don't want to harm your pets, but I will if I must." To prove his point, he closed in and Perrie and August stepped back. Perrie was prepared to bolt as she examined the location of her and August's pickaxes on the ground. They couldn't reach them in time.

The Huntsman raised his axe, ready to swing, when Maisie leapt from a tree and crashed onto him. He released a loud grunt, the force of her attack knocking him to the ground with her landing on top of him. Maisie's fierce expression remained on her face and she didn't hesitate. Lifting her knife high above the Huntsman, she brought it down, slamming it directly into his heart with a sickening squelch. She ripped it out, his body jerking, and she pierced him again. Again and again. Maisie continued stabbing him until his body remained still, no longer moving. Dead.

Perrie watched with wide eyes, not knowing Maisie had it in her, but after being murdered seven times, one could only take so much.

"Run!" Maisie screamed, still holding the bloodied knife, the entire front of her dress splattered in scarlet.

Together, they took off running through the forest, carelessly snapping every twig, branch, and leaf within an inch of their path.

They just *ran.*

Perrie hit the barrier first and bounced back to the ground. August stopped before he smashed into it. He reached out his hands, feeling for the barrier, but no breeze of wind stirred.

Maisie joined them within seconds and pushed on it. "This is what happened when I made it here last time."

Rustling echoed through the bushes. It couldn't be.... The Huntsman, who seconds ago was lying in his own blood, now loomed before them. Completely untouched, as if his clothes and entire body went and had a magical bath.

"There's no way . . ." Perrie panted.

August ground his teeth. *What the hell?*

"Try it again, August," Maisie said in a soft voice, seeming not at all surprised.

"Enough of this," the Huntsman growled. "Are you going to come to me, little doe, or do I have to come for all three of you?"

"Try it again," she repeated, sterner this time.

August reached for the barrier, and it flexed, responding. A strong gust of wind pulled at him, whipping his curls around his face.

Its strength then tugged at Perrie. "Maisie, it's working. Hurry!"

Maisie stretched for the barrier, but her hand was pushed back by it. "Until we meet again," she said, meeting Perrie's gaze and giving a final salute.

Perrie thrashed against the pull of the barrier, fighting it, desperate to get Maisie back, but it was too forceful. August shouted Perrie's name and when she swiped for him, the wind yanked him through. She couldn't escape its powerful pull— it was too late. Maisie winked at her with her uncovered eye before, almost gleefully, darting away from the Huntsman.

Then Perrie was ripped away without Maisie.

Perrie landed on top of a bed, bouncing from the force and colliding with the floor. Darkness covered her face and she screamed. She thrashed her hands, pushing away layers of her own golden hair from her face until she could see. Using the edge of the bed, she pulled herself up.

"August?" Perrie shouted. "Are you here?" No reply.

A light shone from an open window on the far side of the stone-walled room. She hurried toward it and tripped, catching herself against the bedpost. A pile of hair had been the cause of her tripping.

Her gaze fell to the bed where gold hair lay, *her* gold hair. She followed its path across the floor, sprawled against the wall—it was *everywhere*. And all connected to her scalp.

Fuck.

Perrie toed a path in spaces where there wasn't hair to get to the oval window—the only actual source of light in the room. The space was large enough for a person to fit through. When she made it without tripping, she placed her hands against its light gray stone edges and peered out.

Her heart accelerated and a woozy feeling rushed through her. She wasn't in a house, but a stone tower wrapped in thick green vines covered in thorns and vibrant orange flowers, like the color of the setting sun. But while being so dangerously high above the ground, she couldn't focus on their beauty.

"I must be Rapunzel," she murmured. Perrie knew that story like the back of her hand.

For the moment, she was trapped in a tower with long, unruly hair, and of course, no escape. Not a single door was in sight. Perrie searched the floor for the possibility of a hidden exit, but only a cool stone floor and two ornate rugs were there.

As she focused on the bed, then to the table stocked with

fresh fruit and a pitcher full of water, it was as if the Glass Vault was preparing her for a long stay.

Snatching an apple, she rolled it around in her hand, examining the sensuous redness. Then she set it back down beside a banana and an orange.

"I'm going to lose my mind in here," Perrie said to herself.

Plopping down on the bed, she wrapped herself in a scratchy wool blanket and pulled her feet up. *Surprise, surprise—I have on a different dress.* Although, considering the rips and holes along the skirt, it wasn't much of a dress anymore. *How perfect. Here I am, all alone in a tower, warming myself up with an old blanket in rags fit for a rat.*

Everything hit her—*all* of it. Tears pricked at her eyes before raining down her cheeks, a storm all its own. Her checklist was back to zero—no Maisie, no August, and no Neven. Perrie lay back on the bed, helpless. She couldn't save Maisie, Officer Rodriguez, or Josselyn, and she couldn't save herself. Everyone trapped here would continue to suffer, and she felt responsible.

Perrie wondered if August had landed outside the tower, and if so, where? What about Maisie? Was she still out in the forest, running for her life, or was she back in the cottage fighting for her sanity? Were Josselyn, Officer Rodriguez, and Ben still battling their obstacles, or did these things only happen if someone else was in the display? Would she ever find Neven? There were so many displays at the museum—it would take forever to travel through all of them, and that was if she didn't die along the way. It was a never-ending nightmare they wouldn't wake up from—that *she* may not wake from.

"We're all they've got." August's words rang loudly in her ears. He was right.

Abandoning her pity party, a new determination filling her, Perrie returned to the window with her long hair in tow. The hair wasn't very heavy, but it was sturdy, strong. She leaned out and studied the bright greenery which hid the tower away. Rows and rows of trees swayed in the breeze under the shimmering sunshine. She'd always wanted to be surrounded by nature, but after this… *Hell no.*

"August!" Perrie shouted out the window. It might've been an ignorant move but there weren't many other options.

Nothing. Nothing except the flapping of blackbirds' wings around the trees.

Guess that means it's time for Plan B. There had to be another way out of there. With all this hair, she wondered if there was a way she could actually use it to climb down. She stared at the ceiling, around the walls, but there was no real place to put her hair. Maybe she could tie it to the bed, like in the movies when they'd used a sheet. Only, once she was on the ground, how would she cut her hair off?

There had to be another way… But her other options weren't looking too good at the moment.

Her stomach grumbled. Despite everything, she had to feed the little monster before trying to venture into the unknown forest in this display.

Perrie snatched an apple from the bowl of fruit, biting into the round suppleness. The sweet, juicy flavor almost made her moan. *Who knew an apple could taste this good?*

"Screw it," she finally said, deciding to drag the bed to the window.

Before she could execute her plan, a commotion sounded from outside. Perrie rushed to the window, nearly tripping over her hair again.

"Perrie! Perrie, are you up there?" At the sound of August's distressed voice, she could jump right out the window.

"August, I'm here! I'm in the tower," she shouted back.

From the shadows of the trees, August stumbled forward in a full-out sprint. Perrie grabbed for her hair and fished it down like a rope, just as Rapunzel had in her story. He bounded toward the side of the tower, faster than he broke through the tree line.

But, he wasn't alone.

TWENTY-FIVE

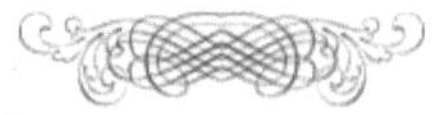

The blackbirds that were seated on the tops of the trees now formed a frenzy. As they dove at August from all angles, their sounds made a thunderous roar, reminding her of the classic movie *The Birds*. He did his best to fend them off, but they pecked and shrieked frantically.

Someone stood at the edge of the forest shrouded in darkness and hidden behind a black hooded cloak. With their lifted hand moving, it looked like he or she was controlling the birds' madness.

August wildly gazed about, seeming unsure of what to do with Perrie's hair dangling in front of him.

"Climb!" she yelled desperately.

As soon as his hands touched her hair, the birds darted back to the forest. The cloaked figure remained, watching them from where they stood. At least, she thought the person, or *creature*, was watching them. She couldn't make out a face from this high up.

"What do you mean, climb your hair? How will that possibly work?" He hesitated, giving her hair a few tugs. Perrie's head moved like a bobble head toy.

"Well, it's not going to fucking work with you pulling on

it like that. Just hurry and climb up before they come back.”

Perrie braced herself against the wall, praying with everything in her that August wouldn’t drag her out the window. She didn’t intend to find out what it was like to smack onto the dirt below.

“Are you ready?” he asked.

“Yes. Please don’t slip and fall!”

A light pressure pulled at her head, but it was nowhere near what she’d been expecting. If she tried this at home, she was sure most of her hair would’ve been ripped out. She couldn’t even tell he was climbing it—she only knew it was working by the sound of his boots scraping against the stone structure.

“You know, I wasn’t even thinking about that until you said it. So, thanks for putting that image in my mind,” he grunted.

“You’re welcome.” Perrie didn’t dare move her head to look down the tower. The only place she was able to stare was to the side, toward the forest, where the blackbirds again rested peacefully in the treetops. Their squawks had quieted, and the cloaked figure was gone.

Perrie’s heart wouldn’t stop its desperate beating. “How far up are you? I’m getting nervous.”

“*You’re* getting nervous? I’m about halfway.”

An eternity seemed to pass before August’s hand clasped the edge of the window, then his other one. The top of his head slid into view, and she grabbed his arms, helping him lift his body up onto the ledge.

He fell softly to the floor with a light, “Oof.”

“Please, no more of this fucking insanity.” He lay his whole body flat against the ground, and brought his hands to his chest, breathing deeply. He turned to face the window and shouted, “I’m serious!”

Perrie hauled her hair back up swiftly. All the while, her heart was still beating beat by frantic beat. After all her hair had been recovered, she collapsed beside August. She grabbed his arm and closed her eyes, practically meditating.

"What's wrong? Did I hurt you?" August studied her.

"No, no!" Perrie tried to catch her breath. "I didn't even feel anything. I'm just overwhelmed."

"What's with all the hair? I know Rapunzel supposedly had a lot of hair, but this is extreme." He lifted a lock of it in his hand, twisting it and pulling the strands apart. His surprise made her want to laugh.

Perrie stopped herself when she noticed specks of blood on his neck and cheek. She sat up and scanned his whole body, shocked by the number of holes in his shirt and pants.

"You're hurt!" Perrie wiped away a trickle of blood on his cheek. The cut on the side of his neck was bleeding, too.

"I'm okay, doll face. It barely stings. It looked worse out there than it really was." He pulled himself up slowly, moving her hand away from his neck and holding it in his lap.

"Really? You sounded pretty terrified." She examined other parts of his clothing—several holes were in his shirtsleeve where the birds had nicked his arm. There were other holes in the shirt from where they'd pecked, but thankfully hadn't drawn blood.

"I was mostly terrified because I didn't know where you were." His legs had a few shallow nicks, but his pants and tunic were made of a thicker material. It seemed to have protected him for the most part. The worst spots were his cheek and neck, but even then, he was lucky the birds didn't do more damage than they had.

Perrie walked to the table where the fruit was and poured a little of the water from the pitcher into the cup. Then she grabbed a pillow from the bed and removed the pillowcase, taking both to August. He was leaning his back against the wall of the tower, watching her.

"What are you doing?" he asked.

"What does it look like I'm doing? I'm not going to let you sit here with blood all over your face and neck."

Dabbing the water with the corner of the pillowcase, she raised it to his cheek and pressed it against his cuts. He sucked in a breath when she wiped away the drying blood. The cuts actually weren't that bad once the blood was removed.

The next spot Perrie drifted to was his neck, swiping away the small streak of blood streaming down to the collar of his tunic. She stared at the exposed skin a little longer than she should've, her stomach fluttering. August seemed to be watching her with the same burning intensity.

"So, what happened when you got here?" she asked, averting her eyes and instead busying herself with his arm. Rolling up his sleeve, she wiped an area on his arm that clearly didn't need cleaning.

"The portal spit me out into a tiny house somewhere in the middle of the forest. I waited around to see if you were going to show up. When you didn't, I went searching for you." He readjusted himself against the wall.

Perrie moved to his legs next, spying the hilt of a sword tucked beneath his thigh. "Looks like you got lucky. You've got a sword and all I've got is long hair for a weapon."

"Luckily I did have it," he said. "I just forgot to use the damn thing."

"What happened?" She set the cup of water and the pillowcase down beside her.

"I couldn't find you, so I went back to where I'd started. Next thing I knew I was surrounded by birds." He rubbed his neck and cheek absently. "They were everywhere. Seriously *everywhere*. Sitting in the tops of trees, sprawled across the branches, trickled over the ground, and resting on the rooftop of the house. As I walked through the forest, the birds didn't budge. You know how normally when you walk too close they'll fly off?"

Perrie nodded.

"Well, not these birds." Hiking his thumb up, he pointed it back toward the oval window.

"What about your cloaked stalker? Did you see who it was?" Perrie knew there was a witch in the story. She'd kidnapped Rapunzel and raised her like her own. But if it wasn't the witch, she wondered if the cloaked figure was another missing person.

"I couldn't see anything underneath the hood. It was . . . just darkness." August folded his hands beneath his chin and rested his elbows on his knees. His blond hair slid forward, delicately caressing his eyebrows.

She reached up and brushed it aside. "How did you find me?"

"We are in these rectangle boxes," he said, and she rolled her eyes. "I wandered around until I saw a tower poking up from the tops of the trees, practically calling for me to come. The second I saw it, I knew that's where you were." He paused. "Then there was a loud crackling behind me, and when I turned, the cloaked figure was there."

"That's it?" she pressed.

"Well, no. That isn't it. I stood there like an idiot, and she lifted her willowy hand with long pointed fingernails—it was definitely a woman's hand. Then she snapped her fingers a few times and the birds went from cool to fucking crazy. I mean, their heads all turned at the same time as if her snapping made them obey her."

Perrie smacked the ground with both of her hands. "And you didn't run away?"

"Fuck yes I did! She pretty much had me cornered. I didn't want to agitate the birds, so I didn't run away at first. Big mistake. She snapped again, and all those birds turned to look at me. Slowly too. Perrie, it was the craziest thing I've seen." He took a deep breath. "And then I took off running like there was no tomorrow. I heard one more snap and those blackbirds collapsed into sheer pandemonium. That's when I started calling for you."

"First, I think you should be a storyteller." Goosebumps

covered her arms. "Second, that creeped the shit out of me."

He whistled lowly. "You and me both, doll face. You and me both."

"Now what do we do?" she asked after a long silence.

"I think we should stay here for the night." August took her hands and warmed them in his lap. "Now, the real question is, what are we going to do with this hair?"

He left her hands and lifted a knotted mess of gold from the floor.

She couldn't help but laugh and agree. "I would've cut it off earlier, but there's absolutely nothing of use here, least of all scissors."

"Do you want me to?" August stroked the sword resting against his hip.

"Yes, please!" If Maisie were here, she would've been blowing into one of those little party horns.

August chuckled and raised his sword, shearing away the golden locks right at her shoulders. When he was finished, an uneven mess fell around her face, but it was so much lighter and freer.

"When we decide to leave," August started, "we'll just tie the hair to something and travel down."

TWENTY-SIX

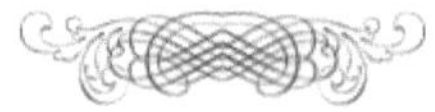

Perrie and August placed the hair in a neat pile in the corner of the room, making sure it stayed untangled so it would be easier to shimmy down. He'd agreed to her original plan, that the only thing stable enough to anchor their weight would be the bed. More than anything, she was relieved her head wouldn't have to be attached to the hair when they shuffled down it.

"Are you hungry? There's fruit in here. No poison apples, thankfully. I would know—*I tried one.*"

August arched a brow, a question dancing in his eyes.

Perrie shrugged. "Sorry, you can't be the only risk-taker to do the job first. Remember the berries?"

He grinned while lazily plucking up a banana. "Fine, I'll give you that."

They sat beside each other, comfortable in their silence as he finished his last bite. Perrie leaned into his shoulder, inhaling the scent of pine and soap. If they weren't in the middle of nowhere, inside a magical glass display, this would be romantic. Yet, it still felt it was…

"So, how are you doing? I mean, *really* doing." August's green irises settled on her. Perrie knew he was asking about

Maisie.

"I don't really know." But she did. The horrible twist of guilt took up space in her chest, an ache there that wouldn't go away until Maisie was safe.

"If anyone can be 'all right' here, it's her. She's tougher than nails." He wasn't wrong. If anyone were able to survive this place, Maisie could.

"What if Neven is like Maisie?" A brutal image sliding in her mind of an axe slicing off his head, the way the Huntsman's had done to Maisie. There would be no more crying. Now, it was about *surviving*.

"I thought about that, too. I for one want to assume he isn't. I mean, he could kick my ass in a fight any day."

"He is tall." She smiled. If she and August were still here alive, then Nev might have found a way to do the same thing.

August changed the subject, and she was grateful for the distraction. Between getting home and the possibility of rabid birds pecking away at her eyes and flesh, his rambling on about nonsense was a relief.

"What's the first thing you want to do when we get home?" Perrie asked.

August slipped off his boots and placed them under the side table. "Eat a whole cake."

"A cake?" She laughed. "After we save everyone from this place?"

He tugged a lock of her newly-cut hair. "Yep. If we're still alive after that, you and me"—he pointed between the two of them—"we're going to have a slumber party and sleep for days. Of course clothing is an option."

Grinning, she tugged one of his curls back. "Slumber party, huh?"

"That's what I said, doll face."

"Then we have to load up on cake first. A big cake, with a lot of frosting. Frosting is my jam." If only Perrie could dive into a swimming pool of cream cheese icing right then, she would be happy for a little while.

"I wish you wouldn't have said that." He chuckled. "I'm going to have frosting on my mind until I can get my hands on some."

"Okay, only about this much frosting then." Perrie held out her hands in front of her about a ruler length apart.

"No, no, that won't do." He grabbed both her wrists and spread her arms all the way open. She couldn't hold her position and toppled backward, bringing August along with her.

All of him pressed against her. Their faces were practically touching, and they stayed perfectly still. Perrie's eyes fell to his mouth, just as his did to hers.

"Maybe you should get some sleep," she suggested with no backing behind her words.

"What if I don't want to sleep?" He propped himself up on his forearms, caging her in.

With August, things had always been easy, even when she was a mess. Besides Maisie, he'd been her best friend, even when she didn't think she had room for anyone else. After what had happened with Neven, she refused to see August as anything but a friend. Following their night out at the prom, though, she started having glimpses of endless possibilities.

Perrie was so incredibly weak with this. If something were to happen and destroy her friendship with him, the way it had with Neven, she didn't know what she would do. She hadn't worn her heart on her sleeve in a long time. She'd wanted to focus on the future, on where her life led, and then maybe she could have the extras.

Her mom was someone who always depended on men—she never worked one single day of her life. Her dad worked hard to support her mom, and in the end, he and Perrie weren't enough for her—they never were, and they never could be.

Love wasn't money or material things. She wasn't sure if her mom ever truly loved either one of them. *I mean, how could she*? If she left Perrie's dad for another man with more money, and he made her dreams come true, couldn't Perrie still be part of that dream? Instead, she left both of them behind and never looked back.

Perrie couldn't do that. There was no way she would end up like her, a parasite that fed off the people who loved her most. She would go to college and find a good job where she could support herself. Then she wondered, *Is there room for someone else*? Could she be in a relationship with someone and still be better than her mom?

"What if I don't either?" she finally said, her voice husky.

"Yeah?" August pressed his forehead against hers.

"Yeah," Perrie whispered back, answering more than just his question. She knew she could be better than her mom.

He was here, wasn't he? He'd even engraved it on a necklace, the same one that the Glass Vault had stolen away. But she didn't need the possession to know how he felt, how *she* felt. August already had a hold on her heart in its entirety, and right now, she didn't think she could ever take it back from him.

"So, you remember the night we kissed, when you pulled me into your lap?" she asked, any nerves she had dissipating. A golden hue shone in his green eyes from where the sunlight struck them through the window.

"How could I forget?"

His mouth was mere centimeters from hers when she said, "I want to continue where we left off."

"What's stopping you, then?" August was close, but she wanted him closer.

"Nothing." Perrie broke out from his "cage" and flipped him to his back. It felt like a true moment of strength when she positioned her legs around his waist and straddled him, like she had the other night.

In this light, August was ethereal. Perrie remembered where they were, and if they were in any other display at the moment, it would be the Rumpelstiltskin one. August's blond hair was like pure gold, and it reminded her of the straw the maiden in that particular story had spun to gold. This wasn't the time or place to be thinking something strange like that, although it kind of was.

As August leaned forward to sit up and draw her closer, Perrie pushed the story away and ran her hands up the back of his neck and into his hair—the curled tips brushing against her fingers, soft as feathers. His breathing quickened at her touch and her confidence grew bolder. She pressed her lips gently against his, tracing his bottom lip with her tongue, tasting the saltiness of his skin. It was cruel to tease them both like this, but she wanted to savor the moment.

August gripped her thighs, deepening the kiss. A volcano erupted inside Perrie's chest and hot lava flowed and spread until her entire body was cocooned in the warmth. Everything felt right, and it was as if the world suddenly made sense. August made sense.

She pushed lightly against his chest, their kiss growing fiercer with the need to be closer. Her heart pounded, the rush of blood racing against her body's adrenaline.

Perrie didn't know if they were going to make it out of Quinsey Wolfe's Glass Vault, and even if they did make it out alive, then what? They would move on to another display, and then another, and another after that?

If something happened to one of them, if they lost each other along the way, then she didn't want to have any regrets. She wasn't going to waste time today, tomorrow, or any other day she had with him.

"August, I love you," Perrie murmured the words against his mouth.

His lips curved into a smile against her kiss, and that was all the answer she needed.

She fumbled with the strings at his chest, loosening the tunic, then hauled it over his head and dropped it onto the floor. He went to help her take off her dress next, but it stuck a few times as he tried. They both laughed and tempted fate once again, letting the fabric pool to the floor.

He then flipped her over, and she unbuttoned his pants, sliding them off and throwing those on the floor, too.

Perrie reached down and grasped his hardened length, loving the feel of it in her hand, and how it would fit perfectly inside her. While she stroked, his chin dropped to his chest, a deep groan escaping his perfect mouth.

When she released him, his weight pressed back down on her as he trailed kisses from her shoulder, up the length of her neck and along her jaw. Then his mouth molded to hers, and he ran his tongue across the seam of her lips before parting them. They kissed again and again, their tongues growing more and more demanding, until there were no other thoughts.

"Are you sure about this? We can slow down," he rasped.

"I'm sure. Are *you*?" She laughed.

"Perrie, I've been sure about you since the day you pressed your cello bow to my chest."

"Really?" She laughed again. "That didn't run you a hundred miles in the opposite direction?"

"No. It left me *intrigued*."

Perrie hadn't felt that way since then, though. He had waited for her to meet him halfway for a while now, and she was finally there.

Their remaining clothing was tossed to the floor, and his skin was against hers, deliciously warm, hard and soft all at once. August's lips tasted like nectar, and she never wanted to stop kissing them, but then he was leaving a path of sparks from her neck to her breasts. Perrie's knees melted as he took a hardened nipple in between his lips, sucking, and turning her bones to rubber. And she couldn't breathe as his hands took over, leaving those heavenly lips free to travel lower, lower, until they were between her thighs, licking, caressing. She moaned, throwing her head back, helpless. Useless. In bliss.

He slid back up to her, kissing her lips once more, his tongue dancing with hers as his hips rocked harder between her thighs.

He pulled back and hovered above her for a moment, taking it all in, their closeness and her. Finally, August pressed inside her with one swift stroke, filling her with everything he had, and it all made sense, even in this nonsensical world because together they could do anything. It was possible perfection did exist.

Performing a gentle rhythm at first, he moved inside her. Perrie dragged his face back to hers, gripping his hair and kissing him, then kissing him fiercer. He seemed to know exactly what to do as he took charge. With each thrust, each touch, she wanted to devour the moment. This was more than she could've ever imagined as emotions roared through her, and her entire body quaked when he tore her world apart.

"Perrie," he shouted, her name echoing off the walls, his slick body collapsing on hers. She wrapped her arms around him, holding him tight, her chest heaving. No words. No words at all.

They were legs and arms braided together for several long moments before he rolled off her. Perrie curled into his side, and shut her eyes, easily falling asleep in his embrace.

She dreamed a dream with no twists, turns, or running for her life.

It started with a normal morning at the breakfast table. Her dad had already left for work and the remnants of her cereal swam in warm milk.

Maisie came to the door in one of her newly-designed eye patches. A giant peach—with the words, *Everything is peachy* sewn across the fabric. Her cousin was excited about starting a new job at a resale-clothing store. She rambled on about her half-price discount and all the possibilities the clothing would supply for materials toward her designs.

Maisie drove them to school, as usual. It was such a

beautiful day. At school they spotted Neven and he waved, joining them and talking about how he'd gotten a basketball scholarship. She and Maisie both congratulated him, and her cousin gave him a high five. August strolled through the doors, his presence causing Perrie's stomach to swarm with butterflies. Neven patted him on the back like they were the best of friends.

August wrapped Perrie up in his arms, dipped her back just like in the old films, and kissed her long and slow. She should've been embarrassed about kissing him in front of everyone, but she wasn't. He brought her back up, and Maisie and Neven were smiling.

"You two need to get a room." Neven laughed. Maisie just stood there, shaking her head.

Perrie left their faces behind, as she slowly woke to the feeling of warmth pressed against her skin. She was definitely not dreaming anymore. *What a strange dream.* To think she and Neven could be friends like that again someday felt right.

Draping her arm across August's stomach, she rolled her head to the side and smiled at him.

"I was wondering if you would ever wake up." He grinned at her, the smile reaching all the way to his eyes.

She pecked his cheek and snuggled against his shoulder. "I was having such a good dream."

"Oh? Were you dreaming about me?"

Perrie arched a brow. "What do you think?"

"I hope so, because it will be the last good dream you'll have for a while."

She didn't have time to think about what he'd said. August swiftly flipped her onto her back and hovered above her, the look on his face devious. His head dropped to the side of hers, swaying lazily, as his mouth tickled her ear.

"Thanks for the fuck."

TWENTY-SEVEN

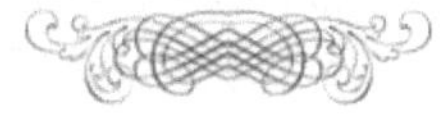

Perrie's body stilled. Everything within her did. *What the fuck did he just say?*

"August?" Her mouth hung partially open, and her breathing increased.

"I have to admit. Out of everyone I have ever pleasured, you are at the top." His face was mere inches from hers.

"What are you talking about?" she whispered. Her body had grown cold.

"I mean, there is one other female who comes close, but not quite. I cannot recall her true name," he said, tapping the side of his head, "but I do remember the red hair. About six months ago . . . at Neven's."

He knocked the wind right out of her. Perrie's mind was spinning, and so was the room. What was he talking about? She'd seen *Neven* having sex with that woman, clear as day.

"That's right. You thought it was Neven, didn't you?" The sides of his lips tugged down, and he moved a lock of hair from her forehead. "Oops."

"August, what's going on?" She jerked forward, but he already had her pinned by the shoulders.

"August," he said the name like it wasn't his own. "That is

227

the name I am going by at the moment."

Perrie's brows lowered and she couldn't release any words. August, or *not* August, cocked his head and stared at her with a form of humor she didn't understand. He observed her like she was a child, a stupid, foolish child who didn't know the simplest answer.

If that wasn't Neven and it really was August, then she was a fucking idiot. Whoever the hell he was, whatever he claimed to have done, she just had sex with him. Perrie tried to force herself up, but his hold was too strong.

"I will let you in on a little secret. My name isn't August. I am whomever I choose to be, whenever and wherever I want. You have known me as August. Others have known less. I am a name without a face, but you, Perrie, I'll tell you my real name." His voice was almost a laugh. "My real name is Vale."

August wasn't actually August? He preyed on her, screwed his way into her heart, tightening the bolt as hard as he could with a screwdriver. She wanted to scream, to kick and flail, and beat his face.

"Get off of me." She wanted to scream, but it came out as a whisper.

"Does it bother you? I have toyed with you, Perrie, for months and months." He lifted a hand toward the ceiling, as if he was proud of this precious tower. A wicked smile spread across his face. "All this time, only to get you inside the walls of my palace."

What? Nausea churned in her stomach and she thought she was going to be sick.

"That's right. This is all mine. Every display, every person you have encountered, they are all part of a very big plan." Vale stood, and though Perrie was free, she couldn't scrounge up the strength to move. "Inside this place they cannot wither away. They are immortal now. I brought them here, to live inside the displays, where they will become the perfect creatures for destruction."

"How?" Perrie asked, her voice weak.

"How? I *chose* who I wanted to see my vault. It is all part of a grand plan that I have concocted to take humanity, and *you*, my darling Perrie, are going to help me lead it."

Perrie took a deep swallow. She had to get away from this bastard.

Before she had a chance to run, he snatched her by the hair and yanked her off the bed. Her scalp burned and she cried out in agony. Each and every single one of the tiny hair follicles was on fire, thumping in sync with the beat of her heart. Perrie screeched as loudly as she could, and the sound of her own scream was even worse than the squeal of squeaky brakes.

"We need to hurry so we are not late to meet your friend," Vale sang as he dragged her across the floor. Then he stopped. "Before I forget. Do you remember the redhead from Neven's room? I recall you mentioning something about recognizing her hair anywhere. Did you?"

Perrie thought back. How had she not noticed it before? She had stood right in front of Perrie in a display.

"Fannie," she whispered.

"That's right. That's right. That is the name she uses now, yet that is not her true name. I never cared to ask. If I need her, I let her come out and play. A small reward for being trapped below with me, after all." Perrie struggled to break from his hold, but his grip only tightened. "Like I said, nowhere near as good as you, though."

Again, with a hard yank, Vale dragged her behind him, making the pain sharper than it was before. He hummed to himself, to her, to both of them, or maybe to no one.

What have I done? I trusted this monster.

Cement scratched at her bare back as she was pulled along. She didn't care about the throbbing of her back, though, she needed him to let go of her fucking hair. *Now.*

The tower became a distant memory as Vale somehow walked through the wall on the opposite end. They passed down a darkened, narrow hallway. She screamed the entire way, right up until he tossed her onto another cement floor like a sack of trash. The pain at her scalp lessened only a fraction, but she could breathe again. Before she could push herself up, something clicked into place—Vale had locked her in a cage.

"I will give you two a few minutes," he purred, before sauntering away.

Give you two a few minutes? Perrie's hands shook, half afraid to see what he was talking about, but she needed to know.

In the corner behind her, someone was sitting against the bars with his head hanging down, pushed as far from the cage door as possible. She knew that shaggy black hair.

"Neven?" *Shit.* Tears flowed from her eyes, and she ran over to him, lifting his face. An iron ring circled his neck, like a collar, with no visible way to remove it. A short chain connected it to a bar that held him back, so he couldn't even curl up on the floor if he wanted to instead.

"Perrie? Am I dreaming or are you really here?" He blinked, his words coming out in a slur.

"I'm here," Perrie sobbed.

"Where are your clothes?" he groaned.

Of course, that's the first thing he asked. She was so relieved about him being alive that she laughed while wrapping her arms around herself as best she could.

"Don't worry about it—not right now," Perrie insisted. "What happened to you?"

Nev looked the same, but not. Scarred lines ran along his arms, neck, and face, as if he'd been torn apart and stitched back together. She inhaled sharply as she *remembered* a particular exhibit.

He was Frankenstein's Monster, the one she'd seen in the museum.

"After I left your house, I wanted to go to the museum again since you had seen it, too. August was there when I pulled up. I thought he was there for the same reason as me." Nev rested his arms on his knees, leaning the back of his head on the metal bars. "We went inside, wandered through the halls and wound up in the display room. Everything was literally made of glass—strange shit. After that, it's kind of been a blur. Somehow I ended up in the Frankenstein's Monster display."

"You don't remember anything after that?" Perrie covered her mouth and shook her head, wanting to rip the chain off the cell to free him.

"Oh, I do. You know that August isn't *August*, right?" Nev said softly.

"Yeah, I know. Go on, I'll be fine."

"He strapped me down to a table, saying he was really Vale and some weird shit about needing immortal souls to become stronger. He went on like that for a while, cutting into me with all these fucked up tools as he *chatted*. I passed out during the process and wound up in this cell. Been chained here ever since."

Perrie hunched forward, tears raining down her cheeks. It was so stupid, but she'd just been so happy, and now, it was a true hellish nightmare. Neven was just like Maisie, like the others.

"This is insane," Perrie said. "He also told me his name is Vale, he said he tricked me, that he was the one with the redhead. He wore your face, Neven." She covered her own face, humiliated. "I don't know how that's even possible."

"I told you, I can make myself into anyone at any time, anywhere." Vale's voice reverberated around the room. She looked back at the door where Vale now hovered.

He wore black slacks and a white long-sleeve shirt that buttoned at the ends. The neck was a collarless V-neck with ruffles that Perrie wanted to rip off and use to strangle him.

With repeated motions, he ran a silver nail file across his fingernails as he examined her. "I have been hidden away for too long, and it is my time to rise and take over. We will bring destruction to everyone. I made this place and filled it one by one with my creations to help carry out my deeds. They may look like glass on the outside now, but after this, they won't anymore. You are to be my last."

"I don't understand," she shouted. "Why me? Why go through all of this? You could have tossed me into one of the displays like everyone else. Why make me—" She couldn't even say the damn words. *Why make me fall in love with you?*

"Why? *Why*? I would not have noticed you at first, Perrie. When you approached me as if you were a queen with that bow in your hand, I felt the light in you, that electrifying energy with a subtle potential for darkness. The minute you walked out of that room with Neven at your side, I knew I wanted you. It didn't matter how long it took for you to give yourself to me, because I could wait. Now that I have you, the time is right." Vale tucked the silver file away into his pocket.

"What the hell is this asshole talking about, Perrie?" Nev sounded drained but fury was there too. She was too ashamed to answer.

"That's right, Neven. As you were sitting here chained to the cell, I had her in ways you can't even begin to imagine."

Nev gripped the bars, pushing hard against them to free himself in his anger. The ring around his throat prevented him from going anywhere, and his face was flushed so red that he might pass out.

"Leave her alone," he roared.

Perrie couldn't even look at Neven's face anymore. Her self-loathing had already taken root—that must've been what Vale had wanted.

Vale unlocked the cage and moved at an inhuman speed, yanking her up by her hair once more.

"What are you?" Perrie seethed.

"To you? A demon, a monster, your worst nightmare. As I told you before, I can be anything."

Perrie could only see half of Vale's face and the gray ceiling above her. With her neck straining at this angle, she couldn't even spit at his face—that perfect skin she desperately wanted to claw off.

"Your soul is mine." Vale stroked her cheek. Then with his inhuman speed, he brushed something sharp against her throat and sliced across.

Pain. Searing pain.

It all happened so fast.

Her hands flew up to her throbbing neck, instantly covered in a warm, sticky liquid—her own blood. Neven's frantic yelling echoed.

She couldn't make the bleeding stop. She couldn't sew the wound shut. There was too much blood. Her body grew weaker with each passing second as a numbness settled. No part of her life flashed before her eyes like she'd heard it did when one dies. Only the desperate urge to live lingered.

Perrie's hands fell limply to her sides, and no other part of her could move. Not even to blink. She waited for all of it to go away, to let the darkness take her.

Vale must've been dragging her. If he was doing it by her hair again, she couldn't feel it. All she could see was the ceiling and part of Vale's black pants. She could hear every detailed sound, like the tapping of his shoes on the hard floor. It was as if the universe wanted her to sit inside of this body longer just to watch her suffer.

"You know, Maisie was right about one thing." Vale lifted her body and set it back down on something solid, then his face hovered over hers. "When you die here, you stay here. She is smart but not smart enough to piece it all together. You do die here and stay here, but only until I am ready to release you. You, my darling, are going to transcend your humanity. When I am done, all that hate in you will continue to grow and gather and lead to true carnage. You will be like the others, like Maisie and Neven. When I bring you back to life, the old

Perrie will be gone. You will be made new. And my Bride will rise."

He brushed his lips against hers. Perrie didn't feel a thing, or she would've bitten his lip clean off. Finally, Vale closed her eyes, and the escape into darkness she'd been waiting for took her.

Epilogue

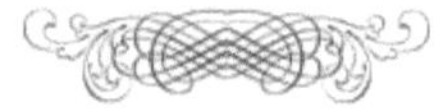

Vale stared down at the Bride, admiring his new creation in all of her glory. She truly was the most exquisite creation he had altered.

Perrie had told Vale she loved him. He didn't know what love was. He still didn't, but she was his. All he had known was satisfaction and ruination.

His heart was darker than midnight, and he liked it that way. The wound at her throat was stitched, the skin healed over, a clean cut with a clean mend. Greater care had been taken to preserve his Bride, as she was the culmination of all his efforts. Like all the mortals inside the Glass Vault, she was no longer human—they were fiends, prepared to feed upon the earth. Their thoughts now matched his.

Vale reached for a lever and fed his Bride the electricity she needed, until the sparks crackled and ceased.

Her eyes burst open with a wickedness that had him giddy with glee.

One by one, sculptures once made of glass, all rose from their cold displays. They were like the living dead thawing out of hibernation, digging through the dirt to reach their destination.

Vale opened the door to Quinsey Wolfe's Glass Vault. The Bride was the first to exit, and they all followed her into the night at the witching hour. The palms of her hands popped and cracked with electricity.

She was ready to strike.

End of Book One

BOOK TWO

BRIDE
OF
GLASS

For Mom
Thanks for showing me the way

PROLOGUE

After the Awakening - The Bride

The electrical current beaded and trickled from the Bride's hands, rolling down her fingertips like whips. They popped with each thrust. One after another, she hurled a long charge toward the civilians in her path. She did it without a thought, without remorse or guilt for what she had done. *And why should I?* The mortals became glass the instant her power touched their frail skin.

Bride watched as their souls abandoned their glass bodies. For every final breath that left their lungs, she felt fulfilled—her appetite sated.

The knocking inside her head had quieted. At first, it was incessant, pounding like a drum as though something was begging to be awakened. She couldn't make it go away, so she drowned it out.

The more Bride crushed, the quieter it became—she needed to destroy. She *wanted* to destroy. Nothing else mattered, not even the others who had followed her out from behind the doors of the Glass Vault.

Nothing.

Except, *him*. He was right beside her—the one she was endlessly drawn to. Together they could be anything—together they could create true havoc. The moment Bride opened her eyes, she had wanted his heart to be hers. His heart sat in his chest without any real force, but it was *hers*. It would always be hers.

Vale.

That was his name. His *true* name. Yet, something continuously beat at the back of her mind, wanting her to remember there was more than that—there was more to him.

"Again!" Vale yelled, his eyes hard and focused.

A white flash of light, her light, struck an entire row of brick homes, bathing them in momentary daylight. The blow was powerful enough to freeze every living soul within the houses' walls. She could feel her electricity snaking its way through each mortal's veins, their every cell heating like desert sand, until their bodies became glass, petrified in their last moments of fear, their souls drawn away to the Glass Vault. Trapped forever.

Bride looked back at Vale. His blond hair stood on end, a lovely mess of curls, from her electricity. He was wickedly beautiful, like a lonely bright star illuminating the night sky, searching for its partner. The friction of her power receded back into her bones until there wasn't a single spark flickering. A wrongness stirred within her. He noticed the shift and his green eyes found her.

Beyond his penetrating emerald gaze, a nightmare was lurking. A nightmare Bride wanted to be a part of. Stalking toward her, he backed her up against a tree. The bark dug into her flesh, and she savored the sting. No matter what happened to her, she couldn't die. Vale treated her differently than the others—she was his Bride.

"Can you keep going?" he asked softly, his lips dangerously close to capturing hers.

She couldn't tell him no. She didn't want to tell him no.

She would *never* tell him no.

"Continue," he pleaded as his head nestled in the crook of her neck.

The knocking in her skull had ceased. Bride lifted Vale's head from her shoulder and gazed one more time into his emerald eyes, a devious smile spreading across her lips. That was the only answer he needed, the only one he would ever need with her. Then his mouth claimed hers in a fierce and devilish kiss, their lips slanting over one another's, their tongues entwining, tasting, devouring. And she relished his kiss—she always did.

Vale's hands roamed over the curves of her body, cupping her backside when she pulled him closer. His hard length pressed against her, making her anticipation for what was to come rise even more. The electricity sparked again in Bride's veins as her power resurfaced.

For him, she would always continue.

ONE

The Awakening - The Bride

Her eyelids flew open, no longer consumed by darkness. She looked around wildly as her vision cleared, and a pair of emerald irises met hers. A young man with golden hair leaned over her, his face mere inches from hers. His bright, dancing gaze tamed her in place. She couldn't remove her eyes from those two beautiful specks of green light. He smiled down at her with a hint of allure, danger.

She *liked* it.

"Welcome to the new world, Bride. I am Vale, and you are going to be the most magnificent creature the world has ever seen."

Bride opened her mouth to speak, but a sharp pain in her chest halted her. An ache around her heart stirred, a craving for chaos and destruction. It sat in the deepest part of her soul, begging to be filled, yet she didn't move.

"Vale." The name, his name, rolled across her tongue like wildfire. She treasured it.

"Are you ready?" The ache in her chest rose with his

question. She knew what he was asking her.

Vale pulled her up to a sitting position. Bride's legs, ready to move, dangled over the metal edge of a cool silver table. A white gown, like a waterfall made of silk, spilled down her body to her ankles. She didn't remember wearing this—then again, she couldn't remember how she had gotten here. With a growing curiosity, she held out her hands in front of her, and a spark popped from the tips of her fingers. A buzzing sensation pulsed through her entire body. Bride focused on it, concentrating on the electricity and gathering it into her palms.

As she thrust her hand forward, a bolt of electricity shot out from her palms, slamming against the wall, shattering like glitter. She smiled to herself with gratification when the bright light created a deafening pop.

"I am ready," Bride said, determination filling her with a will to do whatever he wanted.

Vale nodded and clapped his hands loudly in front of his chest. One minute she was seated on the table, and the next she stood on the floor with glass objects surrounding her. Glass machinery was positioned directly above her. She lowered her head and scanned the area until she found Vale in the middle of the room.

He wore a white shirt of the same material as her dress, ruffles positioned down the center of his chest. His face beamed with malice, and she wanted to be a part of whatever gave him that pleasure.

With inhuman speed, Vale moved to where she stood and held a hand out to her. "Lead us," he instructed.

Bride shook the stiffness from her arms and took hold of his hand. The warmth of his fingertips awakened something positively wicked inside of her. She couldn't help but feel enkindled by his attention and soft touch.

Lifting the skirt of her dress, Bride rigidly stepped down from her box with Vale's aid. Like her, other lovely creatures were leaving their own confinements.

Bride fixed her gaze on Vale as he led her to a hallway. Together, they walked, and they walked, and while they did, a slight sense of familiarity rushed through her, as though she had been down these halls before. Ornate wallpaper lined the walls, and crystal chandeliers hung from above.

Vale came to a stop as they reached the end of the hall, a door standing between them and what waited outside. He pointed to the golden handle and bowed low, waiting for her to make the first move. She pressed forward, throwing open the door in one swift movement, and stepped out into the darkness which called to her very heart. This was what she thirsted for.

With a glance over her shoulder, Bride stared at the others behind her, all of whom had followed her into the darkness. She scanned the crowd, her gaze stilling on a young woman wearing a blue patch over her left eye. A crazed smile was spread across the woman's face—she wanted the same thing as Bride. Something then tugged at Bride, telling her to go after the woman, to chase her down, or cry out for her. But then, unintentionally, a small crackle of light slipped from her palm, striking the ground at the woman's feet.

Bride refocused, the moment forgotten.

As she turned her head back around, Bride searched for Vale, finding him farther up ahead, his eyes narrowed at the other immortals. She caught up with him in a matter of moments, then he placed his hand against her lower back as he spoke to the others.

"This was your home." Vale flicked his hand back at the building. "Within the Glass Vault you have become immortal. Those who you use your power on will become glass, and their souls transported back here. We need as many as we can get for now, but I want them all. You will obey my rules or there will be many ways to be punished. We are going to take everyone. Follow her." He motioned at her. "The Bride will lead us on our path to elimination, and then we will separate to finish."

"I will help lead," a voice called from the crowd.

Furrowing her brow, Bride whirled around to a young woman walking toward them. Her thick red hair cascaded down her shoulders and her silky blue dress swished as she moved.

"Do not belittle me, Red," Vale growled. "You will have much to answer for if you dare speak out again."

She lifted her chin in defiance, slowly approaching Bride, the woman's brown irises boring into hers. "Do you remember me?"

Bride didn't answer.

The woman bared her teeth as she grinned. "My name is Fannie."

Bride studied the immortal, finding nothing familiar about her. The electricity crackled in her palms once more, and she drew up her hand to strike the woman in her pretty face.

Vale was faster, though. He grabbed the back of Fannie's neck and squeezed it. Fannie's grin twisted into a grimace, and Bride smiled.

"I'm warning you. If you oppose the Bride or me, I will end you in seconds. Do you understand?"

Fannie remained quiet, her face pale.

"I said, *do you understand*?" He shook her back and forth like a little doll. One that Bride would make broken.

"Yes, Master," Fannie grunted.

Vale tossed her to the side and she stumbled backward, catching herself before crashing to the ground. He turned his back on her again and faced Bride.

"Don't forget what your father would do if something happens to me," Fannie said, her lip curled into a snarl.

Vale flexed his beautiful hands and balled them into tight fists. He then jolted toward her, slapping Fannie across the face. A thunderous sound clapped as Fannie's head was thrown to the side. With a vicious smile, she slowly brought her face back to him but remained silent.

"Do not mention my father again," Vale ground out.

He settled his gaze back on Bride, and his furious expression turned to one of delectation. "Begin."

Without hesitation, Bride moved forward. She could feel the immortals' eyes on her back as she took her first steps onto a paved road full of sky-scraping trees. Into the night they followed, driven by the need to destroy. Destroy. *Destroy.*

When the first civilian came into Bride's view, she didn't hesitate. She lit up with white crackling light and hurled her first bolt of electricity at the young male. A rush of satisfaction stormed through her as his skin ignited and froze into glass. He didn't even have a chance to scream. His soul would now be at the Glass Vault for Vale to do with as he chose.

The world spun for a moment, a dazed feeling washing over her. But then her body relaxed, and she wanted to do *more*, to taste that darkness again.

After the first soul was claimed, the immortals trailing after her responded in a monstrous uproar. Fueled by their desire, and hers, for more, Bride led them down streets, cutting off electricity, phone lines, and lighting the world up with her power. The more civilians she turned to glass, no matter how thrilled she was, the more she needed to continue. She *ached* for it.

By morning, the civilians in town had become more aware of what was happening, and chaos ensued. They tried to pack their families into cars and flee, but they were too slow. Guns were fired, knives thrown, gasoline and matches attempted to strike, but nothing from humanity could stop an immortal.

After several days, the immortals separated in their own directions, leaving only Bride, Vale, and Fannie. Bride wanted

Fannie to leave—she yearned to have Vale to herself—but the woman remained.

"Can we rest?" Bride asked, her lids fluttering from lack of sleep. Unlike the slap he would have given to Fannie, Vale lifted her chin with a gentle touch.

"Try," he whispered, his emerald gaze locked onto hers. She knew he trusted her and believed in her strength.

Because Bride believed in him too, she held her palms up in front of her and willed the spark to life. A tiny flicker popped, then the light snuffed out.

"I can't." She furrowed her brow, growing frustrated with herself. But he only nodded, while Fannie clenched her jaw and gave her a dark look, dripping with hatred.

They trekked to the nearest house, a two-story with a wide porch and white-washed wooden balcony. Vale charged to the porch and kicked the door open, breaking the deadbolt. A heat flowed through her body at his raw strength and inhuman speed and went straight to her center. She wanted him then and there, flesh to flesh.

Screaming went off inside her, and she shook her head to clear it.

Setting the odd feeling aside, she followed Vale down a narrow hallway to a living room. She took a deep breath and inhaled jasmine and refocused once more. A spark of energy popped in her hands when she found an old couple huddled on the floor behind the couch, their bodies trembling, their eyes open wide in horror.

"Please leave us be," the old man begged.

He gripped his wife's wrinkled hand tightly. Beads of perspiration dotted his sun-spotted forehead. The man pulled his wife closer into his side to shield her as best he could. Bride wasn't the least bit moved by the gesture—she wanted to feel her power again and destroy.

She lifted her hands, willing enough energy to create a spark, then unleashed a bright bolt that illuminated the room.

It hit the woman first, and the man released a choking sob as he held his wife's glass body. Bride listened to his beautiful cries a moment longer before taking him next. A sense of fulfillment rushed over her as the couple cradled each other in their glass positions.

"I will be back shortly." Vale nodded his approval and left the room.

Bride sank into the cushions of an old floral couch while the statues of glass hovered behind. Fannie lingered in the room, watching Bride the entire time. The blue skirts of her dress swished as she approached and lowered herself beside Bride. She propped her elbow on the back of the couch and gazed at the side of Bride's face.

Bride chose to ignore her and examined the many-framed photos of loved ones hung across the wall. It was far more interesting than engaging in a staring war with the one immortal she wanted dead.

"You know," Fannie drawled, "you are only his marionette. Eventually, he will cut your strings and toss you aside. Then there will be a new one to take your place that he will latch the threads onto."

Her words burned, and for a moment, she wondered if he really would do that to her. Toss her aside for someone else? Vale called her his Bride—*the* Bride—and he wanted her to lead, not Fannie. She shoved the words away as if they meant nothing because Fannie was *nothing*.

"You wish," Bride said and continued to stare straight ahead without blinking.

In an instant, Fannie pressed a knife into Bride's throat. Her head pushed back against the couch as the blade bit into her flesh.

"You may be immortal, but that doesn't mean I can't have a little fun with you." She inched the blade closer to the scar at Bride's throat. "Maybe I'll just peel off your skin, bit by tiny bit. I'll begin with this soft little nose of yours. Maybe slice it off?"

Fannie grabbed Bride's nose with her free hand and squeezed, pinching it to the right. Anger brewed within her, creating a storm of wild fury. Bride's fingernails dug into the skirt of her silk dress to keep her power from unleashing.

"And what would Vale do if you delivered on your threat?" Bride asked.

Fannie threw her head back and laughed hysterically. "Vale? What is the worst he can do? Shove me back in my cage or send me back to the Underworld? His father would destroy him. He already has."

Bride frowned—her last words hadn't made sense. "What do you mean by that? How has his father destroyed him?"

Fannie released Bride's nose, but the cold steel remained pressed against her throat. "Tut-tut-tut. Enough talk for now." She pulled the knife away and slipped it back into her dress. "But maybe you're not so special after all, are you, *Bride*?"

Bride brushed her fingertips across her throat, and her nostrils flared. The blade might have been gone, but her anger demanded to be free. She balled her hand into a fist and threw a flash of electricity at Fannie's chest. The immortal flew off the couch and slammed against the sheetrock, her body knocking down a shelf of figurines from the wall. As she crashed to the floor, surrounded by shattered ceramic, Fannie cackled with laughter.

"Silly girl, you can't turn immortals into glass." She stood with her spine pulled taut, her hand rubbing at her chest. "Still, it hurts like fire to the skin."

"Good." Bride smiled, threatening her with another small current in her palm.

Fannie watched the energy in Bride's hand spark to life, seeming hesitant. "Believe what you want, but you truly are only temporary. Have fun with him while it lasts, *little puppet*." With a smirk as though nothing happened, Fannie swayed her hips and sat on the couch. If Bride could sew

Fannie's eyes and mouth shut, she would use the immortal's red hair as the thread.

The front door squeaked open as Vale returned.

"The street is clear for now. We will begin again in the morning after you have time to rest." His eyes and words were for Bride only. The fact he didn't acknowledge Fannie made her chest swell with pride.

"Where should we sleep?" Fannie asked, as though she would be the one riding Vale into bliss tonight.

"*You* can choose wherever you wish to sleep," Vale snapped at her. "Let us find somewhere upstairs." He held his open palm out to Bride, and she took his perfect hand, tightening her fingers around his warmth.

"But—" Fannie stopped short, halted by the hard, icy look in his stare. The immortal could pretend she wasn't afraid of him all she wanted, but she was. Fannie's gaze shifted to Bride, murderous.

"I am going to take a shower. Join me?" Vale's face softened as he asked Bride. His eyes mirrored the same emotion that danced in hers—he wanted her as much as she wanted him.

Bride's lips tilted upward and she grasped him through his pants, his hard length ready for her. "Yes."

A low groan escaped his throat as she gripped him harder before releasing him. With that final exchange, Bride led him up the stairs to create a storm of their own.

TWO

Before-Josselyn Shaw

Fuck this place, Josselyn thought as she toted a six-pack of beer from the rundown gas station in her shitty town. Tonight was different than any other night—she was going to drown her sorrows away, alone in her apartment.

Josselyn's "best friend" Emma had stood her up earlier, even though Emma had known how much Josselyn needed her. Josselyn's ex-boyfriend broke up with her the night before because he said they were *too different*. Yeah, but not too different to have sex with her before he'd told her that. *Fucking asshole.*

Screw him and screw Emma. She didn't need anyone except herself and the beautiful pack of beer hanging in her hand. The clinking of the bottles was practically chanting her name, so she pulled one out before climbing into the driver's seat.

The engine purred to life after she used her keychain to pop the lid on the beer. She knew she shouldn't be drinking, but she didn't give one single shit. Josselyn brought the tip to her mouth and took a swig, humming along with the car as the coolness slid down her throat and drifted to her stomach.

"Where to now, Josselyn?" she asked herself, peering out the window at the little bit of daylight that was left.

"Time to get this party started," she answered, revving the car and swerving violently from the parking lot.

Josselyn continued taking swigs from her beer as she turned left on Oak Street, almost finished with beer number one, when she slammed hard on the brakes. A building, a rather *big* building rising high from the shadows of tall trees, had caught her attention. The structure had never been anywhere on Oak Street before, and it was out of place in a town like hers.

She shouldn't be buzzing from her first beer already. At least, she didn't think she should be—drinking had never been her thing, until tonight. Reckless just so happened to be her new middle name.

Josselyn put the car in park and stepped out, bringing her almost full pack of beer with her. She cracked open another bottle and took a long drink as she approached the building.

It wasn't the aged stones around the base of the building or lack of windows that drew her focus, but rather the door. It was large enough for an elephant to fit through.

"Okay, that's an enormous door," Josselyn said. She nearly dropped her beer when it suddenly flew open, her heart pounding.

A young blond guy emerged from inside, halting when his green gaze settled on hers.

"Need something?" he asked as he pulled the door shut behind him.

"Um, no?" Josselyn furrowed her brow. "Well, maybe. Has this place always been here?"

Though she'd only taken this route a couple times, she had never noticed a building at any point. It was quite possible she couldn't remember or just hadn't paid much attention. *I would've remembered a building like this though, right*? There would've been people talking about something like this coming to Deer Park.

The guy's gaze stayed locked on hers, and a smile tugged at his lips. "Yeah, we recently cut the trees surrounding the building to make it noticeable for customers."

Josselyn's eyes darted back and forth between the guy and the stone of the building, curiosity blooming inside her. "What is it?"

"It's a museum with glass statues displayed in different artistic ways. We are currently closed, but you can check it out if you want." The blond guy pointed toward the door with a large grin spread across his face.

Maybe it was the beer, but Josselyn felt her curiosity grow into excitement at seeing something so unique. She definitely wanted to go inside and take a look. Running her hand through her short blonde hair, she said, "If it's okay with you, I will."

The guy opened the door for Josselyn, ushering her in with a wave of his hand. Butterflies danced in her stomach when she took her first steps forward. The idea of being alone inside a museum was both creepy and electrifying.

"Take your time," he purred after her as the door closed. Josselyn stared at the wood and golden knob, not knowing what to think.

"What a weirdo." Slowly, she turned around and peered down a long hallway. Clutching the bottles close to her side, she took another deep drink of the bottle in her other hand.

She walked down the long entrance, which led to another hall, which led to another before she froze. Displays were everywhere, aligned in a circular fashion from her left, looping all the way around to her right.

"Now the party can officially start."

Josselyn stepped to her right, passing several fairy-tale displays where the statues weren't in a very fairytale-like state. She stopped in front of one with a large bridge—three grotesque trolls sat underneath it, and a goat broken into small glass pieces rested on top of the arch. The precision in the glasswork was almost life-like. She shivered, the scene leaving her impressed and shaken at the same time.

The second beer bottle emptied, and she cracked open number three as she passed by the next display. She stopped in front of it, surprised by the description: *Jack the Ripper*. The longer she looked at it, the colder she became, so she hurried on.

The next glass scene displayed a large sign with the words *Sleepy Hollow* written across it. *I love that movie and book.*

She was about to take a drink when something tugged at her legs. Frowning, she looked down, but nothing was there. Just as she chalked it up to her imagination, it pulled at her again—harder this time, and strong enough to knock the beers out of her hands. They crashed to the marble floor, shattering on impact. Her heart slammed inside her chest, and her body trembled as she glanced around the empty room.

The invisible wind pulled one more time and her feet dragged across the floor while she screamed. Josselyn then smacked to the marble, falling into the cool liquid and shards of broken beer bottles. She screamed louder and clawed at nothing, crying out for help. With one final pull, she was yanked into the display.

Once the tugging stopped and the wind dissipated, Josselyn jumped to her feet and hauled ass. She didn't get far as she struck a wall and fell back, landing on the ground with a hard slam. Josselyn rubbed the sore spots on her ass when she realized it wasn't a wall she'd hit. There wasn't anything there to block her way, yet she couldn't walk through it. Instead of something solid, she stared out at grass and trees. She shouldn't have been seeing grass and trees—she should've been seeing displays and glass statues.

"Where the fuck am I?" she shouted, running as hard as she could at the invisible barrier. It shot her backward. With each try, she rebounded harder.

Josselyn fell once again and rolled onto all fours with a deep breath. Blonde hair spilled over her shoulders and she pushed it away, annoyed. One tendril continued to dangle in her face. A horrified scream escaped her when she realized her blonde hair was no longer short. It was now long and curled, the way it used to look when she was younger. *This has to all be a dream.* Josselyn sat back on her heels, and peered down at her lap—her T-shirt and jeans had been replaced with an old-fashioned gray dress that had seen better days. Her hands shook and her voice was trapped in her throat as panic took up the space within her.

Josselyn stood on wobbly legs, the dress swaying against her body and bare feet. She gripped the fabric of the dress until the skin on her knuckles turned pure ivory. Trees and bushes surrounded her with only one direct path ahead. It was in the opposite direction from where she'd fallen. Josselyn didn't know what to do until she took a deep breath and decided to run for the path laid out in front of her.

She trampled through bushes and branches, stopping only for a second to see the same Sleepy Hollow sign from the display. The wind blew at her hair, cold against her warm back. *This was impossible.* A fog settled around her, and she took off running again, jogging into a town with rows of rotted houses lined on either side of the field. Her heart pounded harder. She didn't stop, didn't think, she just ran.

As Josselyn finally came to a halt, the wind paused and the world became silent. The hairs on her arms stood on end at the eeriness of it all. She didn't know where to go, what direction to take, but then she didn't need to know—a graveyard rested before her. Littered in front of every headstone sat a severed head, their blank dead eyes seeming to be focused directly on her. They were everywhere. No bodies, just bloodied, abandoned heads. She gasped loudly and covered her mouth.

The ground beneath her feet shook with a deep vibrato.

Pound, pound-pound, pound. The sound of it was deafening in the silence of the graveyard, yet it only grew louder. Josselyn couldn't move, couldn't think, as the first living thing she'd seen, since the guy at the museum, barreled through the fog.

A man on a horse approached. She was about to yell for help when her mouth fell open. To her immediate horror, he had no head. No *fucking* head at all. Josselyn closed her eyes tightly and swallowed hard. If this was, without a doubt, *the* Sleepy Hollow, then that could only mean the man on the mount was the Headless Horseman.

"This can't be happening. It's only a dream." The beat of hooves on dirt came closer, each step louder, and she begged herself to wake up. For one split second, a searing pain tore at her throat, then it faded away as quickly as it had come.

Katrina awoke in a wooden chair in her sitting room. "What was I doing again? Oh yes, I need to start cooking. I must finish everything before the Headless Horseman returns, when I will have to fall silent again."

THREE

Maisie

An eye for an eye.

That was something Maisie no longer believed after the shenanigans she had to face once she'd been set free from the Glass Vault. She'd managed to avoid the other immortals ever since they'd all gone their separate ways.

Maisie had followed Perrie pretty much the entire time without her notice, while pretending like she was wreaking havoc on Earth, as August, no wait—Quinsey, no wait—Vale barked out his demands. She should've been shocked by the whole Vale-being-some-type-of-demon thing, but after dying and coming back to life so many times, nothing could surprise her these days.

Then she'd lost them.

Now, today of all days, Maisie stumbled upon Josselyn Shaw, AKA Katrina Van Tassel. She barely gave Maisie more than a side-glance, yet Maisie knew the immortal was watching her since she hadn't joined in on Josselyn's turning people to glass excursion. Freezing people into glass wasn't

Maisie's idea of arts and crafts, but then a young man with black hair passed them. Josselyn reached out and touched him, just barely, but it was enough.

The guy's body stilled, his eyes wide open in shock as his skin turned into a clear glass. He looked just the same as the ones that had once been inside the museum's displays, minus his glass being clear instead of having color. His neck cracked, and his head slowly slid off his shoulders to the ground, causing a *clink-clink* ripple effect. *Hmm, that's the tenth time she's done that in a row, and the heads never break.* Maisie's main thought was, *Why do the heads fall off her statues if she isn't the Headless Horseman?*

"Darn, that was to be mine," Maisie yelled, shaking her fist in the air, pretending as though she wanted to help destroy these lives. "I'll get the next one."

"Not if I get to them first." Josselyn grinned wide, her long blonde hair sashaying with the wind.

"I think it's easier for you to see them since I only have one eye." Before, Maisie wore patches to show that people with one eye could liven up their look. But now that she did only have one, it wasn't so bad since she was already used to the patch.

Josselyn ignored the comment and strolled away.

What? Maisie had *only* been giving her a true statement. *Okay, what do I do now?*

Maisie followed behind Josselyn and contemplated how to get Perrie out of this huge mess. Weeks ago, after a couple of days out of the Glass Vault, Maisie was able to pull herself out of her locked-and-lost-in-her-own-head stupor. That meant there *must* be a way to do the same for Perrie.

When she and the immortals first walked out of the museum, Maisie was hidden, safely tucked away somewhere in her own brain. It was like an out of body experience—she'd been shut off from everything, while Crazy Maisie, as she now liked to call her, had full control.

Crazy Maisie had been insane—constantly skipping up to civilians, talking gibberish, grabbing onto their clothing and singing to them until their flesh turned to glass. She knew Snow White liked to sing for no reason, but that was ridiculous.

Somehow, like always before, she traveled her way back to the surface and kicked Crazy Maisie aside to wherever she'd come from. At least Maisie's eighteenth birthday hadn't been totally wretched that day. And since then, there'd been no sign of the lunatic.

Everyone in town was gone—her parents, her uncle, schoolmates. Maisie had cried silently on the inside because she'd missed them so much, but she had to cut it off. It was already done.

She couldn't stop it when the immortals had gone down her and Perrie's old street because she'd still been Crazy Maisie. Perrie had been farther behind, down the road, while Maisie had skipped up to her old house to sing her own family into glass. But when she'd gotten there, some little, creepy immortal kid had already done the job.

Once freed, after being locked away behind Crazy Maisie, the memories hit. A part of her had felt content that she hadn't turned her family to glass. In a weird way, she was thankful her parents and uncle were together when they'd turned. It helped to know they weren't alone in that moment, and Maisie was eighty-nine percent sure Perrie would agree.

She *had* to find her cousin.

Maisie blinked and realized she was no longer walking—she'd completely lost sight of Josselyn. A relieved sigh escaped her at being alone again. Then the ground trembled beneath her feet, her teeth clattering together as the shaking became stronger. The only thing to do was pluck up a glass head laying unbroken on the cement—the warmth penetrated her hands. One would think the glass would be cool to the touch, but it wasn't.

With its already-frozen mouth open in horror, Maisie sang to the severed head, "Little head, you must forever remain glass." The ground rumbled harder. She froze in place, trying to sing another melody as a giant troll from the Glass Vault pounded his way across the street. "Glass is the only way to be in order to help us conquer the lands."

The troll didn't give Maisie one look as his matted hair blew off crumbs of filth with the breeze. She tried hard not to stare at his long length in between his legs flapping about. If the other immortals had to wear clothing matching their display scenes, then couldn't the trolls at least be covered in a loincloth or something? She shivered in revulsion, then gently rested the glass head back on the ground.

Maisie blew out a breath. "That was close."

"Maisie?" a deep voice asked.

She jerked upward and whirled around to find herself face-to-face with another immortal.

"Who is Maisie? My name is Snow," she said, attempting to get back into character, role play, or whatever this was.

Entering Crazy Maisie mode, she lifted her head to give a delighted and creepy smile, baring all her teeth. Despite the ripped black T-shirt and new scars, Maisie would recognize this guy anywhere.

Neven.

"Hello, um, Frankenstein's Monster," Maisie sang. "How are you on your mission to end it all?" She didn't even stutter when she met his light brown eyes.

Neven palmed his forehead with his scarred-up hand and shook his head. A vibration started from the tip of his scalp and ran through to his toes, shaking his entire body.

"Are you okay?" Maisie reached out to touch his arm but ripped it back.

Then it broke out. A laugh. A hard rumble of laughter escaped his mouth. She darted her eye side to side to plot her best escape. But she didn't have any blasted time. He grabbed her by the shoulders, holding her firmly in place.

"Cut the shit, Maisie." Neven's laughter stopped, his brow furrowed. "I know you're *you*. I've been following you around for a while now, not sure what state of mind you were in at first. I just didn't want to say anything until I was sure. That thing you just did with the head was a little overdone, though." His gaze peered over at where she'd safely set the head next to its body.

"So, you are you?" Hope, relief, and happiness all played tug-of-war inside her head.

Neven smiled sheepishly and ran a hand through his shaggy black hair. "Yeah, I've been me since we stepped out the door. As for everyone else, seems like they're all lost in their own little world."

Oh, thank goodness for that! Excitement bloomed in her chest, so much so that Maisie could wrap him up in a hug, but she held back. There was no way of knowing who, or *what*, else might be creeping about, so it would be better to leave things as they were.

She nodded and silently agreed with herself.

"We can't stay out in the open like this. Let's find somewhere and go," Neven said, searching up and down the cracked and broken street.

Placing her fingers to her temples, she thought back to what she'd passed by earlier. Then it came to her. "I know a place. Follow farther behind me and look grim."

His face was already set in his normally non-smiley face.

"Okay, that's perfect."

Neven's one un-scarred eyebrow popped up. "This is my normal face, Maisie."

"It's *perfect*." She grinned.

Neven staggered behind Maisie as she led the way. The place wasn't too far back, but she did remember a barbershop on the strip, sitting alone beside a few abandoned buildings. She doubted anyone had lingered in that area for long, so it was her best idea.

The shop's red, white, and blue pole, no longer spinning, slipped into view. Thin mini blinds covered the cracked windows, and a small white and black sign on the door read: *Open.*

So that means it should already be unlocked. Gripping the handle, Maisie pushed open the glass door and peered inside.

Immediately, she took a step back, slamming her head against Neven's solid chest.

"What is it?" He slid past her and stepped inside.

"Nothing," she said to his back. "Only three glass statues over there."

Neven shook his head, and Maisie knew he was rolling those brown eyes of his. Chewing on her thumbnail, she followed him inside.

The shop was small with only two seats and mirrors, 1950s barbershop photos lining the walls, and an old black and white checkered tile made up the floor. Maisie headed to the back to confirm there were no signs of immortal life. Nothing was there except a closet-sized bathroom and one person break room.

"Nobody's here," she said, plopping down on one of the two barber chairs. This was the first time in a while since she'd been able to sit down, and the pleather red seats were unbelievably comfy. Neven dragged the other chair closer to hers and took a seat.

While studying the small room, she noticed the phone on the wall, but it wouldn't dial out if she tried. After weeks of immortal destruction, phone lines, car engines, electricity—it was all gone. Who would she call anyway? *It would go over really well when I say there's a demon out loose on the street with immortals tearing down the city with different powers.* It sounded like a pretty good movie, though—she shrugged to herself.

Her gaze stayed locked on Neven, a scowl planted on his

face as he sulked. "Mopiness isn't going to do anything, Neven."

He shot her a glare from beneath long lashes. "Well, it's not like I'm going to go back out there and pretend to murder people, Mais. I'm just … thinking."

"You know, you could've just said you were thinking."

He rolled his eyes and shook his head. "I'm trying to figure out what we can do, but I can't think of anything we can do on our own."

"I can't think of anything either." She tapped her chin several times. "Although, I thought it'd be possible to snap people out of their trances at one point, but I doubt that would have gone over well. I'm sure someone would've run off and tattled to Vale."

Neven ground his teeth. "When I find him, I'm going to kick August's ass *hard*."

"You mean Vale," Maisie pointed out.

"Whatever. Same difference. Vale is going to be sent back to hell."

"Hey, you know that almost rhymes."

"You know people are dead, right? Everyone is gone. My *mom* is gone." Tears beaded at his eyes, and Maisie's heart thumped a slower tune. She kind of felt bad for making light of everything, but there was nothing else she could do in this apocalyptic situation.

Maisie knew how close he'd been to his mom, how hard it must be to lose her so soon after his dad died. She hadn't talked to Neven because she thought he'd cheated on Perrie. Even then, it was hard for her because she'd cared about him so much. But Perrie was her best friend and her cousin—how could she not have taken her side?

If only Maisie could read Perrie's mind to locate her. There was the one time when they'd been twelve and performed a blood oath by pricking their fingers to become official sisters versus cousins. They'd touched the small tips of their fingers together since they hadn't been ready to go gashing their palms. If only that connection could lead Maisie to her...

Maisie now knew it wasn't Neven who'd cheated on Perrie. But she didn't know the whole story either, only that Vale was responsible. Even without her pencil and notepad, she was able to put two and two together once she'd left Crazy Maisie behind.

Neven wouldn't look up as he hung his head, grieving for his mom. Maisie bit the inside of her cheek and traded her seat for his lap. She leaned to the side so she could wrap her arms around him as best she could.

"I'm sorry, Neven," she started, lying her head against his warm chest and inhaling his familiar minty scent. "I shouldn't have stopped talking to you, but after everything that happened, I couldn't help but feel betrayed, too. I know now it wasn't you, and I'm sorry I didn't figure it out sooner."

He lifted his long arms and circled them around her, sobbing softly as he rested the side of his face against the top of her head. Maisie had never told Perrie how much she missed him because she knew it would hurt her, but she did. She missed his laughter, his rare smiles that would pop up throughout the day, and his friendship. But Perrie's was more important to her. It wasn't like Perrie had forbidden her from talking to him or anything, but Maisie couldn't, not after finding out what she'd thought he'd done. What *they* had thought he'd done.

Neven's sobs finally slowed and he lifted his head away from hers. Maisie peered up, studying his face for a brief moment, reassured by his calm. She then hopped off his lap and straightened the skirt of her dress. "Are you okay now?"

Pursing his lips, Neven closed his eyes and shook his head. But then he started laughing while rubbing at his temple with the back of his hand. "I don't think I'll ever be okay, Mais, but you made the day a whole lot more interesting."

She gave him a soft smile, glad she could semi-cheer him

up. Now he could help her release more immortals from their mental prisons. "You know what we have to do now, right?"

"What's that?" He looked her straight in the eye and arched a brow.

"We have to get Perrie back."

FOUR

Before-Vale

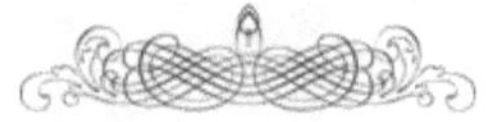

The day Perrie Madeline poked Vale in the chest with her makeshift weapon he knew he had to have her. The very moment her cello bow had connected with his chest, a gateway inside of him opened. It may have been an obsession, but the shining light within her had a subtle potential for darkness that matched his own. He had felt his Bride resting inside of her, dormant—he could make her his equal when she rose. She needed him, and he needed her.

Before Perrie, anyone else would have suited him fine. He would have chosen a mortal who was easier to manipulate, someone with inherent darkness, but it had to be Perrie. No one else made his fingers yearn for the cool metal of a scalpel more than her. It was her throat he ached with longing to cut into—the day her light had called to his darkness.

Vale had slowly slinked his way in, careful not to be too quick about his work. Besides, she was too wrapped up with Neven Lee and that needed to be handled *delicately*. Neven could never have satisfied her in the long run, and Vale had to show her he was the only one who could.

As Vale walked out from the Glass Vault, followed by the redhead, he could not care less about anything except Perrie. The redhead trailing behind him was a means to an end, and her attempt to woo him by tugging the front of her shirt lower was pathetic. He did not care to know her true name because she meant nothing to him, so he only referred to her as Red. His father, on the other hand, seemed to believe otherwise about her.

Red slid her hand down Vale's arm, and he withdrew it from her grasp. The immortal huffed, seeming perturbed by his rejection. She was a touchy one. It was true in the past he may have enjoyed their plotting and fucks, but she never mattered. There was one plot, one focus, and it all revolved around Perrie Madeline.

He felt it every time he saw her, that little glow of light waiting to be snuffed out—for him to eclipse it. But he could wait. The Glass Vault still needed to be filled. The process had been slow, but when the time was right, the pace would pick up. By the time the Glass Vault was stocked with his army of immortals, he planned to have Perrie sitting on the edge of his blade.

"What do you think of the new additions?" Red asked, a smile slowly spreading across her face. She wanted Vale's approval like the little servant she forgot she was. He never gave it, knowing she had a hidden agenda—most likely with his father.

"They work." Vale had built the outside structure, an architectural masterpiece, while Red came up with the ideas for inside it. Her past-life experiences contributed to much of the décor. She had felt the need to include real-life horror, historical aberrations of past events, and altered human fairy tales as grotesque curiosities. By turning modern horror films into panicked chaos of unpredictability, Red had wanted to transcend human entertainment. Vale did not care. He only needed the souls.

"Follow me," he demanded.

This was the first and only time he would let her out of her cage. Unlike the other immortals, she had a little more freedom to roam around. She could go up and down the halls of the museum or walk between the trees outside the building, but she was prohibited from going farther than the tree line. Vale made sure of that.

"So, you appreciate the fact I added the trolls?"

"I said they work, did I not?" Vale came to an abrupt halt, glaring at Red. "Why are you asking me this again?"

"But you said nothing else." Red rubbed her palms together, and all Vale could focus on was how filthy her nails were. He shuddered.

"I said they *work*." Vale clenched his teeth so hard his jaw throbbed. He was not fond of pointless drawn-out conversations—he already knew she wanted to have several displays that used the corrupt souls and the hellish beasts from the Underworld.

Despite his harsh tone, Red beamed, appearing genuinely pleased by his answer. His fingers itched for a blade to use on her, but she was needed for his plan.

It was time to make his move, and his play was Neven Lee. Vale had been stalking his home for weeks, which meant he knew Neven's schedule inside and out. He studied Neven's behaviors, his habits and ticks.

Neven's two-story house was a familiar sight as they made their way to the end of the long drive. If his timing was correct, and it always was, then Neven would be heading out for a jog. The sound of the front door cracking open confirmed his precision and also caught Red off guard. Vale shoved her to the side of the house, and her body crashed into the brick with a loud smack. He smirked at that.

Vale easily scooted beside her, watching around the side as Neven closed the door behind him and descended the porch steps. It took a special concoction to put Neven out for half a day, but he managed to slip a little into his drink at lunch the day before. Vale was especially careful on the dosage as too much could have killed Neven instantly. A small dose, like the one in his soda, was potent enough to give Neven a sense of "food poisoning." As planned, Neven failed to show up at school.

Vale was confident enough in his prey that he knew Neven would not skip his daily run. Like clockwork, Neven's illness cleared by the time Vale and Red arrived for the male's usual routine. Being the loyal and responsible girlfriend, Perrie would visit Neven after school to look after him—Vale knew it. It was a certainty.

What a pitiful human being, Vale thought as Neven jogged away. He and Red had ten minutes to prepare before Perrie arrived.

"This way." Vale peeled himself from the wall the second Neven was out of sight and darted for the front door.

Red grinned as she caught up with him.

As expected, the door was already unlocked when Vale twisted the knob. He was unsurprised by the living situation inside. The entire dwelling was mundane with its boring cloth furniture and photographs of Neven Lee throughout the house. Vale skipped the sightseeing and headed for the main stairs.

Once on the second floor, he found Neven Lee's bedroom door wide open. The putrid stench of the mortal's soiled basketball clothing violated Vale's senses the second he walked in. Dirty clothes lay on the floor in a pile, neatly tucked into a visible corner of the room. Humans like Neven were filthy and pathetic.

"Time for part two," Vale said as he reluctantly faced a grinning Red. She was clearly delighted by what was to come, her fingers already at the button of her jeans, but the thought of her skin on his again left him disinterested. "Undress."

With eager motions, she unfastened her pants and shoved

them down. Vale removed his own clothing, tossing them beside the bed next to Red's. Not once had he held interest to look at Red's naked flesh as he walked to a dresser covered in band stickers. He turned on Neven's vintage stereo and cranked the music up like Neven Lee would. Even Neven's taste in music unsettled him.

Vale brushed away his distaste for the music and sauntered to the bed. Red was already sprawled naked on the mattress, her back arched, her nipples peaked, wetness pooling between her thighs. Her brown eyes locked on his, the hunger of her want for him obvious. If it were not for the plan and the dying sound of a car engine, he would have walked away.

Now Perrie Madeline was on her way, and she would discover what he wanted her to. The thought of the mortal reminded him of all the things he yearned to do to her—kiss her, taste her mouth and in between her legs, sink into her heat as she shouted his name. Then, like the end to a perfect symphony, his blade slicing clean across her throat so his Bride could rise. Those thoughts had his length hard and ready.

Vale called on a glamour, which shaped his facial features into Neven's. He was used to changing his face when needed, and that was how he knew his plan would work. With one last look at the open door, he leapt onto the bed, colliding with Red's naked flesh, her breasts bouncing. She let out a squeal of pure pleasure as he rolled beneath her and sank into her heat.

As Red moved back and forth on top of him, her filthy nails dug into the skin on his chest, and those fingernails were all he could focus on.

The recognizable sound of Perrie's footsteps echoing outside the room was enough to distract himself. He closed his eyes and imagined it was Perrie Madeline grinding her hips into him instead, or more so, the darker version of herself that would one day find him.

FIVE

The Bride

Exhaustion swept through Bride's body, and the electricity at her fingertips barely flickered to life. Vale was right behind her at the next turn, waiting for her to spark up again. They had been at this for weeks now.

"I'm in need of rest," Bride said through gritted teeth, irritated that her energy was running low.

"We can stop for a little while." Vale raked a hand through his blond curls, moving his lower jaw side to side. She knew he wanted to keep going—as did she.

"I'm frustrated too, Vale."

His hand cupped the side of her face, and his thumb rubbed gently against her cheek. "You've done beautifully, my Bride."

His words were the key to lifting her spirits as her shoulders relaxed. Vale was pleased with her work, *their* work. Such elation flowed through her that it felt as though she was floating.

"Where will we go for the night?" Bride asked, fiddling

with the buttons on the front of her dress. Dirt and filth covered the hem of her white gown, proof of their long and strenuous journey.

She brushed a curl from his forehead—even if he wouldn't admit it, he was tired too. A smile, not quite a full one, but close enough, slipped onto his face after her touch. It was a precious gift reserved only ever for her.

"There is an old house a few miles from here that Red is securing for us." His smile dropped, his face becoming unreadable, as he awaited her answer.

A low growl escaped her throat, catching Vale's immediate attention. There was something about Fannie that Bride didn't like, more than the way the immortal was toward her.

"You know she means nothing to me." Vale lifted her chin with a touch of his fingertips. "If I could get rid of her in a second, just for you, I would. But my father wants her here."

With a nod, she clamped her teeth down on her lower lip to keep from speaking words she would rather keep to herself. She had been having more and more thoughts slide in recently, but when she nearly grasped them, they vanished.

Vale held her gaze for a moment longer—his yearning mirroring hers—before he released her face, leaving her missing his warmth. He then silently trekked ahead of her and led the way as she followed behind.

Statue after statue stood frozen, their glass shining beneath the glowing ball of sun in the sky. She smiled at their work, at how complete devastation lingered in their path. Houses destroyed, trees fallen, and streets broken beyond repair. Her smile faltered when a feeling seeped down to her bones—she wasn't fulfilled by the chaos. She needed *more*.

Perhaps sleep would renew the spark within her.

They eventually stopped in front of a Victorian two-story house, surrounded by lush green bushes and a strong iron fence. Bride's feet twitched with a strange warning and for a moment, as she waited at the bottom of the old wooden porch, something within her begged her to run. This would be the perfect opportunity to escape—Vale wasn't paying attention to her. But where would she run to, and why would she want to?

Bride clutched the side of her head and took one step back, then another.

Vale turned to face her and watched her intently. Something like affection sparked in his gaze. "Is something wrong?"

Before she could answer, he scooped her up into his strong arms and carefully towed her through the front door.

The feeling that was inside her vanished, and the sense of safety washed over her instead. Vale was her safety. She rested her head on his shoulder as tiredness took over, hitting her even harder. Bride closed her eyes for a second before Vale set her gently on a soft green couch that her body sank into. She opened her lids and gave him a warm smile.

"Give me a moment," he said and exited the room.

Bride reclined against the back of the couch. The clack of familiar heels sounded as they descended the wooden stairs. Fannie. But Red to Vale. Unfortunately, Bride's moment of peace was now ruined.

Bride hoped if she ignored the immortal that perhaps she would go the other way, but that wouldn't be like Fannie at all.

The immortal bounced into the large living room like a peacock. She appeared clean, her dress pristine, and her red hair wilder than ever. Fannie narrowed her eyes and stepped in front of her.

Bride clenched her jaw. She wanted to tear the immortal's head off with her lightning.

"You're still here, I see. But it won't last. Nothing ever lasts for him."

Baiting her. That was what Fannie was doing *again*. But, Bride stayed.

Fannie sneered, her face turning a bright crimson. "Don't worry, you'll get what's coming to you." She turned on her heels and stormed into another room. The immortal seemed to relish in repeating the same things about Vale to Bride, but when Bride didn't react, that only ignited Fannie's fury.

When they had first walked out of the Glass Vault weeks ago, Fannie had tried to take control, pushing Bride out of the way as much as she could. Bride had stood her ground and Vale had put the immortal in her place once more.

Vale rounded the corner with a shiny metal object, taking a seat in front of Bride on a coffee table cluttered with magazines. With his emerald eyes focused on hers, he picked at his nails with the file.

Bride had noticed this habit for a while, but she wasn't certain what made him do it. Either way, the back-and-forth movements sent a rush of heat straight to her core. As soon as Vale finished, he took out a cloth handkerchief and cleaned the file. Fannie, who had been lingering in the doorway since his arrival, watched him. The way the immortal's eyes danced and the way her chest rose and fell, proved that Fannie was ready to rip his clothing off in the middle of the room just from watching him file his nails. But Bride was too.

"Give me your hand," Vale said softly.

Bride peered up from his file and back into his piercing green eyes. Without a word, she reached toward him and placed her hand in his.

He picked and removed the dirt from under her nails, repeating the same sensual cleaning ritual as before. Once Vale finished, he drew her hand to his mouth and softly blew away the small debris. Bride shivered at the feel of his warm breath on her flesh. A pleased smile crossed Bride's face as she glanced at Fannie, who studied them with revulsion.

"Why don't you ever clean my nails, Master?" Fannie asked while sinking down beside Vale on the table.

He didn't say a word and Bride only smiled wider.

"Come"—Vale released her hand and tucked away his file—"I have something I want to show you."

A new energy rose within her, sweeping the tiredness away. She stood from the couch and followed him down a short hallway, past the flight of stairs, lined with photographs of smiling faces along its beige walls. The people in the photos were dead now, their souls part of the Glass Vault. Bride didn't linger on them long as Fannie clicked her heels. She could tell the immortal was watching her, waiting for Bride to show any sign of weakness.

They passed a large kitchen, and a rotten smell invaded her nostrils. In the center of a table rested a bowl of fruit where tiny flies buzzed around the blackened produce.

Just past the kitchen, Vale pulled open a door that revealed a set of stairs leading down into a dark cellar. Farther down, small candles, already lit, danced in the darkness, their little flames bobbing against the damp breeze of the basement. They could go out any second.

Bride's heart became a steady pound against her sternum.

The descent was slow, and with each step she took, the wood groaned beneath her weight. Her hands slightly trembled, and she didn't know what was happening in that moment—she never felt nervous. Gritting her teeth, she found herself once more and her hands stopped shaking.

Bride pressed closer to Vale, knowing Fannie would attempt to push her down the stairs. She refused to be humiliated by her or anyone.

"And here we are." Vale jumped the last step with an impish grin, making his ethereal face become even more so.

At the bottom of the steps, Bride's gaze settled on a disheveled woman tied up on the cement floor. Her hair was coarse and knotted, her yellow dress caked with mud, and her dark brown skin coated in sweat. The woman lifted her head wearily from the ground, and her brown eyes drifted between the three of them, halting on Bride before growing wide.

The mortal's body shook as she attempted to let out a string of muffled words, despite the cloth around her mouth. Bride felt nothing at the woman's pathetic desperation.

"Pick her up, Red," Vale barked.

Fannie swayed her hips between Vale and Bride, knocking Bride sideways into the wooden rail. Bride's nostrils flared at the slight throb in her back and lightning crackled at her fingertips.

With one hand, Fannie lifted the woman up by her hair, then shoved her down on a metal chair. "Hello, Catherine," she cooed.

Fannie knew her? As Bride squinted her eyes to get a better look, the woman wasn't a stranger—she was one of them.

"We only left you for a moment," Fannie continued, jerking the woman's head back. "I told you we would return."

Bride studied the immortal's features, when something slowly seeped in, becoming familiar… Familiar… A crack of thunder rumbled inside her head, throbbing, spreading. Images flashed before Bride so quickly that she could barely make them out. Lying on a graveled street, in a pool of her own blood, rested a mangled woman wearing a satin yellow dress. Half of her face was mutilated. But the other half? It was the same face as the woman in the chair. Bride inhaled sharply.

"Why is she tied up? Why isn't she out on the streets?" Bride demanded. Something stirred within her, telling her she should not be there, but she ignored the nuisance. Time was being wasted because this immortal wasn't out there gathering more souls.

"We have to send her back," Vale finally said.

Catherine launched herself out of the chair, but Fannie yanked her by the hair and placed a knife at the woman's throat. Fannie slowly led her back to the chair, and Catherine carefully lowered herself down. The knife stayed planted against the immortal's flesh, and a thin line of scarlet ran down Catherine's throat.

"Do you think they're beginning to remember?" Fannie asked Vale.

He cocked his head and stroked his chin, seeming to consider her question.

The question nagged at Bride. *Who is starting to remember? And what are they remembering? Is that what keeps knocking at the back of my mind?* She kept her gaze trained on Catherine and her expression neutral as both Vale and Fannie focused on her.

Fannie's eyes slid from Bride's to Vale's like a slithering snake.

"I don't believe so." Vale dropped his hands to his hips and shook his head. "This one wasn't meant for the Glass Vault. Her life was built upon bringing down crime, and in the end, that need to better the world drew her back out." There was an edge to his voice as though he was sickened by the thought. Bride was even more so.

Catherine mumbled hysterically, her muffled wails falling on deaf ears. It was as if she was trying to only tell Bride something, not the others.

"Hand the knife to Bride," Vale instructed Fannie.

Fannie huffed, loud and frustrated. "Why do you keep favoring her, Master? Catherine is *mine*. She's been mine. I should be the one to send her back to the Glass Vault."

"Don't you dare try to undermine me," Vale growled. The hair on Bride's arms and neck stood on end from the deep, enraged tone of his voice, exciting her. Bride was used to Vale's moods with the other immortals. Fannie deserved it— they all did.

Fannie narrowed her eyes at Vale, not even a drop of fear slipped out as she spoke, "I said, she's *mine*."

"Do I need to send you back with *her*?" Vale appeared calm, but that single sharp note in his last word said it all.

Fannie released Catherine's head with a forceful push. Vale then slipped behind Catherine with one hand on each shoulder.

Fannie sauntered toward Bride with the blade forward as if she wanted to plunge it into her stomach. The immortal curled her lip in disgust at the last second as she flipped the knife and passed it to Bride.

"You are forgetting what she was meant to be used for," Fannie said, staring hard at Vale, "and you are becoming too attached to her. It's starting to feel as if Cupid's arrow has hit you as well." She then stomped up the stairs, slamming the door behind her.

Bride arched a brow at the door before connecting her gaze with Vale's, who was now watching her with a haunted look. Like an emotion was stirring within him, as though he was recognizing something.

Throat bobbing, he turned to Catherine, a new expression on his face taking root, one of pure darkness. His eyes met hers once more, signaling anticipation. "Join me?"

Bride stepped toward him, yet she was uncertain how to go about this. The woman was immortal. If Bride stabbed her, it wouldn't kill her. She would heal. "What do you want me to do?"

Vale's smile grew wicked, every perfect tooth on display. "This one has been a naughty, naughty little thing, trying to stop what we are attempting to achieve. Catherine here will be going back to the Glass Vault with the other souls."

Those were not answers. "She's immortal. Catherine can't go into the Glass Vault, and she will only heal."

His grin slowly fell. "Immortality can be taken away if I choose—if you choose. So will you decide this with me?"

A thrill shot through her. "Of course. And Fannie as well?"

"All in due time, my Bride." This time, his smile became even more vicious. "We have to torture her until she is knocked unconscious, then I can send her soul back before she awakens."

Bride clenched the knife—an emotion washed over her of

how wrong it was, but the other half wanted to slice this immortal in two, then watch the blood pour out of her. Bride had only turned civilians into glass, their souls disappearing as soon as they were turned. This was *different*. Gleefully different.

Her hand tapped the knife silently at her thigh while her heart pounded violently at Vale's pleased expression. She yearned for the gratitude and pleasure he would give her afterward. As easily as her next breath, with her whole darkened heart, she fully gave in to what was right.

Vale held the immortal's head back, her throat ready to be sliced. Tears streamed down Catherine's face as she continued to try and shout at Bride. But her words wouldn't have mattered to Bride, only what Vale and she could do to the immortal together. Lifting the edge of the blade to Catherine's soft flesh, digging in, Bride sliced a crisp line across her throat. Bright red crimson spilled out from the wound—a slight sickness settled in Bride's stomach that should not have been there. But she pushed past the strange emotion and savored the rest with a grin on her face. She then plunged the blade into Catherine's heart.

SIX

Before-Officer Elise Rodriguez

Officer Elise Rodriguez was thorough with her investigation. She'd driven up and down Oak Street two times, deftly aware that she had left no ground uncovered.

She'd gotten out of the car and surveyed the area on foot, inspecting the tree line a multitude of times. There was nothing but trees—some freshly cut down, just like Perrie Madeline had said. Despite her efforts, she couldn't locate the company who'd cut them down in the first place.

Elise had wondered if Perrie fabricated the story, but there was something about the young woman that made her believe she'd been telling the truth. Over the years, Elise had encountered countless, desperate individuals who'd spilled their stories in the same manner as Perrie. Even though it was hard to believe, her gut told her Perrie Madeline was different.

One more time, Elise promised herself at the sound of the toaster. Another early day meant another chance to sweep Oak Street for some peace of mind.

Elise sipped her coffee, lazily tearing at a bagel as she

examined her notes. This case took up more of her kitchen table than her actual desk. Once the reports came in, it was hard to leave them behind at the office, so she'd brought them home. She thought she could piece them all together, find the link that made the puzzle fit for all the missing persons.

If only it were that simple.

The missing civilians all seemed random, except for Maisie Jaser and Neven Lee. She knew from experience that rebellious teenagers often fled their home with a significant other to make a point, especially if the home was chaotic. For Maisie and Neven, it was the perfect answer to the question of their disappearances.

As Elise set down her coffee, she gazed at the cartoon sheep sprawled across the mug, feeling just as tired and hopeless as she had the last few days. It was hard to admit, but she wasn't getting any closer to solving the mystery behind the disappearances. If it wasn't for the phone ringing, she would've drifted off at the table, face planted in her notes.

Elise looked at her phone and didn't recognize the number. "Officer Rodriguez speaking."

"Yes! Officer Rodriguez?" a man's voice frantically asked. "My daughter's missing."

Another missing person? Her shoulders slumped at the thought. The man on the other end was making no sense, his babbling incessant and hard to understand. She rubbed her eyes and took a deep breath. "Slow down, sir. Did you go down to the police station and fill out a missing person's report?"

"I'm headed there right now, but my niece, Maisie Jaser, was reported missing already, and now my daughter, Perrie Madeline, is *gone*. I didn't know what to do, so my sister gave me your number." The man tried again to speak, but his voice trembled with every word. "She said you could help."

Hold on. Now Perrie is missing, too? "Are you sure, sir?"

"Yes, I'm sure!" he cried.

Elise's chest tightened and she rubbed at the spot. Something strange was going on and it went beyond the rapid disappearances. "Go to the police station, fill out a report, and I'll meet you there."

"Okay." Perrie's father's voice faded into the background as Elise tore the phone from her ear.

One more time, she thought again. Already dressed in her police uniform, Elise strapped on her gun and grabbed the rest of her things—notes and files included.

Elise planned to figure out what was going on before anyone else could go missing. She couldn't let it happen again, so she hurried out of her house and hopped in her car, flying down street after street until she reached Oak.

The sun broke through the tops of the trees, casting its light down the street. Elise tapped the brake to slow the car, sighing heavily and feeling defeated once again. All there ever was on Oak Street were trees, and that was all she was seeing now. She thought maybe this time would be different, but she should've known better. Strange stone museums didn't appear overnight.

Then, just as she put her foot on the gas pedal, something appeared in her peripheral vision. She slowed to a stop, her eyes widening in shock by the apparition beyond the tree stumps. A gray stone building now stood there, its large structure casting an eerie shadow across the ground. She'd become an expert on this road alone, and there was no doubt in her mind that this had never been here before.

"This isn't a traveling carnival on wheels," she muttered, studying the old building and its windowless outer walls.

Elise parked the car and rushed out, her heart beating to the pace of her running. She was going to solve this mystery and catch the person responsible. And it was going to happen that day.

She approached a tall wooden door with her gun in hand. A golden plaque was displayed on the door with the words

Quinsey Wolfe's Glass Vault written across in black script, just as Perrie Madeline had said. Elise removed the safety from her gun and held it close—loaded and ready.

To her surprise, she found the door unlocked, which should've alarmed her. Everything about this should've set off warning signals. The door swung gently open without making a single sound. She peered inside and listened for any noise, but was met with silence.

A few feet inside the carpeted hallway, Elise was convinced this area was empty. The door behind her closed with a loud, powerful slam, vibrating the walls. She startled and a streak of sweat slid down her cheek as she aimed her gun at the door. Ignoring the perspiration, she ran back to the exit, and turned the knob—it was locked.

Mother Fucker! she shouted inside her head. But she'd been through tougher obstacles, had been shot at numerous times, had watched her old partner die from one of those bullets.

Blowing out a breath, she pulled herself together and continued onward, down the lantern-lit hallway. The issue of the locked door would have to wait—there were people who needed to be found.

Several hallways later, Elise came to a stop in front of a circular room lined with displays along the wall. Her heart pounded harder as she gazed at what was inside each display— colorful glass-made horrors that made her stomach churn. Some were so violent in nature she couldn't help but gag. As a police officer, she'd dealt with real-life crime on a daily basis, but horror movies gave her the real nightmares.

They always had.

The worst one by far was a display of Jack the Ripper. She knew very little about the cases, but the idea that the sick bastard had never been caught chilled her to the bone. Still, despite the unsettling nature of the museum, Perrie Madeline had been right. Elise fumbled with her phone as she withdrew it from her pocket. The station needed to be notified that the sighting was solid. She scrolled through the cell for the number, ready to hit call, when a violent wind struck the phone from her hand.

"What the hell?" She looked around the room for an open window or door. "Where the—"

A stronger gust slammed into Elise, knocking the words and breath right out of her. She fell to the marble floor, her gun sliding across it and out of her reach. Elise ignored the pain radiating through her body and flipped onto her stomach to crawl to her weapon, but another big burst of wind pulled at her. Screams escaped her as she kicked and clawed at the marble to break free.

Nothing could stop the wind from giving one final pull, throwing her into the display. She instinctively shut her eyes and lifted her hands to protect herself, then waited for the shatter of glass. But it never came.

Elise was off the ground in an instant and bounced onto the wet pavement, finding old buildings on either side of her. The displays had vanished. The museum was gone. Now was the time for panic. Mouth agape, hands shaking, she took a step back and tripped over her own feet. She peered down and gasped when she noticed her shoes were concealed by the skirt of a yellow vintage gown she now wore.

Taking a deep breath, careful of the skirt, Elise pushed forward and bumped into something—*someone*.

"Hello, Catherine," a taunting woman's voice cooed.

"I'm not Catherine," Elise said to the stranger, backing away from the covered woman.

The person in question stood out, dressed in black—cloak, gloves, hat, and shoes. The lamppost nearby, lit by a golden flame, reflected on a lone red curl that escaped from beneath the stranger's top hat.

Who the fuck is this? Elise was too distracted by the odd clothing when the cloaked person charged at her. The stranger was swift, quicker than Elise, and as the lithe figure struck, Elise screamed. A burning pain throbbed at her shoulder.

Elise looked down at her wound, blinking rapidly at the sight of a long red gash torn into the fabric of her dress. Warm blood spilled out from it, sliding against her brown skin, and staining the yellow gown. Adrenaline then hit her and she thought fast, running at the figure and slamming her fist into the stranger's face. The woman stumbled backward, her entire head covered in black cloth beneath the top hat. Without any hesitation, the stranger came back slicing the air with what looked to be a long butcher knife.

She swung her arm up and over, knocking the blade from the woman's hand. Elise punched the stranger in the face again and again until her hand ached. The woman finally collapsed to the ground, out cold.

Elise picked up the knife and ran. Heels clacked hurriedly against the pavement, fabric swishing against fabric as she tore down the cobblestoned street toward a light coming from a building. A *pub*.

Inside were silhouettes of people—people who could help her. The closer she got, the clearer the faces in the window became.

She stopped, her eyes growing wide as they settled on a familiar face. Seated at a table with a young and handsome blond man was Perrie Madeline.

Elise reached out, her fingers nearly brushing against the door handle. Relief filled her at the safety awaiting within the pub—then it was ripped away by two strong hands yanking her back into the shadows. A hand closed hard over her mouth, just as she tried to cry out and scream for help. She brought her arm down to elbow her captor in the ribs, but it was too late. The sting of cold metal burned against the flesh of her throat as hot liquid poured from the wound.

Her words came out gurgled and she struggled for a few more moments, not wanting to give up the fight.

Then the world went black.

Catherine stood outside the brothel trying to remember how she'd gotten there. The stomping of feet down the street distracted her from her thoughts. A woman slipped into view first—Mary Kelly. A young blond gentleman with a lean and strong body ran beside her, one who Catherine would like for herself. "Hey, Mary," she called. "How about you lend your gentlemen to me for the night."

SEVEN

Maisie

The plan was … that there was still no plan. Maisie had been sitting around with Neven for more than an hour with nothing between them besides glass bodies. The concoction of a plan on how to get Perrie back had turned into a gaping failure.

Saving Perrie was still the mission, but neither of them could come up with an idea of where to start. If Maisie's parents were still alive, they would've known what to do.

With them gone, nothing was the same.

No more of her mom's extreme cooking, no more big birthday parties, no movie nights, or her dad's jokes. There was nothing at home to go back to, only what was left behind. But at the end of it all, there would still be Perrie.

And yet, the notepad in Maisie's lap remained blank.

Earlier, she'd searched around the desk drawers at the barbershop, managing to find a pad of yellow sticky notes and a pen. She'd planned to use them for any ideas they could come up with. Not as good as a small spiral pad and pencil, but they would work.

"Do you really need to use the notepad, Mais?" Neven asked, cocking his head. He sat on the floor across from Maisie, while she twirled her pin around her thumb.

"You should know that answer by now." She winked. "Now, are you ready to tell me what happened to you, and how you know August doesn't exist?"

"I never thought this would happen when I went into the museum." Purple bags rested below Neven's eyes, and his lids appeared heavy with exhaustion as though he could crash at any second. He hadn't been open about his experience inside the museum yet, and Maisie had been waiting patiently for the past hour. That had to end now if they wanted to get to Perrie.

"So, are you ready to tell me what happened back in the Glass Vault?" she asked, her tone firm. "If it helps, you can even write it down." She shoved her notepad in his face.

"Are *you*?"

"I never said I wouldn't tell you." She tapped his knee with the end of her pen. "You never asked."

With a groan, he said, "Well, you first. You're not going to like what I have to say."

Maisie inhaled three times since that seemed like the magical number to prepare herself. Her dad had never understood the point of her doing that, but she'd always told him it was because three was her lucky number. Then he would just smile and pat her on the shoulder.

The calm finally took over. "When we were in the Glass Vault, you know, frozen as glass?"

Neven arched a brow.

"We came to life like zombies, right? But not like the breaking out of the coffin and slowly clawing out of the dirt until you break through the surface kind." Pausing, Maisie waited for Neven to say something.

"Do you need to stop every time and wait for me to respond? Just get on with the story in its entirety. You're doing masterfully." He gave her a sarcastic thumbs up and she straightened.

"I'm going to ignore this mood of yours and finish my story."

"You do that." His lips twitched before turning into a smile, one that she couldn't help but mirror on her own face.

Scratching her head with the pen, Maisie gathered her thoughts. "Anyway, when we turned into flesh and began walking out of the museum, and Crazy Maisie started attacking people—"

Neven lifted a hand. "I'm going to stop you right there. You have a name for your alter?"

Why wouldn't I have a name for her? "Yes, don't you?"

He squinted his brown eyes, seeming to mull it over for a moment. "No, because it's still me."

"Well no, it isn't. It's you but some of your emotions are shut off, so it's a new you. But anyway, back to what I was saying before being interrupted. After several days of mass destruction, I was able to escape her claws."

"Can we talk about what happened with you in the Glass Vault?"

Closing her eye, Maisie tried to not let the past tear down the strong walls she'd built for herself. She'd done everything she could to save Perrie back in the Snow White display, and her cousin had still ended up like Maisie.

Neven's warm hand pressed against her cheek, and she didn't open her eye. His opposite hand then trailed up the side of her other cheek. The touch was nice, gentle, and she almost leaned into it. But as soon as she realized what he was doing, it was too late when he reached for her eye patch.

"Don't," she screamed and yanked her face out of his reach, turning away from him. She wasn't sure why she didn't want him to see her missing eye. It wasn't as if he was used to seeing that eye anyway.

"Jesus, Maisie. I just wanted you to look at me with both of your eyes for a minute. I wasn't trying to do anything."

Is that what he thinks I'm afraid of? Maisie adjusted the patch, making sure it was in its proper place before facing him. "That's not it, Neven."

He scooted closer to her, his lips forming a tight line. "Then what is it?"

"My eye is gone."

"What?" His brows furrowed together in confusion.

"I said my eye is gone. Like, it was apparently plucked out by dwarves."

His eyes widened and his jaw tightened, forming an interesting mixture of anger and shock.

"Before you get too mad, when I got sucked into my display, the eyeball was already missing once I got there. I did, however, inherit some memories from Crazy Maisie."

If she had to be honest with herself, those memories were pretty insane. Mutilated dwarves, their eyes, ears, and tongues in a bucket, bloody animal carcasses, and a Huntsman who was in love with chopping off her head or piercing her heart. Once again, she swept those little terrors under the rug.

"What do you mean your eye is gone?" He ignored her last sentence, mouth hanging open as his gaze zoomed in on the patch.

Maisie recalled the time when she, Perrie, and August had reached the barrier to exit the Snow White display. She'd already known she wouldn't be able to make it to the next scene, no matter how hard Perrie had wished for her to escape with her.

When Perrie and August were sucked through, Maisie had darted away from the Huntsman—his hair all flowing in the wind like there was a fan right there blowing at it. It was weird that when she'd looked at him, she had thought of flying hair at that moment, but then his hand came down with a dagger to her chest, and she'd woken in the cottage, the bloody animal fur back in her lap.

The bright side to this apocalyptic situation was the

Huntsman hadn't been trying to hunt Maisie down since they'd exited the Glass Vault. She slid that memory under the rug, too.

"Well, I mean it's gone. Like, there isn't one to display for you inside my eye socket."

He leaned forward and stretched his large hand out again.

She twisted out of his reach. "Stop, Neven!"

"Let me see it, all right? It can't be any worse than me. I have scars all over my body."

"They make you look rugged." Her gaze fell to his visible scars on his arms, hands, face, and neck. In her opinion, they weren't bad at all—slightly raised, pinkish, and spaced a good distance apart. No bolts rested on the sides of his neck, but there were two small circular scars where she supposed they once may or may not have been.

"Did you just call scars all over my body rugged?"

"I did. They look good on you." Maisie lifted her chin in defiance. Flaws were her favorite thing about people. A birthmark here, a scar there… For a moment, she wondered if there were more below his clothing… Her gaze drifting lower, lower still, until she snapped her gaze back up to his face. *Bad, Maisie.*

He cocked his head, his face serious. "Then show me your eye."

Mulling it over for a few seconds, Maisie figured it would only be fair to show him hers since she'd seen his. Slowly, she lifted the blue eye patch and set it in her lap, then continued to stay facing Neven head on.

He studied her for a moment, probably hiding his disgust, but then he smiled. "You look daring."

Unable to stop herself from smiling too, Maisie placed the patch back over her eye socket. Relief washed over her after showing him—it had felt good. As she opened her mouth to tell him the rest of her story, the glass door burst open.

Neven startled, and Maisie leapt up, pressing her hand

against one of the warm glass bodies—a tall man with a comb in his hand. *Had he been planning to use that as a weapon*?

An immortal swathed in shadows took long strides through the door, his gaze fastened to Maisie.

"Ah, you got to them before I did," Dr. Jekyll … or Mr. Hyde said in a raspy voice. She could never tell who was who in this world since both his personalities were a bit on the insane side.

Show time. Maisie skipped up to Dr. and Mr. Evil and screamed to the ceiling. "I sang him a song, a song about dead bloody birds." She giggled and spun round and round.

"What else did you do? What else? What else? *What else*?" He bared his teeth, a deranged smile spreading as he hobbled toward her. Grime caked his crooked teeth, and his hair stood on end as if it had been struck by Perrie's electricity. He wore a disheveled old suit, the sleeve of his blazer ripped at the shoulder, a few of the buttons of his vest missing.

"He got the other ones!" Maisie sang, hysterically jumping up and down, pointing at Neven. She then slapped the pleather of the chair as she watched her friend.

His serious game face was already there, as always, ready to rock and roll. He didn't say a single word, only grunted a poorly-constructed Frankenstein's Monster sound. It seemed good enough for Mr. Two Side, but apparently he'd never seen the movies.

"Tell me more. Tell me more," Mr. Hyde seethed, gripping his hair and yanking out strands. "Jekyll, Hyde, Jekyll, Hyde, Jekyll, *Hyde*!" he shrilled. Turning back around, he took long strides again, this time directly out of the barber shop, still chanting his two names down the broken street.

Maisie bolted to the door and locked it, which she should've done the first time around. She took several deep breaths before pushing away from the door.

"Now," she said to Neven after that rude interruption, "I can finish my story."

"Okay, Maisie. Let's just pretend *that* didn't happen. But go ahead and continue."

So she shrugged, plopped down on the floor, and spilled to him her story of how she'd gotten to the Glass Vault the night she was supposed to start working there. Neven's warm hand slid forward and clasped hers as she continued. She went into detail about how she'd gotten murdered by the Huntsman, her thinking she'd killed him, and how she'd thought she had saved Perrie.

"I have to tell you something, Mais."

"It can't be any worse than my story."

He drew his scarred hand from hers and ran it through his dark hair before looking back at her. "I couldn't do anything. I was chained to that damn wall."

Everything stopped. "What do you mean you couldn't do anything?" When he didn't speak, she urged, "*Neven?*"

"After I came to the Glass Vault, I found August and ended up in the Frankenstein's Monster display. There, I discovered August was Vale. He revealed his plan and plot as he broke me apart. I don't know why he told me all of it, except for the fact I think he knew how much I cared about Perrie and how much it would hurt. Vale put her in a cell with me, completely unclothed. They had … been together, I guess." Bright scarlet seeped into his face and neck. "He killed her in my cell by slitting her throat while I couldn't do *anything*. Then he made her into what she is."

Maisie shut her eye and let his words sink in. She was a firm believer that everything happened for a reason, no matter how lousy. And this was beyond that. Vale had pretended he was August, slept with Perrie, then killed her. To anyone, it would be a tough pill to swallow, but she and Perrie could work with it. Her cousin was still alive and that was what mattered, even though Maisie didn't know if Perrie would be able to get through all of this. But Maisie would be there to help her, always.

Opening her eye, feeling a new-found sense of hope from that messy darkness, she rose to her feet. "The only thing left to do is find Perrie and save her. Using her lightning power with my singing skills, and your strength, we will get Vale back in his vault somehow."

Neven blinked several times, his lips pursed. "We don't even know where to start. I haven't seen Perrie since before we left. I mean, do you even know where she is?"

"No. Do you have a better idea?" she challenged.

He rolled his eyes. "No."

She offered him a hand to help him up. Neven's lips twitched before he gave her a half smile and clasped his hand with hers. It was mostly him pushing his tall body off the floor than her doing the work.

Spotting the small over-the-shoulder purse she'd found earlier, Maisie picked it up and emptied its contents on a chair, in case the owner ever came back to claim them. Most likely that wouldn't be happening, but she took the top sticky note and scrawled a short note, apologizing that she'd needed to borrow his or her purse. Then she pasted the yellow sheet directly next to a small wallet.

Neven rolled his eyes again, which must've been his main habit of the day—even more than usual. She took two candy bars from a desk drawer and tossed one to Neven. He easily caught it with one hand, and she gave a nod of approval, quite impressed.

"You know we don't have to eat, right?" Neven asked as he unwrapped the chocolate bar.

Maisie had figured out the first day that she never got hungry, yet she still delighted in eating what she could find. Besides, her taste buds were still there—she wouldn't want to deny them their bliss. "We need to have some pleasure in immortal life—chocolate is the answer."

She unwrapped her bar and stuffed it into her mouth as she led Neven out of the barbershop. For now, she swept what had happened between Vale and Perrie under the rug. Placing a hand to Neven's strong chest, she looked both ways to make sure the two-sided maestro was gone. He appeared to be.

Neven's brow stayed lifted while he studied her hand.

"What?" she asked, slipping it back by her side.

"Nothing, Mais." He shook his head and smiled. "Nothing at all."

They'd only made it a few feet away from the glass door when a body darted around the corner of the building and slammed hard into Maisie. Her candy bar went flying, and she crashed to the ground, her head striking concrete.

For an instant, Maisie thought she was dead with blood pouring out of her throbbing skull—a heaviness strapped her down to the cement.

The weight then lifted as a loud smack echoed from somewhere. Neven knelt beside her, holding her head up.

"Are you all right? Please tell me you are," he pleaded.

Maisie guessed he'd forgotten they couldn't die. "Immortal, remember? Where's my candy bar?"

A deep chuckle escaped his throat as she sat up and located her delicious treat. She brushed the dirt off it and looked up at Neven, who had vanished from her side. A guy with white hair was now in Neven's grip, backed up against the wall, lifted so his toes were dangling off the ground.

"What are you trying to do to her?" Neven demanded, then continued with a line of similar questions. Maisie stood by watching while she finished her chocolate.

"I'm not like them," the guy cried, his pale skin flushing a bright pink. He was an immortal, but he was right, he wasn't lost in la la land.

Maisie folded her arms and leaned against the wall beside them. "Neven, quit acting like a beast and set the poor guy down."

Neven lowered him, but didn't release his grip on the guy's shirt.

Staring at the immortal for a moment, Maisie blinked in recognition, her mouth opening in awe. She lifted her index finger in the air, ticking it back and forth. "I know you! Ben Johnston!"

He backed up all the way into the wall for safety as though she was going to sing him to glass right there, even though he was an immortal.

"You know, I had my own plan prepared to search for you before I went missing myself." She grinned.

No one said anything, both guys just stood staring at her. With a shrug to herself, she asked Ben, "How and when did you come back to yourself?"

Ben's fright seemed to wear off a bit, but based on his rigid shoulders, she figured he would bolt soon. "I don't know how. It was only a few minutes ago—before I took off running. I had been feeling more and more myself as the days went by until the memories hit me all at once."

I wonder why that is? Why we aren't getting all our memories back at the same time or not at all. Nothing was easy to piece together. If Perrie were here, Maisie was sure they could draw some conclusion together like they always had— whether it was games or real-life situations.

"Do you want to come with us? We're leaving to save Perrie." Three would be much stronger than two since going up against Vale would be a difficult task.

Ben furrowed his brow. "I have no idea who Perrie is— I'm sorry."

"She's the Bride of Frankenstein. Well, really it would be the Bride of Vale." Not that they were married, so Maisie didn't know why she was referred to as the Bride. Vale *was* like Victor Frankenstein by making the monsters, though.

A look of pure horror crossed Ben's face. "Absolutely not. No way." She probably shouldn't have mentioned the Vale part...

Maisie reached out to stop Ben, to reassure him they had a

plan and that everything would be fine. "But—"

"If I were the two of you," Ben cut her off. "I would steer clear of any path that might take you to Vale. Your friend, this Perrie, she's his now." He turned to leave but stopped just short. "Good luck, though. Also, if you see the redhead named Fannie, stay away from her." Throat bobbing, he scurried off without a backward glance. His boots thumped against the pavement, growing fainter, until only quiet filled the air.

Perrie had told her Ben's story, of what had happened to him in his display, and it wasn't the prettiest of tales. Maisie hoped Ben didn't run into anyone who could hurt him again. However, that was not in the stars for her and Neven.

Neven worried at his lower lip.

She wrapped an arm around his waist and drew him close. "Let's find Perrie."

EIGHT

Before-Ben Johnston

Ben unzipped the fluorescent-orange fanny pack at his side, and drew out his handy pink bottle of sunscreen. The day was an excellent day to take photographs. He'd been trampling through the wooded area of Oak Street for the last hour, snapping photo after photo of the lush green foliage. The day had been mostly cloudy, but now that the sun was coming out, he needed to re-apply.

He fired open the spray and let the cool beads hit against his exposed arms and legs—it was refreshing, to say the least. Then he fished out a stick of sunscreen from his pack and spread it generously across his face. Sometimes the sunscreen felt more like an addiction than a necessity, but with having such pale skin due to his albinism, he needed to keep the rays out.

Ben placed the items back in his fanny pack and zipped it up with one quick pull. He raked a hand through his white hair, shaking it out before lifting his camera up to his face. A twisted old tree with gnarled limbs and a crooked trunk, not ten feet away, practically shouted his name.

"Hello."

Startled by a female voice and the snap of the camera, Ben stumbled back and caught himself against the base of another tree. Thankfully, Oak Street was lined with them.

Ben felt the light touch of a hand on his arm and glanced up, meeting two brown irises.

"Oh, I'm sorry." A young woman with bright red hair smiled. "Are you okay? I didn't mean to frighten you."

His heart thumped wildly. "I'm fine." He pushed himself up and checked the lens of his camera for any scratches. Truthfully, he wanted to avoid her eyes, which were focused on him. He wasn't good at talking to women.

"So, what are you taking pictures of?" Her voice was soft with an English accent.

Ben finally looked up, positive the blush on his face was as red as a ripe tomato. He scanned her up and down. The swells of her perfect breasts didn't escape him, as her chest was the first thing he couldn't tear his eyes away from. He swallowed his nervousness and hurried to meet her face before she thought he was a pervert. But he couldn't stop the question from slipping into his head of what her breasts would feel like in his hands.

"Um, just some trees," he stuttered. Finally calming himself, he then noticed her unusual outfit. "What are you wearing?"

Her blue dress was completely out of place in the middle of Oak Street. It was old-fashioned, adorned with vintage buttons, a stiff bodice, and a full skirt that flared at her hips. Her hands, which she clasped below her chest, were covered with olive gloves. He found the whole scenario to be more than weird.

"Oh, this?" She chuckled and brushed her gloved hands over the skirt of her dress. "It's part of my work but it's been slow, so I decided to take a break and go for a walk. Did you think I would actually be wandering around town wearing this?" A smile lingered on her face.

Ben smiled in return and ran a hand along his jaw. "That must have been a long walk then."

"Not at all. I work at the end of the street."

He wrinkled his nose. "There isn't anything on this street besides trees." Maybe she'd meant she was practicing for a play somewhere close by. Theater kids would do that all the time at the park on the other side of town.

Still smiling, the woman twirled a wild curl with one of her gloved fingers. "You didn't know? There's a museum at the end of this street."

A museum? There wasn't any museum out here. She either had to be mistaken or she was screwing with him.

Sensing the question hanging between them, the young woman giggled playfully. "You don't believe me."

"I didn't say that." Ben tugged at the collar of his shirt nervously.

One of her auburn eyebrows rose. "Have you been to the end of the street today?"

He shook his head. "No, but I was at the end of the street last week and there wasn't anything there."

"Why don't you follow me, then?" The redhead turned on her heels and swayed her hips as she sauntered away.

Ben didn't want to stop talking to the pretty woman. Without hesitation, he jogged after her. "What's your name?"

The edge of her lips quirked up, and she wrapped her hand around his bicep. "I'm Fannie."

"Fannie," he said softly. He liked the taste of her name on his tongue—he liked the touch of her hand on his bare arm even more.

"And yours?"

"My what?" he asked, startled.

"Your name, silly." She gently swatted at his arm, causing heat to creep into his cheeks once again.

"Ben. My name is Ben Johnston."

They trekked slowly through the trees, a mysterious redhead on his arm—he couldn't complain. As they walked, he snuck quick side-glances at her, noticing the light sprinkle of freckles running across her nose to her chest. He hadn't seen them from afar.

Up close, she was more than pretty—she was *beautiful*.

In his twenty-three years, Ben only had a handful of short-term girlfriends. It had been more than two years since his last, and he was ashamed of himself. It was hard to have a meaningful conversation with another person when one was a hermit. Fannie seemed nice though, unaffected by his condition, and genuinely sweet. He wouldn't mind hanging out with her sometime.

"And here it is," Fannie said.

Ben's pale blue gaze flicked from Fannie to the end of the street, and he gasped, his eyes bulging. A building much older than anything built in town stood tall before them. It was magnificent. There was an angle in there somewhere just waiting to be captured—he could feel it buzzing in his fingertips like anxious bees.

"You weren't kidding, were you?" He turned his head from Fannie to the large stone structure, then back at her. "This … this wasn't here before."

She looked at him as if he was crazy. "It's been here a while. You must not have been paying attention."

He wiggled out of her grasp. "Look, uh, Fannie. I come out here every week. Believe me, I would've noticed this place. How could anyone not notice it?"

"The trees were cut the other day." She pointed at the tree stumps surrounding the building.

Ben narrowed his eyes at the trees like they were hiding all kinds of secrets. "Something isn't right here, Fannie. I think I better go and talk to someone." Who was he going to ask? His non-existent friends and family? He could ask one of his neighbors, though.

"Wait." Fannie grabbed his arm again, tighter than before—a little possessive even. "Come with me inside, and I can show you around. It's only me today."

Ben studied the curved arch of the doorway, skeptical of the mystery as though it still wasn't real. He couldn't believe his eyes. His gut told him to go back the way he'd come, back to the safety of the forest where he could continue taking pictures. But that pleading expression on Fannie's face pulled at him more.

"Okay, but only for a bit." He could talk to his neighbor once he got back home.

"Perfect." She tapped the tip of his nose with her index finger.

Once they crossed the archway, Fannie reached for the golden knob and opened the door. Ben closed it behind him and followed her down several hallways, paying more attention to the sway of her hips—how they dipped from side to side—than any of the surroundings. A heat spread through him, shooting straight to his length. Ben adjusted his pants, but he could still feel himself straining. He started counting backward before he embarrassed himself. If she turned around and peered down at him, he would bolt.

Just as he relaxed himself, Fannie came to a complete stop at the end of the hallway.

"Where are we?" he asked, moving past her into a circular room.

"The belly of the beast."

He took a hard swallow—the room they were in was oddly arranged with various glass statues. There were no windows and no doors in the new territory he was about to enter. The gruesome and unique aspects of the glass statues had Ben reaching for his camera to capture the moment, but Fannie entwined her fingers with his and pulled him to the middle of the room.

His gaze fixed on a display and he wandered away from Fannie, taken by a glass scene of Peter Pan. This was one of his favorite stories, and to see it so twisted and different made his fingertips twitch with the need to snap a picture. Peter hovered in the air above Wendy, a knife hidden behind his back. Wendy's hand was in his other, following wherever the Lost Boy might lead. Her expression was taken, wondrous even, because a boy could fly.

As Ben raised his camera, he somehow knew Wendy wouldn't be able to escape the danger.

"This way, Ben," Fannie drawled. He turned around and walked to where she was standing, now in front of a Jack the Ripper display. "This one is my favorite."

"I can't believe they never solved that case." Then again, the technology wasn't as sophisticated during that time. Ben took another photo, wishing he'd brought his digital camera instead of his vintage film one.

"*She* was incredibly smart."

He puckered his lips. "It wasn't a woman." It wasn't that he believed a woman couldn't commit the crimes, but rather what the evidence had said. The letters were signed by Jack.

Fannie smiled, a bit too wide, and something about it didn't feel right, snapping him out from the distraction of this place and her. Ben always found himself caught up in taking pictures versus what he should be doing. He needed to leave.

"I gotta go." He stepped to the side, placing him in front of a display that held a large bridge, naked trolls underneath, and a broken goat on top. *Three Billy Goats Gruff.*

"Sure." Fannie cooed, her grin growing wider.

Before he could respond, a violent wind knocked Ben to the floor. His face smacked into the marble, sharp pain radiating through his teeth. Warm blood filled his mouth as he tried to push himself up. The invisible force picked up again, pulling him and his camera toward the display.

High-pitched laughter echoed in the room that could've

only come from Fannie.

Ben closed his eyes. The feeling of falling was harshly interrupted by the impact of his body against solid ground. He opened his eyes, blinded by the bright rays of an orange sun hanging overhead. Was he back in the forest? He had to be dreaming.

Fannie was nowhere in sight.

Slowly, he pushed himself up to all fours, still dizzy from whatever had happened. He was right about one thing—he was beside a forest with the beginning of a path that led to a hulking bridge. Ben brought himself to his feet, eyes on the bridge as he reached absently for the fanny pack at his waist.

Only, it was *gone*.

In its place was a sword. His whole body trembled as he spun in a circle, trying to spot anything familiar. Nothing.

Panicked, he shot forward and sprinted for the bridge, hopeful he would just wake up if he kept running. Halfway across the stone structure, he tripped over a small rock, losing his footing again. For the third time that day, he was knocked to the ground. He'd never fallen so much in his life.

This is madness, he thought. He started to push himself up and came to an abrupt stop when a naked woman with olive skin and thick black hair lifted herself from over the side of the bridge. His jaw fell open as she walked toward him with rosy peaked nipples and perfect dark curls between her thighs.

"You are mine," the enchanting woman growled. She was extraordinary, radiant, and sparkling like sunshine. He couldn't rip his gaze away from her, even if he wanted to.

Ben yearned to kiss down her throat, feel her nipples in between his teeth, press his digits into the heat between her legs. He wished he had his camera to keep a piece of her. The actual sunshine from the sky blinded him for a split second, and once it cleared, he was no longer face to face with a gorgeous woman. Instead, he met the eyes of a malformed beast with saggy skin and rotten teeth who stood as tall as a giant. What was in front of him, he'd only seen in books or movies. There was no way it was real—but then again, the sword on his hip was tangible.

Troll.

Heart pounding out of his chest with fright, he spider-crawled backward to avoid the beast. Ben stopped as something washed over him, as if a spell was drawing him to the creature, its allure. He closed his eyes tightly to push the pull toward the troll away as he stood to take off running. The scent of decay invaded his nose and his lids flew open. He shouted as the beast's monstrous hand swiped at him, plucking him up from the ground. Ben's ribs bit into his lungs, cutting off the oxygen that he was desperate to drink in. He wanted to rub at his throat for air, but his arms were trapped in the troll's deadly grip.

As the sun scorched his pale flesh, all he felt was the burning and lack of air supply, until there was nothing left for him except blackness.

Billy rubbed at his head, feeling a little dazed about where he had just been. He stared at the foliage around him and out toward the bridge farther ahead. It was about time he took an adventure, so he began his journey to discover what lay on the other side of the bridge.

NINE

The Bride

Bride helped Vale carry the remains of Catherine's body up the stairs. Fannie was nowhere in sight. The dejected deviant was most likely skulking about through the city, searching for any remaining mortals. Vale's decision to let Bride lead the torture was enough to spark Fannie's anger. Despite the notion of torture, Bride was more pleased by the immortal's dramatics than anything.

As they stepped out onto the backyard patio, Vale tossed the limp body onto the pyre. The heap was made from old tomes and the stack of chopped firewood beside the garden shed.

Vale picked up a can of gasoline, a token he'd found earlier in the garage, and sloshed it over Catherine's body. The pleasure of torturing another soul had brought Bride a sense of foreboding. She pushed it away and focused on the scarlet splattered on her own arms, wondering what it would taste like. Victory? The strike of a match drew her away from her thoughts, and she watched as Vale tossed it toward the bloodied corpse.

Fire ignited under the dark sky, crackling and burning while each flame licked away Catherine's flesh, peeling it away from the bone. Bride couldn't conceal the sparks at her fingertips as giddiness stirred within her at the sight. If Vale were able to use his stronger abilities, she could only imagine how powerful the fire would have been. Outside the Glass Vault he was limited, but inside he could do anything.

He longed for power. Sometimes, Bride believed she craved it even more.

Together, they mourned how great Catherine could have been. Even with her betrayal, she was still one of them. The flames continued to eat away at the immortal until she was nothing but ash. Vale's eyes hadn't once left the blazing orange, but as the last flicker snuffed out, he turned toward Bride.

"You were miraculous in there," he murmured, pressing his forehead to hers, his fingers trailing the length of her spine.

"I felt miraculous, Vale." She was the only one allowed to call him by his true name, even Fannie had to refer to him as Master.

"Because you are. You are remarkable. You can get cleaned up if you wish. There is a shower on the second floor." He lifted his forehead from hers, his expression now unreadable.

What Bride wished in that moment was to be with Vale right here in the open, surrounded by Catherine's ash, but her skin ached to be washed, for her to remove the dirt first.

With a nod, she went back inside the house and up the stairs. A throbbing came at her chest, similar to the pounding in her head, but she ignored it. Bride needed a distraction, and she found it as soon as she stepped into the bathroom. On the countertop, a towel and rag were already set aside for her. Bride stared at her reflection in the rectangular mirror hanging above the sink, and she didn't recognize her face beneath the blood and grime.

Long, brown hair, wild and untamed, hung below her shoulder blades. A thin streak of white hair rested on each side of her temples, weaving themselves into the tangles. Deep brown eyes rimmed with black circles from lack of sleep peered back at her from the glass. They focused on a part of her throat hidden in shadow. Just a few inches above her collarbone sat her pale scar.

It seemed to smile at her, as though it knew something she didn't.

For a moment, Bride didn't know who she was or *what* she was. The ache in her chest pulsed faster, sharper. She gripped the fabric above her heart and took a deep breath, knowing who she was, what she was. She was the Bride. Vale's Bride. She was his chosen leader, his Queen of the Glass Vault and all living creatures inside of it.

Shedding her blood-smeared gown, she took a step into the shower.

Cool beads of water pelted against her flesh as it washed away the grime, red and brown mixing with the clear water. Bride gathered her electricity and ignited it to heat her skin. As her current crackled, the liquid now felt warm when it hit her skin. The dull pounding in the back of her head shot forward, sending a path of shocks through her body, and she couldn't fight it anymore.

Bride's knees buckled and she caught herself on the floor of the tub just before slamming her head against the wall. A flash of pain still twisted inside her skull, crashing into memories she had never once seen.

A shadow... It morphed into a young woman with obsidian hair and a bright blue eye. This was no stranger—she was the same immortal wearing an eye patch that Bride had seen at the museum. She squeezed her head between her hands. The pain … it wouldn't go away, and the more it pounded, the clearer the vision became.

Nev came over to watch movies while Perrie's dad was at work. Her dad hadn't looked himself this morning, and she knew why. It was the anniversary of when her mom had left them. Years might've passed, but to her dad, it was like yesterday. She preferred not to think about it.

They were waiting for Maisie to show them her surprise. Her cousin had told them a week ago that she'd come up with an idea but wouldn't let either one of them know what it was.

Maisie had said she planned on starting it in a month when summer break began after their sophomore year, but she apparently couldn't wait a second longer.

Nev sat in the chair, already enchanted by an old werewolf movie Perrie had turned on for him. He hadn't seen many of the old classic horror films, so Maisie had made it a purpose for him to start a few weeks ago.

"What do you think she's going to surprise us with?" Perrie asked, fiddling around with a Rubik's Cube that she could never fucking solve.

Nev cocked his head and smiled as he seemed to mull it over. "I'm thinking it has something to do with what she's been into recently, which has been pirates."

That was true. Maisie had been carrying around a lot of different books lately. Perrie believed two of them may have had a pirate ship on them. "So, your guess is a pirate accent?" She laughed.

Rolling his eyes, Nev looked back at the TV. "If she got this worked up over a pirate accent, I'm going to be thoroughly unimpressed."

A knock came at the front door, and Nev bit his lip anxiously toward the sound. Perrie frowned, unsure what he was nervous about. It was only Maisie, not a werewolf creeping out from the TV screen.

Perrie checked the peephole and released a birdy whistle when she confirmed it was her cousin. Maisie stayed turned to the side as she whistled in return.

As Perrie swung open the door, Maisie jumped through the space and waved her hands in the air. "Surprise!"

Nev leapt around the chair and ran to Maisie, cradling her face in his hands. "What the hell happened to your eye?"

Maisie's smile grew wider, and she patted his hand away. "You like it?"

Okay, so Nev was right. *"Pirates, remember?"* Perrie said, glancing toward him as he studied Maisie.

"Damn it, Mais." A scowl crossed his face for a brief moment before he smirked, most likely impressed with himself for knowing her surprise had something to do with pirates.

Perrie took a closer look at the blue and red eye patch, appearing to be well crafted. The patch part itself was the body of a parrot. A head poked out on one end, tail feathers on the other, and tiny feet at the bottom.

"I'm surprised you didn't add a pirate hat with a skull on top of it." Perrie laughed.

Maisie tapped the side of her head with her pinky finger. "I'll add that thought for another day to my growing list."

"What list?" Nev piped in, his interest piqued.

Clapping her hands together, Maisie brought them in front of her mouth. "I'm starting my own business. Time to do away with boring black eye patches. Those with one eye deserve to express that you don't have to hide the eye, you can embrace it."

"Technically, the eye would still be hidden behind a patch," Perrie pointed out.

Maisie waved her index finger around like a pirate's sword. "That's true, but the barrier protecting the eye can be vibrant. To show my support, I will wear one from now on."

It was a Maisie sort-of-idea, but Perrie liked it. "Go ahead."

Nev shook his head and sank back into the chair, seeming to not quite get what the hell was going on.

With a laugh, Maisie rumpled Nev's hair to bug him, then

plopped down on the couch.

The image disappeared. It all vanished. There was something there—Bride knew it. She tried to bring the pieces back, but she couldn't. It was gone and she was here in the shower, the water once again cold. Bride pressed her hands to the sides of her head and squeezed, urging the memory to resurface, but it didn't. Instead, she was left with a dull throbbing in each temple. Grounding her teeth, she slapped the bottom of the tub as hard as she could, the small puddle of water splashing against the walls.

Beads from the shower head continued to pour down on her, and she slowly felt herself once more, no longer caring about what had been there. Bride turned off the water and wrapped herself in a towel while staring at the fog-covered mirror. She leaned forward, lifting a finger to the glass and drew a picture of a flower.

"Strange," Bride said to herself, wondering what would make her do something so pathetic.

Shaking her head, she finished drying off and bent down to pick up the dress from the tile floor. The ensemble was back to its impeccable condition—pure ivory, not a speck of dirt or blood. Stepping into the silky material, Bride buttoned it back up.

As she opened the door, Vale leaned against the wall, file in hand. His hair was damp and curled slightly against his forehead—he must have showered as well.

"Took you long enough," he said almost playfully, running the file across his perfectly-shaped fingernails.

Shame slithered forth within her as she thought about the weakness she had just experienced in the bathroom. She was too ashamed to confess the words aloud, even though Bride knew Vale would help her. He always answered any questions she would ask.

"I wanted to make sure I scrubbed my nails thoroughly and made them extra clean," Bride lied, holding out her hands and splaying her fingers for inspection.

Vale ran the tip of his tongue across his lower lip, his smile turning into something like a dare.

His luscious, full lips drew her gaze. Everything was forgotten, the world *forgotten*, except for him. With a grin, she whirled away from him and slowly walked toward the bedroom, knowing he was following behind. She *wanted* him to follow her.

The room appeared clean, finely decorated with a large bed, a white-washed vanity, and an antique desk with a closed laptop resting on its surface.

Quiet filled the room, and it was all theirs for the night.

"You know the effect you have on me, don't you?" Vale pulled her to him, turning her in his arms. He placed his forehead into the crook of her neck for a moment, breathing her in, before reuniting his eyes with hers.

She did. These were the times when Vale was almost vulnerable. These were the times she went mad with lust. Bride's hands traveled up his chest, stopping at the place where his heart sat, but nothing beat against his rib cage.

Vale lifted his hand and gently trailed his fingers along the scar on her neck. "You never asked me how you got this," he said softly.

"Because I don't care." However Bride became what she was, she truly didn't care—she relished in what she was, loved doing the things she did. She felt powerful.

"I will always answer anything you ask. *Anything*."

"How about you tell me tomorrow, then. There are more important matters at hand." Bride licked her lips, inching closer to him. To her delight, his breath quickened.

That was all it took.

Vale's mouth crashed to hers, his body pressing into every part of her. The kiss was so rough that Bride tasted metallic on her tongue. They plunged back into the desk and her thighs pushed into the edge of the surface. She kissed him with the same level of intensity, but her body ached for more.

Vale flipped her around, and Bride steadied her hands against the desk. His fingers skimmed down the sides of her rib cage and to her hips. Everything within her ignited at his caress, the rush it sent through her. Releasing a growl, his digits dug into her flesh, tugging her closer.

Bride's heart sped with yearning as he pressed into her from behind. His touch captivated and rendered her nerves senseless.

Vale's warm breath fluttered against her ear as he purred, "Should you hike up your dress, or shall I?"

He removed his hand from her waist and ran it along the inside of her thigh while the other hovered just below her breast. She let out a moan that she didn't want to hold back when he cupped her breast and did wicked things with her nipple, even with the cloth barrier between them.

"You do it," Bride pleaded.

Vale released a low groan. The zipper of his pants slid down, the only other sound besides their ragged breaths, then he yanked up the skirt of her dress. He trailed rough kisses down her neck and nibbled the skin just below her ear.

With one quick stroke, Vale buried himself inside her, and she inhaled sharply at his delicious movements. Again and again, he thrust—each time she moaned louder, needing even more of him. He seemed to know exactly what she wanted as he increased his pace.

When his fingers came to her center, circling in an enticing pattern, she shouted his name for more. And he answered with *more*.

Bride closed her eyes as her electricity lit up the entire room, roaring with bliss. She never wanted him to cease.

The smell of clean cotton sheets disturbed Bride from sleep.

Her eyes fought against exhaustion as she turned onto her side, pulling the covers back up to her shoulder. The muscles in her legs ached, but it was an exquisite feeling to have, knowing that Vale was still beside her. He had dozed off to a well-deserved rest after he had taken her multiple times, but to her disappointment, he was on the edge of the bed, out of reach.

Always when they slept, he drifted farther away and didn't touch her, as if he was afraid of letting himself feel too much. Bride reached out to him, and he rolled onto his back at the last second, straight into her extended hand.

It happened so fast she couldn't stop the little spark that escaped her finger.

Vale jerked against the light jolt, and Bride yanked her hand back, horror on her face. She waited for his eyes to flick open, worried she may have hurt him, but it didn't happen. He was still sound asleep—not a hair on him had been moved out of place to cause a disturbance in his slumber.

"Vale?" He didn't answer, so she touched his chest again and felt it against her palm. *Thump … thump … thump.*

She withdrew her hand and hurriedly placed her ear to his chest. It pumped, though weak and labored, begging to be heard. Its voice was tinier than most, but his heart was crying out. Possibly for her.

Vale's heart was *alive*.

Frantically, Bride tried to shake him awake. Vale rolled toward her with hooded eyes.

She sighed in relief as he studied her.

"Perrie," he murmured. A small boyish smile appeared when he said the word—the type of smile Vale never wore.

Bride didn't recognize what he had said. Before she could speak, Vale reached for her waist and drew her closer. He rested his forehead on hers, one hand lightly cupping her cheek, then he softly brushed a kiss against her lips. Something slammed inside her, trying to break free—it pressed against the back of her skull.

Ever since Bride had first awoken in the Glass Vault, Vale had never kissed her in this manner. Their kisses were more passionate, never this subtle, this tender. His caresses tingled against her lips, sweet and gentle like the soft brush of a feather. His hand drifted to the small of her back, lightly stroking the area—then he pulled her even closer.

Vale trailed delicate kisses along her jaw, down her neck to her collarbone and right back to her mouth while gracefully entangling his fingers through her hair.

Vale kissed her gently one more time before Bride rolled away from him, a strange emotion pouring over her. He settled behind her, encircling her mid-section and resting his forehead between her shoulder blades. His heart barely thrummed against her back. But that kiss felt *wrong*—something was wrong with *him*.

This wasn't *her* Vale.

Before she could sit up to shake him back awake, the pounding in her head returned with a ferocity unlike before. It was the same as in the shower, only this time she could *feel* the memories falling back into place, like tiny pieces to a puzzle. Names, faces—they all came flooding out from the depths of her mind. A tidal wave that consumed her.

Warm blood poured down Perrie's throat, Neven chained to a wall, Vale dragging her by her hair as she thrashed. Then she was lying naked in a bed with a flushed August—there were crazed blackbirds flying before that—then the Huntsman was going after Maisie. She remembered it all, right up to the moment she entered Quinsey Wolfe's Glass Vault.

Everything was on rewind, and the sting of hot tears filled her eyes.

She couldn't stop the memories from coming—part of her tried, but she fought back. Perrie had forgotten about everyone—including herself. She'd lost everything inside the

Glass Vault and then, because of her, she lost everything outside of it, too. Her dad, Uncle Jaron, and Aunt Krista—they were all dead.

The pounding in her head lightened to a dull throb, then it was gone, leaving behind a terrible panic. Fear rose inside her, clawing its way into her chest as she realized where she was— and *who* she was with. His arm was looped around her waist, an anchor that had her trapped in the middle of the ocean away from any sort of land or freedom.

I need to get the fuck out of here. Now! Her heartbeat kicked up.

Tears streamed down Perrie's face, but she needed to keep quiet. After she got out of here, she could scream all she wanted. Slowly, she lifted Vale's warm hand away from her stomach. She prayed to any god listening to let Vale not wake up. Just this once, she desperately hoped someone would hear her prayers. *I have to get out of this house—I have to escape.* She repeated it over and over again in her mind until Vale's arm was safely removed.

With a steady hand, Perrie lowered Vale's arm to the bed beside his hip. He rolled to his back with a low groan and she froze, waiting. His eyes remain sealed, undisturbed. Carefully, she shifted her feet to the floor and pushed up from the mattress, glancing back only once to check on him. Her chest tightened. He looked like August Hartley, but he wasn't. The sleep-tousled blond curls and peaceful expression couldn't conceal the monster underneath the boyishness anymore.

Perrie tip-toed across the carpet toward the door, grateful the floor wasn't wood that could squeak. She left her boots behind and wouldn't risk her safety for a pair of shoes. No matter what, barefoot or broken, she would be running for her life. And if what she knew about Vale was true, then she would most likely never stop.

As Perrie descended the stairs one slow step at a time, Fannie rounded the corner from the living room. Perrie folded her face into a blank expression when everything inside her was shivering to the bone, her heart screaming.

Fannie sneered as she passed and clicked her heels down the kitchen tile toward the basement. Perrie breathed through her nose, a little too rapidly and loud for her own comfort. When the immortal closed the basement door behind her, Perrie padded toward the front exit and turned the knob.

The door swung open and she closed it behind her with a soft click. Relief thrummed in her veins, but it didn't last long—she wasn't far away enough yet.

The early morning welcomed her with a warm breeze. Stumbling down the steps of the porch, Perrie inhaled as much fresh air as possible. Her body tingled, and adrenaline vibrated in her toes, urging her feet to move faster. Perrie might be free, but she wasn't safe yet, so she ran to her goal number one— the sidewalk. Then she reached goal number two when she passed the second house. Then Perrie struck fucking gold when she hit the third, and she continued to root for her achievements as her legs pumped as hard as they could. The only thing she held a firm grip on was her scream.

Wind rattled in her ears—the sound of her feet slapping against concrete flushed out the damn insanity, and everything in the world she passed became a blur.

Even when she'd distanced herself, she kept running away from the house, away from Fannie, away from Vale, away from it all. She didn't once look behind her, afraid if she did, Vale would be there to catch and drag her back by her hair to his world of hell.

TEN

Before-Neven Lee

Neven started his car and left Perrie's house in a rush. He hauled ass to Oak Street, pissed off at Perrie. Why couldn't he just let the girl go? She was obviously out of her damn mind. She'd been in a delusional state over something that never happened.

He took several long minutes to think about how she was with August, and he slapped his hand against the leather steering wheel. It was different. She looked at August with a completely different intensity than she'd ever looked at him. She may not be aware of it, but he was.

In a way, the day's events had helped him understand after all that had happened between them, they could just be friends. Now, if only she would talk to him. Just the other day he'd thought they were the real deal, but everything had changed. He would prove he'd never cheated on her, though. That situation was a fucking mess that boiled the blood beneath his skin every time he thought about it.

Neven turned down Oak Street to confirm to himself that,

yes, there was a museum, and David and the other guys were full of shit.

He sped down the street and came to an abrupt stop when he spotted August's silver car. "What the hell?"

August's blond head moved closer toward the stone building. The squeal of Neven's tires caught August's attention—he stopped in his tracks, turning his head back to Neven with an expressionless face.

A run-in with August these days was a bucket full of fucking fun, and this was one encounter Neven didn't want to deal with. August used to be cool, but ever since he'd thought Neven cheated on Perrie, that had changed. Then again, if the situation was reversed, and he'd heard August cheated on Perrie, he'd be damn angry, too.

Hopping out of his car, Neven slammed the door shut and jogged up to August. "What are you doing here?"

August lifted a blond brow. "I could ask you the same thing, Lee."

Neven and August stared at each other for several seconds, neither saying a word. "Okay, this is dumb as shit," Neven said to cut the tension. "We know we're both here for the same reason."

A crease appeared on August's forehead. "We do?"

Standing out here with August was getting Neven nowhere. "Yes, we do." He shifted closer to August, hovering over him.

August's lips twitched and pulled into a smirk. "Lee, you have no idea."

"Moving on." Neven shook his head, stepped back, and pointed straight at the wooden door. "You see this building? Where the hell did it come from? And why did it appear out of nowhere?"

August cocked his head as if thinking *really* hard about the building. "You think I know these answers?"

Neven let out a long, exasperated sigh. "No. I don't think

you know the answers, but I thought you might've drawn a better conclusion than I could've. The guys I asked at school haven't seen this place."

"We can go inside and take a look." August shrugged and strolled toward the door.

"I already came here this morning. The door was locked, so I can guarantee you right now it's still going to be," Neven said, following closely behind.

Once they stood in front of the door, August brought his fist to the wood—a loud bang that screamed to whoever was inside.

"What are you doing?" Neven yanked August's hand back.

"I'm seeing if anyone is here. Isn't that obvious?" If Neven could've punched August, he would've, but it would only piss Perrie and Maisie off.

They waited around for about a minute, and no one answered. August twisted the knob, and the door opened without making a single sound.

"I guess it isn't locked," August said with a cocky smile. Neven rolled his eyes, vowing to himself that he *would* punch the jackass later.

"I guess it's unlocked now, but it wasn't this morning," Neven mumbled.

"Do you want to go in, or do you want to go back to your car?"

Ignoring August's sarcasm, Neven brushed past him with two long strides. "I'm going in."

"Your choice." August closed the door, his words trailing behind Neven.

Coming to an abrupt stop, Neven turned around to face August. "Enough already, okay? I get it. You think I cheated on Perrie, and I didn't." Neven marched toward August and poked his index finger to the idiot's chest. "Even if she doesn't completely know it, I see how she looks at you. She never looked at me like that, so I'm done trying to be with her, but

I'm going to get my friend back."

August stared him down with that stupid blank expression again. "I understand."

Neven shook his head and continued down the carpeted hallway filled with lanterns. "Now that we have that settled, we can maybe get some sort of answer around here about why this place came out of nowhere."

"Good idea," August called from behind.

The lanterns' shadows swayed along the walls as Neven walked to the end of the hall, then turned down another. A single line of chandeliers hung from the ceiling in the new hallway. He ignored the rest of the decor and proceeded down the corridor when, eventually, he needed to take a turn to another long hallway.

"Feeling lost yet?" August asked.

Neven glanced over his shoulder at August and shot him a glare. "How can I feel lost if the hallways are leading me in what direction to go?"

August let out a dark laugh, and Neven chose to ignore that too. The end of the hallway neared, and he entered a room filled with displays of some sort. He moved at a quicker pace until he stood in the center of the room, able to view the details more clearly.

"What is all this shit?" Neven asked more to himself than to August. Everywhere he looked, there were statues made of glass. He strode to a display with a crooked sign that read: *Beware the Black Plague*. Inside rested two glass statues. One of the man's arms was missing, while a blackness spread from fingertip to elbow on the other.

"This is strange," Neven said as he faced August, but he was no longer there. "August?" Neven stepped away and scanned the different scenes, as if August would creep out of one of the displays.

"August? This isn't funny, man." Neven observed the new scene before him for a moment, wondering what the hell to do.

Before him stood a glass statue of a man wearing a white dress shirt and black slacks, positioned with his back to Neven—an empty medical table at his side. He turned away from the scene to search for August, when something tugged his shirt.

"Cut it out, August. That was stupid of..." His words trailed off as his gaze connected with no one except for the statue. He gnawed on the inside of his cheek, knowing it was time to bolt. Whirling around, he lunged forward but was thrown back with one forceful pull from an invisible wind. He flew through the air, landing hard on his back against the rough floor inside the display.

Groaning, Neven stared at the ceiling for a second as pain radiated through the length of his spine. He brought himself to a sitting position and studied the display, his chest heaving. No, not a display, a cage. Heart pounding, he rose to his feet and ran toward the metal bars. He shook the door, making it bang throughout the entire room.

The sound of squeaky wheels rolling down the hall echoed against the walls. Neven paused, his hands still gripping the bars. August strolled toward him, pushing a silver tray on wheels. He now wore black slacks and a white shirt with ruffles down the center.

"When did you have time to change?" That was the best thing Neven could think to say because he had no idea what the fuck was going on as confusion swirled within him.

August's upper lip curled. "I am going to avoid that question, but I will answer one from earlier. I know you did not cheat on Perrie because that was all me."

Neven stilled. He felt like all the reasons for the strange things happening were about to be revealed, and shit was about to hit the fan.

"First, I'm going to explain it all to you." August glided his hand over a set of tools on the tray before lifting a pair of medical scissors. "Then, we are going to have a little fun."

ELEVEN

Maisie

The past couple of days had gotten Maisie and Neven nowhere. If only Maisie had some sort of psychic ability to locate Perrie, but she didn't even know if they were heading in the right direction.

She and Neven had stayed to the trees, away from the main streets. From the look of things, it seemed as though all the immortals had already left to set sail on their own adventure to their continuation of ruination.

The first night after she and Neven had left the barbershop, they'd made themselves a little camp in the forest nearby. *By camp, I mean one of us would fall asleep in the grass while the other kept watch for anything strange.* While Neven had been dozing off, Maisie left their hideout and decided to poke around near the edge of the forest, in hopes she would find *something.*

The sound of loose rocks scraping gravel had come from straight ahead, and Maisie prepared herself to go in for the attack and save her cousin from Vale. Maisie's shoulders had slumped as soon as she caught sight of the scraggly mermaid. Her dark skin, cerulean hair and matching tail, all seemed to glow beneath the silvery moon. The creature had slowly dragged her body across the gravel, her tail half ripped from her abdomen. Something oozed from the wound, leaving a liquid trail in its wake. Maisie hadn't been sure whether to be impressed for how many weeks the mermaid had towed herself across the land, or worried she might spot their camp. She leaned more toward being impressed.

After the mermaid crawled on by, Maisie had made it a point to stay by the fire.

Day two had been anything but action-packed. No immortals were anywhere to be found, only an endless supply of their finished business—glass statues. The town was so deserted, even more broken than the last, that she'd expected to see a troop of tumbleweeds pass her, but that most likely came from another movie.

Now, at the end of the day, Maisie couldn't focus on anything else except for how much she missed Perrie, her family, and the eye patches crafted by her own hand.

"Neven?" she asked, leaning against a tall tree, its pinecones scattered around her.

"Yeah?"

"Do you miss Perrie?" A look of confusion spread across his face, so she needed to break it down further—as if it wasn't obvious enough, though. "I mean, do you *miss* her, like are you still in love with her?"

Neven frowned for an entire sixty seconds. Maisie knew because she counted.

Finally, he shook his head. "No. I think it's more like I miss her friendship. Besides David, I was always around the two of you, and then I wasn't. I did love her, and a part of me always will, but I was wrong about a lot of things."

Maisie let his words sink in. She wasn't sure if she believed him. Just a couple days before he'd vanished, Neven was all about getting Perrie back. He hadn't lurked around corners or anything to talk to her, but he'd still tried every now and then.

"What?" He shot her a hard stare. "You don't believe me, do you?"

Maisie bit her thumbnail and didn't say anything.

"Believe what you want."

"I don't know, Neven. You seemed pretty persistent about getting her back before you disappeared."

He sighed. "I know, but after I left her house that day, something hit me, and I knew she looked at August differently than she ever did at me."

"Okay, but just because you thought she felt something more toward August, it doesn't counter your feelings or make them vanish."

"Look, I can't explain it, but I cared more about our friendship than anything else and that's why it was so important to get her back. Yes, I told Perrie I loved her when I left her house, because I do. It's just not in *that* way anymore. Does that make sense?"

It did. His words did make sense, but she still wasn't sure.

As Neven stared out at the fallen and cracked telephone poles near the street, something in his eyes grew distant, and an old feeling stirred within her as she watched him.

"Speak, don't forever hold your peace," Maisie said.

He whipped his head to hers. "Seriously?"

"What's wrong now?" Maisie scooched closer so her arm was pressed to his. He needed someone in that moment, and she wanted to be there for him.

"I thought maybe I could help be a hero after what happened to my mom, but the past few days proves I'm just a monster who can do nothing."

"You're not a monster." Maisie patted his back. "You're going to be a hero with me. Frankenstein's Monster was never the villain of the story."

Neven slung his arm around her shoulders and held her close. "Easy to say, Snow White was the ultimate innocent."

"Ah, my dear friend, but I've actually turned people to glass, while you were fine and dandy after exiting Vale's funhouse." Neven was luckier than all of them, and she was glad for it.

"Under all that upbeat attitude you always have, you're *still* positive and I sort of admire it, even though it's a very oddball reaction to this new existence."

"Why, thank you. I couldn't have said it more perfectly myself."

He didn't look as miserable for the time being, and Maisie didn't want to rehash and think about his feelings for Perrie. So while the sun set, Maisie stayed pressed against Neven, his comforting minty scent enveloping her, as they studied the cracked streets, the stalled cars, and the smoke curling into the air farther away where buildings had been burned to the ground.

Once Vale was gone, Maisie, Neven, and Perrie would help to return this world to its former glory. That was a promise.

As the sun's rays crept out for morning to bring about the day, Maisie's eye flicked open. A feeling of adrenaline pulsed within her. She was fresh and pumped to continue their mission in the next town.

Maisie propped herself up against the tree trunk and shook her legs out to get them ready to roam about. Neven yawned as he stood and stretched his scarred arms toward the sky. The insides of her stomach performed a little dance as she studied the sliver of skin where his shirt was lifted. A trail of dark hair rested below his belly button, leading to… She hurried and looked away. That old feeling had been there, a link to the past, and a part of her kind of *liked* it.

"Ready to go?" Maisie pushed herself up from the cool grass and brushed off the dried leaves and specks of dirt clinging to the skirt of her dress. Neven plucked a tiny leaf stuck to her back, and his touch sent a thrill through Maisie. She maneuvered away from him as she pretended to adjust her patch.

He chuckled. "More walking, right?"

She peered up at his face, and the light hit his jaw just right. He had an intriguing jaw. Maisie shook her head, needing to not think about his features. Any of them. Regardless of how pleasant they may be to look at.

"So, no walking today? We're just going to stand here?" He pointed to the ground.

"No." Somehow, Maisie tripped over that one-syllable word. "I mean, yes, we're going to walk." She pivoted on her heel and headed to the street, becoming her own compass since she lacked one.

Neven jogged up beside her. "You're acting weird, Mais."

She laughed, feeling back to normal, *focused.*

"Well, weirder than usual." He cracked a half smile.

"I adapt to my environment."

Debris and broken branches littered the road and leaves crunched beneath their feet. They hadn't talked to another living soul since Ben. Maisie wondered how far he'd gotten after leaving them in the dust. She hoped he'd made it to somewhere safe. What about Josselyn? Had she managed to snap out of it, or was she still out there creating headless glass statues? Maisie may not have been able to save her parents or Uncle James, but she was determined to save Perrie. Unknowingly, Maisie shook her fist in the air.

"You all right?" Neven asked, latching onto her arm. His hand was warm, comforting.

"Yeah, I'm fine. I'm just thinking."

"About what?"

"Ben. Josselyn." She paused, taking in a breath. "My family."

He nodded, understanding. Since the world turned to glass, Maisie doubted he'd stopped thinking about his mom once.

"Mais, listen—" Neven didn't finish his thought. A loud rustling in the trees stirred, directly above them.

They halted and exchanged a glance. Maisie thought for a second that it could be animal life, maybe squirrels or a raccoon, but a decaying odor permeated the air, and she knew she was wrong. Something twisted in the branches, shuffling through the leaves. Maisie squinted her eye to get a better view.

Without hesitation, the thing dove from the tree, and Maisie pulled Neven out of the way just in time.

"What the hell is that?" Neven's words echoed above her head.

They slowly backed away as the questionable thing rose from the ground. Human eyes stared back at them, unblinking, from a mask of rotted flesh. The greenish skin, which was far too large and sagging in places, revealed a hidden wooden body beneath its surface. The putrid smell of decay became stronger, drifting straight from the creation. If it weren't for the long wooden nose and too-big wooden hands protruding from the flesh, she wouldn't have known who it was.

"It looks like Pinocchio in a skin suit," Maisie whispered.

"We need to run," Neven hissed in her ear.

"We can't run. He knows we aren't part of the club anymore." Besides, if they escaped his presence now, then flesh-wearing Pinocchio might locate Vale before they had the chance to find Perrie. Then the whole saving Perrie mission would be finished before it had even begun. "Stay here—I've got a plan."

"Oh fuck, not another one."

Pinocchio hadn't moved a single wooden muscle—his

dark eyes remained unblinking, possibly waiting for them to make the first move. Maisie put on her best soothing face and inched closer to Pinocchio. He held his stance, chest puffed out, proudly wearing the dead skin.

Preparing her ammunition, Maisie cleared her throat before softly whistling a little melody. Pinocchio's head tilted to the side, creaking with each twist of his neck. It was working—Maisie had his attention.

A tune escaped her lips, one she sang just for him, "Pinocchio wants to be a live boy. He created his own clothes out of skin. It's time to fall fast asleep and—"

"What are you *doing*?" Neven demanded, hauling her to him, her back pressing against his firm chest.

"See, it's working. I'm hypnotizing him with my powers!" She pointed frantically at the wooden boy.

Maisie's gaze latched onto Pinocchio's and she opened her mouth to sing again, when he lunged at her. With each step, a groan sounded as he bent his knees. They whirled out of the way right before his hands connected with her throat. She should've known her ability wouldn't work on an immortal.

Pinocchio spun around to attack again, but Neven charged forward first, slamming the immortal into a tree trunk. The wooden boy clawed violently at Neven's chest, shredding his shirt and skin until blood bloomed to the surface.

Heart pounding, Maisie had to help Neven. Searching around the forest, she spotted a fallen tree branch on top of a bush that she could use as a weapon. She barreled for it, hoping Neven could hold the immortal off. Neven's power was strength, after all.

Pinocchio viciously gnashed sharp teeth at Neven's forearm as Maisie snatched the branch. She rushed back, swinging for the savage immortal's head until she finally thwacked the heavy wood. He howled an ugly sound, distracted enough by the blow to lose his grip on her friend. Neven took the opening and grabbed for Pinocchio, pinning the immortal's arms and legs to the ground.

The wooden creation hissed as Maisie lifted the branch over his head once more. Without hesitation, she brought it down hard, over and over again. He bucked and thrashed, shaking Neven's body with the movements. No matter how many times Maisie struck Pinocchio, he didn't surrender, wouldn't give up his battle.

"I don't know what else to do!" Maisie yelled. "Nothing's happening to his head."

"Screw this." Neven took Pinocchio's head and twisted it side to side. The immortal's sharp, wooden teeth snapped at Neven's hands, and she wondered if Neven's finger would grow back if Pinocchio bit it off.

Neven gave the head one more good twist, then it cracked off. Pinocchio's body turned limp and something like sap oozed from his neck. Neven's shoulders relaxed and he appeared pleased with himself as he tossed the wooden boy's head to the side like a piece of dirty clothing.

"Well done." Maisie grinned.

"Thanks, I—holy shit!"

Pinocchio's body sprang to life where Neven was kneeling. Maisie hurled herself toward Pinocchio's arms while Neven went for the legs. It had been too soon to celebrate. Using his inhuman strength, Neven ripped both legs away with a snap, then finished by cranking off the arms.

Neven hadn't even broken a sweat. Maisie, however, was drenched, and beads of sweat trickled down her flesh.

"Now what?" Neven asked.

"Do you think he can magically put himself back together?"

It was entirely possible. In her display, Maisie had killed the Huntsman once, and he'd poofed right back to life. From her experience, dead things didn't always stay dead.

"I don't know," Neven started. "Maybe we should bury him? Well, his pieces I guess."

A finger twitched on Pinocchio's severed arm. "Maybe bury them separately," she said.

"Good idea."

Neven found a patch of dirt and clawed at it with his hands. He dropped one twitchy leg in and hurried to cover it.

He made quick work of the remaining limbs while Maisie hunted down the head. Pinocchio's eyes were glazed over, glassy like the statues left behind. She pressed her fingers into the cool dirt and tried to make a grave for his head, even though she couldn't tear the ground up like Neven.

Giving her a lopsided smile, Neven patted her shoulder and gently took the head from her hands. "I got this."

Pinocchio snapped his teeth at Neven, but he buried the head casually, as if it was totally normal to dig a hole for an almost-dead marionette.

"So, singing to Pinocchio, *really*?" He laughed deeply when he stood.

Placing her hands on her hips, Maisie jerked her chin toward the fresh plot. "It's not like I knew for sure it wouldn't work on him, but I kind of forgot he wasn't human."

"The dead skin, wooden head and hands didn't give it away?" Neven held his hands in the air, and she gave each one a high five. He laughed again, the beautiful sound singing in her ears, as they headed toward the street.

"How's your chest?" she asked, lifting his torn shirt to inspect the wounds, but they were already healed. Only blood and taut muscles on his strong chest were there.

"I'm all right," he said, voice low as they stared at one another.

Swallowing, she dropped his shirt and peered down at her hands. "Can we find somewhere to scrub this syrup off *unless* you want to go search for some pancakes?"

"That's fucking gross, Mais."

Maisie laughed. "Come on, I'm pretty sure there are some houses a couple blocks away." She took one confident step forward before Neven stopped her.

"Look, I know you want to get Perrie back, and I do too, but we need to be more careful. That was close, too close," he said, his voice firm. But his expression held something softer, concern.

Even though the expression on his face made her heart sing, telling her to take a step toward him, she had to take a step back. "Aw, are you worried something's going to happen to me?"

"I'm serious!" His shoulders slumped. "I'd miss you, Mais."

"You've been fine without me for months and months, you'd be okay. If something happens to me on the way and it helps save Perrie, that's fine—she's all that's left of my family. There's no one else."

Neven tugged at his hair with a dirt-covered hand. "I didn't try to talk to you because you were harder to get through to than Perrie, and that's saying a lot."

His big brown eyes found hers, and she could tell he wanted to say something else. But then he just shook his head and scowled. He didn't have anyone left either, so she understood where he was coming from, but she needed to try. Perrie had come after her without a second's hesitation when Maisie had gone missing.

"Let's get going." She patted his back a couple of times with a reassuring smile.

He ran a hand down his face, then surprisingly, he laughed. "That's it? You give me a pat on the back and everything's fine now?"

"Yes. Now let's get going before Pinocchio becomes *Day of the Dead*."

"That's the best idea you've had so far."

TWELVE

Maisie

Maisie and Nev headed down a street where several crashed cars rested. A truck was smashed into a tree with a family of four inside—all glass. Another had taken a nose dive into a grassy ditch. Two smaller vehicles were rammed into one another, pieces of their cars scattering the ground. Maisie blew out a breath and pushed forward.

A few roads down, past a shattered gas station, rows of houses lined unbroken pavement. Thankfully, it hadn't been a long walk from Pinocchio's graves to sunshine in suburbia. Every house was the same exact make and model with a couple alterations in windows and mailboxes.

Maisie threw her hand out to the side, stopping Neven. She looked both ways before they crossed the street, making sure she didn't see any sign of another immortal. When the coast was clear, she grabbed Neven's hand and booked it across the street with him in tow.

"You know, Mais, you don't have to be my protector. I did just defeat that thing back there." Neven drew her to his side as they came to a halt.

"Sure, Neven." She patted his back.

Maisie believed he could take care of himself, but he wasn't the best at observing situations. Maybe she wasn't either because neither one of them had spotted Pinocchio up in the tree. She wouldn't say it was her fault though—his woodenness had blended in with the tree, while the hunk of skin he'd worn was a shade of green that fused with the leaves. A little chameleon, he was.

"Take your pick," Neven said, scanning the mostly beige houses.

"The middle one."

"Why the middle?" He cocked his head, clearly skeptical of her choice.

There was always a method to her madness. "Besides for it looking rather cozy in the center? Strategically, it's the safest point between the beginning and the end."

"How?"

"If anyone is looking for us"—Maisie gestured at both ends of the street—"they'll check the first couple houses. They won't keep looking if the first two are empty—they'll just move on." Plus, she would feel more protected by the barriers of the other homes.

Neven palmed his face in both hands and groaned. Sarcasm laced his next words. "And what if they choose the middle house first?"

Maisie chewed on her thumbnail for several seconds, pondering what he'd said. "But what if they don't?"

"You can't answer a question with *another* question!" he hissed, his voice cracking.

She couldn't help but giggle. "Trust me, Neven. The middle house is the safest place to be. Come on"—Maisie strode toward the house in the center—"and join the fun side."

He gave her a side stare and attempted to conceal a grin.

Overgrown grass and lawn gnomes surrounded the house.

Not one or two small little smiling men, but about fifty. This house was right up her alley, other than the statues slightly resembling the dead dwarves back in the Snow White display. But since there were more than seven, relief washed over her.

"Are you sure you don't want to pick another house?" Neven asked, lifting the closest gnome from its place beside a bright pink flower. The figure held a watering can and his grin took up half his face.

"No. It's perfect," Maisie said, placing a hand on her hip. "You know they aren't real."

He arched a brow and set the gnome back on the ground. "I know, but it's still fucked."

Maisie brushed past him and reached for the knob, finding it locked. Neven shrugged, rising on his tiptoes to look through the half-window above the door.

"Looks like there's a backdoor," he said.

They walked around the house to the back, not completely away from the gnomes since more littered the backyard. The backdoor didn't do them much good with it also being locked and all. Neven discovered another entrance by punching through a window.

"I'm not paying for that." She grinned.

Neven rolled his eyes. "Whatever, just get over here so I can help you inside." He cleared away the rest of the glass with his shirt and lifted her up. His fingers trailed down her sides as she crawled through, and a warmth spread through her. She ignored the feeling and unlocked the door for his larger frame.

Maisie set her borrowed bag down and decided to search the house while Neven patched up the window. It was a quick process—three bedrooms and one bathroom. The living room and the kitchen were connected, both appearing clear—no villainous immortals and no glass statues. Photographs lined the hallway and several more stood on a shelf beside the TV. It looked to be a single mom and her two high school kids. Maisie wondered if they were caught on the street in one of the cars she'd passed, or had they been able to escape?

She rooted for the latter.

"All done with the window," Neven said as he joined her in the kitchen.

"Shower time. You go first."

"Oh no, ladies first." Neven tried to prod her to the door in the hallway.

Maisie wiggled out of his arms. "I don't think so. You're covered in more of Pinocchio's sap than me, Neven. And I need time to brainstorm."

"You do that."

"You seem to enjoy saying that," Maisie called to his back.

A few seconds later, the sound of the shower turned on and a string of loud curses followed. She softly laughed to herself—it seemed Neven had forgotten the water wasn't going to be hot.

Maisie took a seat at the perfectly-round kitchen table, her fingers silently tapping the wood as she thought of a strategy. Finally, she wrote down, *Make sure to have a weapon.* That was all she had... She needed a distraction. The fridge took up a corner right next to her, practically begging her to look inside. She drew the door open. And … she should've kept the forsaken thing closed.

A rancid odor invaded her nostrils and she gagged. Not that any of the food would've still been good without power, but she would've probably still eaten the cheese slices if they didn't have mold growing on them.

The pantry, however, had her bouncing in place. It held a box of crackers, a can of spray cheese, and a few packs of breakfast bars. Maisie snatched the crackers and cheese can before resuming her brainstorming.

By the time the shower turned off, Maisie had managed to jot down a few more ideas.

"Be prepared. The water is freezing." Neven padded into the kitchen, shivering.

Maisie took a blanket from the back of the couch in the living room. Opening it, she laid the fleece across his shoulders as he watched her with a curious expression.

"What?" Maisie asked as she tucked the ends together for him to hold.

"Nothing."

Not really an answer. But then Maisie remembered her notes. She grabbed her notepad and handed it to him. "Here."

As he scanned over the notes, a large bead of water slid down his cheek. She reached to wipe it away with her fingertips, and he threw his head back as if she'd struck him.

Maisie frowned, confused. "What?"

"Nothing," he muttered while avoiding her eye.

"You had water on your cheek."

At that, he looked at her, his lips set in a tight line. "Thanks. It was just unexpected."

Is he thinking about what happened with Vale? Maybe he had a problem with being touched after what he'd gone through with that monster. Even though she'd already touched him several times… "You know you can talk about it."

"What?" A puzzled expression formed on his face.

"I get it. Your situation with Vale caused you to not want to be touched." Maisie wanted to reach out and put her hand on his arm, pull him close, but the reaction might cause him to fold into himself.

He slapped his forehead and slid his palm slowly down his face, shaking his head. "You don't even know the half of it. But no, I'm fine about Vale. I mean, as fine as one can be after having your body torn apart, but I don't have any of those effects from it." He handed the notes back to her before she could give him a response. "What I'm more concerned about is that the maniac who did these things to me has Perrie. We're going after him and all we've got to defend ourselves is a little notepad with a bunch of useless ideas. You have no hows." Neven caught himself at the last second, seeming to realize what he'd said.

"Well, how about you write the hows while I take my shower then," Maisie mumbled, tapping the notepad three times in his face before tossing it back on the table. She stomped away without looking back.

"Maisie, wait!" he stammered. "That's not what I meant— I'm sorry!"

Bring weapons! Find Perrie! Put Vale in a display in the Glass Vault! Destroy the Glass Vault! Those ideas are good! Maisie slammed the door shut and practically ripped off her dress. She threw it at the floor, along with her eye patch. Anger rolled through her in waves and she didn't realize how mad she was until she stepped into the shower. All because of Neven. She never got mad—occasionally frustrated, but never angry. Taking a deep breath, she focused on something else— eating the cheese on those crackers once she finished showering.

Her hand drew the curtain closed, and she turned on the shower. When the freezing blast of water pelted her skin, Maisie released a high-pitched shriek. She'd forgotten to prepare herself for the blasted cold.

"Maisie? Are you all right?" Neven shouted, his voice shaky as he barreled through the door.

She startled before clenching the curtain and wrapping it around herself. "I'm fine. I just forgot the water was going to be so cold," Maisie said, trembling while peeping her head out at him.

Relief filled his eyes as he stared at her, his hand clutching his chest as he worked to slow his breathing. "Next time, can you not scream like that?"

"I would have prepared myself if you hadn't made me mad earlier," she pointed out.

Neven pinched the bridge of his nose. "Look, I didn't mean what I said. Your notes are more than what I have."

Maisie's teeth chattered as the cold drops met her flesh.

"Are we going to stand here and chat all day? I need to finish."

Neven's cheeks reddened when his gaze focused back on hers. It must've hit him that she was showering while they were having a chat. A grin spread across her face. She didn't know why he felt embarrassed—he was only seeing her head, and the curtain concealed her entire body. Really, he'd seen more of her earlier in the dress with her arms exposed.

"You're forgiven!" Maisie yelled as he hightailed it out of the bathroom. She leaned back against the wall of the shower, finding his reaction rather cute. Then she remembered he was in this very shower just before her… Images of him naked while washing floated in her head, and now *her* cheeks were heating.

Cheese. Crackers. Cheese. Crackers. She repeated the words like a mantra in her head as she finished showering.

Once Maisie slipped her magically pristine dress back on, she headed into the living room, clean but shivering. Neven pounced on her with the blanket she'd used on him earlier.

"Why thank you, Neven." Maisie snuggled down into the soft fleece.

"No problem, I knew you'd be cold since I'd been." He smiled, resting his hand on her shoulder.

Maisie's eye locked on it, remembering her earlier shower thoughts. As if reading her mind, he drew his hand away. She tugged the blanket around her until she was as snug as a burrito, which reminded her of food, which reminded her of cheese in a can. Darting for the table like her life depended on it, she halted when she reached the now-open can.

Throwing the blanket to the tile floor, Maisie lifted the can and cranked the tip to the side. A remnant piece of yellow cheese rose to the top before falling to the table. Her heart plummeted.

Maisie slammed the empty can down on the table, releasing a metal clank throughout the room. She shut her eye, her chest heaving as she took deep breaths.

That's twice in one day and less than an hour apart? Frustration coursed through her veins, and her fingers vibrated from how mad she was. Neven hadn't spoken a word, but she knew he stood a few feet away, silently watching. She opened her eye and turned to face the culprit. He didn't so much as blink.

"My cheese!" she finally shouted, marching up to him with her fist shaking in the air. "If I could sing you to glass right now, I would!"

His eyes widened. "How the hell was I supposed to know you wanted that cheese? It was just sitting there!"

"*Maybe* because it wasn't there when we came in? *Maybe* because it was sitting next to my notepad? *Maybe* because it was right in front of the chair I was sitting in!"

Suddenly, her feet were off the floor and she squeaked, finding herself in Neven's strong arms. He carried her to the couch and plopped down onto the cushions. His gaze held hers, and she could feel the beat of his heart against her. He then gently set her beside him.

"What was that for?" She laughed.

"You were getting a little too intense—*over fucking cheese.*"

"Well, it was *mine*, and I would have happily shared half the can with you if you'd have waited." She rumpled his almost dry hair, messing it up like she used to do, feeling back to herself.

"Next time I find food, I'll ask first. Do you want me to get you the box of crackers?" He rose from the couch, and she pulled him back down beside her.

"A cracker without a partner isn't fun."

He rolled his eyes *hard*. "I'll stack it with two crackers, then."

"Fine," she drawled. "If you insist."

Neven left her on the couch, her gaze sliding down his flexing muscles to his backside. She swallowed and looked away.

He returned from the kitchen with both the blanket and crackers in hand. With a smile, and a rush of something else pulsing inside of her, she dug into the box. As she bit into a cracker, she was still reminded of what amazement the crackers could've become if only she'd had that cheese. But the warmth of Neven beside her made it all better.

THIRTEEN

Maisie

"What do you think Vale's doing with all the collected souls?" Maisie asked.

Neven handed her the last two crackers. He'd been generous enough to let her have more than half the box since he *did* eat all the cheese.

He considered her question a second longer, staring deeply into the darkness of the empty cracker box. Maisie waited patiently so as not to disturb his train of thought.

"I don't know." He shook his head. "I mean, I may possibly have a clue."

She perked up and pulled the blanket tighter against her body. "You do? Why didn't you say something before?"

"I didn't think it was important?"

"It's definitely important now, Neven!" Maisie practically jumped into his lap, which caused him to fall back on the armrest, dropping the empty box.

"Aug—I mean Vale—mentioned something about power. He said the Glass Vault was the source of it all."

"It's a start."

"Now if only—" Neven didn't get to finish his sentence as the vibration of a violent tremor shook the couch.

No, not the couch, the entire house!

The walls, the windows, everything quaked. Neven grabbed her arm at the same time she leapt to the floor like a flying squirrel, arms opened and all. He dove next to her as the wood beneath them rattled, her teeth clacking together from the movement.

"What are you doing?" he whisper-shouted.

She put one finger to her lips and another to his, giving him the quiet signal. His lips were soft against her digit, but she didn't have time to think about that as she pulled it away. The briefest of pauses occurred between each tremor, which made Maisie wonder if it was footsteps and not an earthquake. Maisie pointed toward the window at the front of the room, ignoring Neven's dirty look, and army crawled to it.

Neven sighed and joined her, peering over the top of her head as she peeled the curtain back a fraction of an inch. Her eye widened when it fell on a massive troll stomping along the wide street, creating craters in her wake. This troll was just as filthy as the last one Maisie had seen days ago. The immortal's flesh sagged, her large breasts flapping against her belly, and matted hair clung to her back. Maisie scooted away from the window and leaned against the wall. Neven followed suit, his arm shaking as he wrapped it around her shoulders.

"What was the point of that?" Neven hissed in a low voice.

"I had to see what it was."

"What would you have done if the troll was coming in here?"

"We would've run out the backdoor." She shrugged—it was that simple.

Neven rolled his eyes and drew her closer.

As if on cue, a loud crash tore through the air at the end of the street. The ground rumbled once more, lasting for only a few seconds before everything turned silent. Neven's chest heaved, his breaths coming out rapidly through his nostrils. Maisie wrapped her arm around his waist and held his free hand to quiet his nerves. The crashing hadn't been too close, so her nerves weren't as loud.

The antsy part of her wanted to run outside and see what had happened. She attempted to calm that part of herself by stroking Neven's hand with her thumb, drawing soothing circles to help his fright at the same time.

After about fifteen minutes, Neven's breaths came out even and she couldn't control herself any longer. Maisie unfolded herself from him and jumped to her feet before racing for the front door. She drew it open and hopped down the steps past the gnomes.

"Oh, come on, Maisie!" Neven called.

At the end of the driveway, past the curb and mailbox, she peered out at the end of the street. Dust billowed upward from a pile of rubble. The troll seemed to be long gone.

"What?" Neven rasped when he caught up with her. Then he spotted the destruction, his lips parted before giving her a hard look. "Don't even say it."

Maisie couldn't help it—her lips curved into a wide grin. "So, we should've chosen a house at the end of the street, right? Not one in the middle?" She laughed, gesturing to the crushed one-story home at the end of the road. To see a house in shambles like that was still a devastating sight, but no worse than anything she'd seen thus far. Thankfully, no one was likely there to get crushed, but turning to glass wasn't a much better option.

Neven tried to hide his smile. "I was talking about us staying at the *other* house at the *other* end of the street."

"Sure, Neven."

The sun was quickly fading, the sky turning hues of red and orange. The moon, the stars, and the night would be peeking out soon, so they headed back inside in case troll number two decided to venture back.

"We should probably hit the sack." Neven yawned.

"You can take one of the beds." She nodded in the direction of the bedrooms.

"Where are you going to sleep?"

Maisie held out her arms, then fell gracefully onto the cushions of the couch and closed her eye. "Right here."

"Why not a bed?"

"I would, but I don't know the people who slept in it, or how clean the sheets are. It's too weird." Plus, some people slept naked in their sheets, and who knew what sort of bodily fluids leaked from them there. Just because she was immortal didn't mean she stopped thinking about things like that.

"But you're going to let *me* take a bed?" he countered.

"Yes." She opened her eye, her expression sheepish.

"Gee, thanks," he said, folding his arms and inching closer to her. "Move over and make room."

"What?" Her heart slammed against her sternum, but not from fright as he stood above her, waiting for her to make room—something else.

"Look, we stay together." Neven pulled at the edges of his hair. "If that thing comes back and we have to bolt, I want us to be ready to go."

"All right." That made sense, yet it didn't stop her heart from singing to her.

Neven took the other side of the couch and lay down, his body too long to fit on it comfortably. As he adjusted his head, her heart sang louder, thumping and thumping. And when his arms opened up for her, the blasted organ screamed.

"*What*?" she asked, her voice high-pitched.

"Seriously, Mais?" Neven sat up and drew her down with him. "You're not going to sleep with my feet in your face, and I'm definitely not sleeping with yours in mine."

After nervous laughter and awkward shifting, they settled into a comfortable enough position. Neven wrapped his arm around her waist, and her back pressed against his firm chest. She could feel every single one of his deep breaths, every single one of his heartbeats.

It was actually kind of perfect. *Perfect? No, I can't be liking the snuggling session with Perrie's ex!*

Maisie was about to break out of his arms and go for a bed, regardless of a stranger's potential semen, blood, or sweat. But then Neven held her tighter, and she didn't know what to do. He was warm and comfortable, and she fit perfectly in the pocket of his arm and chest.

Stop it! Maisie needed her notebook to distract herself, but it was across the room, and by the sounds of his laborious breaths, he'd already fallen asleep.

But the tiredness she'd been feeling had already left as her mind raced about all the wrong things concerning Neven. He was Perrie's. He'd always been Perrie's, ever since the day they'd met.

They would rescue Perrie, and her cousin and Neven could live happily ever after. That was the way it was supposed to be. That was the way it always should've been.

A memory sprang forward from the rug she'd shoved it under. Despite her best attempts at sweeping it away, it found its way back out in her dreams when she'd finally fallen asleep.

"Perrie, are you sure you're going to be okay?" Maisie asked.

"I don't know. I may die tonight, and you'd have to figure out a way to revive my corpse." Perrie tried to smile, her skin pale, while she clutched her stomach, still on the verge of throwing up.

"Eh, you'll live." Neven shrugged but still looked concerned as he waved her a goodbye.

After Maisie closed the door, she turned to face Neven. It was always the three of them, Neven and Perrie, or Maisie and Perrie. But she would give it a little variety this time and make it Maisie and Neven. "You coming to watch the movie?"

"I can walk home." He glanced out toward the door.

"You want to leave?" Maisie asked, confused.

"No. No. Only if you don't want me to come." He smiled, a flush creeping up his neck.

"Nah, I don't want you to leave. You're going to be my movie partner in crime." Too bad Perrie was going to miss out on such a Phantom-tastic day.

Maisie ran into her room as soon as they made it over the threshold and grabbed two masks—one was hers and the other Perrie's. She tossed a mask to Neven when she padded back into the living room. He rolled it over in his hands, giving it a peculiar look over.

"Put it on," Maisie said, but he continued to stare at it. "Here. Let me help you." She took the mask from Neven's hands, and he hunched down a little so she could easily bring the elastic cord over his face. Her fingers brushed his skin, and she found it to be one of the softest she'd ever felt. "Perfect. You look exactly like the Phantom."

His eye on the masked side shifted from side to side. He didn't speak a word, just continuously blinked at her, seeming unimpressed.

"Let me put mine on." Maisie tugged the elastic cord over her head, slid the white mask onto her face, and smiled. "There."

Neven grinned and shook his head.

Now that they were in character, it was the perfect time for her to start the movie.

During the film, Neven's arm brushed hers, but she didn't think too much of it besides it feeling nice. Their bodies were pressed close together, but Maisie always relaxed like this with Perrie too.

Throughout the remainder of the movie, Neven fidgeted and tapped his knee constantly, making it jerk. Maisie wanted to ask him if he was trying to perform the knee-check-thing a doctor did, but she let him continue his leg dance.

As soon as the Phantom drew to a close, she glanced at Neven to see what he thought about it. Only, he already faced her, watching her nervously. He then leaned forward and pressed his lips to hers, soft and warm. She'd never felt anything like it before. A crinkling came from their masks when their noses rubbed together. He was like the perfect Phantom.

As she realized what was happening, she froze, then pulled back and released a small scream.

Leaping from the couch, she booked it to her room, shut the door, and locked it behind her. Hands shaking, she backed away, like Neven might possibly break it down.

The mask was stiff against her face and it reminded her of the kiss, so she took it off, burying it underneath her bed.

Did I want him to kiss me? Maisie wasn't sure, but if he did it again, she would want him to. She would want to feel those soft lips on hers one more time. Her heart quickened at the thought, the anticipation. This time she wouldn't run off screaming like a sacrificial animal.

After Maisie calmed the singing birds in her stomach, she casually unlocked and opened the door, walking out of the room as if nothing happened. Neven still sat on the couch, his spine stiff, but the mask was no longer on his face.

"So, about the movie…" He then started to talk about the film for a long time. There was no mention of the kiss, and her chest was struck with disappointment. It was as though her Phantom had left her. But she wasn't brave enough to bring it up.

Maisie's eye flew open, and she was now fully awake. The memory-turned-dream played over and over in her head.

She'd been only fourteen, and she'd never had a crush on anyone before. Even after that day, neither one ever brought up the kiss, not for the rest of ninth grade or the following year. It was as if it had never happened. Not even Perrie knew about it.

Maisie couldn't tell Perrie how she'd felt about him—he'd been her cousin's best friend.

Then the summer Neven's dad passed away, Maisie had been in Turkey visiting her family. Perrie had been there for him when Maisie wasn't. Perrie was the one who'd made him better, not Maisie, and then they fell in love. Maisie had selfishly wished it had been her who'd been there for him, because maybe he would've fallen in love with her instead. But then she'd seen Perrie and Neven together. She'd known then that it was right, *they* were right, so that was when Maisie brushed everything under the rug.

Maisie closed her eye with Neven's arm still tightly wrapped around her, pretending for a moment that she'd told him back then how she'd felt, before *everything*. She was about to drift back to sleep, when an ear-piercing scream roared through the street from outside. Neven and Maisie jerked up at the same time, and she could see the fear in his face.

Another wail tore through the dawn, accompanied by thunderous crackling. Lunging for the door, Maisie ran out into the morning light and discovered the source of the noise.

It was *Perrie*.

FOURTEEN

Vale

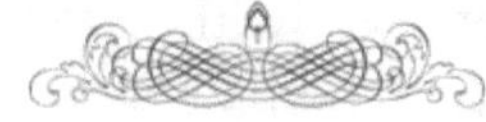

Vale woke to the blank space of a white wall and a throbbing headache. His eyes focused in and out, the pain in his head blurring his vision. This was something new and entirely unwelcome. He wanted to rip his brain out and slam it against the wall, if only that were possible.

He couldn't remember anything from last night after falling asleep—it was almost as if he had woken from hibernation. After he blinked a few times, the pain faded.

The day was new, yet something did not feel right. He rolled over to wake his lovely Bride, but found she was not there beside him. The covers were pulled back, revealing a cold and empty spot.

She normally woke him by nibbling on his neck. What the fuck was going on? He forcefully slapped the empty spot when a thought crossed his mind. Elise Rodriguez had come back to herself. What if…

No. Impossible.

He pushed himself out of the bed, throwing the door open

so hard it crashed and broke into the wall. Without a pause, he raced down the steps and called, "Bride?"

Nothing. No answer.

Vale brought a hand to his chest. If his heart could beat, it would have exploded with fury—this could not be happening. It *was not* happening.

He searched everywhere, including the front and backyard. Then he thought maybe she had gone downstairs to the basement, to relive the bloodshed. Opening the door, he hurried down the steps and found nothing except burned down candles.

Vale rushed to the living room where Red was sprawled across the couch, snoring quietly with a line of drool trailing down her cheek. *What an insignificant waste of space.* He could not understand what his father ever found in her that was worth saving.

"Red!" he roared as he approached her.

The immortal's eyes burst open and almost popped out of their sockets. He then slammed his hand around her throat, tightening his grip. Red's eyelids fluttered as the air in her lungs cut off. She clawed at his chest, but he only squeezed harder.

"Where is she?" he demanded, his voice low, frenzied.

She only shook her head and gripped the couch cushions, those filthy nails of hers digging in. Lifting her by the neck with one hand, he flung her to the floor.

Red brought her hands to her throat and lurched forward. "What was *that* for?" she seethed.

Vale sauntered toward her, prepared to rip her apart in the slowest way possible. She was no innocent—after her mortal death, she had come to the Underworld after all. He knelt beside her, fastening his gaze on hers. "Now, where is she?"

"The Bride?"

"Who the fuck else would I be talking about?" Vale growled.

Red had to go soon—she had irritated him since day one. She was a tick that would not go away, a parasite that had found its way into his father's bedroom. If he could dispose of her without consequence, he would do it in an instant.

"I don't know. I saw her earlier this morning when I was heading to the basement," she stuttered, running her hands through her hair, trying to press it down. "I assumed she went back upstairs with *you*." He could sense by the way she said the last word, she was not as nervous as she was pretending to be. In fact, she seemed elated to find out the Bride was gone.

Fiery flames coursed within his veins, sewing their way throughout his entirety. His anger wanted to come out and play a vicious little game with Red.

"Where did she go?" His voice was a calm, deadly whisper.

Her mouth hung open, and he could see her tongue stroking the inside of her cheek. If she did not come up with a good answer, he was going to cut it out and make her choke on it.

"I don't know." She shrugged. "I warned you that you were becoming too attached to her, *didn't I*?"

Running a finger through one of Fannie's curls, he gave it a hard yank and she yelped. "If I do not find her, I am going to rip this red hair, you so dearly cherish, out piece by piece and then move on to different body parts. Isn't that the way you like to torture your victims out here?"

"I understand."

"If you find her before I do, your punishment will be lessened a fraction." Vale whirled away from Red, then stopped and glanced over his shoulder. "And clean those nails of yours, you disgust me."

Fists tightened, he burst through the front door and out into the daylight. The sun's rays beamed down on him as he ground his teeth. The answer he did not want to think about earlier was there once again. He knew without a doubt his Bride was gone and replaced with Perrie Madeline.

The anger inside him needed to be released. Vale threw his fist into the first thing he came into contact with—the tree cracked under the powerful blow. He smacked his fist against the trunk over and over, watching bright crimson leak from his knuckles. Chest heaving, he lifted his hand and studied the red liquid as it trickled to the ground. The sight of his blood relaxed him for a moment. He swore to himself then and there that he would find Perrie Madeline.

The Glass Vault would have enough souls very soon, giving him the power to locate her. He would rip Perrie Madeline apart, then put her back together again and again, until she became his Bride once more.

It was impossible for him to love, but what he felt for the Bride, what he did not know he could feel, was stronger than anything he had ever experienced. She was his and *only* his, and he knew with everything in himself that he belonged to her.

FIFTEEN

Maisie

A few houses down the street, Perrie stood, her wild hair blowing in the wind, her white gown swishing around her. She released scream after scream, hurling bolts of lightning toward anything and everything. A stream of sparks struck a long, thick tree branch above Maisie's head, snapping it off. It crashed to the ground, missing her by an inch. Perrie's face looked pale with fear written in her expression. Maisie tried to take a step forward, but Neven tugged her back.

"How do we know it's actually her, Maisie?"

"It's her. I know it." She inhaled a deep breath, got in a runner's stance, and prepared to lunge toward her cousin.

"We're both going to get her. Just don't try to army crawl after her." He sighed, raking a scarred hand through his hair.

"That would be a better idea, but I wouldn't be quick enough." Before he could say another word, she sprung forward, thrashing her arms in the air. "Perrie! Perrie, it's me! It's Maisie and Neven!"

Neven shouted something at Maisie, the sounds of his feet

pounding right behind her. Between Neven's shouting and her running, Maisie saw the horror of recognition cross Perrie's face just as she released a bolt of power. Pure white light slammed into Maisie's stomach, sending her flying backward. Her body smacked against the pavement, her spine cracking into two.

"Maisie!" Neven yelled, falling to her side in an instant. His arm looped behind her neck, and one of his comforting hands clasped hers. "You're going to be okay."

As the world spun, she peered up at his perfect face and smiled. "Of course I am. I'm immortal, remember?"

"Oh my god! Fuck!" Perrie screeched, her voice filled with panic. "I'm so sorry, Maisie. I'm so, so sorry!"

Maisie could feel her spine fuse back together, each fiber connecting. Chest heaving, she sat up with Neven's help. Perrie stood frozen in place just a few feet away, her brown hair wilder, matching the expression on her face. Her cousin's shoulders relaxed, relief seeming to hit her once she found Maisie sitting, no longer harmed.

"See? I'm good as new." Maisie grinned.

Perrie's lower lip quivered as her eyes filled with tears. Her legs buckled and she collapsed to her knees, gripping the white strands of her hair as she sobbed. The sound of her agony pierced Maisie straight to her heart—it was worse than anything she'd ever experienced, even her own deaths with the Huntsman.

Neven pulled Maisie to her feet and they ran to her. Perrie rocked back and forth on her knees, her hands covering her face. They needed to get her inside before someone found them.

Neven made it to Perrie first and scooped her up in his arms, her tears spilling onto his shirt. "I've got you, Perrie," he said in a soft, soothing voice. "I've always got you."

Maisie touched Neven's shoulder and ran her hand through her cousin's curls. "No, Perrie, *we've* got you."

Perrie turned into his chest, racked with sobs, as they walked back inside the house. Neven took her to the couch, lowering himself as carefully as possible, so as not to disturb her. Maisie closed the door and locked it back up before joining them on the floor. She stroked her cousin's hair again to calm her.

She'd hoped Perrie would be her usual smiling self when they found her, but her cousin remained in this position for a long while, crying, not looking up at either of them. Maisie could only imagine how this must be for her, to know that August wasn't ever real. The word devastated wasn't strong enough to describe it.

Maisie didn't know how much time had passed when her cousin finally lifted her head, her tears slowing as she looked at them. "I'm so glad you two are all right," Perrie said with a ragged breath.

Neven moved Perrie from his lap and set her on the couch beside him. She took his hands in both of hers, squeezing them tightly. Maisie studied those joined hands, and her heart raced in her chest, singing louder. She couldn't make it stop, so she kept her gaze trained on her cousin's face.

"Hi, Perrie." Neven's voice was low, gentle.

"Oh, Nev," Perrie stuttered, tears sliding down her cheeks, "this is all my fault, I'm so sorry."

Neven wrapped the blanket he and Maisie had been sharing around Perrie's shoulders. It wasn't Neven and Maisie. It was Nev and Perrie. Maisie had to remember that. She stepped back and swallowed the tainted feeling stirring within her.

"I'm going to take a quick lap around the neighborhood to make sure it's clear," Neven started. "It will give you two some time to talk."

Perrie reached for Maisie and drew her down beside her. All Maisie wanted was for her cousin to be okay, inside and out.

"We were coming for you, Perrie. We've been looking for you this whole time and you found us!" Maisie squeezed her cousin's shoulder, breathless with relief.

"It must have been our blood oath." Perrie smiled, then it slipped from her tired face. "I've done terrible things, Maisie."

They both had.

"I did bad things, too, but we can't hold onto that. You've got this. You have to be strong here. I know the world is a wild carnival ride at the moment, but it could all be worse. There is *always* worse."

"How can it be any worse than it already is? There's a demon that basically murdered people and turned them into things that can't die, who by the way, are now wreaking havoc on Earth. Then to top it off, this fucker pretended to be someone I'm in love with. I killed a lot of people."

"Were in love with," Maisie pointed out.

"*What*?" She jerked, the color draining from her face.

"You just said *I'm in love with*. You meant were, right?" Maisie ran her thumbnail along the edges of her front teeth as she awaited Perrie's answer.

"That's what I meant," she said in a rush.

Was it? Maisie wasn't in Perrie's position, so she didn't quite understand. But she believed she would've been thinking of all the ways to kill the demon instead of crying over him.

She took Perrie's hands in hers and gently squeezed them. "Do you remember what you said to me back in Snow White's cottage? You told me Crazy Maisie wasn't me, and we were pretty much two separate people. So you're going to have to look at it like that in this situation, too. The Bride isn't you— it's your alter. She's not who you really are, nor the actions you would've chosen."

Perrie sighed heavily. "I didn't really understand the situation then, and now that I see the memories are all mine, I was still the one out there doing everything."

"You're going to have to separate them. That's what I've

been doing, or you're not going to be able to live with yourself." Her cousin could do this. Maisie knew she could.

"You're always so smart with things, you know that, Maisie? But everyone we know is dead. Dad, Uncle Jaron, and Aunt Krista." Perrie let out another rack of sobs, and Maisie circled her arms around her cousin.

Perrie's grief felt as though it was transported to Maisie when she thought about what had happened to her parents and uncle. "I know they're gone, Perrie, but are they really? All we know is their souls got sent to the Glass Vault, but their glass statues are still here. Maybe there's a way to bring the souls back to their statue?" She desperately wanted that to be true, but she didn't know if they were really lost forever.

Perrie shook her head. "I don't know, Maisie. You haven't been with Vale this entire time. I don't think there's a way to defeat him."

That might be true, but Perrie would know better than anyone if there could be a way. "Um, Neven told me you crossed paths with him in the Glass Vault."

Perrie's body hunched forward, but not a single tear escaped her this time. "As you probably know, August is Vale. I confessed to August that I loved him, gave him everything I had, and I've never felt that way about anyone. Then he dragged me naked by my hair and tossed me in the cage with Neven. And the outcome was this." She trailed a hand across the scar at her throat.

A rush of anger rolled through Maisie, and she wanted to find a pickaxe like she had back in the Snow White display. She would slam it through Vale's darkened heart when she crossed paths with him again. Her fingers fidgeted with her dress as she thought about something else, almost too afraid to ask, but she pushed herself to do so. "How bad did he hurt you outside the Glass Vault?"

Perrie lowered her head and avoided Maisie's stare. "He—he didn't."

Maisie's nose wrinkled and her eyebrows became one long caterpillar. "What?"

"He treated *her* much differently than he did with me. When he had me in that tower and in the cage with Neven..." She blew out a breath, then hurriedly changed the subject. "Anyway, all Vale's trying to do is fill the museum with more souls so his powers grow stronger. I don't know a way to stop him."

"Yet. But we will." Maisie would fight in every way she knew how to come up with something. Her thoughts turned to Neven outside, and all Vale put him and Perrie through just to break them apart. The feelings of wanting him as more than a friend had resurfaced back to the correct setting like a Rubik's Cube. But no matter how much she wanted them to, they couldn't stay, so like before, Maisie twisted them inside her head so the colors were mixed up once more.

This was the moment for Perrie to get her happy ending. Defeat Vale, Perrie and Neven together, and Maisie joyous for everyone.

Maisie nudged her cousin's elbow. "You know, you can be happy again once we get the world back to normal. Neven's right there. You two would still be together if it wasn't for Vale. Now's your chance to make things right."

Perrie lifted her brows and fought a small smile. "So, it's like one of those action movies where the world is practically destroyed, but people still kiss and make up at the end as if nothing ever happened?"

"Why yes, yes it is." Maisie silently pleaded for Perrie not to sink back in her hole, but she would always be there to help dig her out if she did. Before the Glass Vault, sometimes it took people longer to heal over things, but in this new world, there wasn't time for that.

"Look, Maisie, I'm not going back to Nev. I know you have some plan brewing to bring down Vale, and I'll help you, but we'll only ever be friends."

"I don't understand." Why wouldn't she want him back?

Perrie wrapped her arms around her stomach, tears beading her lashes. "This isn't going to make sense. It doesn't even make sense to me. Technically, August is Vale, but if I have to admit it now, I will. I'm still in love with August who doesn't exist, yet the way I felt for him was deeper than it ever was with Nev. So it wouldn't be fair to Nev. Our relationship was rooted with friendship more than anything else. With August, those roots flourished into a beautiful blooming tree, so I wouldn't go back to anything that offered less. In fact, I wouldn't go to anyone."

Maisie cupped Perrie's warm cheek and brought her cousin's head to her shoulder.

"As horrible as this situation is," Perrie whispered, "I know if you're with me, things will be better."

"Does that mean you're ready to plot?"

"I'm ready to plot." Perrie said, lifting her head from Maisie's shoulder. And as Perrie smiled, determination radiated from every inch of her cousin.

The door creaked open and Neven walked in, unscathed by his brief journey. He grabbed the box of breakfast bars from the pantry and tossed one to each of them.

Opening up a bar, he said, "Don't worry, we're all alone. No trolls and no crazy girls shooting lightning at pedestrians."

Maisie held her breath, waiting for Perrie to cry, but she didn't. Her laugh filled the air, and it was the sound Maisie had been missing.

"Time to plot." Maisie looked to Neven, giving him a wide grin, when Perrie stopped laughing.

"Ah, yes, more plotting," he said sarcastically and settled in a seat at the kitchen table.

Perrie sank down across from him, and Maisie took the chair in between them. Maisie peeled off the top paper of her notes and stuck it to the back of the sticky pad. She then wrote down a question.

Maisie was about to open her mouth when Neven held up his hand. "Before we begin on a long journey of plotting as Maisie would call it, the most important question is, where is Vale now?"

She lifted the pad directly in front of Neven's face. "As I will have you know, that's the first question I have on my list."

"It's also the *only* question you have on your list."

"Don't worry, I have more coming your way." Maisie peeled the sheet she'd stuck to the back, wadded it up, and tossed it at Neven's head, hitting the bullseye.

He reached for it and tossed it back, but she dodged out of the way, laughing. Maisie glanced at Perrie, her lips parted while her gaze shot between Neven and Maisie.

Neven cleared his throat and focused back on Perrie. "How did you escape?"

"I just ran. I woke up, remembered who I was, and I ran away." She frowned, burying her hands into the skirt of her dress. "He was still asleep."

"Do you know where he is now?" Maisie asked, not wanting to dig too much into their sleeping arrangement.

"He could be anywhere if he knows I'm gone."

"Then we should keep moving." Maisie stood from the table and threw the notepad in her borrowed bag. "Hopefully, he doesn't know which direction you ran in and we can stay ahead."

"Never eat her cheese." Neven rolled his eyes while they trekked through a wooded area.

Perrie arched a brow. "I could've told you that, Nev."

Speaking of food, Maisie needed to find more breakfast bars. Immortals may not have to eat, but her taste buds were yearning for something.

Neven filled Perrie in on mostly everything. Perrie didn't go into great detail when she spoke next, but she did give them bits and pieces of what happened while they'd been separated. The things she'd done were ruthless, but again, it could've been much worse.

"Remember Ben Johnston?" Maisie asked Perrie.

"Troll display. Yes."

"We ran into him a few days ago. I tried to get him to join our team, but that didn't pan out. However, he did have his memories back."

"You know who else did? Officer Rodriguez. She— she…" Perrie covered her mouth with her hand and took a deep breath. Maisie placed her arm around Perrie's waist and Neven wrapped his around her shoulders. "She did, too. But me and Vale … we murdered her. She's gone."

"An immortal?"

Perrie straightened, wiping a few tears away before explaining to them how an immortal could die at Vale's hands. If he could make them, then he could break them too. Sooner or later, Maisie believed everyone would have their memories back—if they were still alive anyway.

"After I finished with Officer Rodriguez, Vale sent her soul back to the Glass Vault," Perrie said.

"How does that work?" Neven sounded confused—looked it too.

"We're bound to the Glass Vault, same as Vale," Perrie started. "That's why he wants the souls. It makes him stronger. It's like—"

"The Glass Vault is a battery?" Maisie interrupted.

Perrie nodded, and the skeleton of a plan took shape in Maisie's mind. They *could* set the Glass Vault on fire. If they destroyed his source of power, then maybe it would make him weak—maybe it would kill him altogether. And maybe Vale wasn't as invincible as he believed he was.

"I think I know what to do. Originally, I was going to have

all the immortals gang up on Vale. Bind, gag, and bring him to the Glass Vault," Maisie said, striking her fist against the open palm of her other hand. "They would only be going up against a demon from the Underworld. No big deal."

"If everyone is like Ben, that wouldn't have worked," Neven pointed out.

"Precisely, but I think if that big museum is Vale's main generator, burning it may actually work. I just—"

Before she had a chance to finish her plan, Maisie's feet were ripped out from beneath her. She landed flat on her face, a sharp pain throbbing in her nose and cheek. Something took hold of her leg and yanked her backward. A powerful scream tore from Maisie's throat, vibrating violently in her ears. Neven and Perrie latched onto her arms, their teeth clenched, unwilling to let go.

An excruciating pain radiated through her abdomen as both sides of her body were pulled. It felt as if her stomach was going to be ripped apart. All she could think of in that bizarre moment was what a way to go. She at least hoped Perrie and Neven would be left with the upper portion, so she wouldn't have to watch herself be eaten or torn to shreds.

Neven gave one hard tug, saving Maisie from the unknown's hand. She flew straight into him and landed on his chest with a forceful blow, knocking him to the ground. His fingers dug into her waist as she sat up, her knees cradling his hips. Taking a quick swallow, she didn't have time to focus on the position she was in on top of him—she sprang to her feet.

"Maisie!" Perrie screamed. "Look out!"

A flash of Perrie's white light struck the dirt a step away from Maisie's feet, rumbling the ground. Then a scream pierced the air, a foreign voice, as Maisie searched for her attacker. And there she was, the mermaid sloth who'd slowly crept her way down the street the other night. *How did she make it the same distance we have without falling apart?*

Then Maisie's gaze fell to a sparkling pond behind Perrie.

Oh, that's how.

The mermaid recovered quickly enough and shot forward, not at a snail's pace any longer. Unhinging her jaw, revealing a set of needle-sharp teeth, the immortal screeched and launched her body at Perrie. The lightning bolt didn't release from Perrie's fingers in time as the mermaid hit, burying her pointy teeth into Perrie's shoulder. Perrie wailed, struggling to yank the mermaid's head away by her blue hair.

Half the mermaid's blue tail still dangled from her upper body like it had the other day. Maisie jolted for it, grasping her tail in both hands and pulling on it, hard. The immortal howled, tossing her head back, Perrie's blood fresh on her dark lips.

The mermaid lunged for Maisie and sank her teeth into her neck. Maisie released a shrill scream. With all her strength, she pushed roughly at the immortal's chest, but the mermaid was glued to her throat. As Maisie wriggled, she wasn't quite sure if this creature was trying to be a vampire or a zombie.

Her flesh throbbed even more as the mermaid began sucking. Blood pulsed beneath Maisie's skin, leaving her veins as it entered the immortal's mouth. She needed to get this leech off of her, and as she shoved, the immortal was ripped away. The creature was in Neven's grip on the ground while he tried to wrestle her down. But she continued to screech and whip her body and tail about.

"A little help would be lovely!" he called.

"Team effort!" Maisie yelled as she and Perrie rushed to his aid, each taking an arm while Neven put his weight on the mermaid's tail. With half of the creature's body dangling, she still showed no sign of weakness.

"Do it," Maisie said, remembering what helped them the last time. "Just like with Pinocchio." The mermaid seethed at them, speaking in a language Maisie didn't understand. "Sorry, I can't hear you, little mermaid." It probably wasn't worth hearing anyway—she doubted the immortal was begging for her life.

Neven pulled, his face turning red, until a loud bone-crunching sound drowned out the mermaid's voice entirely. The blue tail thrashed in his grasp and he tossed it aside.

Next came the arms, then finally Neven removed the head. Green blood leaked from the missing appendages, surprising Maisie. She figured it would've been blue.

Perrie held a mermaid arm, staring at the still-wiggling fingers and asked, "Now what?"

"Bury time," Maisie yelled.

"Déjà vu?" Neven cracked a smile at Maisie as he went to dig the first grave.

"Déjà vu," she said back.

"You two have done this before?" Perrie asked.

"Oh, I forgot to tell you"—Maisie grinned, clapping the dirt from her hands—"Neven and I had a run in with creepy Pinocchio in the woods recently."

"It got pretty fucking ugly," he said.

"Neven kicked his little wooden behind, though."

"I'm glad I wasn't there for that one." Perrie tilted Maisie's head to inspect her neck wound, but it no longer ached.

"You didn't want to try *singing* again?" Neven gave Maisie a teasing shove.

She pushed him back playfully. "I really do have the worst power. You can still rip immortals apart, and Perrie's power knocked the mermaid down." Maisie hadn't tried singing to the mermaid, though. Maybe this time it would've worked if she had. She would have to try it again when they encountered another wicked soul. That was what she should've been calling them all along.

Neven looped his arm around Maisie's waist and pulled her in close, surprising her. She breathed in his minty scent, and her heart fluttered.

"Like you said, Mais"—Neven leaned in close—"team effort."

Laughing, Maisie glanced up and her gaze met Perrie's, who must've been watching them this whole time. A sinking feeling dropped to the pit of her stomach and she left Neven's warmth.

SIXTEEN

Perrie

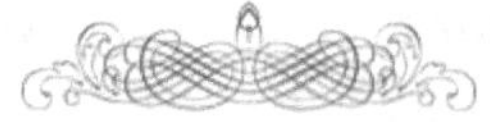

After their encounter with the mermaid, Perrie was even more exhausted. Every single part of her body and mind was.

She, Neven, and Maisie stumbled upon a, hopefully safe, place to sleep, far away from the fresh burial plots. There hadn't been any other sign of life along the way, only more and more glass statues. *Would this ever fucking end?*

They each took a shower, and Perrie curled up in bed beside Maisie in the abandoned room. Worry poured through her thoughts, almost all of it about Vale. Throughout the day, she'd wondered where he was, how damn close he could be. Maisie and Neven weren't overly concerned—they were too confident he wouldn't find them. Perrie knew better, though. Her gut told her he would find her, and that it would be before they were prepared to fight him. Yet, she didn't think they could prepare for him at all. Tomorrow they were going to continue toward the Glass Vault. It would be days before they got there, but they would attempt to destroy the museum as soon as they reached it. Maybe Vale wouldn't expect them to return to that hell.

She felt so … lost.

There were moments between Vale and the Bride that she wouldn't think about, that she *couldn't* think about. Perrie would rather hold on to the time in the tower when he'd snatched her by her hair and dragged her down the hall. That drive was what would help them win.

Maisie rested beside Perrie, fast asleep, her chest rising and falling. Most likely dreaming about sunshine and rainbows. Her cousin almost wouldn't sleep in the bed, until they'd found a spare set of sheets in the linen closet. Maisie was so lucky. Perrie wished she could borrow her damn optimism, even just for a little while. After all her cousin had been through, she was still just as strong as she was before the Glass Vault.

Much more than Perrie was. But she was going to force herself to push forward, like she'd done when she was inside the Glass Vault's displays.

As Perrie listened to Maisie's soft snoring, relief filled her again that she'd found her cousin. If she hadn't, Perrie didn't know where her dark thoughts would've taken her if she'd still been alone and on the run from Vale. She honestly didn't know if she could've survived. Even if they defeat him, Perrie wasn't sure if she would ever truly be free of him.

He was the reason she wasn't asleep, snoring softly like Maisie. When Perrie closed her eyes, she was back there in his bed, or on the metal table, bleeding out. She could see his green eyes, dancing in the shadows, following her wherever she went. Eyes she longed to gaze into, and eyes she wanted to run from. She saw his image in the faces of the people she'd let down—her dad, Aunt Krista, Uncle Jaron, and Neven.

Maisie.

Herself.

Gritting her teeth, Perrie pushed the covers away and padded quietly across the room. Maisie fidgeted, readjusted, then went back to snoring. Careful not to wake her, Perrie closed the door and headed into the living room. A dull lantern illuminated the room, casting shadows on the wall. Nev glanced up from the couch and offered her a small smile. The light lent itself to his pinkish scars, reminding her of another time, in another cell. And guilt seeped its way into her once more—she was the reason he went to the museum that day.

"Can't sleep?" he asked.

"No." She shook her head. "Why don't you get some rest? I'll take watch. Shouldn't let a good night's rest escape the both of us. It's better if someone gets some sleep while they can."

A loud whinny broke the silence from outside, followed by the hard thumps of hooves beating the ground. Perrie stilled as a rush of memories hit her of the time she'd spent in Sleepy Hollow—Josselyn as Katrina, bloodied severed heads in the graveyard, the Headless Horseman. Nev raced to the door, pulling Perrie out of her frozen state. She hurried to the window and peered out into the night. It was dark outside but she could see just enough to catch the alabaster fur coat of a horse as it passed by.

Not the Headless Horseman.

Perrie sighed, her body relaxing. *Am I going to get this worked up every time I hear a horse for the rest of my fucking life?*

"Get some rest?" Neven lifted a brow as they sank back on the couch. "I don't think I could sleep if I wanted to. I'm a mess, you're a mess, and the world is a mess."

"Maisie's not a mess." At least ninety-percent of her didn't seem to be.

"Well, Maisie's special," Neven said quietly. He could barely bring himself to look her in the eye as he'd said it too. Perrie knew what was going on—she'd heard it in his banter with her cousin only hours ago.

He could hide it from Maisie, but he couldn't hide it from

Perrie.

"You like her!" Perrie whisper-shouted, fighting a smile.

He opened his mouth to say something, but no words slipped out.

"Don't lie to me."

Nev pursed his lips, as if he'd eaten something sour. "I haven't ever lied to you, and I told you I never lie about anything."

Perrie jabbed a finger at his chest. "No, but I can tell you want to now, don't you?"

"It doesn't matter." Nev sighed, hanging his head after a few seconds passed. "The world has too many fucked up things going on, and nothing else matters except figuring shit out that doesn't make sense. None of this makes sense."

Perrie grabbed his hand and intertwined his fingers with hers. The gesture didn't stir that rush of butterflies like it used to, just the comforting thought that he was her friend. A friend she hadn't talked to in a long time. It was like coming home, and everything was the same as before, only this time, they really were only friends.

"I'm sorry about your mom," Perrie whispered. "I know if anyone loved someone more than life itself, it was you."

"Me too." A few tears slid down his cheeks, and he wiped them away.

"It's okay to cry. Cry as much as you need to, I know I did. I'm right here, and I promise I'll always be your friend, no matter what." Perrie pulled him into a hug, holding him tight as he cried.

After his tears subsided, Neven sat up and concealed his face as if he'd never needed that moment.

"Now, tell me the truth. You like Maisie, don't you?"

His mask finally broke, and he was as relaxed as she'd seen him in the last few hours. Then he nodded.

"Since when?" she asked.

He shrugged. "Since forever ago. Since recently."

"When we were *together*?" Perrie hissed. "What's fucking wrong with you?" *Okay, maybe our rekindled friendship is back to being dead.* She started to stand, when Nev tugged her back down by the wrist.

"No, Perrie. It was never like that, I swear." He threw his hands up cautiously, as if that could stop her from punching him in the face. "When I was with you, it was only ever *you.* Even after you broke up with me." He closed his eyes and stayed silent for several seconds. "But I liked her before *us.*"

The hell? "What? What do you mean?"

"Back in ninth grade, and most of tenth too."

Perrie's eyes shifted side to side as she thought back. That was when they'd all met, when they first started hanging out together. He'd never told her any of this. How did she *not* see it? "Why didn't you tell me? Why didn't you tell *her*? Is this why you were weird around her sometimes? I assumed that was because you thought she was odd."

He stayed quiet, not giving any damn answers, so Perrie elbowed him.

"Ow." He chuckled and rubbed his arm.

"Shut up, that didn't hurt. Tell me."

"Okay, but please don't be mad if I tell you this, and don't run off and tell Maisie. I know how you like to tell her everything."

"I swear. I won't say anything. Scout's honor." She held up two fingers, fighting a smile, anxious to hear about this new side of Nev.

He rolled his eyes and lifted another one of her fingers. "It's three fingers."

"What the fuck ever." Perrie smiled.

He bit his lip and gripped the back of his neck, appearing nervous. "You remember that time you got sick back in ninth grade? It was pretty bad, you were out for a few days."

"Yeah?" Where was he going with this?

"We were going to watch a movie, then after you left I

stayed with Maisie." He took a deep breath. "That's when I knew I liked her, for real. I had a crush on her before then, back when she would make those crazy bracelets before the eye patches became her thing." A shy smile played at the corner of his lips as he touched his wrist.

Perrie had almost forgotten about those. Maisie would take slap bracelets and place little pom balls in the center to make a design, whether it was a face, fruit, or something else. They'd been really cute and Perrie used to have a ton of them in her top dresser drawer.

"You never said anything to me. Or to her?" Perrie flicked his hand hard.

"Ow. Quit doing stuff like that." Neven rubbed at the spot dramatically. "I never told you because she was your cousin, and you were my friend. I didn't want it to mess up our friendship and make it too weird. But…" His voice faded, and he stopped talking.

"Go on." Before she got the chance to pinch him again, he continued.

"We were watching the Phantom—while wearing masks—and after the movie I sort of kissed her, sneak attack."

Perrie's jaw fell open, and she softly shouted, "You did not!" She then snorted because she remembered those masks. One time she and Maisie even made Aunt Krista and Uncle Jaron wear them during the movie.

"I did." He cringed. "She was wearing this really awesome perfume. I got a whiff of it when she helped me with my mask." Maisie didn't wear perfume, but Perrie knew what he was talking about.

"Banana berry bread," she stated simply. Neven cocked his head, seeming to not understand. "It's her shampoo. She uses that stuff religiously. Sorry, go on."

"Right." His brows creased together. "It was right after the movie ended. I kissed her, she screamed, then ran away."

"Shut up." Perrie laughed. "She ran away?"

"She came back out after a while."

"Then what?"

"Then, nothing. We didn't talk about it." He shrugged.

"That's the stupidest shit I've ever heard. You kissed her, and both of you pretended like nothing happened?" Perrie couldn't hide her shock. Neither of them had said a word to each other or to her. Maisie wasn't especially good at keeping secrets, and Perrie was surprised her cousin had held onto this one for so long. She was tempted to wake Maisie up right then and ask her about it, but she'd made a promise to Nev.

"Yep."

"If you ever do make another move, you have my approval, Nev."

"Thanks," he muttered, his expression becoming serious again. "But don't ever think I settled for you. I wouldn't take it back—I wouldn't take any of it back."

Perrie folded her arms around him again, remembering their first kiss, their first time together, and all their special moments. Their chapter had ended a long time ago, and a new one, though different, would begin. "Me neither, Nev. You should try talking to Maisie about how you feel since you never know what's going to happen."

"I don't think I want to make her scream and run away again." He chuckled.

Perrie didn't have an answer for him because this time she didn't know what Maisie would think of this. Her cousin hadn't ever liked anyone that she knew of.

They then talked for a while and their friendship felt as it always had, before Vale came into the picture. As Perrie's thoughts drifted back to Vale, a light shuffling came from the room behind them.

She released her hold around Nev, and they both looked behind them to find Maisie's shadow standing at the now half-open door. Maisie slid to the side out of view and didn't come out. Perrie rolled her eyes. *Does she think she's invisible?* Nev frowned at the doorway then turned back around.

"I better go see what that was about," Perrie said.

"Goodnight. Also, ask Maisie if she army-crawled back to bed." He smiled.

Perrie headed into the bedroom and glanced to her left where Maisie had slid to. But she was already gone, lying in bed like they hadn't just spotted her. Perrie crawled into bed beside Maisie, her cousin's body already cocooned into the blanket. Maisie didn't just wrap herself up into an angry burrito for no reason.

"Psst." She poked Maisie in the side.

Her usual response would've been a laugh. Instead, she didn't move and only whispered, "I'm sleeping."

"No, you're not," Perrie said to Maisie's back. "We saw you in the doorway. Look at me." Maisie finally rolled over, still bundled in the blankets. "What's going on with this attitude?"

"Nothing. Sorry I interrupted you and Neven."

Then it hit her. Perrie should've seen it earlier, but she'd only been seeing how Nev felt about Maisie. Her cousin was friendly with everyone, so it was harder to notice it. But it all made sense now. "You like Nev, don't you?" Perrie murmured.

"What? No, I don't," she answered hurriedly.

"I told you already we weren't getting back together."

"You should get back together. Plus, you were already cuddling," Maisie snapped. Perrie could hear the jealousy in her voice.

"We're just friends. You know, if you ever decide to get with Nev, you have my approval." Perrie smiled. Maisie may not see it, but Perrie knew she heard the smile in her voice.

"Wouldn't that be incestuous, though?"

"Maisie, how would that be incestuous? You aren't related to Nev," Perrie said, incredulous.

"No, but I'm related to you, and you've had sex with him."

"I think there are stranger things going on in the world than that right now." Perrie had more things to be worried and angry about, and she would never be upset with Maisie about this. She was her cousin, her best friend, and she wanted her happy.

"Thank you for the approval if I ever decide to go in that direction." Maisie unraveled herself from the blanket and spread it across the both of them. Her cousin liked him, more than liked. This was odd to Perrie because she didn't think Maisie ever crushed on anyone. She kind of liked that her cousin did have a few hidden secrets. Perrie had promised Nev she wouldn't say anything and she would keep that damn promise, but that didn't mean she wouldn't give Maisie a nudge in his direction.

SEVENTEEN

Perrie

*P*errie sat on the edge of the Galveston Seawall—her feet dangled and swung back and forth, lightly tapping the stone as they came down.

The night had already fallen, but lampposts lit the unbusy street behind her and August. They'd settled on a portion of the Seawall that wasn't too high from the ground, yet still enough to make her stomach flutter.

Waves crashed into the sand, and each time gravity hauled them back, it felt like her life. The sounds relaxed her as she closed her eyes. It was almost as unwinding as when she and August played cello together. August's leg pressed against hers, and he leaned back with his palms propping him up—his blond curls scattered in all directions.

Perrie watched him for a moment, something she didn't normally do, but he really was beautiful. He was more than that, though. August looked off in the distance, and if she could read his mind right now, she would want to know every minuscule detail that was there.

"What are you thinking about?" she asked.

"Hmm?" He lazily slid his eyes from the darkness toward her. "Oh, I was just thinking about things."

Perrie lightly kicked her foot against his. "Like what?"

"The world." He smiled.

Perrie thought about the world all the time, too. The future. How when she was younger, she knew what direction her life would go in, but a child's mind was a dangerous one. Thoughts were innocent, and life wasn't. "The world is a pretty damn big place, August."

"Then we will conquer it." His smile grew wide, and he leapt from the wall.

"August!" Perrie shouted as he fell through the air.

His feet slapped the sand, and he spun to face her, laughing as he said, "Your turn."

She peered down at the long distance. It wasn't far enough where she would break anything, but a dizzy feeling still swam through her. "No way."

August chuckled, then jogged over to the stairs and went up them. Perrie watched as he rounded the rail and strode up to her. He hovered above her while she gazed up at him, and she shook her head. She knew he wanted her to leap, but she wasn't going to.

"Come on, doll face. Just do it."

"Is this peer pressure, August? You know I stay away from those situations," she teased.

"Give me your hand." He reached his out for her to take, and she hesitantly put hers in his, feeling the comforting warmth.

Pulling her feet from the edge of the Seawall, she faced him, and he helped her to stand. They walked right to the edge, and she gazed over. "I don't know about this. It's still a rough landing."

He turned her face to his and murmured, "Together?"

Chest heaving, Perrie looked back down. It didn't seem as

*daunting with his hand in hers. "Fine. Together," she agreed.
Then they jumped.*

Perrie shot up in bed, her chest tightening. "August? We have to leave." She turned to August to tell him they needed to find a way out of the Glass Vault, but no one was beside her.

Maisie crashed through the door with Nev at her heels.

"What are you shouting about?" Maisie asked as she hurried to Perrie's side of the bed.

Perrie's heart slammed against her rib cage, beating on overdrive. She didn't know if she could get it to slow down. Maisie crawled next to her and pulled Perrie to her chest. August wasn't here. August didn't exist. Perrie wanted to rip out the memory—all the memories of him, and bury them somewhere in concrete.

"Nothing. It was only a dream."

Nev watched them with his arms crossed, then moved toward her. "It sounded like more than a dream to me."

"It's okay. I'm okay," Perrie told herself more than them. The dreams or nightmares she could handle, because that was what they were. She could separate the two—she had to think about it in a different way. It was as though August was dead, and Vale would be fucking dead, too. And Perrie was the one who was going to end this, end *him*.

"Do we need to stay here a little longer?" Maisie asked.

"No," Perrie said. "We're going to head to the Glass Vault now." She would shatter every inch of it until it was completely destroyed.

"Let's go then." Nev unfolded his arms and waited for Perrie and Maisie to follow him into the living room.

As Perrie went to hand Maisie her purse, a loud knock at the door rumbled through the house, shaking her bones. She froze, Maisie's eye bulged so wide it might pop out, and Nev scowled at the door.

Maisie was the first one to shake off her shock and tiptoed

toward the door.

"What are you doing?" Perrie hissed.

Maisie threw her head to the side to look at Perrie. "I'm going to see who it is." When she turned back around toward the door, Nev was already there, peering through the peephole.

He whirled around to face them, his expression bewildered. "No one's at the door."

"Don't open it," Perrie whispered. The hairs on her arms rose as the electricity inside her crackled to life. Something wasn't right. And that something may have to do with a certain vicious demon from the Underworld.

"I wasn't planning on it," he replied.

Maisie pushed past Nev and glanced through the peephole. Perrie rushed to her, sliding Maisie away so she could look. From what she could see, no one was there, only a brick porch with potted plants.

Perrie wasn't going to linger around, and Nev and Maisie seemed to have the same thought as her.

"Backdoor," Maisie and Perrie said simultaneously.

"Start running now," Nev whispered.

They booked it to the door. Maisie reached it first, throwing it open and leaping over the patio. Nev passed through next with Perrie right behind him.

Maisie and Nev were a few feet ahead of her, and she was trying to keep up. Nev had his running experience with basketball, and Maisie was just ridiculously fast. The two of them swiftly leapt over the short iron fence. Perrie's hands gripped the top bar roughly and she hopped across, but part of her dress snagged on something sharp. Heart in her throat, she gave it a hard tug and ripped the material free.

They entered a lush green field, and not a single soul seemed to be in sight. Perrie chanted silently to herself, *Don't look back at the house. Don't look back at the house.* But she did. No one was behind them. She smiled to herself in relief and continued to run.

After close to a minute of hauling ass, Perrie must've been lagging, because Maisie yelled, "Keep going!"

Nev slowed his pace and glanced back over his shoulder at her to make sure she hadn't fallen too far behind. The Glass Vault hadn't improved her running skills by much because cramps were already churning in her stomach. Nev's determined expression switched to one of horror.

"What are—" Perrie started.

A hand jerked her back by the hair, wrenching her body to a hard chest. A raspy cry of pain escaped her throat. Perrie knew this particular type of hair pulling. An image of her being dragged down a hall by only her hair flashed through her head. This time she bucked her head as hard as she could, not caring how much pain shot through her scalp.

"Ah, you didn't think you could hide forever, did you?" Vale's hot breath struck her ear.

Despite his rough grip, Perrie kicked her feet at the demon and attempted to elbow his ribs. She focused on her power, unable to summon a single spark to electrocute this monster.

Nev and Maisie darted their way, but Vale didn't move an inch. He only grabbed her by the jaw, squeezing with enough pressure that she feared he would rip it off. "Oh, you did? How sweet." He smiled, baring his teeth.

"Let her fucking go!" Nev charged full force, and with his strength, he could tear Perrie away from Vale's clutches. It would give her enough time to try and gather her electricity.

Vale lazily tossed up a hand. Nev flew back about fifty feet, landing in the grass with a heavy smack.

Maisie looked at Nev, concerned, then dashed toward Perrie, her expression turning fierce as she tried to sing with her immortal ability. Vale's amused laughter echoed around Perrie as he threw up his hand again, flinging Maisie farther back than Nev.

"Stop!" Perrie shouted.

Maisie and Nev were off the ground, once again rushing

toward them, but then Vale lifted that fucking hand of his once more. This time, they still raced in her direction, yet they were going no farther, as though running in place.

Vale spun Perrie around, a murderous gleam dancing in his emerald eyes. "Listen to me, *now*."

Perrie didn't listen. She didn't want to listen. She would never listen to him. Not now. Not again. Not ever. If he wanted to slit her throat a hundred times, a *thousand* times, then so be it. She would *always* try to escape.

"You will return my Bride to me!" He shook her roughly, and her head bobbled, sending a jolt of sharp pain shooting through her neck.

Perrie peered into his green eyes, holding herself steady, remembering him and his Bride. The way he touched her, tasted her, made her shout his name in pleasure, how he'd done the same with hers. She would never give her back to him again. "No."

"What was that?" He crushed Perrie's arms and tilted his head, bringing his ear closer to her, as if the fucker didn't believe what he was hearing. As his fingers dug into her flesh, her eyes fluttered, but she held them open.

"I said, *no*," Perrie said, gritting her teeth. "I made sure she's gone, and she's never coming back. I killed her."

He then gripped the sides of her skull in between his hands—his nose rubbed against hers. "Then I will make it so you can't come back, and she does. We both know she wants to stay here with me."

With those words, he took a step back and slammed her head to the ground. It bounced slightly, hit again, then she fell to her stomach. Perrie's skull rattled, her brain shook, and the veins throbbed. She was dead. She had to be dead. This was what death would feel like, even worse than having her throat slit.

Before she could stand to spit in his face, Vale yanked Perrie forward by her hair. *Can he quit with the fucking hair already*? She wanted to stop him, retaliate, but her entire body was weak, exhausted.

"We are going inside to tuck you away, by any means necessary." The grass prickled her arms as he dragged her through the field. He began to hum, a soft melody, and Perrie recognized the tune—they'd always played it together on their cellos, back when she thought he was August.

A roar rumbled through her veins, and she gathered that inner strength, letting the anger fill her. As her head pieced back together, she geared up to make a move. With his casual strides, she could do this. Perrie's gaze became predatory while watching each leisurely step he took. He moved as if he had an eternity with her. *Well, he doesn't.*

She quietly brought her arms up from her sides, attempting to block out the pain at her scalp. Thanking the grass that he had her on her stomach and not on her back, Perrie picked her body up by her hands, lifted herself to her knees, and shot forward. Perrie's body collided with Vale's back, and she knocked his ass to the ground.

He released a loud grunt, and she beamed with satisfaction as she leapt onto his back. She raised her hands and tried to ignite the spark, but her electricity still wouldn't come, so she pummeled her fists against his muscles. Hard, harder, wanting to tear him apart like he'd done to Nev.

Vale moved with his inhuman speed, flinging her from him. Perrie landed on her backside, and she ignored the throbbing. But before she could jump to her feet, he pushed her back down, holding her by the arms.

"Enough!" he roared as heavy breaths hit her cheek, his voice seeming to shake the entire field. Rage filled his eyes and his mouth twisted into a harsh sneer. "You don't want to go inside? Fine! I'll break you apart right here with my bare hands. I need her and she needs me! Give her to me!"

He took hold of Perrie's left arm tightly and with one swift, forceful pull, she howled in agony at the loud snap. Her arm had to be gone. Numbness and burning soared through her. Perrie's head fell to the side, finding her arm there but out of the socket. Tears pricked at her eyes at the pain of it all.

Then Vale grasped her arm and brutally shoved it back into place—hot tears streamed down her cheeks as she screamed. And then, the masochist did it again to her same arm—nausea swirled in her stomach and bubbled up her throat. She was going to vomit—she was going to puke all over his damn face. More powerful than before, he shoved it in place, and she didn't think she would ever stop screaming. She *would not* become *her* again, no matter how many times he did this. He would never accept that his Bride was gone.

"That was only practice. Now, I'm ready to truly begin." *Please no*. Perrie didn't even want to think about what he would do to her next. So she focused, harder than before, letting determination fill her more than she ever had. His grip on her right arm loosened. *Please work damn it*.

Yanking her arm away, Perrie pushed her palm against Vale's chest and prayed the electricity would come. In answer, a flash of white light shot out, igniting the world around her in sparks. The explosion of her power barreled into his chest, sending him backward.

As he stumbled, Vale's gaze fastened on hers, a true look of pain on his face, before slumping to the ground. Perrie believed the pain wasn't even from the spark, it was because he knew his Bride was gone forever.

She shakily stood, inhaling deeply as the throbbing lessened in her arm. Perrie frantically searched for Maisie and Nev, then sighed in relief when she saw they'd escaped Vale's invisible hold and were headed her way.

Perrie's body relaxed as she studied Vale resting on his side, his eyes shut. Did her electricity work? Was he dying? When she stepped closer, a loud piercing shriek escaped him and she jumped back. Vale's hands cradled his head and his body curled into a tight ball. Fat tears rained down his cheeks while he howled in desperation. She should've moved forward to do to him what they'd done to Catherine, but she took another trembling step back. Maisie and Nev halted beside Perrie. She sparked up as Nev tightened his fists.

With Vale's hands still pressed against his skull, he slowly peeled open his lids. He settled his bright green irises on *her*. One word softly slipped from his lips, and it wasn't Bride. "Perrie?"

EIGHTEEN

Before-Vale

Vale was born in a damp room in the caverns of the Underworld. After hours of labor, his mother, Yorna, gave birth to a beautiful demon male—the first and only with a live heartbeat. That steady beat thrummed up and down the dark halls of the Underworld. She could not hold him with her wrists bound to her ankles, but she lay beside him, whispering words in his ear.

After unlocking the cell, Vale's father charged into the room, scooped up the little infant and tossed him to the ground away from Yorna.

"What have you done?" he yelled at her.

Yorna quaked and shook violently from the sound of her master's voice. "I did nothing. Please, don't take him away." She attempted to crawl to her child, but the chains held her back.

Yorna wouldn't call herself good. She lived her life destroying and tearing apart souls by any means necessary, obeying her master's orders. Things became different for her when she discovered she was with child. Her master's child.

She reveled in each passing moment as her belly grew, until the day was bestowed upon her that she knew she had to leave. The child could not be raised by her master—so she ran.

Yorna attempted to escape out of the realm but failed before being dragged back to her master in thick and heavy chains, binding her wrists to her ankles. The remainder of her pregnancy was spent with clangs of her metal chains echoing through the cell.

Yanking her chin in his large hand, Master narrowed his ebony eyes at her. With the sneer on his face, she knew this would not end well. "Please, Master. Don't separate Vale from me," she pleaded. Yorna had known a demon should never beg, yet she had done it anyway.

His sneer turned into a devious smile that warned Yorna what would become of her. She would not see Vale again. Yorna's dead heart grew frantic as her eyes slid to where her little Vale rested. Master now watched the baby with a curious expression. Curled on his side in a snug ball, Vale did not wail, even after being slung to the ground. His heartbeats were miraculous music, singing to her his lovely song.

Master released Yorna's chin and thrust her face to the side. As her black hair flung into her eyes, all she could do was watch. Lifting the baby off the freezing floor, he stared into the peaceful, unconscious face. Then his gaze shifted back to Yorna. "You did this, you made him this way with your witchery."

Yorna loathed her master, wished flames would burn him until he was nothing. She wanted to gut him to pieces, take the baby and run, but it was useless. He always got what he wanted.

Master lifted his hand and placed it over the tiny infant's chest. A current popped and crackled until Vale's heartbeat quieted. No other sound could be heard, except for the continuous soft breaths of the child.

He gingerly set Vale back on the ground as though he hadn't taken away the one beautiful thing here. With no time to react, Master ran at Yorna with speed quicker than a flash of light. "The child is only mine, Yorna." Then he twisted her neck with a loud snap before vanquishing her soul.

Nine-year-old Vale's eyelids bolted open. He knew exactly where he was—his cage. Father made him sleep in one at night when he could not keep an eye on him.

Vale brought his frail hand to his chest and felt the beat that had come back to life. Letting out a small sigh of relief, he left his palm over his heart, absorbing the *thump, thump*. With the organ's movement, he was able to remember his mother. Despite how short their time together had been, he had loved her. But then he remembered his father, and what he would do once he heard Vale's heartbeat had restarted.

At that moment, he thought maybe it would have been better if his heartbeat had never come back at all because he knew what his father would do next—to him.

Vale leaned forward, pressing his small chest against the cool floor, trying to conceal the vibrato as long as he could.

There was no escaping the iron bars, so he relished his new thoughts and shoved out the memories of his father—imagining perhaps one day, he would have enough strength to leave his prison.

His thoughts were interrupted when he heard loud, heavy footsteps—the sound of anger, of hate.

Vale didn't rise, though. He remained on the floor with his eyes hidden behind the darkness of his lids, attempting to summon a power that would make his father disappear. But he didn't have the strength to bring forth any energy. The gate wrenched open and slammed against the wall. He still did not open his eyes as he tried to hold on to wishes and hopes.

Two hands lifted him by his shirt and shoved him against the wall, his lids flicking open. Vale then met the two darkened irises of his father.

"Vale? Is it already time for a lesson?" His father's lip curled, his eyes gleaming with a hidden thrill.

"No, Father." There was no use pleading or begging because as Vale had learned, it only made him more vulnerable and his father more pleased that he was at his mercy.

"Oh, I think it is." Father dropped him, and Vale's small arm roughly hit the ground.

As soon as he lifted his head, Vale gazed toward the open door, ready to try and make an escape. His father waved a hand in the air, slamming the gate shut, and locking it, as though he had read every one of Vale's thoughts of desertion.

His father pulled out a long brown whip hidden behind his back, the edges lined with sharp metal spikes. Father would give Vale his lesson before snuffing out his heart once more.

Vale did not cry, did not scream as the whip cracked down upon him, time and time again. Thick blood poured out from his wounds, and before they would heal, the whip would snap down again, harder than before. With each heavy crack, Vale tried to hold onto his hope of the possibility of one day escaping. As much as Vale wished for his father to stop his heart and the pain, he wanted to keep all his memories more, so he could eventually find a way out. One day he would be happy because he knew it did exist, even if for the time being it was only hidden in his dreams. Always, he would try to find it.

As Vale grew, there were moments when his heartbeat would

return on its own, and he would remember every detail from the instant he was born. When the memories would strike through him like lightning, he wanted to run, tried to run, but his father could always hear the heartbeat when he drew close enough. Then, all of himself, including his wishes and hopes, was buried back into the depths of his mind where there would be no remembering.

Vale's father had taught the dark part of him well. He'd shown him everything there was to the Underworld, including the souls he would one day torture.

That time was now.

"Vale, grab the scalpel." His father pointed to a tray lined with a variety of sharp objects. A thrill flowed through Vale's limbs at his father's trust in him to help perform his duties.

"Yes, Father." Vale padded to the tray and lifted the cool steel into his palm, rolling it delicately back and forth. He absorbed the moment.

Rows of cages filled the room—in one sat a woman, bright red hair falling past her shoulders. She crouched on all fours and stared at him, smirking. "I want that one." Vale pointed in her direction and sauntered toward the cage.

A strange tightness formed in Vale's chest, as if something was knocking at his ribs. Something sparked in his head, an image of an emerald-eyed female he had forgotten existed, who he would have called mother, followed by a rush of wrongness for all these souls in cages. He needed to escape the Underworld as his mother had whispered in his ear when he was first born.

Vale would get out. He would leave this place. Hastily, he turned toward his father, ignoring the surprise crossing his face, and thrust the scalpel into his chest and ran.

He was quicker than his father. Endless times Vale had done this but was always found and dragged back. This time would be different. The burn in his chest felt good, and he did not want it to go away again.

He passed by the darkened stone halls where souls endlessly wandered, others locked in more cages, and none remembering who they were. With certainty, he knew he could not become like them again. Not now and not for all eternity.

Vale reached the dim black hall, where a bitter, salty smell invaded his nose. Everyone there might be dead, but they still bled. Again and again and again.

The barrier was not far away, and he believed he would make it out this time. His father would not be able to get through, but Vale could. Hurling himself at the obsidian stone wall, he was roughly tossed back. Vale lunged toward it four more times before the pounding of his father's heavy footsteps slapping against the ground drew near.

"You cannot get through with a heartbeat, and when I shut it off again, you won't remember." His father's lips curled into a calculated smile as his dark gaze penetrated Vale's.

Father cocked his head. "I will tell you something, Vale. I figured a way to shut it off so it does not come back easily this time. You will do as I say, and you will come up with a plan to serve as I do down here, except you will do it up there with the humans." Vale's hands trembled as he planted himself against the wall. He tried to back up farther, even though there was nowhere left to go.

"I will not perform what you tell me to, Father. I'll remember. I always do." Vale lifted his chin in defiance at his father, even with fear coursing through his veins.

His father savagely arched an eyebrow. "Not this time." Vale felt a hit to his head and blackness darkened to nothing.

Vale awoke in the same room with the rows of cages from earlier. The tray of torturous devices rested across from him, prepped for his choosing. Swallowing deeply, he blinked several times to rid the blurriness of his surroundings.

It was near impossible to push himself up to a sitting position as he found his wrists were chained at his ankles. He was not surprised. This was the same tactic his father used endlessly. But he finally managed to bring himself up to a sitting position.

Vale turned his head side to side, and there was nothing to see. All he could do was listen to the screams reverberating from the hallways. His father was not there, but he knew he would be back. His father would shut him down again, but it was temporary. It would always be temporary, and he was strong enough to find his way back. He had to.

When Vale looked back at the rows of cages, his gaze stopped on the one with the redheaded female. Without fear and only confidence, she watched him. He slid his eyes away from her—something was not right with the female, more than the other corrupt souls there.

"I ripped them to shreds up there," she cried out.

Vale chose to neglect the mad creature and peered down at his knees. At that moment, he desperately yearned to be out of the chains and away from her. But she continued to speak, seeming not to care that he was not listening to her.

"You will, too."

He turned to her then. "Listen. I do not care what you are talking about. I am not going to tear apart *anyone*—up there or down here."

Her expression turned smug. "I may be the first for you to torture once you turn back into your better self, but I will get your father on my side. Since you are special and are able to bring souls with you, I will help. I heard what your father had to say about you."

Vale ignored the mad female, but her words continued to tap at him. She rambled on about how everyone believed Jack to have been a male and that made the situation easier for her.

Why was she the only one down here who remembered

their past life? Vale thought.

The redhead's words were cut off by his father's entrance. "Vale, it's time. You are to begin on these souls, *now*." Before Vale could protest, his father held up a new device he must have crafted himself. As it pulsated with an electric current, Vale tried to move away, but his chains only caused him to stumble to the ground.

In an instant, his father's instrument was now pressed at Vale's chest. As his body vibrated from the instrument, Vale wondered if maybe this time he would not wake again. And in a moment of weakness, he decided he would be fine with that. But no, he shook that awful thought away because that would mean his father would have won.

Vale's memories gradually faded as his heart slowed, but he fought to keep them from escaping. He held his eyelids tightly together, not looking at his father, the strange female, or the instruments he knew he would be picking up if he let the memories vanish. His heart barely pumped, taking two more sluggish beats before ceasing.

He unclenched his eyelids and studied the male in front of him with black eyes, blond curls, and his jaw grinding. His father, his master.

"What do you remember?" the male asked.

Frowning, Vale tried to touch his head, but his wrists were chained. *Remember?* An eagerness stormed through him until he grinned with pleasure. "I was about to get started." Vale's dark gaze fell on the corrupt souls in their cages.

His father smiled a wicked grin in return. "Good. Now let us begin. You are master to all these souls." His father, glowing with pride, held his arm up and dragged it across the air in front of the cages.

Father unlocked the chains binding Vale's wrists and ankles. As they clacked to the ground, Vale rose to full height and walked to where his father motioned at a tray of instruments.

"Now, as we were before. Pick one," his father demanded.

Vale ran his tongue across his teeth while staring at the shiny instruments with longing. He lifted a scalpel from the middle and focused on the cages. His father was already moving to the one with the redheaded female covered in filth. She crawled out, and a smile tugged the edges of her lips that Vale did not understand.

He did not care, though—he was going to slice her up in ways that would make her never stop screaming.

NINETEEN

Perrie

Tears continued to pour down Vale's face, and the lightning crackled in Perrie's palms as she prepared to strike him with her power again.

"Perrie," he gasped for the second time, releasing his hold from the sides of his head. "I am sorry." He pushed to his knees and dropped his hands to the ground, his fingers gripping blades of grass.

A desperation crawled onto his face, in his eyes, while Perrie's heart thundered, conflicted. She stared at her feet so she could think, concentrate. An image slid into her mind—the night she escaped from Vale. A kiss. Him calling her Perrie instead of Bride. A heartbeat. Her sparking him.

Realization struck, and she lifted her gaze to meet his, her entire being pleading. Perrie took off running toward him with hope blossoming in her chest.

"Perrie!" Neven shouted.

"Stockholm Syndrome," Maisie yelled behind her. "Stockholm Syndrome! Don't!"

Ignoring Maisie, she came to a stop in front of him, falling to her knees as he peered up at her with those green eyes that called to her. She pressed a trembling hand to his warm cheek, her lips mere inches from brushing his. "August?" Perrie whispered.

The expression in his face fell, no longer appearing desperate. Something like empathy stirred within his eyes while they moved side to side, as if he was trying to keep up with a metronome.

"August does not exist," he said softly. "I am Vale."

Perrie jerked her hand back, her entire body recoiling from him. Maisie pulled her out of her shocked state, tugging Perrie to her side. Nev yanked Vale up by the collar of his white shirt, holding him in the air, his toes scraping the grass. Curling his other hand in a fist, Nev delivered a hard blow to Vale's face— a loud cracking sounded as his head was thrown to the side.

Vale held up his hand, and Nev released him. Nev floated backward through the grass, punching air, and slowly dropped to his knees.

"Stop," Vale whispered, his voice calm as he hovered above Nev.

Perrie now had a clear shot, and she hurled a whip of light at Vale's chest. But he was too fast, swinging his other hand up, her lightning dissolving to small sparks that fell to the ground. She tried to launch another, yet she couldn't do anything. Couldn't move her legs, only her upper body, but no ability would come. *Shit.*

A humming drifted through the air, coming from Maisie who seemed to be immobilized too. Vale cocked his head. "You can stop. That isn't going to work on me."

Blood trailed down the side of Vale's mouth from Nev's hit, and he swiped it with the tip of his tongue. Then he brought the sleeve of his shirt to his mouth to wipe the rest away, marring the white silk.

"I'm going to tear you apart this time, you fucking

asshole," Nev threatened, spewing out all the ways he was going to do it. Perrie shook her head at him, telling him to stop talking.

Lines creased Vale's forehead as he lifted his hand and snapped.

Perrie's heart hammered, panicked, expecting the world to split into two. But Nev remained whole, except no words spilled from him as he still tried to shout.

Maisie was also at a standstill, attempting to sing again, but only silence escaped her mouth.

With what appeared to be hesitation, Vale stepped toward Perrie.

"One more step and you're dead," she threatened, hiding the fear pumping through her veins.

His gaze dropped from her face, to her feet firmly planted in place, then drifted back up to her eyes. "I do not think so."

"Your Bride is already gone. I'm not going back with you, and I'll find a way out. We all will." Perrie would claw and claw at him forever, until he decided to rip her hands off if he wished. The Bride may have treasured the earth Vale walked on, but she sure as fuck didn't.

Sighing in defeat, Vale shook his head and ran a hand through his blond curls. "Look, Perrie."

"So what, you're fine with me being Perrie now? Not *Bride*?" she spat.

Vale frowned, wounded, like he was the one who'd been torturing the world as someone else. "I—I don't want the Bride. Can you listen to me without talking for a moment? You need to hear this."

Perrie shook her head. "More lies?"

"No. Not more lies. Only truths." He held up his empty hands showing no weapons, but the fucker must've forgotten he was full of invisible ones. Dirt covered his hands and fingernails, and she was surprised he hadn't taken out that damn file to pick at those stupid nails of his.

"Don't you need to clean your nails first?" Perrie hissed.

Vale blinked. Blinked again. Then a rumble of laughter poured from his mouth. The sound reminded her of her partner back in the Glass Vault. But that wasn't a real friend, a real lover, it was an enemy.

Vale stopped laughing and studied his filthy hands. "That is what I am trying to talk to you about if you will drop the stubbornness and listen closely to what I have to say. *All of you.*" He exchanged a glance between the three of them.

Maisie no longer tried to fight and watched him intently, as if she might be considering being on Team Vale. Perrie waved her hand to get her cousin's attention, then Maisie turned to her to speak. Nothing came out, but she nodded, pointing from Perrie to her ear. She wanted Perrie to listen to what Vale had to say…

Perrie threw her hands in the air, while Maisie kept tapping at her ear. Maybe she knew something Perrie didn't? When she turned to Nev, he shook his head *no*.

But they were glued to the ground with really no other choice except to hear what Vale wanted to say. Perrie folded her arms. "If you let Maisie and Nev speak, then I'll listen."

Vale bit the edge of his lip. "Only Maisie for now. Neven will continue to interrupt."

"Fine, but after, you will release him," Perrie demanded, though her heart still thundered. She was sure he wasn't worried since she couldn't even move her useless legs.

Vale snapped his fingers, releasing Maisie, her breathing making the lightest of sounds.

Maisie's eye stayed open wide as she spoke, "Perrie, I have a theory, but first you need to listen to him."

A *theory*? Perrie shot her cousin a surprised look before turning to Vale. "Go ahead."

He continued to chew on the side of his lip for a moment, and he looked more human than the demon he was.

"As I was trying to explain to you earlier, Perrie, I am not

August. He does not exist and never has. I am Vale."

Perrie could feel her anger rising, her hands shaking as she narrowed her eyes.

He hurried on, "But I am not *that* Vale."

What? Perrie took a deep swallow, her tongue thick in her mouth. He had to be lying. But she would play along until he unrooted her from the ground, then she would make a move. "I—I don't understand."

He blinked at her several times like he didn't understand why she couldn't grasp the concept. "You had your emotions disassembled, but your heart still beat in your chest. My father completely shut my heart off, causing me to no longer be myself. I was like the Bride, Snow White, Frankenstein's Monster." He paused, his lips set in a thin line. "Except I was more vicious with my emotions completely shut off. I couldn't escape my prison the way you did"—he pressed a hand to his heart—"and I was locked inside this body."

"I knew it! You have an alter too!" Maisie shouted.

Maisie's voice drew her attention away from Vale. "You believe this shit?" Perrie asked. "Vale may not have had many emotions, but he sure as hell could pretend to have some when he was August."

She lifted a shoulder and shrugged, apologetic. "I believe him. What would be the point of him saying all this when he could just as easily take you away again?"

"I don't know! What was the point of him acting like August, if he could easily have just thrown me into one of those displays like you were in? And by the way, you didn't think August was a demon either." Perrie glared.

Maisie ran her palms against one another. "That's true, but Vale also wanted to unleash havoc on the world at a rapid pace once we were out. What would be the point of him slowing down now, only to pretend he's good?"

"Let's say this Vale is actually the real Vale," Perrie started, "what makes you think he's a 'good guy?'"

Maisie wiggled her finger side to side. "This Vale…" Her words faltered mid-sentence as she looked at Vale, who watched them with wide eyes. "Why doesn't your alter have a different name? This is getting confusing even for me, since you're both named Vale."

He cocked his head, his arms folded in front of him. "Because *my father* continued to call me Vale."

"Okay, well we will refer to him as Bad Vale from now on." Maisie slid her gaze suspiciously to Vale once again. "And what do you mean *me,* if you're not him?"

He exhaled slowly and said, "You may sit here and call these sides of yourselves whatever you want, but they are still you, only a darker version of you. A deadlier individual."

"Why do we have memories from the displays, then?" Maisie asked.

"I was going to get to that. The images of Snow White having her eye ripped out by the dwarves was all a game to 'Bad Vale' to toy with you." He brought his fingers up to quote.

"Did you just *air quote*?" Perrie asked, taken aback by the movement.

His hands gripped the sides of his head. Perrie's chest tightened, her body still. In a moment, she knew he was going to laugh, then say how this was all just a game of him toying with them. After that, he would continue to play with her arm sockets, demanding his precious Bride be returned to him.

But then Vale released his hold on his head.

"I remember all of Bad Vale's memories as if they are my own, including the human things from when he pretended to be August, and they are my images now. I know all Vale has done." He stopped and stared her in the eye, and something like sorrow flickered in his gaze. "I know all August has done."

Perrie pinched the inside of her wrist to keep from looking down. She didn't know which parts he was thinking about.

She'd tried not to think about Vale and the Bride's relationship. Besides them both being sadistic, there was something between them that was pure. She hated it. Hated that they could've been so happy together after what they were doing. If he was thinking about her and August in that tower, then he knew Perrie at her most vulnerable. And she hated that too. Instead of anger stirring, her cheeks heated with embarrassment and she couldn't stop herself from looking down. But if what he said was true … then he was a prisoner, just as they were.

It took a moment, but Perrie gathered her courage and lifted her chin high to face Vale. She still saw the sadness he held for her in his eyes, and she didn't want it.

He snapped his fingers—her knees collapsed, and she fell to the grass. Perrie swallowed hard, past the lump in her throat, then rushed to Maisie.

"You really believe this bullshit?" Nev shouted after Vale released him.

"Yes," Maisie said simply before Perrie could get a word out. Perrie thought about Vale's words again. She needed to be sure, but something nudged her to agree with Maisie. And a part of her was irritated at herself for it.

"You would." Nev glowered, pissed. Perrie completely understood why he would be.

"Then why did he free you?" Maisie asked. "And why is nothing happening now?"

Vale observed them, but didn't make a deceitful move. He only stood there, quietly, patiently.

"Damn it, Mais." Nev's nostrils flared. "You've been right a lot so far, but so help me if you're wrong about this and something happens to either one of you, I'm going to find your ghost and shake you."

A wide grin spread across her face. "I'm not wrong."

Nev palmed his face.

As for Perrie, her emotions were being pulled in every

direction imaginable. She studied Vale, his face the exact replica of August's, and she wished it were different. But it was never August's face to begin with—it was Vale's.

Perrie thought about something he'd voiced earlier, and she took a few hesitant steps in his direction. "What's this about your father? Even back with Fannie, you mentioned him several times."

Vale clasped his hands together, then rested them right below his bottom lip. "My father is the one who concocted this plan to begin with, and Bad Vale was the one who grew the seed into this nightmare. I think Red has a hidden agenda with him, but I am not sure what it is."

"Where's your father now?" she asked.

"He cannot come here—he is down in the Underworld, ruling it."

Maisie slipped up right behind her, craning her neck over Perrie's shoulder. "Like a king? So, that makes you a prince?" *Is she fucking serious?*

Nev rolled his eyes, and Perrie didn't think he would ever stop. He then said, "Next, you're going to ask if we should bow down to him, and I really don't think you need to be bowing down to evil."

Maisie stepped around Nev until she stood right in front of Vale and poked the demon in the arm. "He's not evil, but he's still a prince."

"It is not quite like that." Vale's brows drew together, seeming confused.

This whole conversation has gotten too strange and too damn odd. I mean, people are dead here. There were creatures from the displays and souls turned immortal out in the world killing people.

"What about serious matters here?" Perrie focused on Vale. "What are we going to do about what's happening? What are *you* going to do about it?"

He rubbed at his chin and held her gaze for a long moment

before he finally nodded. "Follow me."

TWENTY

Perrie

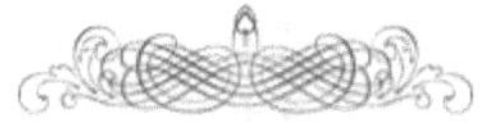

Follow him? Perrie wasn't sure where in hell Vale wanted to lead them. She hadn't budged, and neither had Nev. But then Maisie took the first steps forward.

Vale's powers were much stronger than any of theirs, and Perrie wouldn't let Maisie go with him alone. Nev seemed to have the same thought as her as they both followed them back to the house they'd started in.

Perrie came to a stop on the front sidewalk beside Vale and looked up and down the street. "This is where you wanted us to come?" she asked. "A *damaged street*?" A deep, crooked crack ran up the pavement, seeming as though the earth was being pulled in two different directions. Small craters, resembling pockmarks, were scattered throughout.

Vale searched across the street farther down, his gaze focused on a brick house with all its windows broken. "We are not alone."

Perrie stiffened.

"Come out," he called, a light breeze rumpling his hair.

Perrie wasn't sure if they'd made the right choice in following him. She didn't know who or *what* was going to slither out from his call.

A loud swooshing sounded, cracking like thunder from the direction of the brick house. Perrie threw her hand up, trying to get her electricity to stir—it didn't. After his little paralyzing spell, he'd never returned her power.

The heavy beating turned louder as a shadow took shape, rounding the corner and heading straight in their direction. Not slithering, but *flying*.

"What the hell is that?" Nev asked, his chest heaving.

A strong gray body with cracks marring its flesh, as if it were made of stone, stormed toward them. Paper thin wings, covered in thin veins so dark they looked black, beat heavily against the wind. The creature's face appeared human except for its pointed ears and flat nose. *Gargoyle.*

Maisie, Nev, and Perrie backed up as the creature came closer. Vale lifted his hand and the gargoyle froze midair, its wings continuing to crank.

Perrie squinted her eyes to get a better view of the male gargoyle, her heart beating erratically. Bright blood caked its chin and razor-sharp teeth jutted out from its mouth. A protruding spine detailed the middle of its back so tightly that if the gargoyle bent any farther, the thin skin looked like it would rip.

If Vale held any fear, his nonchalant persona did a fucking good job at covering it up. "It is only a gargoyle."

"You mean a wicked soul inside the gargoyle," Maisie pointed out.

"Yes." As though bringing two long-lost lovers together, Vale gracefully clapped his hands in front of his chest, their sound almost musical.

The gargoyle was there one moment and gone the next.

With wide eyes, Perrie scanned the street, not seeing any sign of the gargoyle. "Where the hell did it go?"

A hint of a smile touched Vale's mouth. "Back in a display at the Glass Vault."

"And what about the rest of them?" Nev asked, glowering.

This time when Vale slammed his palms together, a loud boom pierced her ears. Her hands automatically covered them, but nothing seemed to change.

"What did that do?" Perrie narrowed her eyes with suspicion.

His smile grew a tad bit more. "All the corrupt souls are back at the museum now."

Maisie's mouth was open in awe, while an inner battle on what to think stirred inside Perrie.

Nev didn't appear to buy it. "You're telling me all you had to do was clap your fucking hands together, and everyone returned back to that shit hole? How are we still here, then?"

Oh, he has a damn good point. Why didn't they return there too? A chill ran down her spine, and she silently pleaded for Vale not to clap his hands and send them back to the Glass Vault. Nev should've kept his mouth shut.

Vale's smile slipped. "As Perrie knows, Bad Vale didn't have all his powers earlier because the Glass Vault hadn't consumed enough souls, but as more have gone in, the stronger he got—I got. That is how he was able to locate you. I cannot do everything, but since they are connected to the Underworld, I could send them back." He slammed his hands together in another explosive clap. "And I can do this."

Perrie panicked for a moment, feeling her arms and chest to make sure she was still whole, then to see if she'd been transported somewhere else. But she was still here. Her stunned gaze remained on Vale, words trapped in her throat. Maisie and Nev stood quietly beside her.

"No questions?" Vale asked, sarcasm dripping from his voice.

A part of her wanted to laugh, but she didn't. "Well?" she finally said.

"I took away everyone's powers and restored their memories." His smile this time was only for her, and it was a captivating one. She felt drawn to it for a moment but shook her head to clear it. Did he want her to thank him? Bow down to the demonicness?

"Again. How do we know you aren't making this shit up?" Nev folded his arms across his chest. "You already took away our abilities, and we already remember everything."

Maisie perked up, pulling back her shoulders. "I believe him. So is everyone not immortal anymore?"

Perrie couldn't manage to think straight. Too much was going on, *way* too much had happened, and too much had changed in the last few days.

Vale grimaced. "Now, that is the problem. There won't be any more destruction, but since all of you died within the Glass Vault, it is not something that can be reversed."

"What's the real answer?" Perrie asked, tightening her grip on the skirt of her silk dress. Maisie chewed on her thumbnail. Nev just looked confused and pissed. Her heart kicked up again, her nostrils flaring.

Vale rubbed the back of his neck, then gripped it. "You can stay here and remain immortal, or I can deliver your soul to the Glass Vault. When I return to send the souls from the Underworld back to their rightful place, yours can go where it would have eventually gone when you died."

Horror hit Perrie, and her hand slammed over her mouth. Maisie gnawed harder on that nail of hers.

"So, we *are* dead." Nev moved toward Vale, his face inches from the demon. "This is all your damn fault!"

"Sorry I was born." Vale stared him down, even though Nev hovered above him.

Maisie pushed forward, splitting the guys up while Perrie silently thought about what Vale had said. She knew they'd been slaughtered in the displays like it was their own personal horror movie. But she'd thought that maybe since she felt real and still had a heartbeat, she wasn't technically totally dead. *I mean, I suppose immortal isn't dead, but it's not something I'm sure I want.* They still had a heartbeat when they came out…

"Wait!" Perrie shouted. "Why did we still have heartbeats? When yours came back, your memories returned to you, but our hearts never turned off. They still continued to pump as they always have. Why?"

Vale stepped away from Nev's glare, and Maisie tugged Nev to her side. "I am a demon." He shrugged. "Demons normally do not have heartbeats. You, on the other hand, were born human, even though you are immortal now. Without a heartbeat, you would perish, your existence snuffed, and that is why I believe you all were able to remember. With no way to turn off your hearts, the loss of emotion was only temporary."

Perrie let his words seep through her, trying to analyze them. It made sense … even though it also didn't. This was a damn disaster—a horror movie gone more than wrong. She peered out at the glass statues lining the street and raced toward them. Maybe their souls could be returned too.

She slowed to a stop, placing a hand to her chest. A glass child who was maybe about five with hair just below her shoulders, her mouth open in a scream, stood before her.

"What about them?" Perrie asked when Vale pulled up beside her in a split second.

In answer, he clapped his hands together once more. She expected nothing to happen. Or she didn't know? Maybe the clear glass would morph into human skin, a live little girl appearing in its place.

Something did change, though, and it wasn't what Perrie was hoping for. Like snow on a blazing hot day, the glass turned to water, crashing down to the concrete, where the clear liquid pooled around them.

"What happened?" Perrie shrieked, searching the street.

The other statues were no longer standing either, only puddles of water soaked the cement in their places. They'd become nothing but liquid, too.

Vale said nothing.

"What did you *do*?" she screamed. All she could feel was the little girl's warm water brushing her bare feet.

"I had to send them away," he answered, his voice soft, sad.

"Away where? Back home?" Perrie pushed at his chest once. She shoved at it again. Then she bulldozed him to the cement. She straddled his hips, and pinned his shoulders to the ground. He gave no resistance, only stayed lying there, watching her. His defenselessness only made the anger within her roar.

Perrie got right up in his face, her nose a centimeter from his. Her heavy breaths struck his skin, and he still didn't say anything. "Where. Did. They. Go?"

Vale's gaze drifted down to her mouth, holding there for a moment before sliding back up to meet her eyes. "The souls were taken. The bodies turned to glass. It is not how it was in the Glass Vault where glass can turn to skin. This happened outside of it, so they are only glass. That is all of them that was left."

Before he could say another word, Perrie slapped him across his cheek. The sound echoed throughout the broken neighborhood. She pulled her hand back to strike him again, but before she could contact his face, Vale managed to roll her to her back. He held Perrie's arms above her head against the cement, his body on top of hers.

"Stop," he said gently, his expression pleading.

Perrie thrashed and tried to kick, but he didn't budge. She was going to murder him. It didn't matter if he was Bad Vale or Good Vale. She needed to know what happened to her family. "Tell me!"

"I am *trying* to, but you keep lashing out. Allow me to

finish. *Please*."

"Fine," she said between clenched teeth.

He released her arms and took a deep breath. "The souls were sent to the Glass Vault and were prisoners there, feeding their energy to me. They cannot return here, but they are no longer trapped there either. Before you start kicking me again, they are not in the Underworld either unless that is where they were meant to go. Otherwise, they have moved on."

Tears pricked at her eyes. She hadn't known if they'd be able to come back, but she had *hoped* since the glass was left behind. Now her dad really was gone forever.

Vale furrowed his brow. "Did you want them to stay trapped? Now they are not hurting anymore. I can guarantee you, your family is okay where they are now."

Perrie understood what he meant, but she still wanted them here with her. Her dad, Aunt Krista, and Uncle Jaron. Aunt Krista's huge birthday celebrations with all the leftover food would no longer happen. Uncle Jaron with his laid back and funny personality wouldn't joke anymore. Perrie's dad, who was always there for her, with the power of being two parents after her mom left, would never hug her again. *All gone.*

"Do you think I *wanted* this?" Vale paused, his eyes glassy. "You aren't the only one who has lost something here."

Perrie was unable to hold back the sob—it started out small but then she couldn't control it. Vale hauled her into his lap in an instant, letting her cry against his chest. She helped do this, destroy the world. The one thing keeping her from breaking and falling to pieces was the fact that she wasn't the one who'd killed her family. If that had been her, she wouldn't have been able to live with herself.

Perrie circled her arms around Vale's waist, latching onto his warmth. The guilt of everything clawed at her, making it hard to breathe. The tears wouldn't stop—they sang their own melody … for him, for her. Their alters had destroyed life around them, shattering the world as they knew it. And somehow, despite everything, they were meant to go on, to continue breathing.

At that moment, she realized survivor's guilt was a true thing.

Vale's arms held her tight as his chin rested on top of her head. Perrie remembered a time with August, back in an orchestra closet that felt so long ago—the day she'd thought a real friendship had started. Vale tenderly lifted her chin so their eyes met. His soft fingertips brushed across her cheek, wiping her tears away.

Perrie's breath hitched, and she leapt out of his arms, on the verge of running away. She stopped herself, and only stepped back a few paces. Heat flooded her cheeks, embarrassed, for crying in his lap when she didn't really know this Vale at all.

"I'm sorry. I didn't mean to do all that." The words came out in a rush.

He nodded and smiled shyly. "It is okay. I know you do not understand or truly know me, but through it all, I was there with you, just tucked away. I do not want to see you hurt ever again."

"Thanks." Perrie turned away from him, not wanting to hear any more. And yet…

She then froze when she spotted Maisie and Nev. How had she forgotten about them? She'd been too lost in her damn emotions.

Maisie flung herself toward Perrie, and Nev seemed to fight against an invisible barrier.

It took Perrie a split second to realize what was going on. She spun to Vale, who was already snapping Nev out of his temporary state.

"Why did you do that again? Please don't do that anymore," Perrie said. It was too weird.

"I wouldn't have, but I needed to tell you everything, and he was already trying to come and hit me again."

"Damn right," Nev seethed as he strolled up beside Perrie.

"Why didn't you run over, Maisie?" she asked, keeping her gaze on her cousin's solo eye.

Maisie smiled sadly. "I knew there was nothing to fear, except what he needed to tell you, and we all had to listen."

Perrie pulled her into an embrace and rested her head on Maisie's shoulder. "They're gone. They're really gone."

"I know." A lone tear slid down Maisie's cheek, and her cousin reached out, grabbing for Nev.

He inched closer, drawing them both into him. Maisie looped her arm around his waist and Perrie's, so they were all cocooned together—they were all they had left.

They stood there for a long while, just the three of them, before breaking apart. At first, Perrie didn't see Vale, and her stomach plummeted, thinking he may have left them without a goodbye.

But then she found him, sitting nearby, his back against a tree and his knees drawn inward. With his elbows propped on top of his knees, he gripped his hair while studying the grass.

Perrie wasn't sure what to do or say because everything was so fucked up. She still walked up to him anyway.

"Are you all right?" she asked, biting the inside of her cheek. "I know it's a stupid question."

He lifted his head, quickly masking his haunted expression by putting on a smile. But she'd caught the switch. From the memories Perrie had of Vale, she could only wonder how horrific all his past memories must be. She couldn't even imagine what had taken place. She didn't know if she wanted to either.

"Not completely, but I feel better with all my emotions back on." He pushed himself up and fished out something from his back pocket. A silver file.

Her shoulders stiffened, but then he tossed it to the grass. She immediately relaxed—the other Vale worshiped that stupid file. *Good riddance.*

They stared at each other, neither one saying anything. He was the first to break the silence. "I have got to leave."

"Where are you going?" Perrie grabbed his arm, then dropped it when he peered down at her hand.

"Back to the Glass Vault. I need to send it back."

"I'm coming with you." There was no way he could go by himself and not because she didn't believe him, but because she needed to see it disappear with her own eyes.

"No," Maisie piped in. "*We're* coming with you."

Vale chewed on the side of his lip and nodded. "I cannot poof us back there, though, so it will be a few days' journey."

Her electricity had started his heartbeat... "That's fine. But can you give me my power back? In case something happens to your heart again." Otherwise, they'd be fucked.

The crackle of energy lit up within her, igniting each nerve, flooding through her veins. Sparks sizzled at her fingertips as Vale gave her another warm smile.

TWENTY-ONE

Before-Vale

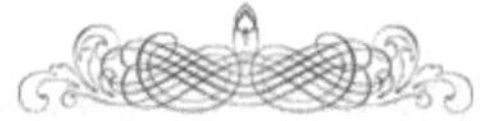

Vale inserted the scalpel in between the male's collarbone. The corrupt soul screamed, pleading for mercy. Closing his eyes, Vale sniffed the air with a greedy suction, as if the sound itself smelled delicious.

Hot blood spilled out from the fresh wound, and Vale purposefully dragged the instrument down the male's fleshy chest. When the metal connected with the soul's navel, Vale lifted the scalpel and set it to the side, gazing at the red liquid as it spilled out. The soul continued to howl in agony and the sound pleased Vale.

Not quite finished yet, Vale dug his index finger inside the collarbone where the wound began. He then glided his digit through the incision until it reached the navel, all while watching the man buck and chew on his tongue.

Lifting his finger, Vale sucked off the excess blood. He inspected his nail and digit, confirming they were now clean, even though they would only become messy again.

A pair of forceps would need to be used next. He clamped

them on one side of the incision and tugged gracefully. As the skin slowly peeled back, he licked his lips in anticipation, then repeated his movements on the other side.

Vale waved his fingers in the air as he gazed at what instrument would take priority. The large knife became his top choice. He picked it up from the tray, then shaking his head, he set the blade back down and reached for a long and thin metal baton. First, he wanted to play a little with the intestines.

Vale bared his teeth into a grin and jabbed the baton into the soul's stomach, digging around the organ so the instrument wound through to the other side. Then he gave it a violent yank, and the man screamed in torment, the soul's eyelids fluttering.

Now, it was time for the knife. Vale picked up the sharp instrument from the table, and admired the blade, captivated by how clean, strong, and beautiful it was before bringing it to his mouth. Slowly, he made contact at the hilt with his tongue and licked his way up the sharp side with firm pressure, until he reached the pointed tip. A metallic flavor burst onto his taste buds, and it may have been his own blood, but he still shut his eyes and felt the rush of ecstasy flow through him.

Now it's time to really play.

The knife hovered in the air over the open stomach, when a female's voice called from the doorway, "Master?"

Fury sewed its way through him, and he slammed the knife into the soul's stomach, ignoring the man's endless, agonizing moans.

"What?" he roared as he turned to Red.

"Your father wants to see you," she crooned.

His anger snuffed as quickly as it had appeared and turned into boredom. "How come he is not here to fetch me himself, then? Why is it you are freely walking around instead of back in your cage?"

Red's lips curved into a seductive smile. "He requested pleasure, and I gave it to him. He's still recovering from it."

She sauntered closer to him, and he hastily brushed past her to find his father.

Vale headed down the long dark hallway, the click of heels echoing behind him. He stopped and calmly turned around. "Why are you following me?"

"Your father never said he was done with me. On the contrary, he demanded I return." She grinned, twisting her finger around a red curl.

He frowned before turning to continue his pace. Red's fucks were not good enough to let her roam around on her own, but it was his father's decision.

Vale entered his father's room—lit candles, casting their glow, filled the three brass chandeliers that hung from the vaulted ceiling. His father, still naked, sat up in bed with his hands laced behind his neck, his blond hair tugged in all directions. The silky black blankets rested in a clump on the floor.

Vale did not care about his father's disheveled state—he only wanted to return to his plaything. "Yes, Father?"

His father did not move from his position as he tilted his head in Red's direction. "The little slave mentioned you have been growing bored with your duties and are constantly trying to figure out new torturous activities."

"Yes." Vale's appetite was always curious for more.

"I think you should go up there." His father pointed to the obsidian ceiling and Vale peered up in confusion. "You can prey on humans instead of the corrupt souls here."

"None of us are able to leave." There had never been a way of escape for anyone.

His father flashed a secret smile. "That is not true. *You* can, and you may choose who to bring with you. I am unable to leave, but I can live vicariously through your actions. And I feel you are ready, my son."

Son. He had never called him that. Vale felt nothing, only cocked his head.

"She will explain to you the plan." His father barely glanced in Red's direction.

Vale nodded. "Let me clean up my work first."

"Very well."

Vale strode from the room, already obsessing about what his father had said.

Red clicked her heels behind him as he walked back down the stone hall to his plaything. The soul still lay in his place. Vale snapped his fingers to light a small fire and began cleaning his work, but only after first pricking a few places on the soul with the blade.

Humming to himself as he worked, Vale watched Red lift the soul, then she returned him to the cage across the room. Vale picked at his nails with a smaller instrument and thought to himself how this was not as delightful as it could be. And that would change.

Surrounded by boredom, Vale wanted those new souls, *needed* those new souls, lusted to feed on them in miraculous ways.

Red stood before him as he turned to her and asked, "What is my father's plan?"

TWENTY-TWO

Perrie

How could so many cars have been destroyed? It amazed Perrie how every car they'd found had the same problem, the engine fried. So, running during the day was their only option.

The new Vale situation had started to finally hit Perrie, and it struck her hard. She didn't show how she felt on the outside—not a single tear was shed. On the inside, however, she was *screaming*. She couldn't look at Vale most of the time because it confused her more than ever—his beautiful face reminded her of August, but then she would think of the other Vale. And it wasn't the Vale from up in the tower as one would think. It was the Vale, who in his own way, treated the Bride as his queen, his equal.

But this Vale was like neither—he was quiet, calm, and offered her apples he'd plucked from a tree. It sent a strange feeling to her chest. Needless to say, she refused the damn apples.

As they turned down a curving road, the sky above dark with flecks of stars shining, she could barely hold her eyes open. Farther up the long and narrow road sat a small wooden cabin.

"Let's stop for the night," Vale said, seeming to notice her tiredness. Relief washed over her when Maisie and Nev both agreed.

After breaking inside, they searched through the tiny home for something to give off light. There was only one bedroom, one bathroom, a living room, and a small nook that would be considered a kitchen. Vale stumbled on two flashlights in a kitchen drawer, which would be good enough.

Perrie's body was too drained to shower, so she crashed on an old, cloth couch, curling on her side.

Vale plopped down on the floor beside her. Perrie's eyes widened at him, unsure about what he thought he was doing.

"What the fuck do you think you're doing?" Nev angrily demanded, stomping to Vale. Apparently, Nev thought the same thing.

Vale stared Nev down with a calm expression. "I am protecting Perrie."

Perrie arched a brow. She didn't think she needed any protecting now that the souls from the Underworld had been sent back to the Glass Vault, and she sure didn't know if she felt comfortable with Vale lying on the floor beside her. It was fine during the day, but the night was a different matter altogether. Night was when the Bride and Vale slept in the same bed, when she rode him to bliss, when he thrust inside her until he brought her over the edge. It was when sexual desire was their only conversation. That, more than anything, scared Perrie because she could still feel that lingering chemistry between them. And she could lie to herself all she wanted, but the fact remained that she wasn't indifferent to it.

"I don't think so," Nev said, taking another step toward Vale.

Vale didn't move a muscle, not even to toss up his hand and freeze Nev in place.

"He's fine, Neven." Maisie tugged Nev back by the elbow.

Nev whirled around and scowled at Maisie. "What do you mean he's *fine*?"

Maisie brought her thumb to her mouth and chewed on her nail, then shrugged.

Perrie didn't have the strength to argue about any of this. "He's fine, Nev. I have the electricity if I need to use it."

Vale bit the side of his lip, seeming surprised by her willingness. But after being through hell after hell, she needed to face things for herself.

"We can all have a slumber party out here if it'll make you feel better, Neven," Maisie suggested.

"No thanks. I'm not sleeping anywhere near that bastard." Stomping away to the single bedroom, Nev slammed the door behind him. Maisie shook her head and studied the door, frowning.

"You should probably go in there to calm him down," Perrie said, hoping they'd have a chance to talk about their feelings for each other. "I'll be fine." *Fine* was probably exaggerating, but it was a word that had to get her through this.

Maisie nodded and exchanged a glance between them, as if she was completely *fine* with Vale. "If you need me, just scream. I'll be out here in a jiffy."

"Okay," Perrie drawled.

Maisie closed the door to the bedroom behind her. So, she really did leave her alone with Vale. He'd been nothing but *fine*, so why was she worried now?

Slowly, Perrie turned and Vale met her gaze. A comforting smile crossed his lips, which provided her no comfort. Not when the image of Vale's face between Bride's legs slipped into her mind.

"Apple?" he asked, offering her one of those absurd ripe red ones he still had left.

"Apple." She huffed but stretched forward and took it from his hand. She didn't want to deny him this *sacred* act he'd continuously been offering her.

When Perrie bit into the apple's suppleness, it reminded her for a second of the same damn fruit in Rapunzel's castle back in the Glass Vault. Hurriedly, she shut the recollection out and chewed determinedly, trying to create a new memory of the fruit, as ridiculous as it might be. But it seemed to work.

"Thanks, Vale." Perrie meant those two simple words—he may not realize the small gesture helped, but it did. Vale had faced cruel things too, and she needed to remember that.

"You are welcome." His green gaze locked onto hers, and she studied the red apple.

Perrie finished half the fruit and glanced up at Vale, who hadn't stopped watching her eat. But he wasn't staring at her, he was staring at the *apple*.

"Next time, just let me know if you want to eat it." She let out a small laugh that surprised her and handed over the half-eaten apple.

Eyes practically twinkling, Vale bit right into the thin skin. "This is a new experience for me—eating fruit first hand."

"*What*?" Perrie slapped the couch and lurched forward. "You've never had fruit?"

"I have never had anything. When I lived in the Underworld, there was nothing. We do not have to eat, remember?" He winked.

Did he just wink at me? Okay, I think I need to sleep now. "Well, I guess we'll have to find more fruit for you to try." Perrie lay back down so he'd get the hint that she was done talking for now. But a part of her wanted to keep the conversation going.

"Good night, Perrie," he murmured, his voice sad.

"Good night," she said, fingers twitching at her sides. Closing her eyes, Perrie listened to each crunch as Vale chewed the fruit, until the sound stopped. She heard rustling as he nestled onto the hardwood flooring, his breathing turning slow and deep.

Perrie rolled to her side and opened her eyes, unable to sleep. She couldn't relax. Her heart thundered. She held out her hand defensively in case Bad Vale crept out and she needed to electrocute his heart to a crisp. Another part of her sang inside her head that he was *fine*. *Is that Maisie singing in my brain?*

After a while of lying there restless with her newly-acquired paranoia, Vale began tossing and turning. Perrie started to reach out to wake him, but decided not to as soon as he settled into a curled ball. He looked … helpless. Taking a deep swallow, she pulled her hand back but still left it open, just in case, as she fell asleep.

The day had been a blur of feelings. With the absence of glass statues out in the open, it only reminded Perrie that those people weren't coming back. *Her family* wasn't coming back. It was going to haunt her for a long time, but when she looked at Maisie and Nev, she held hope. When she looked at Vale, on the other hand, her emotions were scattered, especially when she thought about that morning.

Something poked Perrie's arm and she groggily peeled open her eyes. Her gaze settled on Vale and she smiled.

She should've been terrified when she'd woken, but oddly enough, that emotion hadn't stirred in that moment. As the day went on, she constantly caught herself glancing in Vale's direction, then she got irritated at herself for staring. His movements were strong, graceful, and the way his eyes took in the world was as if he recognized it yet found a newness there.

As the night unfolded, they stopped at an empty house with a musky odor. Nev and Maisie claimed a set of bunk beds in a kids' room, leaving only one bed remaining.

"Do you need new sheets?" Perrie asked with a grin.

Maisie waved her off. "I'll make due. Might have to take them off like last night though."

Nev rolled his gaze toward the ceiling and Perrie shook her head as she left to go and get cleaned up.

"You can take the other bed," Vale whispered as she passed him in the hall. She was about to argue when he'd already gone into the living room.

After a long, cold shower, involving too much damn thinking, she headed down the hall to the master bedroom. She halted when she stepped into the room and found Vale with his eyes open, curled up in a snug ball on the floor. Her heart beat with a familiar thump as she stared at him, and she pushed it away.

"You know you can sleep on the bed or the couch if you want?" She didn't mind sleeping on the couch. In her opinion, it was just as good as a bed.

Vale lifted his blond head to look at her, his lids half-closed. "I am fine right here, and I want to make sure you are safe." A tired smile crossed his lips.

That again? Hesitating for a moment, Perrie decided to ask if he wanted to share the bed. It was a king-size mattress with plenty of room, as strange as it still would be. After the night before, she wasn't scared to sleep beside him. If for some reason his heartbeat shut off, she would be ready to flip the switch.

"Um, you can sleep up here if you want, Vale. You don't have to sleep on the floor. There's plenty of room." Perrie hopped onto the bed and lightly tapped the mattress.

He shook his head. "I am already used to the ground, no need to worry."

Used to the ground? How often *had* he slept on the floor? But she didn't ask as she slipped beneath the covers and shut her eyes.

Perrie laid there for what felt like a fucking month, staring up at the darkness above, her head spinning with too many thoughts. She wondered if anyone would ever return to these cities she'd helped destroy, or if they would always remain empty.

A cool breeze drifted through the cracked-open window. Perrie rolled to her side and pulled the thick blanket up higher, thinking about what Vale had said. They could either remain immortal or move on to the other side … wherever souls go. After all she'd done, she hoped she didn't get shoved down into the Underworld, but she wasn't willing to go anywhere yet.

A tiny whimper interrupted her thoughts, and Perrie jerked up in bed. She scanned the dark room, thinking she'd imagined it, when the sound came again … from Vale on the floor.

Last night, he'd tossed and turned for hours. He hadn't been moaning like this, though.

With a heavy sigh, Perrie threw off the blanket and left the comfort of the bed. She shut the window, then rubbed her own arms to warm them. Her gaze dropped to the floor where Vale's otherworldly face seemed to glow beneath the moon's silvery light, as if it was giving him his own spotlight. Should she let him continue sleeping, or wake him? He shivered, and another soft sound of pain slipped out from his mouth. *Wake him, it is*.

Perrie gently nudged his leg with her foot, waiting for him to stir. Vale didn't, so she nudged him again, a bit firmer this time. A small sob escaped him, yet his eyes stayed tightly sealed. Her chest tightened as she studied him, something akin to sympathy taking root inside her. He looked so helpless, just like the night before. Why couldn't she shut off her feelings?

Then she thought of the Bride, and she wouldn't ever want to turn that emotion or any other one off ever again. She wanted to feel *everything*.

Perrie didn't know why she did it, but maybe because the human side of her ached to come out. Or maybe, because Vale had comforted her the other day in the street, or maybe it was just the familiarity of him.

Either way, she took a deep breath and lowered herself behind him on the carpet. She shifted closer and draped her arm around his waist. Her breathing hitched as he took her hand and slid it to his chest over his own heartbeat, like she was his salvation. Maybe she was? Did he even have anyone? Perrie still had Maisie and Nev, but she didn't know who he had.

Vale's heart increased against her palm, and she lifted her head to peer down at his sleeping face. He wasn't asleep though—he was smiling, his eyes almost fully open. Perrie yanked her hand back.

"Did you just fake all that to get me down here?" She frowned while hovering over him. If he did, she would kick him outside.

"Pretend to do what?" His expression turned serious as his eyes met hers. Maybe he wasn't pretending...

Her frown left her face and she bit the inside of her cheek. "You were crying in your sleep."

"Oh. I was having a nightmare." He rolled over to face her.

Perrie studied the loose lock of hair that fell over his eye, but she left it where it was. Even though her fingers ached to push it back. She adjusted herself on the floor and propped her head in her hand. "Demons can have nightmares?"

A dark blond eyebrow drew up. "Well, I do sleep, don't I?"

"I find that odd too." Before, she wouldn't have imagined a demon could sleep, let alone have a bad dream.

"That I sleep?" He let out a low chuckle.

"Yes!" Perrie whisper-shouted and threw her other hand up.

"You're immortal and *you* still sleep."

"But that's completely different." It was way different. She'd at least been born on Earth, so if she slept here before, it made sense that she still would.

The edges of Vale's lips tugged to the side. "Not really."

"Um, yeah it is."

"We both don't age and live forever. It's the same." They could argue about this all night, but he did have a point.

"So, you were born this size?" *I mean, was he even born like humans are?*

He chewed on his lip. "No, I was born a baby, like you."

"Before this gets any more weird, how old are you really?" she prodded. "You aren't eighteen, are you?"

"No." He adjusted himself so his head was propped up too.

"Please don't tell me you're like five-hundred years old." It was already fucked up that she'd had sex with a demon, but if he was some ancient age, she'd be nauseous.

His grin grew wide. "I am nineteen."

"You could've said that right away instead of just saying 'no.'" Perrie smacked his arm and laughed. Realizing she so flippantly hit him, she tucked her hand between her waist and the floor to prevent *that* from happening again.

"What about family? Friends?" She thought about Fannie who'd followed him around endlessly, but she didn't want to bring that bitch up. The thought of Fannie made her want to find her, then electrocute her over and over. Perrie supposed she did have that aspect in common with the Bride.

The half-smile faded away, and he shook his head. "I've never had any. My father murdered my mother after he found out she had given birth to a demon with a heartbeat. It had never happened before, but with how powerful I could become, he wouldn't have her whispering ways to turn me against him. Father would shut my heartbeat down every time it would emerge, until finally, he found a way to turn it off permanently, or at least he thought he did."

"No friends ever?" Her jaw dropped, taken aback that he was nineteen and never had a single friend, regardless of where he was from. She didn't know much about his father, but he already sounded like an asshole.

"None."

"Oh." Her chest felt as though it had been punctured, the air slowly leaking.

He lifted his shoulder and shrugged. "It is okay. I have the memories of you, so I know what it is like to have a friend."

Perrie didn't feel like that was the same thing at all, not in the slightest. "Well, I'll be your friend." She was surprised by her suggestion, but she believed he needed one.

"I will take what I can get." He chuckled and rolled over.

Perrie started to push off the floor and return to bed, but he wrapped her arm back around his waist.

"What are you doing?" she asked, not sure if she should be feeling uncomfortable about this whole situation, but she didn't.

"Friends help friends, so you can stay holding onto me to keep the nightmares at bay."

"I think this is just a way to keep me down here holding onto you." A laugh forced its way out from her throat.

"Perhaps," he said, giving her a smug look. Maybe he could help keep *her* nightmares from making an appearance too. She thought of Officer Rodriguez and what they'd both done to her. She closed her eyes to escape the woman's frightened face. Perrie and Vale had been through the evilest of things together, and they both needed those memories to stay away.

As soon as her forehead pressed into his warm neck, she drifted to sleep. All her thoughts eroded not into a nightmare, but a dream.

Something tapped Perrie's bare foot, and she drowsily kicked at it. Then the quick pressure came again, and she blinked her eyes open. Maisie hovered over her, smiling, while Perrie was still clamped onto Vale. His lids were already open like he'd been lying there a long time.

Perrie quickly removed her arm, and, with a smile, focused on Maisie. "Did you really have to tap my foot to wake me?"

Maisie gave her a sheepish look. "Neven said you were taking too long, and we need to get moving." Perrie glanced toward the door, finding Nev staring at her and Vale with his brows up his forehead. *You would think he just found Vale and me naked together.*

Then Perrie remembered how they'd been like that in the past, in every which way possible. The breath in her lungs seemed to constrict, and she pressed a palm to her chest, the memories playing over and over. The sex. The blood. The glass. The deaths. Their *romance*…

Vale's expression turned concerned, and Maisie knelt beside Perrie, taking hold of her hand. Perrie didn't rip it away, even though she wanted to melt to the floor like the glass statues had done the other day. She wanted to vanish from everything and everyone.

"Can I have a few minutes with Perrie before we leave?" Vale asked. "Please?"

"It's fine," Perrie rushed out.

Maisie pursed her lips and nodded, while Nev narrowed his eyes at Vale before following her cousin out of the room.

"What is wrong? And do not try to tell me everything is okay." Vale propped his back against the bed, leaving her enough room to breathe.

Perrie was going to be honest with him. The way she was with everyone, especially her friends. "I was thinking about before. With August—with you."

She didn't have to say anymore—he knew exactly what she'd meant as his throat bobbed with a hard swallow. "I am sorry about that. He—he did a terrible thing in the tower. It feels like my fault, if only I had found a way to have not let my father shut off my heart." Terrible wasn't quite the word she would use, but it hadn't been him.

"It's not your fault." Perrie took a few shallow breaths before continuing. "The first time with August, I wanted to, but the outcome afterward wasn't the best." She could've used a more descriptive sentence of how she really felt, like how she'd been hollow and powerless as she was dragged naked across the floor. Then when her throat was slit, and she was still inside, she only wanted death. He knew this. And she didn't want to make him feel any more self-loathing than he already did because he knew what *that* Vale did.

"The other times as the Bride..." Perrie trailed off.

But she needed to talk to him about this because he was the only one who knew how she felt. Maisie might say she understood, but she really wouldn't because she wasn't in Perrie's head. And Nev? He would just threaten Vale even more. They wouldn't understand. She knew it wasn't just the Perrie show here—they'd all been through horrific things. But she couldn't get past her damn emotions as easily as Maisie and Nev.

"Vale? Can I ask you a question?"

"Of course."

"When we were um, together, as the Bride and Bad Vale … I know with every fiber in me that we both wanted each other, every single time. It was never a one-way street. I wanted you and you wanted me. It was like the darkest parts of ourselves chose it, so it wasn't ever a violation. Or was it? Since we didn't choose to have our emotions taken away. *You* didn't choose to have your heart shut off." She paused. "How do you feel about it?"

Vale ran his hands through his hair and avoided her gaze. "I don't really know. I have never had intimacies with anyone when I was me, but I have all these memories and feelings of being with others—with you. Most of my life has been without anything being *my* choice."

Perrie inhaled sharply. She might've been through hell herself, but he'd really gone through it. He had *lived* there.

"And, maybe it is wrong," Vale continued, "but I am glad I have the memories of you. Not the ones after the Glass Vault, but all the ones leading up to it, including when we were together inside the museum getting through all of it side by side. Even the simplest ones where we sat on the couch in your home watching old movies together. I know it wasn't me with you, but those memories … those memories are holding me together. It is the one thing I have that is good. I may not be someone you would like to be around, but I want to do the same for you. If you need it, I want to help hold you together with new memories. Although, I know you don't need me. You are strong enough to do it without anyone."

Perrie remained quiet, but she managed to give him a small smile. His words sank in and she wanted to be brave for herself, but she wasn't sure if her pieces would stay glued together.

Earlier that day, everyone remained mostly silent while they covered a great distance. As they got closer to the Glass Vault, the world appeared even more broken, catastrophic. Every tree was ripped from the ground and thrown like twigs—not a single trunk still stood. Power lines were scattered all around, and almost every house and building lay in shambles.

Perrie stayed focused, quiet, just to make it through the day.

They stopped at a house for the night with several outer walls torn off, but it still stood, so that was good enough. After two more nights, they would be at the Glass Vault.

Maisie went into the bathroom to take a shower, while Vale headed into a bedroom. Nev still hadn't come inside, so

Perrie opened the door to find him sitting outside on a porch step. He hadn't even tried to speak to her that day.

She shut the door behind her and asked, "What's going on?"

Nev stared at a hummingbird yard decoration and watched its spinning wings before turning to her with a frown. "No. What's going on with you? You and Vale were cuddled up together on the floor this morning. You do realize this is *all* his fault, and everything we've suffered through is because of *him*."

With a sigh, she sat beside him on the porch. "Vale isn't the Vale you hate. He may still be a demon, but I'm starting to trust him."

"Like you trusted August?"

It felt as though she'd just been slapped. "That's not fair, Nev. He has no one."

"But how do you even know he's not worse than before?" His stare became hard, as if the answers would all pour out from her soul, but she didn't have them. If he was going to accuse Vale, then he would have to blame her and Maisie, too. They were all a part of this, whether they'd known it or not.

"I don't. The thing is, I've been through a lot. You and Maisie have been through just as much, but I can't live my life wondering if Bad Vale will come back or if things may get worse. I'm giving him this one chance, but believe me, if a third Vale pops out or if this one goes hostile, there will be no more chances."

"I just can't see you get hurt again. I don't want him to do that to you." Nev fidgeted with his hands as he studied her.

"It isn't like that, Nev."

He cocked his head and lifted a brow.

She mirrored his movement right back at him. "It isn't!"

"Maisie and I have your back no matter what, Perrie."

Her heartbeat sped up. The two of them meant everything to her—they were her family. "I know you guys do." She wrapped her arms around his waist and held him tight while he ran his hand through her hair, comforting her.

"But I still don't trust him."

"You don't have to, Nev."

They sat on the porch and stared up at the night sky for a long time, just shooting the shit, until Perrie finally decided to head back into the house. She found Vale still in the bedroom, curled on his side on the floor. His apparent routine shouldn't have surprised her, but it still did. *I'm only staying in here with him in case he needs my electricity to revive him.* Or that was what she told herself anyway.

After maybe two minutes of resting in the bed, Perrie sighed and dragged her pillow down beside him. "Okay, so tell me what the deal is with the floor? Why do you insist on sleeping like this?"

The wooden floor was hard against her back, so she wasn't quite sure why the hell anyone would want to sleep on it versus a soft bed.

Vale rolled over to face her with a weak smile. "It is what I am used to. I have always slept on the ground. I remember *him* sleeping on mattresses outside the Underworld, but I never have."

Perrie's heart sank to the pit of her stomach as she thought about what he'd just confessed.

"Do you want to now? Everyone needs a chance to melt into a mattress." She tugged lightly on his shirt. "You can test it out for yourself. I'll even stay down here while you sleep."

"That would be a stupid idea. Down here is where all the fun happens." He softly patted the wood several times.

"What fun? Bad back fun?" Perrie laughed.

He chewed on his lip in thought. "Re-energized fun."

"That doesn't even make sense. You can get re-energized even better on a soft mattress." Perrie motioned at the bed.

"You can go back up there if you want." Something in his voice seemed to yearn for her to stay.

"No. I think I'll stay down here and keep you company." She rubbed a hand across the wood as if it was her new best friend.

"Roll over."

"Why?" Perrie blinked, twice.

"Do you question everything? Roll over."

She wrinkled her nose, then awkwardly rolled to her side. He folded his arm around her waist, and she melted into his warmth.

Time slowed, and Perrie flipped back over to face Vale as she recalled a moment she'd had with him when she was Bride. "It was you that night, wasn't it? The kiss. Your heartbeat fainter, but it was still *you*."

He didn't answer, and she thought he may not, until he did. "It was. I thought I was hallucinating—I wasn't fully aware of everything because my heart was sluggish." His gaze dropped to her lips, becoming hooded, before focusing back on her eyes. "Now, roll over, I'm going to keep your nightmares away tonight."

Perrie wanted to forget about that sweet moment with his mouth against hers, tasting, caressing. But it continued to linger as it was now her turn for her gaze to fall to his mouth. So, she rolled over.

After they woke this morning, it was another uneventful journey with no sign of life anywhere. Not even a bird, stray cat, or dog. Only emptiness. An ugly quiet that Perrie could feel down to her bones. Chill after chill slithered up her spine, and it felt more and more like a movie she'd seen that she never would've expected to be real.

As night started to fall, and their bodies grew tired, they stopped for their final night at an old apartment complex with half the building still intact.

"You can have the bedroom," Maisie said, not taking no for an answer. Nev stayed with her cousin while Perrie headed into the room.

It was small with band posters covering every inch of the walls. She ignored the smoky odor lingering in the room as she peered around. A vintage stereo system took up the corner and hundreds of vinyl rested in blue plastic crates. Plaid sheets sat in a heap at the end of the bed.

Before Vale could be the first to achieve floor status, Perrie positioned herself on the carpet as he got out of the shower, his soft steps sounding down the hallway. He came to a stop in the doorway when his gaze fell to her, amusement dancing in his eyes. Instead of meeting her on the carpet, Vale closed the door and dove straight onto the twin-size bed. The springs squeaked with the bounce from his weight.

"I think I will take the bed tonight." He peered over the edge, and a grin spread across his face.

Shrugging, Perrie smiled back. "That means the floor is all mine." She stretched her body against the thick carpet.

"We may have to switch positions." In a flash, Vale leapt from the bed, swooped her off the floor, and tossed her on the mattress, her body bouncing two full times before she could process what the hell had just happened.

Perrie laughed a real laugh and rolled to the edge of the bed. She found Vale already on his side with his arm up, ready for her to crawl in. As she hopped off the mattress and curled up beside him on the floor, she told herself the main reason she was indulging him was because this had been keeping her nightmares at bay. But she knew deep down that wasn't the only reason…

After she was cozily tucked into his side, a low muffle escaped Vale's throat. She stilled, then flipped around to face him. "What's wrong?"

"I'm sorry," he rasped. Tears streamed down his face as he

sat up, then turned away from her.

Perrie's shoulders slumped, and she didn't want to tell him it was okay because nothing was okay. She scooted beside him as he brought his hands to his face and sobbed into them. Tears pricked at her eyes and streamed down her cheeks when she thought about what he'd done, what she'd done, what they'd done together. It may not have been them, but it hurt like it was.

"Do you want to talk about it?" Perrie pulled him toward her and lay his head in her lap, letting him cry while she stroked his rumpled hair. Everything was catastrophic and nothing was their fault, but it was. His hand squeezed her knee as his warm tears fell harder.

"I am so messed up. I did such terrible things while I was in the Underworld with my father—when I was *him*. I keep hearing the screams down there when he would perform unmentionable acts of cruelty on the corrupt souls. I hear you scream, too. I—I do not know how to repair myself."

"Look at me." Perrie gently lifted his chin. "I hear screams too from when I was the Bride. I may not know everything about you, but we have been through a lot together, and we are going to get through this together. Maisie will help you, too. Nev might need a lot more time."

Vale's laugh was half sob because they both knew how Nev felt about him.

"If it comforts you at all, the Bride would've loathed this version of Vale. She would've fought to have her Vale back by any means necessary, far worse than anything he'd ever done." Perrie continued to stroke his hair, and with her free hand, she brushed the scar at her throat. The raised skin reminded her every day of a time in her life she ached to forget, but it was also something she needed to remind her how she could overcome anything.

Vale's gaze found hers. "He was going to tell her, you know. He was going to tell her every single thing he had ever done in order to bring her to life."

"I know. She told him to tell her in the morning, but I had already gotten my memories back."

Vale stayed silent.

"She wouldn't have hated him," Perrie said softly. "She would've thanked him and loved him even more because if he hadn't done it, she wouldn't have existed. And together they could be even stronger."

A palpable instant passed between Perrie and Vale as he murmured, "He loved her. That emotion may not have been possible for either one of them, but somehow it existed in its own way."

Perrie looked out the window at the night sky, and it was just as dark as their alters' hearts had been. "Everything in the world could burn except for the two of them and that would be perfect. A twisted romance that would be a superb movie. Now, roll over. I think you need to be held tonight more than I do."

"And in the end, they could both be happy," Vale whispered quietly, so quietly that she wasn't sure if he'd meant for her to hear him. But she knew he was no longer talking about Bad Vale or Bride, he was talking about *them*.

Tomorrow they would reach the Glass Vault, and once the museum was gone, maybe they could start to truly heal.

TWENTY-THREE

Perrie

Perrie woke this morning to Vale robotically poking her arm, and she kept swatting him away, trying to fall back to sleep. Then she shot up when she realized they would be at the Glass Vault that day.

Maisie was already jogging in place at the doorway while Nev stared at her with, Perrie's guess was, longing.

Even though the city was in shambles, the weather was perfect with the sun shining high up in the sky. Maybe the world was trying to tell her that everything would be all right.

They took off on a heavy sprint, running the entire way without stopping once. Perrie's bare feet slapped against the ground and after each step, she felt freer. With how good the earth felt against her feet, she may never wear shoes again.

As they went down Oak Street, a pit formed in Perrie's stomach as the Glass Vault loomed before them. It appeared just the same as the last time she'd walked out from it. They slowed to a stop in front of the building, and she gazed up at its outer shell. She thought that maybe it would've vanished, like it had all those weeks ago when she'd come with Aunt Krista and Uncle Jaron. But no, here the piece of shit was now—existing before them with its tall wooden door, no windows, and gray-colored stones that wrapped around its entirety.

Vale's curls swayed as the warm breeze blew through the strands, a lock fluttering right at his brow. "Let's get this over with and put the Glass Vault back where it belongs," he said, his jaw clenched, determined. No worry sounded in his voice, and that helped to trigger a new-found confidence to bloom in her chest. He stared at the stone museum, barely blinking—the first time he was seeing it in person as his true self.

Perrie reached out and squeezed his hand to give him support, even if he didn't think he needed it. "Let's send it back," she whispered.

The three of them waited for Vale to make it disappear, but instead, he said, "I am going to go inside, and I will be back out in a moment."

Perrie's heart felt as though it stopped beating before plummeting to her toes.

"What do you mean go in?" Nev demanded.

"I mean, I have to walk inside, stroll down each of the halls, make it to the circular room, look at each display properly, return through the hallways, and then appear back out here." Vale cocked his head and stared at Nev.

Nev narrowed his eyes at Vale's sarcasm. "I didn't need all that info. The point is, why do you have to go inside at all?"

"I did not say *you* had to follow me inside."

"Yeah, I'm not following you inside that shit show again."

"I'll come with you." Maisie raised her hand, and Nev shot her a dirty look.

Perrie's stomach was more than tied in knots at the thought of entering this building again. It was bound together by ropes, chains, and locks—all squeezing at her intestines. She didn't want to go back in there, and she couldn't believe Maisie would volunteer to. But it was Maisie.

As much as Perrie would rather have a tea party in the forest, she wasn't going to let her cousin traipse inside by herself. Perrie didn't think Vale would do anything, but it *was* the Glass Vault—who knew if it would trigger some magical slap of brainwash once inside. Then they would be back to square one.

"Me too," Perrie sighed, and reluctantly raised her hand.

"That means we're all going, apparently," Nev huffed, "but you're leading the way this time, Vale. None of that walking behind us shit."

"Fine." Vale shrugged and started for the door, followed by Maisie, while Perrie and Nev watched. She reassured herself by knowing that if they got rid of the museum of horrors, then maybe the world could be semi-okay. Swallowing her fear, Perrie grabbed onto the back of Maisie's dress. Maisie gave her a quick pat on the hand, letting Perrie know everything was all rainbows and roses. *Yeah, maybe black decaying roses and rainbows leading to evil leprechauns.*

Vale opened the door, and they stepped into the long hallway. The lanterns lining the walls were still lit with what must be a magical fire that never dissipated. Not surprising. As soon as they were halfway down the red wallpaper hall, that now reminded her of dark blood, the door slammed shut.

Everyone froze except for Vale who continued walking. *Maybe we should've waited outside.* Vale halted and peered back at them, then rolled his eyes harder than Nev ever had. "It is only an effect. Now, come on." He motioned them all forward to the torture chamber.

A need burned through her veins to help end this, so she hurried and jogged up behind Vale.

They completed their walk through hallway number one and turned down the next, where the chandeliers were practically waiting to drop and crush them below. Perrie wondered about the halls, but she would ask questions about them later. The walls were drenched in blue, like an ocean, but then an image came to mind of blue lips on a bloated dead body.

Perrie gripped the back of Vale's silky shirt, and he offered her an encouraging small smile. Maisie then latched onto the back of Perrie's dress, and Nev fastened onto her cousin's. End of hallway number two was now complete. One more.

"Hallway of doom," Maisie whispered.

Perrie focused on the white of Vale's shirt instead of the green walls as they continued walking in a line that connected like a train. Sparks of lightning crackled within her as her heart thundered.

Once they reached the opening leading to the displays, Perrie lifted her chin, holding her head high, and took slow breaths.

Vale glanced over his shoulder at her. "Here we are."

"Yes, here we are," Perrie said sarcastically. Then she yanked on his shirt, his back meeting her chest. "If we walk in there, we aren't getting sucked into the displays, right?" Sparks sizzled inside her, prepared in case something fucked went down.

"No. You will only be able to go back in if I allow you to."

Vale placed his hand in hers, and she stepped beside him. Perrie remembered the moment he'd taken her hand when she'd awoken as the Bride. But the way he looked at their entwined fingers now, the same way she was looking at them, like it was familiar yet unfamiliar, made her feel strange. But not in a bad way—she couldn't even explain it to herself at that moment.

At the center of the circular room, the displays all still remained, except this time, some of the glass figures were missing. Perrie came across the werewolf scene—the wolf stood in a new position, but Little Red Riding Hood was gone. The wolf's glass fur was the color of tree bark, and a pile of human skin surrounded its clawed feet. She peered at the Frankenstein's Monster scene, finding it empty.

"Why isn't there a statue in that one?" Perrie nodded to the empty display.

Vale bit his lip as he studied the scene. "Because that one is mine, but I do not have to be in it." *Victor Frankenstein. Fair enough.*

"What are you doing?" Perrie watched as Vale walked away, scanning the displays.

"I am making sure they are all here."

Perrie's gaze followed him and stopped on Sleepy Hollow. Glass heads, drenched in bright blood, surrounded the hooves of the rider's horse. The Headless Horseman's blackened buttoned-up coat shone under the light as did his dark brown boots that appeared as though they could crush anyone. If it wasn't for the transparency of the glass, she would think the horse could leap out of the display. *Maybe it still can…* She brushed the thought away and glanced at the other scenes— the victims were all missing, but the villains looked the same. Only they stood in different poses than before.

Vale focused on the Jack the Ripper display, squinting his eyes like he was trying to read the scene. The box held no one. Perrie's heart unfolded like paper origami with stress lines practically tearing it apart.

"She is not there," Vale whispered. He finished searching the rest of the displays as Maisie and Nev watched him closely, but Perrie's eyes lingered on the empty display. She should've known that bitch would be tricky. Fannie seemed to be tamed by Vale, like she was his personal mannequin to do with as he saw fit. But there was always something off about her.

The sound of Vale's heavy feet echoed through the room as he ran to the first display, then studied each one with precision again.

"If only I had a magnifying glass," Maisie grunted as she inspected the scenes.

Perrie rushed to the opposite side and examined slowly. She wasn't sure what she was looking for exactly—if it was supposed to be a glass figure of Fannie in her normal attire or a top hat and cloak, so Perrie searched for both. But she found neither.

Vale scratched his head and turned to face them. "Well, she is not in her display."

"I knew something fucked was going to happen here." Nev struck his leg with his fist, seeming to want to break every statue in this place.

As anger shot through Perrie, her power sparking, she might join him on that damn adventure.

Vale arched a brow at Nev like he was an idiot. "Fannie may not be there." He pointed both his hands like they were guns at the Jack the Ripper display. "But she is here." Then he took his gun-made hands and triggered them at the ceiling.

Perrie marched right up next to him as he lowered his pretend guns. Nev watched them as if actual bullets were going to appear. But in this place, anything was possible.

"How do you know?" She hadn't seen a sign of her anywhere.

Vale glanced at the empty hallway as if Fannie would pop out right there. "Because when I sent the souls from the Underworld back here, I put a barrier up. The front door is sealed, preventing their escape. There is also a seal keeping them from stepping out of the displays."

That couldn't be right because Perrie had seen Fannie with who she'd thought was Neven. "I don't understand. Fannie has been out of the Glass Vault before."

Vale chewed on his lip, as if thinking about the same thing, which he probably was with how fiercely he dug into that lip. "That was only when she was allowed out. At that time, the barrier was open to her, but now it is closed to all of them, including her."

Vale stretched his spine to his full length. "I am going to

have to go in."

"Go in where?" Perrie blurted. He couldn't be talking about what she thought he was.

"The displays. She is in one. But her statue is not appearing because she is not in the correct scene."

"How do you even know that?" Nev asked.

"Because while I may not know which display the corrupt souls are in without seeing their statue in their correct scene, I can still feel her inside the museum." He ticked his index finger back and forth at the Jack the Ripper scene.

"Which display do we all start in, then?" Maisie asked, stepping beside Vale.

Nev ran his hand agitatedly through his hair, seeming more pissed than he was earlier. "Maisie! Seriously! Enough of this. We already traveled through this death house to fulfill your investigation needs. But get real, there's no need to go traipsing through different horror shows here."

Maisie pointed between Nev and herself. "*We* are immortal. Therefore, we'll be fine."

Perrie arched a brow at her. Maisie might be all about venturing back into the displays, but she sure as fuck wasn't.

"If you want to begin at one end, I will start at the other," Vale said to Maisie, then paused. "But when you reach the Sleeping Beauty scene, you will have to stop there and wait for me. You are right about being immortal, but if you enter the Snow White display again, there is no escaping, and you will be heading back with the Glass Vault."

"To the Underworld?" Perrie gasped, taking a few steps back.

Vale slowly nodded, his lips pursed.

"Fuck that. Vale can go by himself," Nev hissed.

Perrie shut her eyes for a moment—she would face this. Opening her lids, she took a deep breath. "Maisie, you stay here. As the older one, I'll do it."

Maisie whipped her head to Perrie. "We're the same age.

You're only older than me by a few weeks.

"Exactly." Perrie smiled. "So you stay here."

Nev shook his head. "Wait a minute, what if Vale becomes 'Bad Vale' in the displays again."

Smart question. Before Perrie could respond, Maisie darted off to a display near the hallway. "Team effort. Perrie with Vale. Nev with me." She waved Nev to her, and he stared at Maisie with wide eyes.

"Two things," Vale started. "Good news, the souls listen to me and should not attack you. Bad news, you have no power inside the displays." He gripped the back of his neck as he looked at Perrie. "That means your electricity will be gone."

Fuck. "None of this is adding up. What if Fannie slips past us into one of the other displays, and we continuously run after her forever? Also, I won't be able to run through my scene."

Vale grinned. "The Bride is special, you can run through your display if you have to."

That's dumb. Then I should be able to use electricity if I'm so special.

Vale clapped his hands together. "Barriers are up."

Perrie wrinkled her nose, confused. "Sometimes you have to explain things a little more to us. I thought they were already up."

"I wasn't close enough to put that barrier up earlier. Whichever display Fannie is in, she won't be able to leave it now that they are up between each display."

"Then why can we walk through the barriers?" Maisie called over.

"Because I am allowing you to. Weapons will be at your waist in case you need them for Fannie."

That must've been answer enough because Maisie looked toward a display, where a glass pond rested in front of a greenish, fish-like creature. Maisie clasped Nev's hand tightly, seeming to wait for the wind, that had pulled them in before, to blow. Nothing happened.

Vale snapped his fingers, and a gust of wind stirred, blowing Perrie's hair around her head. But it didn't tug at her though, only dragged Nev and Maisie's feet across the floor.

"Meet you at Sleeping Beauty," Maisie shouted while waving like she was going on a damn vacation.

"See you then," Perrie yelled back. She tried to appear calm, but inside she was freaking out—she didn't want to be separated from Maisie again. *They'll be okay,* Perrie told herself once they were both gone.

"You know you can wait out here for us," Vale said. "You do not have to go."

Waiting out here would be easier, but Perrie didn't want to do easy. She wanted Fannie to be sent back to where she belonged, and she would help put her there.

"Let's do this." Perrie punched the air as Maisie would've, then followed Vale to a Hansel and Gretel display. She truly believed the world was laughing at her. But then she remembered all the fun times she'd had playing Hansel and Gretel with Maisie when they were kids. Vale did say the immortals wouldn't attack, but was he even sure about that?

Vale held his hand out to hers, and she peered into his emerald eyes. There wasn't fear she felt, only hope, so she gripped it tightly.

"Together?" he asked.

"Together." Perrie smiled.

TWENTY-FOUR

Before-Fannie Caldwell

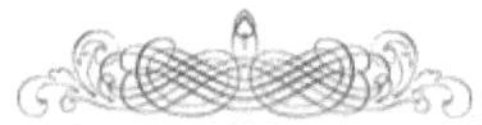

Fannie Caldwell was born Jaqueline Richards. She'd had entertainment while it lasted—murdering whores, slicing and dicing into their luscious flesh. She may have been a whore herself, but she'd yearned for the blood—the warm, red liquid that she loved to lick off her tools after a murder.

She would have never been found out. Her intelligence was beyond anyone's thinking capacity, and that laughable police force would never have been able to discover her.

A common cold turned into bronchitis that led to pneumonia was what had ended her killing spree. Something as simple as that. She would have preferred to be taken down with her skin peeled off—something painful, yet pleasurable. A simple cut was all it would take to light up all her nerve endings. Alas, Jack the Ripper was only a mortal.

Jaqueline had wanted a new name when she returned from the Underworld. She would become immortal, and nothing would take her down this time. Fannie Caldwell was the name that rolled off her tongue.

"I went over the plan with your son," Fannie said, focusing on her master—*her real master*. She only truly wanted him. Not Vale.

"Does he approve?" Vale's father still lay in bed naked, and Fannie thought of all the delicious things she had done with him earlier. Sucking him, riding him. The things she would do again once this conversation was over.

"Yes." She smiled, licking her lips. "With his abilities, he is going to build a barrier of sorts. It is to resemble a museum, and there will be different boxes that will trap individual souls. Those souls will be able to perish inside their box and become indestructible, and they *will* bring more souls into its walls once released."

Master ran his wet tongue across his white teeth, tempting Fannie to obliterate the conversation.

"You did not tell him I will eventually be released once enough souls are pulled from the earth, did you?" His black eyes narrowed into thin slits as if he believed she could be tempted by another. *Impossible.*

"No, Master." When she was pulled from her cage on her first day in the Underworld, after Vale cut into her repeatedly, Master found her. He could see she was not fearful like the others but enjoyed every minute of her torment, so he confiscated her. She told him about the days of her own joy above, and he was astonished she could remember. He relished it, relished her.

He knew she had a purpose, and Vale would be their personal little marionette. Master would hold the strings, but Fannie would keep them from unraveling. That frail, miserable young male she'd watched from her cage, her first day in the Underworld, had been undeserving of the powers he held in his possession. He still was. Those powers were waiting to be fully unleashed, and Fannie and her master would have it all.

"Good. His heart seems to have been permanently stopped, but if it ever beats again, he cannot know this." A deep crease settled in between Master's blond brows.

"As you wish." She took a sultry step toward him.

"Vale must believe you serve him up there." Master leaned forward, staring hard at her. "Do not make a single mistake for him to believe you want this for yourself. He can only believe I want this for him, to help him grow stronger, and he *will* grow stronger. But then his powers will come to me as my insides drain him of all he has."

Fannie nodded, peeling off her dress and letting it drop to the floor. She took another step in his direction, heat pooling at her core, lust filling her.

"When I'm released, you will stand by my side." He held up a finger. "But if this fails, I will find you, and the things you did above ground, the torture Vale presented to you, are minuscule to what I will do. I will shred every part of you there is." Master stuck the end of his index finger in between his teeth and lightly bit it.

Fannie closed her eyes and let those sentences flow through her. Those words were a delicacy she wished to taste. Either way sounded like a triumph to her. She wanted to be ripped into by her master with *her* weapon of choice. If they were above ground, she would still make him do so, with the new power he would possess. That was a true dessert she craved. Her nipples hardened at the thought.

She sauntered to the bed and closed the distance between them. Master's eyes roamed over her naked body hungrily, as if knowing what she wanted from him. And she was going to have him begin now.

TWENTY-FIVE

Maisie

The strong gust of wind flung Maisie to the hardened dirt, the graininess scratching at her forearms. Neven's hand was still firmly in her grasp as his head plummeted to the ground.

"Are you okay?" Maisie asked while Neven massaged his scalp.

"No."

She knew he was talking about more than the pain, but they both leapt to their feet and surveyed the area.

A small pond rested in front of them, blocking their path to the other side of the display. When Maisie glanced to her right, a certain fish man, with light green scales and razor-sharp needle claws, watched her. He was knelt to one knee and looked incredibly similar to the classic horror film character, Creature. But there was a little variance—eerier.

Tiny horns sprouted above each dark eye—eyebrows?—and his teeth were like sharpened sticks of charcoal. His gills oozed thick green slime onto slightly lifted scales. He studied them, but she eagle-eyed him right back. Maisie remembered this little deadly game with Pinocchio. She adjusted her patch to give off the warning vibe that she may only have one eye, but she could see every single movement he made. *I'm prepared for his bag of tricks.*

Neven hastily tapped her shoulder. "Are you going to stare at him all day, or do you want to try to move on to the next display?"

Maisie gave Neven a once over before doing the same to herself. Their clothing hadn't changed—unlike when they'd been here last and their outfits had matched their scenes. But, this time, Vale graciously gifted them knives at their hips, as promised. *No time for playing with these glorious weapons, though.*

The space in this display wasn't the same as in Snow White, or the ones Perrie had traveled through. Instead of going on for a good distance, the display seemed more similar to an extra-large living room—four walls painted like a forest with tall, thin trees and a bright blue sky. Maisie looked at Fish Man, his eyes following their every movement, but he remained immobile. She was ready to pounce if he tried anything sketchy, though—and she *would* fillet him.

"Run!" Maisie yelled as she dove into the freezing pond, ignoring the icicle sting. Slicing through the liquid, she kicked her legs hurriedly. Neven's arms beat at the water beside her, and they landed on the other side in no time. Maisie sprang to her feet, waiting for the wicked soul to follow. The creature's head was now tilted in their direction, his dark eyes focused on them, but he stayed planted across the pond.

"I guess Vale was right about them not coming after us," Neven said, shaking his head like a wet dog. A few drops splashed against her skin.

Squinting her eye, Maisie observed the stretch of land one more time. "I say Fannie isn't here unless she's hanging out at the bottom of the pond." They padded to the edge and gazed around the clear water, not seeing anything.

"Next one." Neven turned toward where their escape should be. Maisie grabbed his hand, and they easily walked through the barrier as the gust of wind sucked them through.

They hopped to their feet as soon as they hit the ground. Another small area. *Good.* It would be much easier to spot that red hair of Fannie's. No red hair, though. Only a vampire with razor-sharp canines in Maisie's line of vision. Long—at least three inches—alabaster claws lazily tapped from pinky to index finger across his knee—all while sitting on the edge of an empty bed covered in magenta satin sheets.

Transparent, chalky-white skin wrapped around his skeleton, a map of thin red veins pulsing through his flesh. He ran a thick black tongue across thorn-like canines.

Maisie wasn't sure if the vamp would stay there and obey Vale. So, she moved her hand to her belt of goodies. This time, wooden stakes of all sizes and varieties were attached at her hip. *This is what I'm talking about.*

Neven frowned, rubbing his jaw nervously. "I think we have to leap over the bed."

Her eye darted around the room. It was empty besides the too-long bed touching the walls to their left and right. Still no red hair or Jack the Ripper gear, but Maisie didn't know if the heathen was underneath the bed skirt. Diving to the floor, wooden stake in hand, Maisie lifted the edge of the bed skirt. Nothing.

Neven hauled her back with his arms wrapped around her waist. "Are you an idiot?" His voice cracked during his whisper-yell attempt.

"We can't very well move on before we search the area, right?"

Maisie received no response from Neven except for a puckering of the lips.

The vamp still sat in his same comfortable position, tapping that knee of his.

"Now!" Maisie screamed.

She took hold of Neven's hand, and they bounced a foot onto the bed, leapt to the floor, and ran for the wall. The heavy suction pulled them through with a clean sweep.

They landed on their feet this time.

Neven tugged her elbow. "Maybe I do want your plans, Mais, before you start getting all gung-ho and doing things without explaining."

"So, you do like my planning." Maisie grinned while searching the area. She didn't spot a wicked soul anywhere. *Oh wait, there it is*. Small bubbles popped within a mysterious green liquid, and two large violet eyeballs blinked in their direction. The slimy substance coasted from side to side, and Maisie just stared at the creation in awe.

"This one's too weird," Neven muttered. "No sign of Fannie—let's go." Grabbing her hand, Neven tugged her forward. They hopped over several toppled metal cans before the gust of wind yanked them to the next display.

Maisie somehow landed on top of Neven, and she gazed at his face. "I think you're the planner now." He didn't lift her off him as she examined the display. She didn't want to leave this position either until … she saw what was in the room with them.

"Run!" Maisie shouted.

Neven shoved himself from the floor in a second with her hauled to him. Before them, a person sat huddled on the ground—blackened limbs barely hung on to his torso, and thick black blood leaked out from the wound. And no Fannie. They barreled across the crow-colored grass, where the infection must've also spread, then they passed through the barrier.

"What was that about?" Neven asked as they crossed into a nursery rhyme nightmare. A woman leaned against a large boot, as tall as the ceiling, with tiny ivory skeletons of children on the ground surrounding her. She lightly smacked some sort of white stick against her palm.

"Black Plague. We had to avoid it." Maisie's chest heaved, trying to catch her breath. Having an arm chopped off would be one thing, but a rotting limb dangling about was a whole different ballgame.

Neven broke into a wide grin and tapped the side of his head, his dark hair swinging forward. "Immortal, remember?"

"I know, but it was still a risky situation. Some scientists believe the plague wasn't spread by fleas on rats. They believe it was airborne!" Maisie shuddered to herself.

"You know that immortal back there could've transferred venom into you and turned you into a vampire." Neven tugged one of her dark curls.

"But my ligaments would've still been intact." She could deal with vampirism but not *rotism*.

Neven rolled his eyes and studied the tall black boot. "I'm not sure what this display even is."

"There's a lady and a shoe."

"Okay?" he drawled, his expression bewildered.

"The nursery rhyme of the lady with too many kids that lived in a shoe." That rhyme was creepy even without it being converted into a horror display—living in a boot filled with kids and more kids was a nightmare in itself.

"Sorry, Mais. I must've missed that one." He shrugged and glanced back at the woman.

Maisie took a better look at the lady—the immortal's black hair was pulled into a raggedy bun, and something red was smeared on her chin. Maisie squinted at the immortal's tapping hand—it wasn't a white stick she was holding, it was a *bone*. One of her children's bones.

"What's coming from her mouth?" Neven should've already known the answer to his question.

"Blood! Time to run!"

The immortal's empty eyes bored into them as they leapt over the skeletons of her dead children. As they passed their surroundings, there was no sign of Fannie. Neven yanked the door to the boot open while Maisie clamped down on his arm. Then a tornado of wind unleashed and pulled them through.

As they stood in the next display, Neven pressed a fist to his mouth like he was about to gag. "I think I'm going to be sick. This was your bright idea, Maisie."

"It's all for the good of humanity," Maisie said and let go of his bicep.

"I think humanity needs to defend themselves." Neven's gaze drifted through the room, then paused.

"Well, we've gone past several wicked souls, so we pretty much have to keep doing the same thing." She followed his gaze until she halted on a woman with metal from wrist to fingertip, gripping her own bloody, fleshy hands.

"What? See sick shit and then run?" Neven watched the blood droplets splatter to the ground in a large puddle that took up almost the whole room. Blood dripping continued to echo throughout the space, sounding like a loud drumbeat.

"That's correct," Maisie sang and nodded as she kept rubbernecking Metal Hands on their sprint to the barrier.

Neven released a loud puff of breath. "Okay then. Let's hurry and make it to Sleeping Beauty."

With no sign of Fannie, they ran and kept on running through scenes. No wicked souls attempted to lunge at them, only staring contests with her and the immortal while Neven avoided this new sport.

Eventually, they were spit out into the Sleeping Beauty display, green walls surrounding them. Maisie should've counted from the beginning to know just how many wicked souls they'd had to bypass to get to this scene.

There weren't any big surprises here when Maisie spotted the dark fairy hovering in a corner. She wore a sleek black gown with a low v-neck reaching her belly button, the swells of her breasts exposed for all to see. Her horns were longer and thicker than Maisie would've imagined. Instead of coming to a single point, the horns looked more like tree branches with tiny limbs sprinkled across them. The dark fairy gripped a deep brown staff in one hand, beating it against the wooden floor with a slow repetitive thump.

Maisie didn't feel like sitting in a room, waiting for Perrie and Vale, with this immortal watching them the whole time. She darted toward the dark fairy and whirled her around, so she faced the corner of the wall. Her staff continued to pound the floor, so Maisie took it from her hand and laid it beside the fairy's feet. The wicked soul didn't move to reach for the staff or turn back around.

"Didn't I say to tell me your plans?" Neven said, seeming more impressed than irritated.

Maisie peered past Neven to look at the bed—it was huge and high off the floor. Large wooden posts with vines engraved in the wood stood at each corner of the bed, and green satin sheets covered the mattress.

Striding to the bed skirt, Maisie lifted the material and found no Fannie. Her heart sank. She hoped Perrie and Vale pinpointed her soon because she and Neven had failed their mission.

With nothing else to do, Maisie crawled underneath the bed as if it was a tent. It even felt like one since she could almost sit to full height.

Neven drew up the skirt from the other side. "What are you doing?"

"Waiting for Perrie and Vale, but I couldn't help but test this out." She stroked the wooden bedframe, her fingers trailing over the thin vines.

Neven rolled his eyes but crawled beside her. Even with his long body, he fit snugly under the bed. "This is weird as shit."

"Would it be weirder to sit on the bed and see the wicked soul?" Maisie asked, peeking through the front edge of the bed skirt. The fairy still held her soldier stance as she faced the wall.

"Point taken."

Under here it was like she wasn't in the room. The quietness felt a little strange, though. Even during the attacks with Pinocchio and the mermaid, there'd been other sounds.

"Do you think Perrie and Vale are going to find Fannie?" Neven ran a hand down the side of his face and rested it on a pale scar.

"I do. Vale is the one who brought the Glass Vault here. As soon as he finds her, this place can be tossed back to the Underworld." Maisie had faith in both of them, no matter how slippery Fannie might try to be.

"I take it you're all about Vale, too. Now that he isn't evil or however you would word it." Neven clenched his jaw while seeming to bore holes into the ruffled bed skirt.

"What do you mean *too*?" Maisie did like Vale. Over the past few days, he'd proven he was like them—controlled by the King of Darkness himself.

"Well, Perrie was instantly attracted to him again once it was revealed he isn't 'bad' anymore." He continued to stare straight ahead, so she couldn't really see his expression.

Perrie hadn't said anything to her, but Maisie had noticed how her cousin observed Vale. She'd thought Perrie had wanted him to be like August, but she was wrong about that. Perrie watched him differently. Maisie wasn't sure if it was only a friendship situation, yet the cuddling at night made her question that aspect.

"So, you're concerned with Perrie liking Vale?" Maybe he did still want Perrie back...

"No. I said *too*. As in, I'm concerned that you're crushing on him, *too*."

What? Maisie's lips parted. "Why would you even think that?"

"Over the past several days, every time, you're the first one to hop on the bandwagon of doing what Vale does." Neven worked his jaw back and forth, frowning.

"That's only because I believe him." She couldn't explain it, but she somehow knew what he'd said was true.

"But why?"

"I could just feel it." Before Maisie had known August was an evil demon, she'd had no idea. But now that she knew Bad Vale pretended to be this person, she could see how they were connected. At times, August would have the same empty expression Vale had, except he would disguise it quickly. Now, even if there was a neutral expression, his eyes didn't feel empty.

"That's not logical."

What was he even getting at? She didn't like Vale in that way. She liked Neven, but she didn't want to shout it in his face.

"Every time Vale did something or said something, you were right—"

Maisie didn't want to scream how she felt, so she quickly pressed her lips to his. His mouth was like a fluffy pillow against hers, and she wanted to melt into the touch. Maybe now Neven would be quiet about the Vale stuff. His eyes opened wide, and his jaw dropped slightly when she drew her head back.

Heart racing, Maisie smiled at him mischievously. "I didn't run this time."

"Or scream." A nervous laugh escaped him, but then he turned serious.

Neven reached out and ran his hand across her cheek to the eye patch. She closed her lid and let him tenderly slide it off. He scooted closer to her, leaned forward, and softly kissed where the eye was missing. His lips then trailed kisses down her cheek, all the way down her neck, until his mouth was on hers once more.

Nev kissed her gently, a soft caress, and she mirrored his movements. He then rolled to his back, bringing her on top of him. The tip of his tongue traced the seam of her lips, and she parted them for him. His tongue danced with hers as his hand pressed on her back, drawing her closer. As their kiss deepened, grew bolder, and the warmth in Maisie's body became hotter, she had to pull back for now. She wanted desperately to continue the moment, but duty called. They needed to monitor the dark fairy in case she really did try to pull some sort of stunt.

"We have to keep an eye on the fairy, but we'll continue this later," Maisie said, kissing him deeply one more time before crawling out from underneath the bed.

Neven followed her and swooped her into his lap before leaning against the wall. While he circled his arms around her, she couldn't stop herself from smiling. Snow White didn't find a prince or a huntsman in the end, instead she found Frankenstein's beautiful monster.

TWENTY-SIX

Perrie

The strong gust of wind wrapped its invisible leash around Perrie and Vale, then easily glided them through the barrier. After their feet hit the ground with a slight stumble, Perrie anxiously scanned the small area with blue frosted and sprinkled walls. The room didn't have an odor, not even a sweet scent from the frosting. Her gaze connected with the plump witch sitting on top of an old-fashioned stove with her legs crossed at the ankles, leisurely swinging them up and down.

The witch's dark brown hair was styled in a long braid, and she appeared much younger than Perrie would've expected, not a single line creasing her beautiful face.

Chocolate chip cookies rested on a metal tray in her lap, and Perrie waited for the witch to try and shove a dessert down her throat. But she didn't, only observed them with a twitch of the lips.

"Why is the room so small?" She thought back to how most of the displays she'd been in held large forests and had felt like a real place.

"After everyone was released," Vale started, "the Glass Vault returned the displays to their normal size. The illusion of something larger is not needed any longer."

"Okay then." Perrie peered down and found a belt around her waist, loaded with a variety of tiny knives. When she'd come to the Glass Vault last, she'd only been given a small dagger in Billy Goats Gruff.

"She is not here," Vale said, scanning the space.

He took hold of her hand, and they moved to a frosted wall. The gust of air came to life, rumpling her hair and dress before sucking them through. This would be easier than Perrie had thought, since the displays were miniature versions of themselves. She only hoped finding Fannie was as simple.

Still clasping Vale's hand, she searched the new room. Old headstones, broken and cracked, covered the sparsely grassy area, but she didn't see anything else. And she didn't see a sign of Fannie anywhere either.

Something to Perrie's right moved, catching her attention like a flare in a night sky. She whirled to the side and pushed Vale out of the way, nearly knocking him down. He steadied them both before they crashed into the dirt of the cemetery.

A long arm with a slight greenish tint protruded from the ground. It had somehow managed to claw its way out from the dirt one way or another. The ring and pinky fingers were ivory bone, while a loose flap of flesh hung against the hand. A thick yellow liquid ran down the other digits, the skin there appearing as though it wouldn't stay attached much longer. That sight alone put *Night of the Living Dead* to shame, and it was only a damn hand.

"I told you they would not do anything." Vale watched the wiggling digits like he was confirming what he'd said.

"That doesn't make it any less creepy, Vale!" It wasn't as bad as the giant trolls ripping apart bodies and goats, though. She could easily stomp on a hand if she needed to.

They skirted around a few of the grave markers and rushed for the next scene. Their pace increased as she got used to seeing a sinister immortal studying them in each display. Still, Fannie wasn't in any of them—no bright red hair or Jack the Ripper clothing. They then traveled to the next scene, and then to the next, and then to the next after that.

As they continued crossing new world after new world, it felt like it would never end, that they would never find her. But when they stepped into the next display, Vale stiffened. "She is here."

Old stone cathedrals were painted on the walls in neutral shades. To Perrie's right rested the gray gargoyle that Vale had made disappear days ago. The beast sat crouched in a position that resembled a real statue. But as its broad chest heaved up and down, it clearly indicated the gargoyle wasn't one. Its large wings spread fully, the tips reaching toward the heavens. Black veins were set in a leafy pattern that throbbed against the appendages' thin skin.

The gargoyle's left wing twitched, and Perrie just happened to catch a glimpse of a lock of red hair behind it.

Perrie's hand reached for her belt, pulling out the longest knife there. Even though she couldn't spark up, she still tried to ignite her electricity. *Of course nothing, damn it.* She waited for Vale to make his move—possibly clap Fannie away, or telekinesis her to them so Perrie could stab the immortal in her devious heart. Something besides standing there with a crease between his eyebrows and looking lost.

"What is it?" she hissed, clenching the knife harder.

He snapped his fingers. "Something is off. My power is not working in this one."

"What do you mean?" Perrie screeched, glancing back at the gargoyle with its sharp protruding teeth.

"Stay here."

What the hell is he talking about?

Vale lunged for the gargoyle. Perrie waited for Fannie to

run at her and proudly held up her knife, ready for the bitch.

Fannie didn't pounce as Perrie expected, but the gargoyle did. The beast tore forward and rammed Vale to the floor, restraining him by the shoulders. The gargoyle then dug its clawed feet deep into Vale's thighs, blood seeping to the surface. Vale winced but didn't release a scream.

Movement came from where the gargoyle previously was. Fannie rose from her kneeled position, smirking. A beat of wings cracked behind Perrie, and she glanced back at Vale— the gargoyle's stone-like hand now squeezed Vale's throat. Her heart roared, louder and louder.

Should she try ripping the gargoyle off Vale? *No…* She couldn't do that because then Fannie would try to do something to her from behind. Perrie didn't think anymore— she charged at Fannie. But the immortal spun to the side, somehow ending up across the room. Thinking back to their Ripper times, Perrie remembered how fast Fannie was when she'd sliced Perrie's arm in the display. How sneaky she could be. She still was.

Perrie charged at her again, swinging her knife like crazy. Fannie bent backward like she was doing the fucking limbo, and Perrie missed her completely. Even mid-movement, Fannie still managed to turn around and slice the back of Perrie's arm. Perrie gasped at the sharp sting, warm blood oozing out from the wound. She'd had enough. Enough of this. And enough of her. Fannie was going to die.

"You know, little puppet, we can do this all day long." Fannie beamed, running the bloody scalpel across her lower lip. Perrie's chest heaved, but she was far from stopping. "We will be returning to my only master, *your* master." The immortal's gaze shifted to Vale, who choked as he attempted to speak. The veins at his temples looked like they would burst, his face turning a bright cherry red.

Perrie desperately tried to reach into herself, to somehow gather that spark, but she couldn't.

"Option one did not work out, so we are moving on to option two," Fannie said. "Vale is coming back with us to his father, and you, dear *Bride,* are coming along. I don't want your soul to travel anywhere except with us to the Underworld." Her smile was laced with pure venom.

Perrie was *not* going there, and Vale wasn't either. She couldn't let his heart be shut off again by some sadistic fuck, then have this whole process repeat. Vale didn't deserve that. With the knife still tight in her grip, she thrust herself at Fannie.

Perrie had the immortal's movements down. Just as Fannie was about to spin to the side and flip around, Perrie shot forward against her back. She lifted the blade and slammed it into Fannie's right side, piercing her lung, all while knocking her down.

Before Fannie started bucking, Perrie ripped the knife from the immortal's back with a sickening squish. Perrie straddled Fannie as the immortal began to lift. Without a pause, she yanked Fannie's head back by her red hair and sliced a half circle at her throat to match Perrie's. Blood poured out from the wound.

The gargoyle still had Vale pinned down, and Perrie needed to figure out how to get the beast off him. But first, without a care, Perrie flipped Fannie over to her back—she wasn't going to risk it, so she shoved the knife into the immortal's heart. As Fannie choked on her own blood, her hands desperately clawed to her throat.

Not satisfied yet, Perrie stabbed over and over and *over—* she didn't want Fannie or anyone else here to tarnish any more innocent people. She didn't want whatever humanity was left outside the Glass Vault to go through what she or any of the others had. Maisie had done this to the Huntsman back in the Snow White display, but Perrie stabbed Fannie even more.

The immortal's laborious breaths slowed before turning into nothing, her chest still. Perrie didn't know how long it would take before she woke again, so she needed to hurry. With her knife at the ready, Perrie leapt off Fannie and dove for the gargoyle. An odor of burnt feces struck her nose, the only thing she'd smelled thus far, coming from the beast. She yanked it by its paper-thin wings, but the gargoyle's hold on Vale's throat didn't release. Perrie lifted her knife high above her head and stabbed it in the back, ignoring its shrill shrieking as blood splattered the walls. The gargoyle's wing was next, and she sawed at it.

Vale managed to slide out and get to his feet, then hauled ass toward Fannie. The gargoyle flapped his wings, creating a large gust of wind that flung Perrie backward. It then whirled around and backhanded her in the shoulder with its thick skin. She went flying into the wall, her head slamming against it with a powerful bang. The room spun as she crumpled to the floor.

Perrie shakily rolled to her back, nausea bubbling up her throat. She prayed Vale was achieving something with Fannie. He had to.

When Perrie lifted her head, two massive gargoyles hovered over her, then her double vision cleared. Before she could make a move, the beast pounced on her and raised its knife-like claws. The gargoyle slashed them across her chest, her stomach. Again and again. Perrie screamed at the top of her lungs, pain, so much pain, roaring through her. She wished the first slash had killed her because, with each strike of a claw, the agony only became worse.

By now, her organs must be displayed for his choosing. Most likely to eat. If only she had her electricity… Perrie closed her eyes and blood seeped into her mouth. A cracking sound echoed when the gargoyle's hand plowed down into her chest where he would rip her heart out.

But then the slashing stopped.

Everything stopped.

Her eyes fluttered open, her gaze locking on an angel and

cloud-covered ceiling. She tried to lift her head, but it only stayed rooted to the floor. This pain was the worst she'd ever suffered, including her own death before.

Perrie was about to close her eyes again, beg to the heavens above for her body to either heal or let her die, but then a beautiful mess of blond hair and an angelic face leaned over her. *Am I hallucinating?*

"Hold on," Vale murmured as he scooped her into his arms. Perrie wanted to reassure him that she could walk, but all she tasted was blood on her numb tongue. His green irises stayed locked on hers, and she didn't look away. Those two emeralds were the only thing grounding her in this horrific moment.

Vale lay her on the hard marble, and an uncontrollable cough escaped her throat. She struggled to cover her mouth, but she managed, and her hand came away with droplets of blood.

"You are going to be okay, Perrie," Vale said softly as he stroked her hair, but worry shone in his eyes. Her hands trembled—her body wasn't mending, and she felt tattered and torn to pieces.

Vale leaned forward and pressed his lips gently against hers, and they came away with speckles of her blood. She was too numb to feel anything in the kiss. But she wished with everything that she had.

"Wait here. I'll be right back." And then he was gone.

Where is he going?

Everything faded, growing darker… Everything gone. Then she was gone too.

"Perrie?" She knew that voice. Her eyes were too heavy to open. "Perrie?" There it was again, that female voice.

Perrie finally jerked her eyes open. "Maisie?" Three heads awkwardly hovered above her face. She sat up as they shifted back.

The first thing she noticed was her dress, ripped and drenched in blood. It was practically saturated to where there was more red than white. Then it all hit her—Fannie and that monstrous gargoyle.

Vale sat beside her with his hand against her lower back, propping her up in case she fell. But she was okay now. No more pain.

"How are you feeling?" he asked.

Perrie swallowed, peering up at his concerned face, and she didn't want to look away. "Remember that hand we saw sticking out from the ground?"

He nodded but also looked confused. "Yes?"

"That's how I feel, except like I crawled out of the heavy dirt and am relieved I'm out. I thought I was gone."

"Immortal, remember?" Maisie piped in.

Perrie's attention stayed focused on Vale. "But Officer Rodriguez was immortal, and she still ended up dead."

"That is because after she died, *he* sent her soul away," Vale said in a weak voice.

"So, I did die." *Again.*

He slowly nodded, chewing the edge of his bottom lip. A much better habit of his than the compulsive nail picking. "Did you wish I would have sent your soul away?"

"No!" Perrie practically yelled. This immortality would take some getting used to, but she didn't want to die yet.

"Good. I kind of wish for you not to leave." Vale grinned. She smiled back at him.

"Now we have to finish getting rid of the Glass Vault," he said, seriously.

"Okay, but what about Fannie and the gargoyle?"

"She is over there." He gestured toward the Jack the Ripper display. A panic flowed through her until her gaze settled on one lone glass form, hidden away beneath a black hat and cloak. She guessed that answered her earlier question—Fannie wasn't wearing the dress.

"How?" Perrie asked while Vale helped her stand.

"My abilities were off in the display with Fannie and the gargoyle, but after you killed her, they re-appeared. Before she came back to life, I transported her to the Ripper display. It took me longer than I liked, or I would have gotten to you sooner." He closed his eyes, clenching them tight.

"I'm glad you didn't, Vale," Perrie rushed out the words. "I mean, what if you went after the gargoyle first and then Fannie woke back up leaving you powerless again." She would've withstood any amount of pain, as long as Vale was able to send Fannie away.

"I know, but you still had to go through all that. I knew you would be okay, but I did not want to screw anything up for you any more than it already has been. If I did not get Fannie to her display, it would only have made your life worse, and I could not have her send you down there to my father."

"It's okay, Vale. I under—"

"Then," he interrupted, squeezing at his hair, "when I turned to you and saw what the gargoyle had done, I was so angry. I brought you out and went back into its display first, punching the gargoyle over and over until he told me everything. Fannie and my father were using the gargoyle as a spy when she was not around. She had a charm that would be able to shut my powers off in a display that wasn't her own, and Father was going to use me when I became fully charged. He wanted to drain my powers into him so he could rise. Then I dropped the gargoyle and immediately went and found Maisie and Neven because we have to close up the Glass Vault."

Perrie listened to everything he said while Maisie and Nev watched. Nev was the first to speak. "Then what the hell are we doing here still talking? We could've done all this after."

"Let's go," Perrie said, wondering what their next move would be. Vale waved them over, and they hurried down all three hallways. As soon as Vale touched the gold knob, the door opened.

Once outside, and even though it wasn't over, Perrie could truly breathe for a second. She inhaled the fresh air, peered up at the sky, and listened to the rustle of the wind through the trees.

Vale took a few steps forward in the direction of the Glass Vault and clapped. This time before he separated them, he slowly bent his knuckles, leaving the outer edges of his hands together, like he had something in between them. Where the museum once stood was now only a lot of land, as if the Glass Vault had never been there at all.

Perrie gasped. Maisie watched in wonder. Nev sighed in relief. With his fingertips still touching, Vale rotated his hands. One faced the grass, the other the sky—he lifted the top hand gracefully away. A miniature form of the Glass Vault now rested in his palm, and Perrie wished he would bring his other hand down to smash it.

"What are you going to do with it?" Maisie asked, tiptoeing up to the tiny building and inspecting the small structure.

"Crush it?" *Nev is in the same thinking boat I'm in.*

Vale shook his head. "I have to transport it back through the barrier that leads to the Underworld."

"How do we get to the barrier from here?" Perrie hoped it wasn't too far.

Vale gave her a sly look. "Right there." He walked to the spot where the Glass Vault once stood, tossed the little stone building into the grass, snapped his fingers, and poof, the small toy-like building vanished.

Fucking finally. "That's it?"

"That's it." He smiled.

"What now?" Perrie asked, her heart pounding. "You're

not going to go back, right?" She hoped he wasn't going to jump into the grass and disappear too.

"No. I cannot go back. Father would try the same thing, but this time maybe my heart would never beat again."

Perrie didn't want him to go, not only because she didn't want the Glass Vault to come back, but because she didn't want to see Vale hurt again either.

"But what if your father still tries to escape?" What would they do if this *king*, as Maisie would say, were to come up?

"I cannot dissolve the barrier, but it is sealed. I will only have to monitor it every now and then to make sure the seal remains strong."

This little portal reminded her of her dad's favorite 80s horror movie, *The Gate,* only it wasn't in her backyard. She wished with everything in her that her dad was here too, but he wasn't.

"So, what now?" Perrie asked.

"That is the question." Vale tilted his head. "What now?"

Perrie stepped out of the shower after thoroughly scrubbing away all the blood from what had happened in the Glass Vault, as well as the memories of everything the Bride had done. Her silk dress lay sprawled out on the floor, and Perrie kicked it aside—she was never putting that damn thing on ever again.

She was home now. Well, she wasn't sure how long it would be her home. It felt strange and heartbreaking to be there without her dad, and she caught herself before she could cry. Maisie had gone with Nev to get some of his possessions from his house before they went back to her place. Perrie had told them she'd meet them there in the morning, then they'd head off wherever they decided to go. Besides, she wanted to stay at her house for one night and pretend as if everything was normal. Even though it wasn't.

A noise penetrated through the crack under the bathroom door, and Perrie closed her eyes as she listened to the sweet, graceful strokes of a bow across four strings, intertwined with a mixture of chords being pressed. This melody from the cello fractured her heart with brutality and delicate sounds. He was good, better than anything she'd ever heard from August before, and that was saying a lot. Her ears drank in the notes as she wrapped a towel around her body.

Stepping to the mirror, Perrie drew a quick picture of a heart with broken vines on the glass. She thought about her mom and wondered if she was out there somewhere, but then stopped. Her mom wasn't real family after she'd abandoned Perrie. Even now, she still couldn't stop drawing the mirror doodles they'd always done together after bath time. It was their thing before her mom had left, but it was all Perrie's now.

Knowing what she was about to do, Perrie took a deep breath and padded down the hallway to her bedroom as the music continued to play.

She stepped into the room wearing only her towel, her wet hair brushing her skin. Vale faced away from the door, sitting in her desk chair. Perrie's heart thumped as she inched toward him, and he startled when her cheek met his warm one. Her right hand looped around to lay on top of his, ceasing the bow's movements, while her left rested atop his fingers on the strings.

"Show me?" she whispered, wanting to play this song with him.

Vale didn't speak, only began to play. Perrie lightly kept her fingers pressed against his and they moved together as if they were one. The music felt like his, like hers, like *theirs*.

The melody drifted for a long time, notes swaying in the air around them. And when he finished, they stayed there, breathing deeply together before she removed her cheek from his. His eyes were closed, then he finally opened them as she stepped back.

Without looking at her, Vale got up to set the cello against the wall. He then turned to face her and stilled. His eyes grew wide, and she just stood frozen in her towel, not saying anything. He didn't say anything either. Heat flooded her cheeks, and she felt ridiculous, stupid.

Perrie closed her eyes, reopened them, and shakily took a step forward. Vale's lips parted, and she continued to walk until she stood right before him. But he didn't move away. So she reached out and stroked his soft cheek, and those perfect green eyes of his closed as he leaned into her touch.

"Be with me," she whispered.

He lifted his head and bit his lip. "Why?"

Perrie brought her other hand to his chest and rested it against his rapid heartbeat. "I want to be with you knowing that *I'm* choosing this, not the Bride. I want to be with you because I'd like to see what can come from this. More than anything, I just want to be with you."

"I am not August." Vale said it in a way that made her believe he was envious of someone who never existed.

"I don't want you to be." She wanted him to be *this* Vale.

"You are not in love with me." His gaze shifted from her eyes to her lips and back up, seeming to search for an answer in her face.

"But one day I could be." And Perrie meant it. If he could care about her after seeing what the Bride did, even though it wasn't her, then why couldn't she feel the same way about him? She was already attracted to him and his kindness.

Vale's hand met hers at his chest, his thumb gently rubbing her skin. "I do not want to get hurt. Not anymore."

Perrie didn't know everything he'd been through, but she knew it was awful, and she wanted him to eventually confide in her—his entire story.

"I wouldn't hurt you." She took their hands from his chest and intertwined their fingers. "I've been through a lot. You've been through a lot. Maybe we can help mend each other. Both of us could cross a tunnel on our own, but together? Together we could be *stronger*."

Taking a deep swallow, Perrie unwrapped the towel at her chest until she was baring everything before him, including her emotions.

He reached out without any hesitation to bring her face to his, and his soft lips molded to hers. Vale's hand shook, and his kisses were gentle and sweet, like him, until they weren't anymore. He hauled her to his body as his back hit the wall, and they melted together to the floor. Vale pulled her to sit on top of him and she moved back, so he could yank off his shirt.

Vale watched her for a moment, deliberating about something he wanted to say. "Perrie, I—I love you. I fell in love with you through the memories, and the feeling has not gone away. It has only intensified. I choose to always be your strength in any way you need, even if you never feel the same way."

Perrie may not be there yet, but she knew she'd catch up. She had to do it before with August, when she'd thought Nev had cheated on her, and she wanted to do it again. She didn't think she would ever want to, but how quickly something could change. Her heart was already waiting to open up for him, but her head just needed to deal with everything that had happened in order to get her there. For now, she would give him all of her—at least, what was there for her to give.

Her mouth crashed to his from his lovely words, and their lips sailed across each other—he caught her bottom lip in between his teeth, giving the area a soft lick. Perrie kissed along his jaw to right behind his ear, and he pulled her tighter against him. As she tugged on his blond curls, she softly bit his earlobe.

He rocked her against him while they kissed for a long time, until they both needed him to remove his pants. "Do you want the bed?" he whispered against her ear as she helped him out of his clothing.

"I want the floor," she whispered back. They were already used to sleeping there anyway.

He gave her a beautiful smile that was all Vale, and with a smile in return, she drew him closer. His hands touched everywhere—she arched as his fingers trailed feather touches down to her breast, then ventured between her thighs, circling with beautiful movements that had her on the brink of shattering completely.

And Perrie wanted nothing but to show him how good he was making her feel. She grasped his length, stroking him as he groaned in the crook of her neck. His lips came to hers once more and she continued her pace until they both needed him inside her.

Vale carefully lay Perrie down on her back and kissed between her breasts. He then flicked a nipple with his tongue and brought it in between his teeth, making her moan. With a soothing suck, he released it and kissed his way back up to her lips.

She could feel him at her entrance, and she threaded her fingers through his curls. Her body was singing to his, and his was calling to hers. He pushed inside her, and she gasped in pleasure. His body trembled as they stared at one another.

"Are you all right?" she asked.

"With you, how could I not be?"

Her mouth collided with Vale's and his trembling subsided. Perrie gripped him tighter when he started to move inside her, holding onto him with everything she had. Then they showed each other how through the darkness that hibernated in them all, the light could always subdue it.

EPILOGUE

Six Months Later - Perrie

Trying to get back to normal hadn't been easy. There were moments when Perrie needed her dad, Aunt Krista, and Uncle Jaron. Other times, she was okay because she had Maisie, Vale, and Nev.

So many areas had been destroyed throughout the Americas. The first thing they'd decided to do was search for everyone who'd become immortal in the Glass Vault.

The main reason they did this was because Perrie had wanted the immortals to have the same option Maisie, Nev, and she had—whether they wanted to stay here or let their soul move on. It took a while to find them all, but they did.

Most of the immortals had wanted to stay, but if and when they changed their mind, they could search Vale out. A few of them had decided to move on, such as Josselyn. She was too haunted over the headless statues she'd created. There were times when Perrie couldn't cope with what she'd done, but then she forced herself to remember that the Bride wasn't her and if she'd been in her right mindset, none of this would've happened. Fannie, however, was a whole different story. As vicious as it may be, Perrie could honestly have stabbed her as many times as needed in order to save everyone.

Earlier, they'd found the last immortal—Ben Johnston. He'd chosen to stay immortal and was just glad he could take photographs for an eternity while not having to worry about sunscreen any longer. Then he'd ventured back out on his own.

"How do you feel now that our mission of finding lost souls, as Maisie would say, is accomplished?" Perrie asked, studying Vale as he watched Ben fade into the distance. They would have to let Maisie and Nev know they completed this final task. To search more quickly, they'd gone in one direction and Maisie and Nev in another.

"It was all for you." Vale looped his pinky with hers.

"That's a lie. You wanted to do this, too."

There were still nights when he woke up trembling, and Perrie wrapped her arms around him to let him know she was there. Sometimes his nightmares were about his father and the Underworld, other times they were about the people who had normal lives before and were left with no choice but immortality after.

Some nights it was him who held onto her, when the past crept into her mind.

"I could have found better ways to occupy my mind." Apparently, he could start joking for a bit since everyone had been found.

"Cello, right?" Perrie grinned.

"Definitely the cello." He ran a finger across his lower lip.

Something about his expression, the way the sun hit his blond curls, the glint in his eyes… She didn't know exactly what did it, but her heart filled with so much emotion, tears threatened to fall. Before she could talk herself out of it, she rushed to Vale, practically tackling him to the ground. Her arms wrapped around his waist, squeezing him with all she had.

"I love you," she murmured.

Vale froze, then sighed softly above her head, like everything had been set right with him. "I should have mentioned a long time ago how much I *love* that cello occupies my mind, then maybe you would have said those magical words sooner." He chuckled as he brushed a kiss right at her temple.

"That's totally what would've made me say it sooner." Perrie smiled, listening to the beautiful beat of his heart while it played its own symphony just for her.

Life wasn't always straightforward, and immortal life was even less clear, but with Vale, Maisie, and Nev, they would continue to hold each other together and make sure the barrier remained sealed.

If it ever broke, they'd be ready.

End of Book Two

Turn the page for a special epilogue scene from Maisie's POV

HEART OF GLASS

Maisie

Some immortals' hearts were like glass, easy to shatter.

But not Maisie's.

Maisie pedaled her old bike down the dusty abandoned road. This thing had been sitting in her garage for years before it helped her to venture across the country. Two months had passed since the world almost came to a dreadful end, when a demon prince and his wicked souls had run the show. *But hey, the world survived.* Just as Maisie had. Although, she was immortal. Forever and ever.

"I think I see her, Mais," Neven said as he pedaled faster, catching up beside her. The wind blew his shaggy hair back, exposing his perfect scars even more. Since they'd started dating, she couldn't get enough of him, couldn't believe the guy who she'd ran from after their first kiss, when she'd been fourteen, was now hers.

Vale and Perrie had separated from them for a while, so they could each track down the turned-immortals from the Glass Vault. It had been time to ask them a higher-power of a choice—live or die.

Maisie squinted her eye and found a lone woman curled up beneath the shade of a maple tree at the edge of the woods. Her gray dress was a raggedy mess and her blonde hair hung in knots down her back. *Yep, there's Josselyn.*

With a smile, Maisie hit the brake at the same time Neven did. Hopping off her bike, she released the kickstand and clapped her hands with a smile. *Another immortal down*!

Maisie held a finger over her lips, telling Neven to stay silent as they walked to her. She didn't want to frighten Josselyn and have to chase after her. They'd already had to do that twice now with two other immortals.

As she peered at Josselyn's form, she wasn't sure if she was dead. Then the immortal's chest rose and fell. *Nope, not dead.* Even if Josselyn had tried to pierce her own heart or something less messy, she wouldn't have died anyway. Vale, who was no longer Bad Vale, but Good Vale, was needed to perform that duty.

Maisie crouched down at the sleeping woman's side and shook her arm. "Josselyn," she whispered.

The Immortal's lids jerked open and she screamed when her gaze met Maisie's.

"It's okay." Maisie tightened her grip on Josselyn's arm, while Neven grasped her other one. "It's just us. We were once part of the same wicked club, remember?"

Josselyn's body trembled, her eyes widening in fear. *Maybe I shouldn't have brought up the club just yet.*

"No one's going to hurt you anymore," Neven said softly. Josselyn seemed to relax a fraction at his words.

"Vale is good now," Maisie started. "Bad Vale is gone. He's giving you a choice if you want to live or die." And then she explained the rest to Josselyn, everything that had occurred in the Glass Vault, all that had happened between Vale and his father, how he was hurt as much as they'd been, and how he was willing to look for every last immortal, no matter how long it took. To give them this choice.

When Maisie finished, Josselyn pressed her hands to her face and sobbed.

Maisie patted Josselyn's back. "There. There. It isn't so bad."

"Isn't so bad?" Josselyn glanced up at her as though she were back to being Crazy Maisie. "Look at the world. Look at *us*."

Neven shrugged. "I mean, it's better than it was a few months ago."

"I can't do this," Josselyn cried, tears streaming down her cheeks. "I just can't."

And she wouldn't have to. Maisie understood the immortal life wasn't meant for everyone. She pulled her backpack off her shoulder and fished out her notepad and pencil from the front pocket. Josselyn's brow furrowed while she watched Maisie write down the address to where she could wait for Vale and Perrie.

Tearing off the note, she handed it to Josselyn. "Meet them here and your wish shall come true. No more tears."

"I don't know if I trust this." Josselyn's lip quivered while taking the note. "But it can't be worse than what's already happened."

Things could always be worse, but Maisie kept her lips zipped as not to upset the immortal more.

Josselyn rose and slowly walked down the dusty road, her shoulders slumped and her head lowered.

"Wait," Maisie called after her. She jogged to her bike and pushed it toward the immortal. You don't have to walk there. Take this." It was the least she could do.

"Thanks." Josselyn smiled warmly, placing her palms on the handlebars. She pulled her dress up a bit to take a seat on the bike, then took off down the road to get her happily ever after somewhere else.

"Now"—Maisie whirled to face Neven, a huge grin on her

face—"I have a surprise for you."

He arched a brow.

"I swear it's a good one this time." She laughed, remembering the last time she'd taken him to a cave and they couldn't find their way out for days. Before he could reply, Maisie yanked him by the hand into the woods. She hadn't planned to do this here, but spontaneity was the answer.

The leaves crunched beneath their feet as she drew him a bit deeper into the trees. She whirled around and grasped both his hands in hers. "Today's your birthday."

"Yes?" The edges of his lips curved up as if he was still unsure about what she was planning. At nineteen, Neven should've started college with his basketball scholarship already, but maybe he still could once the world was healed. He would have to be hush-hush about the immortal thing, though.

Maisie released his hands and set her backpack on the ground, then drew out two cans of spray cheese and placed them next to her backpack.

"Are you sure you don't want them both?" He grinned, watching as she pulled out a box of crackers and put it beside the spray cheese.

"Hey"—she stood and poked his chest—"I won't deny that, but I at least share."

He rolled his eyes. "I don't think you'll ever let me live that one down."

"Before our little picnic, I have something else for you first." She held his hands once more, his calluses beautifully rough against her skin. "We're going to have sex."

Neven coughed, choking. Then laughter poured out from his mouth, his body practically convulsing. He grabbed her by the hips and drew her to his chest, then pressed his head to hers. "I love how you're so fucking forward. But are you sure you want your first time to be here?"

It didn't matter where she took him at, and out here, in the woods, with the wind blowing and the sun shining, was the right choice. "Yes, unless you're not ready."

"Oh, I've been ready." His fingers dug into her hips. "Are you sure?"

Maisie had been ready since their kiss in the Sleeping Beauty display, but she figured they'd needed to go slow. By that, she meant do almost everything but sex. "I want it more than the cans of cheese." She grinned and bopped his nose before taking a step back to peel off her eye patch. "So let's get undressed."

"Yes, ma'am." She could tell he wanted to laugh again, but he only smiled and lifted his shirt over his head.

They removed their clothing, item by item, their eyes locked all the while, until they stood naked before each other. To the majority of the world, it may not be the most romantic concept to talk about sex before having it, then study each other's naked forms before crashing into one another. But it was to her.

Maisie looked at Neven as she would an art sculpture, taking in each one of his pale pink scars, his tan skin, his charming face, his strong hands, and the part of him that was no longer soft.

"You're beautiful," he whispered, his gaze traveling across her body like he was studying a map, wanting to take in each line, each curve.

And then, Maisie closed the distance, drawing his head to hers. She brought her mouth to his, and he lifted her so her legs wrapped around his waist. Neven carefully lowered her to the grass as though she were made of glass.

"You won't break me, Neven," she said as his body hovered above hers, the heat of his skin warming her perfectly.

He rolled his eyes, then kissed the tip of her nose. "I love you, Mais."

"I love you, Neven." Heart pounding, she trailed her fingers across a light scar on his cheek. She then cradled his face and brought his mouth to hers. "We can do foreplay later. I just want you right now. Then break for the cheese and go into round two after."

Neven brushed a lock of hair away from her face. "You may hate round one."

"Then that's what round two will be for. Good or bad, I don't care." It wouldn't matter—it was him, her Frankenstein's Monster, and that was all she needed.

"Here goes round one then," he murmured. His gaze trained on hers, his expression turning serious. "Let me know if I need to stop or slow down, all right?"

Maisie nodded, her fingers entwining with his hair as anticipation coursed through her. His lips softly pressed to hers, then he slowly pushed into her. A sharp ache filled her and she gasped. She'd been through worse, felt worse. Still, was this what everyone liked feeling? But then, the pain subsided and it was just Neven inside her, them peering at one another. Neven and Maisie.

"I'm still good," she whispered.

In answer, he pulled back slightly and rolled his hips forward. Her heart sang at the movement and the new magical thrum pulsing within her. Neven then did it again … and again. Maisie needed more, needed to feel him everywhere. She pulled his mouth to hers—kissing, nipping, tasting. His hand trailed to her breast and cupped it, his thumb softly circling her nipple, sending wonderful shivers through her body. She skimmed her fingers down his spine to his backside, then gripped it as he moved. Neven's pace picked up as she held him tighter. She felt him down to her bones, in her mind, *everywhere*.

Her heart sang higher as a pleasureful feeling rose within her, peaking out of its hidden depths. She'd felt this before from his fingers, his tongue, but this time, it was more powerful. A roaring, an explosion, spread through her as her heart continued to sing. Maisie didn't release a scream or moan, just as she always did when he touched her, tasted her, only heavy puffs of blissful breaths. But when Neven followed down her path, he was much, much louder, same as he always was when she touched him, tasted him. Yet this, this was different, and it was oh so heavenly.

Both their chests heaved, Neven's gorgeous face slick with sweat. He peered down at her with a smile and ran his thumb across her bottom lip.

"That was fun." Maisie grinned, softly nipping his thumb. "Now we can eat, then do it again."

He wrapped his arms around her, laughing as he rolled over, tucking her into the crook of his arm. "I fucking love you."

Did you enjoy The Wicked Souls Duology?

Authors always appreciate reviews, whether long or short. If you enjoyed the Wicked Souls Duology, then you may want to check out **Clouded By Envy**, Boon One in the Cruel Curses Trilogy!

He only ever wanted to be human. She only ever wanted to save him. Sometimes the very thing you wish for, is your undoing...

Brenik has always been envious of his twin sister, Bray. Everything always came naturally to Bray, even after crossing through a portal from their fae world, while Brenik spent his time in her shadow. So, when Brenik discovers a way to get what he has always desired—to become human— he takes it. However, the gift turns out to be a curse that alters him in ways he never saw coming.

Bray can't help but be concerned for her brother, more so when he vanishes. While waiting for Brenik to return, she meets two brothers who realize she isn't human. Her dark bat-like wings are proof of that. But somehow, an aching bond forms between Bray and the hot older brother, Wes.

When Bray reunites with Brenik, she finds he has an overpowering need for blood stirring within him. If Bray doesn't help Brenik put an end to his curse, it will not only damage those who get close to him, but it could also destroy the steamy romance blooming between her and Wes.

Subscribe to Candace's Awesome Newsletter for the latest news and giveaways!
Join Candace's Facebook Group: Candace's Pretty Monsters

Check out Candace's other books!

Wicked Souls Duology
Vault of Glass
Bride of Glass

Marked by Magic Duology
The Bone Valley
Merciless Stars

Cruel Curses Trilogy
Clouded By Envy
Veiled By Desire
Shadowed By Despair

Faeries of Oz Series
Lion (Short Story Prequel)
Tin
Crow
Ozma
Tik-Tok

Cursed Hearts Duology
Lyrics & Curses
Music & Mirrors

Immortal Letters Duology
Dearest Clementine: Dark and Romantic Monstrous Tales
Dearest Dorin: A Romantic Ghostly Tale

Campfire Fantasy Tales Series
Lullaby of Flames
A Layer Hidden
The Celebration Game

These Vicious Thorns: Tales of the Lovely Grim
Between the Quiet
Hearts Are Like Balloons
Bacon Pie
Avocado Bliss

Vampires in Wonderland
Rav (Short Story Prequel)
Maddie
Chess
Knave

Demons of Frosteria
Frost Mate (Prequel Novella)
Frost Claim

Acknowledgments

This duology has a special place in my heart. Perrie, Vale, Maisie, and Never are four people who I would want to team up with if monsters ever did take over the world. Nothing is black or white, and the grayness is what makes us all that more human. Thank you so much, lovely readers. Also a huge shoutout to these amazing people for being wonderful friends and helping me so much! Amber Hodges, Elle Beaumont, Didi Oviatt, Donna Weiss, Christis Christie, Hayley Roe, and Jenny Hickman.

About the Author

Candace Robinson spends her days consumed by words and hoping to one day find her own DeLorean time machine. Her life consists of avoiding migraines, admiring Bonsai trees, watching classic movies, and living with her husband and daughter in Texas—where it can be forty degrees one day and eighty the next.

Connect with Candace:

Website: https://authorcandacerobinson.wordpress.com/
Facebook: https://www.facebook.com/literarydust
Twitter: https://twitter.com/literarydust
Instagram:
https://www.instagram.com/candacerobinsonbooks/
Goodreads:
https://www.goodreads.com/author/show/16541001.Candace
_Robinson or ignore that and just try searching for Candace
Robinson!